THE EYE OF HERMES

A Minerva Novel

W I L L I A M   H O W A R D

Cold Pizza Publishing
Philadelphia

ISBN: 069282829X
ISBN 13: 9780692828298

To Bonnie

Chapter 1
YANICK DCCULLEN

Yanick DcCullen, inmate 3249 of the Minerva Penitentiary, could never resist taking advantage of a business opportunity. So when he learned he could get his claws on some choice pharmaceutical items, he decided to take action.

In pursuit of this profitable venture, Yanick had managed to convince a fellow inmate, Buddash Kyo, to sign up with him for a repair and maintenance detail in the prison tunnels the day after tomorrow. Once they were escorted to their work location, they would create a diversion and make their way to the candy store that was the prison dispensary. Following the robbery, Yanick would sell the drugs to accrue some extra jailhouse credits. Now, jailhouse credit was very different, and in some ways more valuable, than your average currency. It came in the form of assistance from other cellmates in handling delicate matters such as exacting revenge upon an individual who had wronged you or avoiding being the recipient of a beating yourself. And sometimes having jailhouse money meant the difference between survival and extinction.

The main problem with drugs was transportation and storage of the goods, since there was little chance of Yanick being provided with a storage case as if he was doing a day's shopping at a Ruddarian open-air market. But he realized too, that with any venture of this type the biggest dilemma was working out all the minor details.

Luckily, he had a plan. Buddash had a cousin, Hunash, a Venusian pleasurist who provided services to the facilities' primary medical physician, Dr. Rabun, on a bi-monthly basis. Her next appointment with the prison doctor was for the day after tomorrow. It was common knowledge that the Zanuck Corporation, which owned and managed Minerva Penitentiary, provided their employees with female pleasuring to ease the burden of having to deal with society's undesirables. Yanick also knew that the medical specialist often forgot to lock his door on nights when he had a scheduled appointment with a pleasurist.

Buddash and Yanick had scheduled their next-to-last meeting for that morning. They had agreed to meet by the anti-gravity ball court towards the far side of the center, hopefully away from prying eyes and ears. Yanick — who was a blue and green skinned Trionyx — was sitting comfortably on a swing seat waiting, trying to look nonchalant and unintimidating. However, it was hard to be inconspicuous when you were seven-foot-two, with spikes down your back protruding from your android-green-jumpsuit and had razor-sharp-claws on your paws and feet.

Yanick was truly beginning to believe that Buddash had gotten cold padded feet and would not be coming at all. However, these concerns evaporated as he spied Buddash walking towards him. His partner in crime wore the self-same android green prison attire. However, this was their only similarity. Buddash was a member of a race known as the Cranitian. Their skin was cheddar-hued, had large saucer-shaped eyes on either side of their oblong faces, giving them a sullen look. Yet, Buddash's personal body armor — a scaled protective layer that covered him from the back of his head to down below his ankles — sent a very clear message. Buddash Kyo was not a character to be trifled with.

As Yanick met Buddash's gaze, he whispered, "Wasn't sure that you were going to make it."

"I was unavoidably delayed. There is a third party who has expressed an interest in our business venture. I was preoccupied bringing him up to speed on our plan."

Yanick involuntary took a step back as he held up his claws. "I thought that I made myself clear. This deal is just between you and me and I ain't lookin' for any additional partners. I'm going to have a hard enough time trusting you with my back turned in those tunnels. And now, you want me to put my trust in two slime balls? No Fuctur way. You and your new friend want to pull off this heist on your own, then be my guest. But unfortunately, I can't guarantee you that I won't be taking a stroll to Legate Prime Buzz's office this afternoon with a lovely little tip about a possible heist."

"You Reptilia slime mocker, Diabolix is the third party who wants in on the job. The truth is that my protection account with him is currently in arrears and he made it clear to me that letting him in on this job would make us square. So, last night, Diabolix and I, with the assistance of some of his personal thugs, came to this arrangement. And I am sorry there was nothing that I could really do about him requesting a cut. But on the bright side, he seems to only want one thing from the dispensary. He asked me to get him a sample of pure Enhanced Energy gas.

Yanick had a very bad feeling about Diabolix's intentions but was beginning to feel that he really had no choice in this matter. He took a minute to compose himself before he spoke again. Yanick looked down at his claws. "Did you fill Diabolix in on my plan? The three of us will be sneaking away from the repair and maintenance detail to tunnel into the dispensary."

"Oh, it won't be Diabolix himself. He would never dream of getting his hands dirty like that. His representative will be in charge of acquiring his merchandise."

Yanick briskly moved onto the next step. "After the three of us start to work on removing debris in the tunnels and making patch repairs, Buddash, you will create a diversion. You start screaming that the walls are closing in on you or some nonsense. Hopefully, a guard will escort you back to the transport shuttle. At your first opportunity to have a little privacy with your escort, you knock him unconscious. Meanwhile, Diabolix's associate and I will use your theatrics as an opportunity to make our way to junction 42. You'll have to meet us there. While we are busy with tunneling, Hunash will keep the doctor occupied."

Buddash tried to keep himself from imagining what perverse acts Hunash would be performing on Dr. Rabun during the robbery of the dispensary. He took a deep breath and listened to the rest of Yanick's plan. "While Dr. Rabun is otherwise occupied, we'll be hard at work gathering items from the medical cabinet to complete the orders for our customers. The drugs will temporarily be deposited in the rubble and debris buckets that the guards will graciously provide for our repair work. When we are done, the three of us will slip back down into the tunnel and return to the work detail like nothing ever happened. Hopefully, the drugs will not be missed until the next scheduled inventory in two weeks' time. At that point, there will not be a damn thing they can do about it because the drugs will have been digested."

"You failed to consider one element, Yanick."

"And what is that?"

"We can leave our stash of drugs in a safe hiding place after we leave the dispensary. But Diabolix is probably going to want delivery of his stuff by the end of the evening."

Yanick smiled. "We will just let his 'associate' worry about that." As Yanick and Buddash got up to walk towards the door and the rec period was coming to an end, sirens suddenly began to blare as the room was bathed in a sickly magenta. In short, all hell had broken loose.

While Yanick and Buddash had been discussing their plans for the dispensary heist, Buzz, the Legate Prime of Minerva Penitentiary, was awaiting the arrival of a very important prisoner. Legate Prime Buzz was a nine-foot-tall winged Polistine who had the appearance of a Pangean bumblebee with eighteen-inch stingers. Buzz was in a particularly disagreeable mood that morning because the warden, Sobek Bokhun — a giant shelled creature who belonged to the race Hawking Brain Beetle — had assigned him to work with two Beetleguise guards, each seven-feet-long and resembling hissing cockroaches. The prisoner, Hotfire, was a member of a species known as the Chamyx, a close cousin of the Trionyx, Yanick's race. Hotfire could have easily been mistaken for a Reptilia dragon on ancient Pangean, especially since he was able to shoot fireballs from his tail. Hotfire had been convicted by the Polistine government for committing acts of terrorism on behalf of the Beetleguise Trotsnexus. The Beetleguise and Polistine had been at war with each other for five hundred years. In fact, Minerva was the only place that the Polistine and Beetleguise tolerated each other.

Hotfire had no particular feelings of animosity against Buzz's people, but at the same time, had not been able to resist the temptation of the enormous payday that came along with this covert operation. He had been instructed by the Beetleguise Central Secret Service to swallow several pounds of liquid explosives in a dormant state for transport to Insectvore. Once he arrived on the planet, Hotfire was ordered to make his way to the Ministry of Justice and then secretly lay the explosive eggs in the sub-basement. He was then to send a signal back to the Beetleguise home planet of Madagascan, at which time an agent with the Secret Service would activate the devices.

Little had Hotfire known that the Polistine Covert Missionary Police were being assisted by a double agent, Zippo Pulp. While working at Section Seventy-Two, Pulp had exchanged the lethal package with harmless amber. When Hotfire sent the signal for the package to explode, the amber merely vaporized into nothingness. It was then that Pulp activated a homing beacon to alert the Polistine Covert Missionary Police where they could pick up Hotfire. But Hotfire refused to go with the Polistine authorities to prison in a quiet and cooperative manner. The Chamyx managed to send fifteen of the Polistine Ministry of Justice's best agents to the emergency room before day's end. As a result of his mischief, Hotfire found himself in the Insectvore State Correctional facility. Within a matter of weeks, Hotfire had successfully worked out a plan where he was able to use his natural cloaking ability to slip away from his cell undetected and slip down a sewage pipe that led to a dirt sub-basement. Fortunately, the Polistine authorities were able to, almost by accident, avoid an intergalactic incident; namely the escape of Insectvore's most-hated terrorist. A female guard had wandered down to the sub-basement one evening, observed an invisible entity digging a hole in the ground, and used her Taser to electrocute the invisible "something." She then alerted the guards, who recaptured Hotfire.

After barely preventing his exodus, the decision was made to send Hotfire to the more secure facility of Minerva where there would be fewer opportunities for him to seek available means of escape. As for the female Polistine guard who discovered the escape plan, she was put to death for having sexual relations with another guard, per the Polistine penal code.

Because of the attempted escape of the Abomination, as Hotfire was known, it now became the duty of Legate Prime Buzz to ensure that he remained confined until justice was done. Legate Prime Buzz's gaze stayed fixed on the heavy round copper and lead door that protected the air lock to the outside of the prison, the door that was about to roll back to herald the arrival of this most important criminal.

As Legate Prime Buzz waited for Hotfire, his mind wandered back to his days in Polistine Boot Camp. The Legate had an almost savant-like talent for anticipating every military scenario for a given engagement and preparing for that contingency. Many compared him to a mythical Pangean general: Napoleon, from the ancient country of that world known as Paris. But much like that famous general, Buzz felt he had been wrongly sent into exile.

He had been a student at the central hive in the capital city Linnaeus, on Insectvore, when he made the decision to enlist in the Polistine Legion. After yet another act of terrorism by the hated Beetleguise, Buzz dropped out of school to become a defender of his way of life. However, his motives were not completely selfless. The young recruit knew that one of the most effective means for advancement was through military service that often times led to higher political office.

After committing himself to military service, and dealing with alleviating the fears of concerned family and friends, Buzz left on a military transport on a cold Janus morning for basic training on the southern continent of Nectaine. Despite the young cadet's initial enthusiasm, the cold reality of basic training quickly became apparent. He was roused by blaring music from a vladivos — a long tube shaped instrument that expanded into a bell-shaped dome — that was broadcasted over loud speakers just as the sun was peeking over the horizon. The decomposed fruit that the Army almost half-jokingly referred to as "food" was probably just a step below the food given to prisoners of war. His entire training platoon was subjected on an almost-daily-basis to a fifteen-mile circuit flight around the compound of camp Waspatoon. They flew almost to the point when they felt like their wings were going to fall off, and the drill sergeants exercised brutal discipline when it came to infractions by their young trainees. Buzz recalled the forty stinger burns that he'd received one afternoon when he dared to question his drill sergeant about how exactly the daily circuit flight prepared the recruits for combat. His fellow recruits, on the other hand, recognized that there was a future leader in their ranks.

Indeed, the memory of this brutal time in the Legate Prime's life often awoke him from a sound sleep within his cabin on Minerva to a chorus of his own screams. He could still picture his fellow cadets being pushed to their limits. All of the Polistine recruits were brutalized from their ill-treatment at the hands of their drill sergeants: a lack of decent food, lack of sleep, and unrelenting training routines. But even before Buzz finished basic training, he'd distinguish himself from the pack.

As Buzz contemplated his past, and the path that had led him to his current assignment as Legate Prime of Minerva, he saw the darkness outside the port window transform into a blinding light brighter than any sunrise he'd ever seen on Insectvore, Madagascan or any other of the eighteen known worlds of the Venusian system. In short procession after this blinding radiance came a thunderous shaking that nearly knocked Buzz and the two Beetleguise prison guards to their knees. Coming from above them, the trio could distinguish a cigar-shaped tube riding down the shiny cylindrical chamber that led to the bottom of the airlock. This airlock terminated at the main hangar bay located 37 miles beneath the surface of Minerva. Within a matter of minutes, the capsule had eased towards the bottom and come to rest on the landing pad adjacent to where Buzz and the two Beetleguise were waiting.

Within the silvery cigar-shaped craft, Captain Honeycomb, the pilot of the prison transport, *Honeyvein One*, had dispatched two of his ensigns to the detention level to retrieve the Abomination Hotfire. That had been five minutes ago, however, so Honeycomb was a little concerned. He'd completed the circuit of delivering prisoners from various planets within the Venusian system to Minerva penitentiary hundreds of times without incident. And despite the importance placed on this particular run, Captain Honeycomb still considered the mission to be routine. One particular reason that Captain Honeycomb had so many seamless prison transfers to his credit was he sedated his passengers so heavily before each trip that they were lucky to remember their own names after the journey. Still, Honeycomb had the nagging feeling in his thorax that something was about to go horribly wrong. His silent contemplation on the ship's flight deck was suddenly interrupted as the intercom came alive with frantic humming and buzzing, "Sir, we need you to get up here right away. He's gone."

In a skeptical tone, he replied, "What do you mean, gone? Are you sure that you are at the right detention cell?"

"Yes, we are at Cell 17 just like you told us. We are getting ready to drop the force field and do an internal inspection of the area."

Captain Honeycomb opened his mandible to instruct them to come back immediately, but it was already too late. As the two guards stood in the middle of the cell, an invisible force suddenly reached down and picked up one of the Polistine jailors. With a heavy thud, it slammed the Polistine ensign against the bulkhead. The other ensign quickly reached for a container of gaseous vapor mist from his pocket and sprayed in the general vicinity of the invisible form. Within seconds, the outline of a huge Reptilia began to appear on the wall like a disembodied shadow.

"Hotfire, I presume."

"You are going to regret this," Hotfire said with a Cheshire-like grin. Before the Polistine ensign's multi-faceted eyes, there sat an eleven-foot-long reptilian beast with ebony midnight skin and golden patches along his back, some the size of nectar melons. It barely wore a blue and gold jumper around its extended abdomen. Besides his size, Hotfire's most chilling characteristic was his eyes. They were two black and grey stones capable of a penetrating gaze that spoke to the pure evil of his soul. "Let the contest of wits, for which I will demonstrate how truly lacking you are, begin."

As the first ensign took flight with his double stinger abdomen posed for attack, Hotfire simultaneously jumped off the detention cell wall. As the two engaged in a deadly mid-air dance, Hotfire whipped around towards the ensign and knocked him to the ground. The Polistine quickly recovered and flew back up towards Hotfire, and using one of his dual stingers, sliced off the Abomination's massive tail. But within seconds, Hotfire had spawned another tail that appeared to be twice the size and thickness of the first.

"Nice try," he said in a taunting tone. Hotfire spun around towards the valiant Polistine and began launching fireballs from protrusions on his tail in rapid succession. The Polistine was almost instantly vaporized by the incoming fireballs.

The Abomination smirked condescendingly at the smoldering afterglow. "And that, kiddies, is why they call me 'Hotfire.'"

"Good to know," said a voice behind him. Hotfire turned to see Captain Honeycomb facing him with a taser-net cannon. Without missing a beat, the Captain fired a capsule from the weapon that exploded into an electrified webbed netting headed straight for Hotfire."

"Ah my dear Captain, you should have done your homework better. I cannot only make myself disappear but I can absorb any sort of energy, including electricity." The electrified net surrounded Hotfire's upper extremities but, within a moment, the electric charge dissipated like a faulty energy bulb on a Gnasxmas holiday tree. "Now, I am sorry to inform you that I need to hijack your vessel to make my escape. And additionally, I believe you are in my way."

"So sorry to disappoint you but I am not going anywhere." The Captain flew straight up towards the bulkhead of the cell, aiming for a point near the middle of the room. Once in position, Honeycomb triggered a silent alarm that he knew from his time working on Minerva would place the penitentiary on lockdown. He was barely able to activate the warning signal and fly out the door into the corridor before Hotfire leapt after the Captain and cornered him once again.

"I have a pretty fair idea of how you are planning to stop me, but it won't save you," said Hotfire.

"Oh, really," said the Captain. "Well, I am here to tell you that I am about to dazzle you."

"Pretty cocky talk for a walking bug splat," smiled Hotfire sarcastically.

"Oh, I am not dead yet." The Polistine spun in a three-sixty motion until his head was where his bottom had been and vice versa. He quickly began to jab at Hotfire's eyes with both stingers in rapid succession. Unable to determine what damage he had done, if any, while in this upside down position, Honeycomb flew down the nearest turbo shaft as he quickly made his way to the lift's operation panel. He began to swing the wrench device around on an axis to manually open the door. As he worked, Honeycomb could feel the floor begin to shake as the Abomination came storming down the hallway. As he made the last turn, the beast was nipping at his heels but it was too late for Hotfire. Honeycomb slipped down the shaft headed towards the flight deck.

At the end of the shaft, Honeycomb quickly scrambled to an access terminal to activate the lock-out codes so that the ship could not be moved. As he finished, he heard Legate Prime Buzz's voice coming over the intercom.

"Minerva to *Honeyvein One*, do you read?"

"Legate Prime, I am here. The prisoner has …" At that moment, Hotfire launched three fireballs from his tail leaving a gaping hole in the door leading to the flight deck, and pulled the remains of the door away like a child removing a sweets wrapper. Honeycomb tried his best to scramble for the door as Hotfire climbed through the hole in the flight deck, wrapped his tail around the Captain, and began to squeeze.

"Let's see how you enjoy being sedated, my dear Captain," Hotfire quipped as he reached with his foot for a hypodermic from a cabinet where various hallucinogens were stored. With the skill of a med-tech, Hotfire injected the persuasive compound into Honeycomb's neck.

Outside the *Honeyvein One*, Legate Prime Buzz was already radioing to his second-in-command, Legate Beta Zook, that he wanted the Hangar Bay sealed tight. Nothing was to get in or out of the bay until he said otherwise.

"Yes sir. I will make that happen," said Zook.

"And alert Warden Sobek that we might have a possible hostage situation." He pressed a nearby switch to activate the prison-wide klaxon. At that moment, Buzz was grateful for that Chamyx race had a tendency to act before considering their enemy's strategy. In addition, he was thankful that Chamyx's ability to maintain cloaking required a high degree of concentration. A fact that limited the amount of time they could remain in that state. Given that Insectum could go for extended periods without oxygen, Buzz would be able to evacuate the precious gas from the room and seal off all available exits. The only remaining oxygen would be contained within the transport itself.

Inside, Hotfire heard the voice of his old nemesis on the speakers located within the landing tube. Hotfire recalled when the Legate was Commander of the Yellow Z Swarm, and had raided his smuggling vessel for the purpose of commandeered medicine, food and supplies for the Polistine war effort. He had also recently learned that the Legate Prime was the one who had suggested exchanging the liquid explosives for the Ministry mission with harmless amber.

"Give it up, son. You know that there is no way you are going to make it out alive if I have the least bit to say about it."

Hotfire grabbed a headset from the computer console located to the side of the pilot's chair. The communication device looked like a youngling's toy in his massive hands as he struggled to manipulate the headphone into position to converse. "Hello there, Legate. It has been a long time since our last chat."

"Hotfire, I am telling you for your own good that the only way you'll come out of this situation is in a jail cell or an oversized body bag. It is your choice, son. So what is it going to be?"

"I don't appreciate your tone, Legate Prime," Hotfire said mockingly. "I am going to talk to my new friend, the Captain."

Hotfire turned towards the half conscious Polistine Captain. "You are going to activate the self-destruct," he said.

"Never. I'd never help you," said Honeycomb as he struggled to lift his head.

"That really does hurt my feelings. I need to teach you some manners, I think." Hotfire pulled another syringe from the cabinet that held the medications. Honeycomb recognized the compound immediately from the blue color; it was a compound that encouraged prisoners to be more cooperative.

"Have you ever heard the old Pangean expression, Better living through chemistry?" smiled Hotfire as he injected it into Honeycomb's neck.

The Legate Prime did not care for the silence that had overtaken the hangar bay. He knew from experience that a deafening silence usually meant things were about to go horribly wrong. Buzz jumped out of his chair as the intercom crackled to life. "Hotfire, you are going to be one dead Reptilia in less than ten minutes so I would take this opportunity to live. But on the other hand, I am fine if you choose to die in that ship. Your carcass would make a lovely throw rug in my office.

After a brief silence, Legate Prime Buzz received a response but the voice on the other end of the intercom belonged not to Hotfire but to his long-time comrade, Honeycomb. "I will activate the ship's self-destruct and destroy myself, this asteroid and all its inhabitants if our demands are not met."

Chapter 2
KASIDY VULKNER

Even for an astral engineer like Kasidy Vulkner — no stranger to hopping between planets, asteroids and space stations — the vastness of space and the majesty of the solar system through the portal of the *Mjölnir* truly humbled and amazed her.

Possibly, part of this awe could've been a side effect of her exhaustion from the fifteen-hour work shift she'd just completed in the vessel's engine room. As she went zipping through the galaxy aboard this tiny research vessel, Kasidy's mind would often wander back to memories of her child-hood. She'd often lie under her favorite drasill tree at twilight imagining herself fighting aliens and discovering strangely wondrous cultures among the stars. This was one vision of her childhood, though mainly a fabrication of her own imagination. By the time Kasidy turned eight years old, she had few moments that to devote to daydreaming. By early adolescence, Kasidy and her mother had been forced to deal with hardships on a daily basis that would have broken most soldiers.

However, Kasidy could have not anticipated these hardships given her early life. She'd grown up on a Ruddarian biosphere that had been designated as the Rogestran Five Colony. The planet consisted of several environmental domains layered one on top of another. In both the northern and southern regions of the planetoid, there were magnificent plasma seas that contained a variety of sub-surface creatures including the Morpheus — elongated crea-tures with one huge eye and ten tentacles — and the Blownagro, aquat-ic animals who could expand to the size of a small sphere transport when

threatened. The poles of the planet were dominated by snow-covered regions of unrelenting freezing temperatures as well as hundreds of miles of
barren frozen tundra. Only three species of creatures were able to survive
in these harsh conditions. There were the Moosran, eighteen-foot-tall bi-
pedal game animals with antlers that measured twelve feet across. There was
also the Moosran's natural predator, the Lupredator, which was eight-feet-
tall at the shoulder with immense claws and sharp fangs. This beast varied
between running in packs and seeking isolation. It had luxurious fur over
its lupine body that was highly sought after by Polistine and Beetleguise
nobility. When hunted down by ambitious trackers, its fur was tanned and
removed from the body, then thoroughly dried. A skilled tradesman would
be able to get five-to-seven full-length fur coats from one beast.

The last animal claiming the frozen polar region of Rogestran as home
was the majestic twenty-seven-foot-long spike-finned Crustarean. These
creatures resembled the ancient whales of Pangean. However, they had managed to evolve over the millennium from water creatures to animals that
could walk upon the frozen land.

The final region of Rogestran Five Colony was home to its hominoid
population known as the Ruddarians. Kasidy's people lived along the planet's equator. The Ruddarian habitat was dominated by an abundance of thick
jungles with tall trees that often blocked out the sunlight. There was a wide
variety of vegetation available for consumption that were cultivated in the
high canopy of the trees. The Ruddarians also hunted small burrowing and
climbing animals. They had worked hard to develop small village communi-
ties in the jungle, with recreation areas for the children, merchant areas for
the selling of wares, and important civic establishments such as a town hall,
a justice center and places of worship.

The Ruddarians addressed their prayers and thanks to an ancient entity known as the Great Hive Master. According to their creation myth,
the Great Hive Master had traveled to the Venusian system hundreds of
millennia ago to establish a nesting site for his species. Upon arriving in
the Ruddarian home galaxy, the Great Hive Master found a vast emptiness
devoid of stars, suns and planets. Unwilling to allow the potential for life
and growth to go unfulfilled, the Great Hive Master took it upon himself

to weave the fabric of the universe. This weaving process eventually gave rise to stars, planets, and, ultimately, life. Sadly, the process of weaving the necessary chemicals to promote the growth of the universe took so long that the Great Hive Master's own species had gone extinct by then time that he had prepared a home for them to populate.

To the casual observer, the Ruddarians seemed to be living in a garden of peace and tranquility. However, beneath the surface, this community was no more than a holding pen for a highly evolved beast of burden. Within the colony of Rogestran Five, there was a strict policy of compulsory service to the Zanuck Corporation. The men of the colony were away from home for months at a time working on nearby cold and desolate volcanically active moons, engaged in the process of converting super-heated materials such as lava and space debris into useful by-products — raw metallurgic materials for the construction of weapons, ships and houses — and various forms of gases used for industrial production of chemicals and other elements. These raw materials were sent to industrial centers where they were processed into products that made everyday life possible for the members of the Venusian galaxy. Once the materials were processed and separated into solids, gases, and liquids, the miners, including Kasidy's father, Kabul, would place the various substances into compression tubes. These would then be sealed and sent to a processing plant on one of the industrial spheres to be converted into fuel, life-support extract, or other raw material for consumption by customers of the Zanuck Corporation.

Life had been hard for Kasidy but it had been bearable. Yet, a twist of fate had challenged Kasidy and her family to test the very limits of what was a bearable life, thanks in no small part to the Zanuck Corporation.

Kasidy would never forget that evening. She was playing skip cord in front of their modest wooden cabin in the Tuskgrat district when she spied her father emerging from the nearby jungle. She ran towards him instinctively, expecting Kabul to lift her up into his arms, but he merely reached out his pink colored hand and absently moved it through Kasidy's long copper-and- silver hair.

"Father, what's wrong?" Kasidy asked with a befuddled expression.

"Nothing, Sweetie. Nothing."

"Can we go to the park and play before dinner?"

"You go along, Honey. I need to talk with your mom first. I'll be there to get you before supper."

What Kasidy hadn't heard after she went to the park was the yelling and screaming, which eventually became crying, as Kabul told his wife, Zanesta, that he had been fired from his position as a geological extractor after the foreman of the mine had discovered that Kabul had been hording volcanic crystals for his own side venture. Kabul had been grinding the rocks into a fine powder and mixing it with elements of helium and adrenaline extract to create a potent enhanced energy gas. The mixture, when inhaled, promised to raise a miner's work output by 40% percent. He had actually been making a decent profit from this endeavor until he made the mistake of selling to an undercover government inspector. Kabul received a termination slip provided with the greatest of corporate efficiency.

"I don't make nearly enough in the marketplace with my weave crafts to support this family. What are we going to do?" asked Zanesta. "How are we supposed to live?"

"We'll think of something. As long as we stay together as a family, we'll be all right."

But as Kasidy reminisced on her way to her cabin aboard the starship, *Mjölnir*, she mused that the past truly granted a person 20/20 vision. Things were never alright again. Zanesta had done her best to keep their family afloat. She had asked her sister and brother for assistance, which they provided in the form of excess produce and sweet meats. Her extended family also supplemented Kasidy's wardrobe, which consisted mainly of homemade dresses of canvas, and hand-me-downs from her cousins. These supplements to her daily attire, however, did not prevent the other children at school from coming up with creative, and hurtful, nicknames for Kasidy. She was often referred to as "The Raggedy Girl," and "Cloth-Piece Kasidy." But as bad as things got at school, eight-year-old Kasidy knew that when she got home her mom would know exactly what to say to make it all better. Her mom was always her saving grace.

And she knew that, even though they were rough, those hard times had contributed to Kasidy Vulkner becoming the woman she was today. But even with her ability to adapt to difficult situations, she could have never imagined how much worse things were going to get before they got better. She laid the blame squarely at the feet of her once-beloved father.

She was awakened by a clatter downstairs in the living room. Kasidy snuck down to see her father packing gas canisters into a square nylon satchel that he placed over his shoulder. As Kasidy watched Kabul quietly slip out the door, she moved quickly down the stairs and followed him out the door, down the street to her favorite playground. When she caught up with him, Kabul was sitting on the swing set with a distant look in his eyes. Kasidy was not sure if he had just needed some time alone to process all that had happened and contemplate their next move. Or had, Kabul resolved to make a break for it, abandoning his young daughter and wife? Whatever it was, she was beginning to feel that the best decision was to return to her warm bed, out of the cold night air. It was then that Kasidy saw a grey-and-silver sphere descending from the early morning sky.

Shortly after the pod landed, Kasidy watched in amazement as the panels of the ship began to retract repeatedly like a child removing the pieces of a puzzle until none were left. Once the center of the pod was exposed, there in the middle of the craft sat an enormous insect encased in a titan-sized snail shell. The creature had no eyes, merely two whip-like antennae that emerged from underneath its helmet-like frame. In addition, there was an arch-shaped gap located towards the bottom of the shell. From this space, a pair of pincers and a snake-like tongue hissed at her father.

"Greetings, Kabul Vulkner. It is a pleasure to finally meet you face to face. As you might know, I am Atlas Bokhun of the Omnipotent Hawking Brain Beetle Council."

"It is a pleasure and an honor to be in the presence of such intellect," said Kabul.

"Before we begin," hissed Atlas, "I must transport my associates down from my ship."

Atlas spoke into a headset located on the bottom of his rounded slug-like face. "Have made contact with the seller, Kabul. Hotfire, the three of you are clear to transport to the surface at these coordinates."

"Understood, Atlas. We will see you momentarily," said Hotfire.

Moments later, Kasidy saw three red globes appear between her father and the Hawking Brain Beetle. As moments past, the globes began to grow in size and contort until they resembled three rather large reptilian creatures. The first was a blue and green Trionyx wearing a waist length green blazer over an aqua-blue buttoned-down shirt. Accompanying him was a Cranitian sporting a leather green vest that was as bumpy as the humps of his shell, as well as a pair of blue tight pants and heavy military boots. Finally, the third member of the company emerged. She could tell it was a Chamyx but could barely see its body as it was the color of the midnight sky and had a tail of lengthy proportions in constant motion. The Chamyx gazed at her father with eyes that were darker than the deepest abyss in the ocean. When the Chamyx finally spoke, he did so in a menacing tone.

"Does he have the merchandise, Bokhun?" asked Hotfire.

"We were waiting for all parties to join us before getting down to business, Hotfire."

"Well. We are all here so let's get what we came for, and he can get what is coming to him."

"Hotfire, it is simply impossible to take you anywhere without you creeping somebody out."

Hotfire whipped around as he grabbed the Trionyx's throat, "Say that again, Yanick, and kindly smile please, as I choke the life out of you."

"You know, Hotfire, that I never turn down an invitation to settle a score." Yanick made a kicking motion with his feet. Within seconds, Yanick had wrapped his claws around Hotfire's neck.

"This is going to be as much fun as a night with a Ruddarian Pleasurist," smiled Hotfire.

"Oh trust me. You are definitely going to be on your back very shortly."

Just as they were about to tear each other apart, there was what sounded like a sonic boom. "That's enough, both of you," bellowed Atlas. I swear, one of these days I am going to drop the pair of you into a hot vat of acid just for fun." A moment later, Atlas had regained his composure and turned back to Kabul. "I can assure you that we are professionals. I apologize for the sideshow. Do you have the sample of Enhanced Energy Gas, Mr. Vulkner?"

"Yes, it is right here," Kabul said as he handed it to Atlas.

As Atlas tossed the satchel to his Cranitian associate, Buddash produced a wand from his vest and ran it up and down the cube.

"Is Mr. Vulkner true to his word?" asked Atlas.

"Oh, he is extremely true to his word," said Buddash. He extended his mouth into a smile as much as was possible for a Cranitian.

"Good. Very good."

"I can provide a shipment every two weeks with no problem, Mr. Bokhun," said Kabul nervously.

"I applaud your enthusiasm for this venture. But there are two things that I absolutely can't stand in a business arrangement," said Atlas.

"What are those?" asked Kabul innocently.

"Well. The first is having too many moving parts within an operation. My associates and I have worked together for so many years that we are almost capable of anticipating one another's thoughts and finishing each other's sentences. Hotfire, here, is very adept at chemistry and will be able to replicate your formula within hours. Yanick has numerous connections throughout the cosmos that will distribute the product, and Buddash handles all the finances," explained Atlas.

"But I still get the seven hundred thousand credits, right?" asked Kabul.

"See, that leads me to the second thing that I can't abide in a business arrangement."

"And that is?"

"Loose ends."

Hiding among the park bushes, Kasidy could only watch in horror as the Hawking Beetle's antennae glowed with electricity as he shot laser bolts repeatedly at Kabul as he watched in perverse joy and watched the Ruddarian crumpled into a ball of pink flesh. Never one to be left out of the fun, Hotfire produced a laser gun that was the size of a cannon from his black utility belt and blasted the Ruddarian.

Kasidy could take no more. She had to do something. She shouted out from the darkness, "Leave my father alone!"

"It's a kid. Guessing it is his brat. Hotfire, take care of her," ordered Atlas.

"No," exclaimed Yanick. With a fluid motion, he reached up with his claw-like foot and knocked the gun from Hotfire's hand.

The Abomination turned around to Yanick. "Trust me, my friend, I will make you pay for that."

"No kids. No women. That's where I draw the line," said Yanick.

"Hotfire, ignore the idiot Trionyx for now! Take care of that little loose end," exclaimed Atlas.

Buddash ran over to assist Hotfire after witnessing Yanick's unwillingness to eliminate the "problem." Buddash grabbed Kasidy from behind and lifted her exclaiming "I got her." It was then that Kasidy reached back and took a bite out of his face. Screaming in anguish as yellowish green blood dripped down his face, Buddash dropped the girl to the ground.

Once Kasidy was free of the Cranitian, she had no real idea what her next move should be. Hotfire helped her make that decision by pouncing down behind her like a Ruddarian Lupredator. As Hotfire landed on the ground, Kasidy could feel the ground shake as he made foot-falls. She could see his shadow looming over her as she ran and knew it had to be her imagination, but she swore she could feel the icy coolness of his breath on the back of her neck.

She tried to use her size to her advantage in the pursuit. Wherever she could, Kasidy darted through the branches of drasill trees and squeezed through boulders. It seemed every time she did that, a massive tail came thrashing down behind her, slicing off a branch or smashing a boulder to smithereens. In what seemed like an endless run, Kasidy finally glimpsed her favorite gazebo in the distance. She made a last dash for the stairs with her last breath. But as she did, Kasidy felt a strong Reptilia hand wrap around her leg.

As she turned back, Hotfire was grimacing. "You aren't going anywhere, little lady."

With all her might, she kicked Hotfire in the gut and got up to run through the gazebo. She quickly hid underneath the stairs on the other side, wondering how a 45-pound girl was going to outwit a five-hundred-pound lizard. It was then that she spied the gas pipes across from the gazebo that were used for events like electric band concerts and laser shows. Kasidy quickly formulated a plan. She jumped up from her hiding spot and ran towards the pipes.

"You couldn't catch me if you tried, you overgrown salamander," she taunted.

Hotfire reached for his blaster but quickly remembered that it was lying in the grass by the clearing. Just as well. He was ready to show this girl some fireworks. He reached down to pluck a grenade off his belt and threw it towards Kasidy with pinpoint precision. As it flew through the air, he was surprised to see the young girl running back towards the gazebo. But as she moved out of the way, his bewilderment changed quickly to horror as he saw that the grenade landed beside metal pipe emerging from the ground. All he could think to do was yell back to his compatriots, "We need to go, now!"

Hotfire watched as Atlas grabbed Kabul's limp body in his mighty tongs and vanished inside his grey-and-silver sphere. Yanick, Buddash, and Hotfire transported themselves back to the ship in quick secession as it sped off skyward.

In the confusion, Kasidy crawled back under the gazebo stairs and made for the safest place she knew. From countless hours spent watching magic shows in the park, she knew that there was a trapdoor in the gazebo's center connected to a tunnel leading out of the park. She ran through the underground passage that night without looking back until she made it safely home, to her own room in her own tiny house.

But her escape came at a considerable price. She awoke the next morning with a heavy weight of guilt upon her young shoulders, and swore to herself as she lay quietly in her bed she swore that one day she would avenged her father's death.

Kasidy chose not to share the details of Kabul's apparent demise with her mother. Zanesta had enough to worry about at the moment. Shortly after her father's "disappearance," Zanesta learned that Kabul was the subject of an ongoing criminal investigation. It seemed that his late night transaction with Atlas and his companions had not been his first business venture into the trafficking of illegal substances.

Back on board the *Mjölnir*, Kasidy was jolted into the present by the force of an unknown object slamming into the side of the ship. The voice of her captain came squawking over her wrist computer, "Kasidy, get back up here. We have a situation."

Kasidy turned on her heel and headed straight for the chute lift. She pressed the up button and the door swooshed open. She stepped inside, buckled herself into the internal harness, and set the speed of the chamber to maximum. In seconds, the Astral Engineer had arrived at the flight deck of the *Mjölnir*.

As she exited the chamber, she saw Captain Relich Odinord sitting in the center of the flight deck. He wore a navy blue jumpsuit similar to Kasidy's with heavy combat boots and a utility belt that crisscrossed his massive chest. He had piercing blue eyes, wavy blondish locks, and a beard that had begun to turn from bright gold to a darker shade of grey around the edges of his pinkish face.

"Vulkner, report to your post. We have encountered a Polistine battle cruiser. Unfortunately, we may have stepped right into a big pile of dung."

Kasidy headed with all deliberate speed to her console on the far side of the ship. After scanning the readings, she was able to determine that the compression nodes were still in place; there had been no leakage of Enhanced Energy Gas, a key element for the ship's propulsion, since it was also highly explosive.

The *Mjölnir's* defensive officer, Strobjard Kon, shouted directly in Kasidy's ear as he reported that the ship's energy barriers were still working at maximum. Kon didn't bother mentioning what was painfully obvious to the rest of the crew: they could protect themselves with barriers but were limited in their offensive capability since theirs was a mission of exploration rather than war.

Odinord was barking at the communications officer to get him an open channel to the Polistine battle cruiser. Jandar Weingarter, the ship's comm expert, was halfway through making that call when an ominous voice came over the speakers. The chilling voice sounded like a combination of clicking and hissing, as if a battle cruiser had suddenly become self-aware and was barking orders to its crew.

In a primitive tone, the captain of the Polistine ship, Commander Clack, addressed the crew of the *Mjölnir*.

"*Noes crick cuck hull zarno Polistine. Noes stub clock intyo tor spuck. E promcuck noes thich noes'll surick morcrick,*" stated Commander Clack.

Odinord snapped back at Weingarter. "Get me that in a blastard language I can comprehend."

"Translating now, sir. The ship's Querzi also has accessed the language database and will be able to translate from this point forward."

"Thank you," sighed Odinord. "Run that last transmission again."

"You are not of the Polistine. You have come into our space. I promise you that you'll all soon be dead," stated the Querzi, which was the ship's computer system.

"What the hell! Weingarter, get on the horn and tell the Polistine Captain that we are doing peaceful exploration of this area."

"Aye, Captain." Weingarter had established both visual and audio communication with the Polistine vessel. What appeared on the view screen was a chilling sight to some of the uninitiated who'd never seen a resident of Insectvore. It looked to be a gigantic yellow-jacket viewed under a high powered magnifying glass. The creature had no discernible pupils at all but only two large round discs for eyes that were divided into multi-faceted cells that lay on either side of its massive head. Atop his brow sat two antennae, standing at attention. Its mouth was dominated by two huge pincers large enough to grasp a Ruddarian river melon. In constant motion behind the great wasp were two sets of transparent wings that had a span so great that the view screen failed to encompass it completely.

"Greetings, Ruddarian scum. I am Commander Clack of the battle cruiser, *Honey Hive*. We refuse to tolerate lesser life forms occupying Polistine space. Therefore, you will be destroyed."

"Captain, allow me to respond in kind by blasting that winged Blastard out of the sky," Kon said.

"Easy there, Defensive Officer Kon. I am sure that Commander Clack can be reasoned with."

"You are both mistaken," said Commandeer Clack. "We do not reason with creatures that barely have the capacity for rational thought. We merely relieve them of the burden of existence." With that, he clicked off the viewer screen.

Captain Odinord spun around to Kasidy. "I need phase seven velocity now or we are all dead."

"Yes, sir." Kasidy started to do the calculations. But within seconds, the Polistine vessel had activated a disruptor bean aimed at the *Mjölnir*'s main computer core. With a tone of utter helplessness, Kasidy announced what most of the crew had already guessed. "We are locked out of our own ship's computer. We are dead in space and not going anywhere."

Chapter 3
REDHOT AND BLIGHT

Minerva's Recreation Center had been draped in deep, sickening magenta. The blaring, nerve-piercing sound of the lockdown alarm was being blasted over the intercom. The entire yard population, including Yanick and Buddash, had collapsed to the floor paralyzed by a mixture of electricity and chemicals coursing through their veins. This sudden lack of mobility was all thanks to an electronic chip that had been implanted in all prisoners of Minerva upon their arrival.

With absolute military precision, a group of twenty Polistine centurions formed a semi-circle around the room's perimeter. When the Polistines centurions were in position, previously invisible oval-shaped doors slid open allowing them to exit the room. After the Polistine guards' departure, the portals reopened to reveal twenty pairs of Beetleguise centurions who were armed with gas grenades, side arm blasters and a tasers. Within seconds, the portals resealed themselves and again became undetectable.

Once the Beetleguise centurions had made their way into the room, the Recreation Center was sealed as titanium steel walls came crashing down. Now in a lock down, the prisoner's good behavior became the exclusive responsibility of the Beetleguise.

A Beetleguise sub-commander walked to the middle of the room so he could be seen by all the members of his captive audience, "I am centurion Tong. There is an active situation that is none of your concern. All you need to know is you Reptilia will soon be back in your cells."

A tall Chamyx named Redhot, who was similar in appearance to Hotfire, was laying in his incapacitated state thinking to himself, "Big talk for a Beetleguise in a room full of paralyzed Reptilia."

Centurion Tong would legitimately have had cause for concern if Redhot could have moved. Redhot and his twin brother, Blight, were a particularly disagreeable pair of Chamyx. The siblings were serving time on Minerva for a failed attempted to take over the Polistine Ministry of Justice located on Höllenfeuerhalbinsel, the Chamyx home planet. Redhot and Blight had kidnapped the Polistine Colonial Governor, who maintained order in the name of the Polistine Conglomerate. They had demanded 300,000 credits as well as an exemption from Polistine Army service. It had become necessary for the Polistine government to recruit Chamyx to fight in their military because so many citizens had been able to purchase draft exemptions. Therefore, the Polistine army had been on the verge of depletion and defeat. Many Chamyx and Trionyx had been given the option of joining the Polistine army to fight against the Beetleguise or have all their property seized by the government. Blight and Redhot had opted to recover the value of their property through the kidnapping plot. After a standoff of several hours, the twins requested that larva sandwiches be delivered to the Ministry of Justice. The ambitious Polistine Security Officer took advantage of this request to drug the twins' food. Redhot and Blight woke up a day later in identical cells on Minerva.

As Redhot lay on the cold floor paralyzed, he realized that the time had come for he and his brother to take command of this particular situation. He reached up in excruciating pain with his razor sharp claws, ripped his tracker out of his neck and repeated the process for Blight.

"Why the hell did you do that?" asked Blight

"I did it because you ask too may stupid questions. And I need your help taking out Tong."

"That works for me" smiled Blight.

In howling unison, the twins screamed, "Let's get him."

Centurion Tong barely had enough time to turn around to see what all the commotion was about. In an instant, the nine-foot-tall twins were on top of him, holding the Beetleguise down on the ground with their knees. The guards on the perimeter of the room had already begun firing their laser blasters at the pair. With the paralytic influence of the tracker removed, Redhot and Blight were once again able to concentrate on briefly camouflaging themselves. Tong sat by helplessly as he choked on two trackers being shoved in his mouth.

The pair grabbed the seven-foot-long armored bug by head and foot. They began to swing him from side to side in ever widening arcs until he was nearing the ceiling. At the widest of these swings, the brothers released Tong up into the air. The now-deceased Tong went flying up towards the ceiling at a point near the center of the Recreation Center's roof. Upon contact with the sensory device, which lay at the center of this glass enclosure, Tong's body had the effect of deactivating all the Reptilia trackers.

Mayhem commenced. Surprisingly, it wasn't a result of Minerva's convicts being free to attack the Beetleguise centurions, but from the countdown to Minerva's imminent destruction being broadcasted over the intercom.

Down in the Hanger Bay, the *Honey Vein One's* Querzi was still counting down to destruction.

"Twenty, nineteen, eighteen …"

"Buzz, I swear, this is your last chance," stated Hotfire in a calm, collective voice. "You either find me a way off this rock, or your beloved Conglomerate is going to have enough of you left for a burial."

"Seventeen, sixteen, fifteen …"

"You hear that?" asked Hotfire with a slightly quivering voice. "It's telling you to make peace with the Great Hive Master."

"Fourteen, thirteen, twelve …"

"I am not deceiving you, Hotfire," said Legate Prime Buzz. "The airlocks are sealed and you are running out of air. There is truly no place for you to run."

"Then I'll enjoy seeing you burst into flames with my last gasping breath."

"Is proving that you are right and I am wrong really worth dying for, Hotfire?"

"If calling your bluff saves me from a fifty-year prison sentence, then I am more than willing to roll those particular dice," laughed Hotfire.

"Eleven, ten, nine …" stated the *Honeyvein One's* Querzi computer.

"I guess that the rumors are true," sighed Legate Prime Buzz.

"What rumors?" asked Hotfire.

"The ones that say you are nothing, but a coward for all your bravado."

"**Eight, seven, six...**" mocked the Querzi computer.

"I will squeeze the life out of you, and then throw your carcass into the burning remains of Minerva," screamed Hotfire as he nearly crushed the intercom mic.

"I am ready to face you, Abomination. Unless you are too scared to face me?"

"I accept your challenge, you Insectum piece of scum."

Buzz prepared himself as Hotfire came climbing down the side of the rocket. Before he had even reached the ground, Hotfire started to fire energy balls from his tail. Buzz flung himself into the air, avoiding the globes of glowing death. He brought himself down with his stingers facing Hotfire's tail as he repeatedly stabbed at the behemoth's massive rear appendage. Buzz withdrew a stinger like a sword from a sheath and held it in both hands in attack position as he hovered.

"Dear Legate Prime, your colleague, Honeycomb, has already taken one tail from me today. My pride prevents me from losing another to an insignificant insect such as yourself," said Hotfire.

"I am sure that we can reach some compromise." Buzz positioned his sword to catch the beam of a swirling floodlight on the ceiling of the docking bay. When the sword made contact with the light, the bright beam bounced off his sword and directly into Hotfire's eyes, temporarily blinding him.

"You will still all die," screamed Hotfire as he landed with a thud on the floor.

"**Five, four....**" The countdown abruptly stopped.

The Legate Prime grabbed the intercom mike. "I am guessing that you stopped the countdown, Captain Honeycomb?"

"I guess I managed to recover from the mind-control drug sooner than I expected."

"Computer, restore oxygen to normal level in the docking bay. The authorization code is Xi, Xi, Theta, Gamma." Buzz turned to face Hotfire as he absently asked, "Now what to do with you, Rogue?"

Chapter 4
COMMANDER CLACK

"Has the Ruddarian vessel been disabled?" asked Commander Clack of the *Honey Hive's* first officer, Lieutenant Commander Stinger.

Stinger confirmed, "We currently have the Ruddarian vessel in an energy-draining tractor beam."

Commander Clack next turned to the *Honey Hive's* Weapons Officer, Lieutenant Thorn, "Target that ship, Lieutenant Thorn. Fire torpedoes at your discretion."

As Lieutenant Thorn was preparing to carry out that command, the *Honey Hive* was struck by a tremendous force. Commander Clack leapt from his chair and rushed to Lieutenant Thorn's station.

"Where did that blast come from?"

The *Honey Hive's* Navigator, Ensign Swolow, interjected, "Sir, I am detecting three Beetleguise star fighters off our port side and they appear to be coming in guns blazing."

Commander Clack said with a smile, "Then this is far from combat. It is merely pest control."

"Sir, may I remind you that defensive barriers were seriously drained from our last engagement," stated Lieutenant Thorn. "Therefore, we need to choose between defending the ship and maintaining the tractor beam."

"Let the hominoids go, for now. We shall deal with them later," said Commander Clack.

"Targeting Beetleguise fighters," said Lieutenant Stinger. The computer took a moment to pinpoint the position of the lasers. But then everything began to happen almost all at once.

On the Ruddarian vessel, the *Mjölnir*, the crew was breathing a sigh of relief as Kasidy informed Captain Odinord, "We have been released from the Polistine energy beam."

"Best news I've heard all day," said Captain Odinord.

"We may have another problem, Captain," advised Strobjard Kon. "The Polistine beam seems to be having an adverse effect on our phase drive, as well as a number of other systems."

"Well, Kon, can we shut down the engine and place it into a reset mode to purge the particles?"

"That is the other problem, Captain," said Kon. The Polistine beam contains a regenerative element within its molecular structure that allows it to continue to replicate itself even after being purged from our engine drive."

"So give that to me again, in plain language this time."

"Even after the damn Polistine shut off the beam, the regenerative particles had already started to spread throughout all our operating systems, including propulsion and life support."

"So you are basically telling me that the ship is being eaten from the inside out."

"I honestly wish we had that long. But once the regenerative particles eat their way through the protective anti-matter, the ship will explode," stated Kon grimly.

"Couldn't we divert some of the barrier energy from the storage hold where we are keeping the radioactive aquatic samples from our expedition to JL-2413?" asked Kasidy. "It may not stop these regenerative particles, but at least it will give us time to think of other options."

"Why not just eject the core all together?" asked Ensign Jandar Weingarter.

"These particles are resilient little fucturs. They have already weaved a protective energy barrier around the engine which prevents us from ejecting any portion of the propulsion system including the core," replied Kasidy.

"Vulkner, initiate your redirection of that barrier energy. Then you and Kon get down to the engine room and see if you can do anything to prevent our imminent destruction."

"Right away, Captain." Kasidy and Strobjard headed directly for the turbo lift. Once they had strapped themselves in for turbo jump, the doors were opening a moment later and they were both headed to the engine room to save the ship.

Back aboard the *Honey Hive*, Commander Clack was preparing to lead his crew into glorious battle as he barked at his Weapons officer, Lieutenant Thorn, "Target those ships! Fire!"

Lieutenant Thorn activated the *Honey Hive's* neutron gas energy beams from the bottom of the ship's saucer section. It was a direct hit that should have resulted in the disintegration of the enemy craft S but, instead, an ocean-blue glow enveloped the Beetleguise Star Fighter.

"Sir," said Lieutenant Thorn, "the Beetleguise seem to have developed a new form of protective barrier."

"Well, what weapons do we currently possess that would be able to break through these new Beetleguise barriers?" asked Commander Clack.

"Actually, Commander, I think we should be more concerned about the Beetleguise Star Fighter headed right for us," said Ensign Swolow.

"Launch a torpedo mine," barked Commander Clack. "Target that fighter."

"But the ship is too close," Thorn shouted. "The *Honey Hive* will get caught in the after-blast!"

"Lieutenant Thorn, I gave you a direct order," barked Clack.

"I don't care. I know it is treason, but I won't let you kill us all."

"I hereby relieve you of duty, Lieutenant Thorn. Ensign Ispert, take him to a containment cell."

As Ispert guided Thorn towards the chute lift, Commander Clack sprang from his seat and moved quickly towards the station formerly occupied by his weapons officer. "Enjoy your journey to the After Burn, my little brown enemy." Clack moved his pincher upwards along the console launching the torpedo mine directly at the fighter, realizing only too late, as shrapnel and debris began pelting the ship, that Lieutenant Thorn had indeed correctly calculated that the *Honey Hive* had indeed been too close to the Star Fighter.

Lieutenant Thorn was being escorted to a holding cell that no longer existed when pieces of the mangled Beetleguise fighter began flying through the ship. His first instinct was to take out the enemy. However, as he turned to dispatch his captor, he observed that a flying piece of metal had lodged squarely in the middle of Ispert's head. From between those two massive eyes, Ispert stared across the corridor blankly as he slowly slumped to the floor. Thorn watched as the once mighty *Honey Hive* began to crack like the proverbial Reptilia egg. Thorn watched for a minute as sections of the walkway flew into space before his eyes, along with a number of Polistine crew members. As they were sucked out into the void, they tried valiantly to use their wings to hold on to the remains of the ship, but eventually, all of the unfortunate ship personnel met the same awful fate.

Thorn swore to himself that the fate of his comrades would not befall him. He jumped down through a hole in the floor to a level that had not been affected by the devastation of the fighter crash yet. He began running down the passageway towards the shuttle bay, barely keeping ahead of the flying debris that had already reached the lower deck and was moving at a frantic pace.

As he ran down the corridor, Thorn was dodging falling pieces of ceiling tiles as well as jumping over elements of deck plating that seemed to vanish in mid-air as the entire ship began to disintegrate. The Lieutenant had almost reached the exit when he heard a massive rumbling of twisted metal begin to creak. He looked around to see where the noise was coming from. That was when a massive heap of debris slid down before him. If he had advanced any further, he would have been crushed under the sliding avalanche of metal, wiring, and supports.

As smoke and fire encircled him, Thorn looked around frantically for another access point to the ship's shuttle bay. Out of the corner of his multilayer eye, he spied an exposed access tubing that the engineering staff had often used to complete internal repairs. Thorn lifted himself up and zipped inside the conduit but, realized too late that the external gravity was beginning to compress the tube. With his last ounce of strength, he pushed himself farther up the conduit while the tube itself was being crushed. As he spied the tube's exit, it was also being crushed into nothingness. He judged that there was barely enough space left for him to fit through in order to enter the shuttle bay. So he pushed off the wall and went flying across the room like an insect cannonball.

Once Thorn was in the bay, he quickly recovered from his unceremonious entrance only to find that he had yet another obstacle to overcome. His former commanding officer, Clack, was standing in front of him with a taser in hand, apparently looking for a fight.

"Behold, dear Commander, the devastation that you have brought upon us all," said Lieutenant Thorn.

"I am still the ranking officer on this ship," said Clack, "and I have no qualms about executing you for treason."

"You are out of your cranium," said Thorn.

Clack yelled at the top of his lungs as he rushed towards Thorn with the taser in his appendage. Clack appeared to be moving as if engaged in an ancient joust from Pangean. With quick presence of mind, Thorn turned and grabbed the nearest fallen support beam. As he turned around to meet the lance, he knocked it from Clack's hand and pushed the girder into the commander's chest, sending him crashing to the floor.

"Commander Clack, please. There is room in the shuttle for both of us," Lieutenant Thorn said as he extended his appendage.

"Let me tell you, my son, where else there is plenty of room: in the Afterburn for cowards like you."

"Clack, don't be a fool! Come into the shuttle with me."

"Unlike you, I am prepared to do my duty," said Clack.

"You are a good officer. And I refuse to see an officer of your caliber throw his life away."

As Thorn inched forward, Clack revealed that he still possessed his service blaster, which he aimed squarely at the Lieutenant. "Now, I am giving you a direct order, Coward. Get the fuctur off my ship."

"But Commander, listen to reason," pleaded Thorn.

"I said, NOW!" screamed Clack. It was then that Thorn saw the blood spewing from the Captain's mouth. He realized that Clack had already made up his mind that his death would be glorious.

"Aye, Captain." Thorn turned around and entered one of the spherical shuttle crafts. He quickly, and quietly, ran the pre-flight. As he ignited the thrusts, he flew the shuttlecraft out of the bay, watching the once mighty *Honey Hive* burn in space as he sailed away.

Just as the shuttle flew out of sight, Commander Clack felt a red metallic band begin to vibrate and constrict on the third arm on his left side. Clack knew exactly who was trying to contact him, but was desperately trying to ignore the call. This effort to feign ignorance proved ineffective as the golden eye-piece that hung from his multi-faceted left eye clicked on a picture of the Polistine caller.

"Agent Clack, come in. Agent Clack, you are required to respond," said Agent Honey-Runner.

"I am right here, Agent Honey-Runner," said Clack.

"I am contacting you in order to determine if you were able to disable or destroy the Ruddarian ship."

"*The Mjölnir* has been disabled. However, my own ship also sustained heavy damage. It is my belief that the *Honey Hive* will be unable to be restored to full function."

As Honey-Runner slammed the arms on her left side down on the desk, she said in a loud, almost screeching tone, "No one in Section Seventy-Two truly gives a damn whether or not your vessel is destroyed. There is an ancient, dangerous device aboard the Ruddarian science ship, and your one and only task, Agent Clack, was to obtain the Eye of Hermes and bring it to Section Seventy-Two for further study," said Agent Honey-Runner.

"I have failed you, Agent Honey-Runner. I understand that this failure is unforgiveable."

"It is now necessary for me to take additional steps in order to secure the Eye of Hermes. And you are quiet right, Agent Clack. This failure cannot be forgiven."

Agent Honey-Runner pressed a large gold button beneath her desk that sent a signal to an implant in Commander Clack's brain, and a lethal toxin was injected into Agent Clack's circulatory system. As white foam began to ooze from his mouth, he briefly convulsed before falling stone dead to the floor of the *Honey Hive*.

As Thorn maneuvered the shuttle away from the *Honey Hive* burning in space, the clacking voice of a Beetleguise pilot came over the shuttle's intercom. "Polistine, by the authority of the Beetleguise Trotsnexus, you are hereby ordered to accompany us back to Madagascan where you will surrender yourself as our prisoner of war."

"Yeah, that will happen about two minutes after the Afterburn freezes over," said Thorn.

Thorn drove the shuttle at top speed between the two fighters. Each Beetleguise pilot unleashed a barrage of firepower aimed at the shuttlecraft. To their credit, the Beetles did inflict a great deal of damage on the shuttle, basically making the craft inoperable for the moment. But the Beetleguise pilots were already doomed and simply hadn't realized that their fates had been sealed. Thorn repositioned his shuttle to face straight up toward the sky. As he piloted it upward, the two unfortunate Beetleguise pilots wound up firing on each other. Sadly, for the crew of the *Mjölnir*, the force of this friendly fire sent one of the Beetleguise fighter headed on a collision course for the Ruddarian vessel.

Kasidy was working frantically in the engine room of the *Mjölnir*. Every time she and Kon came close to restoring the protective barrier between the Enhanced Energy Gas and its' anti-matter counterpart, the regenerative particles would mount another destructive attack. She turned to Kon with increasing distress. "What if we were able to infuse the regenerative particles with a degenerating virus?"

"Good plan. But what would keep the virus from discriminating between the regenerative particles and the Enhanced Energy Gas?" asked Kon.

"Is there any way to create a centrifuge effect within the chamber?" asked Captain Odinord.

"We are about to find out. Querzi, can you calculate the mass of the foreign regenerative particles currently in the engine?" Kon asked the ship's Querzi.

"I am unable to calculate the weight of the foreign molecules. They are mimicking the propulsion gas too completely for an accurate comparison."

"We'd be able to fix this problem if we had more time," said Kasidy.

At that moment, Captain Odinord's voice came over the intercom. "Kon, you might want to put your work with the engine on hold. Some large ship fragments are headed straight for us."

"Captain, could we install the phase device that we recovered from Höllenfeuerhalbinsel?"

Kasidy looked at Kon, "Aren't you even a little nervous having it on board?"

Kon sighed wishfully. "I believe that everything happens for a reason. I think that some power meant for that device to be onboard our ship in order to save our lives."

"But we could plug that 'thing' into the engine and all be vaporized," Kasidy observed.

"If we do nothing then we still die. I would prefer to go down fighting," said Kon.

The Captain interjected "Very well."

"Sir —," began Lieutenant Kon.

"Lieutenant Kon, "said the Captain, "I wouldn't say anything else if I were you. Just pray that this works and I don't come to my senses at some point. Querzi, transport item, codenamed 'Hermes' to the engine room main propulsion chamber."

"Transfer is not authorized. Item has level Alpha classification, which means —,"

"Yes, I know the meaning of Level Alpha, Querzi. The item is quarantined to the Cargo Bay," said Captain Odinord. The Captain and Querzi did not see eye to digital sensor in this instance. Odinord rushed into the engine room holding a small silver box. "I knew that the damn Querzi wasn't going to let me have it."

"Cap, let me have it so I can install it," said Defensive Officer Kon.

"Stand down, lieutenant. It is my ship so if anyone is going to accidently blow it to the After burn it's going to be me," ordered the Captain.

"Understood, Captain Odinord. Querzi, access proximity sensors. Give me a continual measure of the distance between the debris and our ship," commanded Defensive Officer Kon.

"Very good. Proximity countdown beginning now. Nineteen hundred feet and counting."

Kasidy and Kon watched as the Captain removed the engine panel on the bottom of the console and began to feverishly connect the Green Diamond to the engine.

"Eighteen fifty, eighteen hundred. Contact will occur in approximately seven minutes. Seventeen hundred."

"Sir, the regenerative particles; they are headed for the device," said Kasidy.

"Kasidy, establish a force field around the device. Kon, keep working on maintaining that barrier between the Enhanced Energy Gas and the antimatter gas," barked the Captain.

"Fifteen fifty. Fifteen hundred. Fourteen fifty. Fourteen hundred. Contact with the Beetleguise fighter debris in five and a half minutes."

"Sir, the regenerative particles are migrating to the connection with the device," said Kon, "but the force field is not working as protection against the particles."

"Try reinforcing the energy strength of the field," said the Captain.

"Eleven fifty. Eleven hundred. One thousand feet and closing. Contact in approximately four minutes."

"Captain Odinord, the regenerative particles have broken through the field."

"Daggit. Well, no one can say we didn't go down fighting —" Kasidy interrupted the Captain in a voice of utter amazement. "Sir, the device is vaporizing the particles on contact. Energy gas levels in the propulsion system are returning to normal."

Querzi interjected with her own less-than-happy news. **"Three minutes to contact with alien debris."**

"Cap, switch it on, for the love of After burn," implored Kon.

"What if it destroys the ship like it did those regeneration particles?" asked Captain Odinord.

"I don't know. But we are out of time and out of choices."

"Heaven help me," pleaded Captain Odinord.

Captain Odinord could not believe what happened next as the Hermes device decided to turn itself 'on.' He, Kon and Kasidy watched as every ounce of power on t*he Mjölnir* was drained into the Green Diamond. The lights of the engine room went dark as did the adjoining corridor and eventually the entire ship. The power from all electronic systems including weapons, barriers and life support were quickly consumed by the Green Diamond that Captain Odinord had seen fit to unleash upon the galaxy. Odinord looked out a nearby portal to see that a small shuttle that was also having its power completely drained by the electrical tentacles emanating from the Green Diamond.

Having switched to internal emergency atomic power, Querzi alerted Odinord that contact with the remains of the derelict fighter was a minute away. When the Captain looked, he saw the twisted metal of the Beetleguise fighter headed towards him at an alarming speed. As it moved, the wreckage seemed to be speeding up, getting ready to make contact."

"Final fifteen seconds."

Odinord pressed a nearby comm button, "All hands brace for impact."

"Delete countdown, Querzi." commanded Captain Odinord.

"As you wish."

In that last few seconds, the ancient Green Diamond demonstrated to Ruddarian, Polistine and Beetleguise alike how much destruction the device was truly capable of inflicting upon the universe. A blast of green energy went forth and completely and utterly vaporized the oncoming Beetleguise freighter.

"Querzi, restore ship's systems. Perform vessel-wide diagnostic as soon as possible," yelled Odinord.

"Impossible to complete at this time. Propulsion, defensive capabilities, life support and all other energy-based ship functions will not be unavailable for 25 minutes."

"Why the fuctur not?"

"The Eye of Hermes has drained every last ounce of Enhanced Energy Gas. Like Querzi said, it will take at least 25 minutes for energy levels to return to minimal operating capacity," stated Kon.

"Captain, we are going to run out of oxygen in under 20 minutes," said Kasidy.

"We also have a number of crew who are in need of immediate medical attention," said Kon.

"Then we need to get Dr. Tulare down here if our crew is going to be gasping for air in a few minutes," stated Captain Odinord. "Now, Kasidy and Kon, you need to do something for me." Odinord extended his arm and pointed to the Green Diamond. "Get that thing the fuctur off my ship."

Thorn had only been able to view the scene unfolding before him in helpless horror. The Beetleguise battle fighter was headed on a direct course for the middle of the *Mjölnir*. The ensuing explosion would be a sight to behold for five to ten seconds before Thorn's shuttle was destroyed.

But that explosion never came. Instead, Thorn watched as a long green electrical stream of energy reached out from the *Mjölnir*. The eerie green light managed to gobble up every last drop of the shuttle's power. Thorn then watched as the energy stolen from his shuttle shot out of the Ruddarian vessel as a destructive wave that vaporized the derelict Beetleguise fighter.

"I can't be seeing what I am seeing. There is no possibility that these Pink Monkeys could have developed technology as destructive as this weapon. Even we, the Polistine, had abandoned such destructive instruments of combat because we were unable to control such weapons of destruction.

As Thorn sat contemplating the destruction he had just witnessed, he hardly noticed a creaking sound coming from above him. Before he knew what was happening, a large section of the shuttle's metal bulkhead had fallen on Thorn., trapping him beneath its massive weight. Lieutenant Thorn, weapons officer of the *Honey Hive*, quickly came to the realization that he was alone and trapped in space.

Chapter 5
HOTFIRE

In that moment, the countdown in the hangar bay came to an abrupt stop. The blinding light in front of Hotfire's eyes was fading as his vision began a slow march towards normalcy. And a familiar voice echoed over the loud speakers.

"Legate Prime, have your Bugs restrain this Abomination. Then you may bring him to me. I shall handle his disposition myself."

Hotfire said in a voice filled with bravado, "If you want my opinion, Warden Sobek, I think that you should let me go. Otherwise, you will soon have a serious problem."

"And what would that be?"

"It will be that (a) I will be escaping from your maximum security rock."

"And dare I ask, is there a (b) portion to that problem?"

"Yes, that you have my own guarantee that I will kill you before I make my escape."

"I doubt that."

Hotfire smiled. "I guess only time will tell."

"Legate Prime, bring Hotfire to me."

Buzz released the lock on the access doors on the console. As the door opened, four Beetleguise centurions came running in to escort Hotfire to the warden's office. The Legate turned to the lead Beetleguise. "Lieutenant Trazz, you have my personal guarantee that this malcontent will pay for his crimes with his own blood. Now take this beast out of my sight."

"It seems that he has taken care of that himself, Legate Prime," said Trazz.

"I thought he was too stunned to cloak himself."

Trazz turned to his second-in-command, Hargot. "I want this area covered with genetic detection micro-bots. And I want it done two minutes ago."

"Releasing detection micro-bots," said Hargot, but before he could even reach for the activation switch, an invisible tail knocked the six-foot long Beetleguise to the ground.

"Catch me if you can, my flying gendarmerie," taunted Hotfire.

"Lock down the doors. Nothing gets out of here," barked the Legate Prime.

"Trazz will lock the room." said Trazz

"Oh, at this point, I have no intention of trying to escape. You have crossed a line in attacking me. I will make you pay for this transgression by making you watch your world burn." Hotfire appeared for a moment on the side of the rocket as he launched several fireballs from his tail incinerating two of the Beetleguise.

After climbing back in the cockpit of the *Honeyvein One*, he found Captain Honeycomb waiting for him. The Captain had removed a cooling conduit from the overhead junction. As soon as Honeycomb hear the heavy foot falls of a cloaked entity, he began spraying the deck with the frozonic cooling gas that disrupted Hotfire's ability to maintain invisibility. When Hotfire reached forward to punch the Captain, he had already anticipated this action, and braced himself for impact. What the Captain could not prevent though was being knocked to the ground by Hotfire's massive tail.

Hotfire rose to his full height as he stood over the fallen captain. "Now, where was I before I was rudely interrupted? Ah yes, I know." Hotfire punched a series of buttons on the control panel. After he hit the 'enter' key, Querzi exited sleep mode. **"Captain, are you positive that you wish to resume the self-destruct countdown?"**

"Querzi, please comply with my request, and this time, disable the override command."

In an instant, the transport shuttle's main computer resumed the countdown to destruction. Hotfire sat down in the Captain's chair with a smile of extreme satisfaction on his face. It was then that someone whispered in his ear, "I wouldn't get too comfortable."

Buzz began punching Hotfire repeatedly in the chest. Hotfire tried to shoot fireballs at his opponent but, Buzz repeatedly was able to maneuver out of their path. Hotfire observed that his tactic of trying to singe his opponent wasn't working so he tried a different tact. He wrapped his tail around the Legate Prime's neck and began to squeeze.

"You will never get out of here alive," gasped Legate Prime Buzz.

"Neither will you, my flying gendarmerie," laughed Hotfire.

"I wouldn't be too sure about that," replied Buzz.

Hotfire looked over his shoulder to see two Beetleguise each holding a hypo-spray that they had taken from the onboard supply of sedatives. After they injected the sedative into Hotfire's neck, he could feel his whole body going numb. Buzz then watched as Hotfire slumped in the Captain's chair.

Buzz was well aware that the paralysis would not last for long. He yelled to Trazz and Hargot, "Activate the containment beam and get Hotfire on a Tram. I'll escort him to the *Citadel* myself." The Legate re-entered the cockpit where he re-enabled the override command, "Querzi, cancel self-destruct. Code Psi, Pi, Theta, Omega, Omega, Buzz."

Querzi, replied, **"Reactivation of override command for self-destruct must be authorized by appendage print of two senior prison officials. Four minutes to destruction of *Honeyvein* One."**

"Ah, fuctur," Buzz said to no one in particular as he looked over to see Captain Honeycomb passed out on the floor. Not losing a single moment, Buzz yanked opened a nearby panel and grabbed one of Honeycomb's appendages. "I am sorry, my friend, but this will sting. He unraveled a piece of metal wiring and stuck it in Honeycomb's arm, reviving the Captain."

"Three minutes to the destruction of *Honeyvein One*."

"Why haven't you stopped the countdown?"

"Hotfire disabled the override command."

Without missing a beat, Captain Honeycomb and Legate Prime Buzz placed their appendages on the computer console. "Querzi, cancel self-destruct. Code Psi, Gamma, Theta, Gamma, Omega, Honeycomb."

"Querzi, cancel self-destruct. Code Psi, Pi, Theta, Omega, Omega, Buzz."

"Two minutes to destruct —" Querzi hesitated, **"⊠ override command engaged. Destruction of *Honeyvein One* will no longer occur at this time."**

"Well. I guess that's good to know," said Buzz. "Are you all right, Captain?"

"I am fine. However, Legate Prime, I was negligent in allowing Hotfire to gain access to the Suggestion Sedative. I should have locked that cabinet." Captain Honeycomb suddenly stood straight up at attention. "Legate Prime, I must submit myself to you for disciplinary punishment. My actions in this situation, despite their involuntary nature, could have resulted in Minerva's destruction."

"At ease, Captain, any first year cadet could tell that you were acting under duress."

"Thank you, Legate Prime. That means a great deal coming from you."

"Don't mention it. Now, I have an Abomination to deliver to Warden Sobek." Buzz placed his appendage on Honeycomb's shoulder. "And you have a ship to prepare for its return journey."

"Very good, Sir. Unfortunately, I lost several good soldiers while trying to defend the *Honeyvein One* from the Abomination," said Captain Honeycomb.

"I will assign new centurions within the hour. I will also need a list of the dead so their families can receive the proper compensation for losing love ones in the line of military duty," said Buzz.

"You will have that information before I return to Insectvore."

Buzz walked over to the intercom located in the center of the control panel. As he punched the code that would place him in contact with Warden Sobek's private answering service, the Legate Prime was surprised to discover that it went straight to the recorded 'unavailable' message.

"Where the Hellfire have you disappeared to at a time like this, Sobek," Buzz said under his breath. With reluctance, he left a message indicating that he was on his way to Sobek's private office, the *Citadel*, with The Abomination, Hotfire.

The Legate Prime had just terminated the connection when the loud speakers of the *Honeyvein One* came to life with an urgent call for assistance from a Beetleguise centurion in Minerva's Recreation Center, Lieutenant Hasdot, "We are in desperate need of assistance. Centurion Tong has been killed. The prisoners have removed their trackers and are currently rioting."

Legate Prime Buzz's face grew cold, "Not on my watch they don't." As the Legate Prime and the Captain flew the short distance from the *Honeyvein One* to the Hangar Bay floor, Buzz barked out orders. "Lieutenant Trazz, you and Hargot are going to have to take the Abomination Hotfire on a Tram to Warden Sobek. Captain, you are with me. We are going to go catch some lizards."

At the *Citadel*, Warden Sobek had taken advantage of the fact that his do-gooder Legate Prime was preoccupied with The Abomination Hotfire to glide his way from his main office to the holo-chamber. Sobek's office was a mixture of tropical jungle elements and a central silver mercury fountain as well as high tech implements such as an enormous Querzi system with dozens of view screens that hung from the ceiling. The holo-chamber, on the other hand, was a round antiseptic chamber covered in white panels with a single Querzi access terminal that stood in the center of the room.

As Sobek placed his tentacle onto a nearby console, the scene around him changed from an empty white room to a dark chamber containing a group of Querzies whose diodes flickered on and off with purple lights. Sobek was now surrounded by the holographic images of the Omnipotent Hawking Brain Beetle Council, the entire Hawking Brain Beetle race were also members of the family Bokhun.

Sobek's cousin, a female Hawking Brain Beetle named Osiris, was the first to address Sobek. "Has The Abomination been delivered to you on Minerva?"

"Yes, Council member, Osiris. However, my fool of a Legate has not yet brought him to me."

"Hotfire is an essential element in our strategy to deal with the Diabolix situation. If events do not unfold as the Council desires, you will need to personally persuade Hotfire to come around to the Hawking's way of thinking regarding the Diabolix threat," said Osiris.

"A threat that should have been contained by the Hawking a long time ago," said Sobek.

"Which threat are we speaking of, Hotfire or Diabolix? We, Hawking Brain Beetle, are responsible for them both," chimed in another council member, Ra Bokhun.

"We cannot go back and change the past, Ra," said Osiris. "Our council can only work towards trying to give some of us a future."

"What if Hotfire cannot be convinced to assist us with the elimination of Diabolix? He will not remain trapped in the X-Space dimension forever." stated Sobek.

"Is Dr. Rabun still working on the development of the toxin to eliminate Diabolix?" asked Osiris.

"He has completed the toxin. However, Doctor Rabun has expressed misgivings about using it."

"It might be necessary to use stronger persuasion at some point," said Ra.

"Through his repeated use of the Enhanced Energy Gas as a drug, Diabolix has almost gained immortality. Therefore, I will need to show Dr. Rabun that there is one and only key to eliminating this galactic threat, and that key is his Diabolix toxin." said Sobek.

Sobek then changed his tone from demanding to solicitous, "Does the Council foresee a time in the near future when I will be able to leave Minerva and pass the responsibility of warden to another Hawking Brain Beetle?"

Council member Osiris drew herself up straight, "This is not the moment to discuss you being relieved of your duties as warden. I sense great unrest occurring on Minerva. Go deal with that, cousin."

And once again, Warden Sobek was standing alone in the white holo-chamber.

Back in the Hangar Bay, Yanick reflected that a quiet morning of recreation and, in his case, conspiring to perpetrate a robbery, had turned into a scene of mass confusion in the yard. Through the efforts of the Blight and Redhot,

Minerva's behavioral tracking devices had been deactivated. Despite this taste of freedom, the inmates were awaiting the destruction of the Minerva Penitentiary.

Buddash Kyo was looking towards his partner-in-crime for advice about their next move. "We have got to get out of here, Yanick."

"Wow!" said Yanick sarcastically. "Honestly, that thought hadn't crossed my mind. We are on an asteroid, a million miles from any civilization. Where are we supposed to go?"

"First, let's worry about the escaping part. The details will fall into place later," said Buddash.

"I suppose that there are worse things I could be doing today," sighed Yanick. "In the spirit of this joint venture, I want to thank you for your overwhelming support. In that same spirit of cooperation, I ask your forgiveness for this next action."

"What do you mean?" asked Buddash

Yanick was already ripping the behavioral tracker out of Kyo's orange neck and stomping on it on the floor. He then performed a similar action in destroying his own tracking device.

It was then that Buddash heard the announcement over the loud speakers that the countdown to Minerva's destruction had been averted and that all prisoners were to be escorted back to their cells. "Did you hear that, Yanick? We aren't going to be blown to the After burn."

All that Yanick could hear at that moment was the sound of more guards trying to break down the door to the Recreation Center. "Now, step two, take one of the heavier dumb bell weights off the free lifting bars."

"There is no longer any danger. Besides, I can't leave because Hunash is expecting me to meet her later on this afternoon to fill her in on the plan."

"I am not trading my freedom for some measly little drug heist," said Yanick.

"What part of Diabolix having me rubbed out and turning me into a wall ornament don't you get, you ignorant, overgrown Salamander?"

"Just do as I say for the moment." Yanick could tell that time was growing short as he heard the Polistine and Beetleguise Centurions using portable blast cannons to gain access to the room.

Yanick looked up to see Buddash holding a single twenty-pound weight. "No, that will never do. You are going to need to get something much heavier than that puny thing."

"How heavy are we talking?" asked Buddash mournfully.

"As heavy as you can lift."

Yanick raced over to the nearest lifting bench and grabbed an eighty-five-pound metal weight. As he looked out at his fellow inmates, he saw a yellow flash fill the room. The fact that the prisoners were beginning to collapse to the floor told him that the Polistine guards had reactivated their electronic leashes.

The Legate Prime and the shuttle Captain were lauding over their captives. "Use whatever force is necessary. I want all the prisoners subdued and returned to their cells." Without warning, the shuttle Captain was knocked out of the air and slammed towards the metal floor,

"Did the Beetleguise Centurions let Hotfire escape?" asked Captain Honeycomb, picking himself off the floor.

"No, I have a bad feeling that this is a different animal entirely," said Legate Prime.

Just then, Redhot's brother, Blight, materialized on the arch of the dome in front of Buzz. "Hello there, Legate Prime. Looking for us?"

Blight whipped his tail around to knock the Legate Prime like a rag doll across the room. Buzz decided to respond to Blight with actions rather than words, jumped up to the ceiling.

With one mighty leap, Blight followed Buzz as he landed next to him on the Recreation Center's ceiling. However, before Blight could grab a hold of Buzz, he flew down to the ground and took a neural paralyzer from a nearby Beetleguise Centurion. As Buzz was flying up again, Blight's brother, Redhot, appeared and with an almost imperceptible swipe, Redhot ripped the neural paralyzer from the Legate's Prime hand and removed the protective clasp. Buzz instinctively swirled around and kicked Redhot in the chest, which knocked the paralyzer out of Redhot's hand to the ground below where it sprayed an incapitating mist over a handful of prisoners.

Buzz turned once again toward Redhot and used both of his stingers to stab him in the legs. As Redhot was falling, Buzz followed him down to the ground. Redhot was determined that when he had the first opportunity that he would come crashing down on top of the Legate.

Legate Prime Buzz had a more creative solution. Instead of confronting Redhot, Buzz began to flap his wings furiously in front of the gas, blowing it towards Redhot. The smoke from the grenade had almost reached Redhot when an exhaust fan switched on by itself, sucking the paralytic gas out into space.

"He bothering you, big brother?" asked Blight as he rematerialized.

"Is that your way of reminding me that it is my responsibility to get you out of trouble?" asked Redhot.

"No. It is just fun to remind you that mother would disapprove if anything happened to me," said Blight.

"I concede the point that neither of us wants to displease mother. Now can we please swat this bug?"

Redhot and Blight began to climb up to the dome, Buzz had removed a cable from the broken tracking module, and hit a few buttons that reversed the polarity of the charge. Redhot could only watch helplessly as Blight was shot with about fifty thousand volts of electricity, sending him to the floor. In an effort at self-preservation, Redhot cloaked himself again as Buzz began inquiring of the shuttle Captain, "Where the After burn did he go?" It was then that Redhot observed something that had previously escaped his notice. He detected from his perch on the sidewall that a lone blue-and-green-skinned Trionyx was using a large barbell weight to smack a hole through the floor. His progress was proceeding at a Hawking Brain Beetle's pace.

Moreover, Redhot had the nagging feeling that he had encountered this Trionyx in his limited travels on Minerva. It was at that moment that Redhot realized that he had been played a game of Five Card Gurt – Duchene with a few of his fellow inmates, including this Trionyx. After several hours of consistently losing the financial pot, Redhot had had an opportunity to score a big jackpot. The only thing standing between Redhot and his big payday was the Trionyx. Redhot had placed his cards on the table with a great deal of satisfaction as he revealed a hand of two Zeniths and three Emperors. Quite convinced that he had won the hand, Redhot reached for the pile of credits only for Yanick overly dramatically clear his throat, interrupting him.

"Not so fast, my midnight black friend," said Yanick. "I believe that my royal family beats your full castle." With dramatic flair, Yanick laid his hand on the table: A Zenith, an Emperor, a Concubine, a Fool, and a ten on the table. "Thank you, Gentleman, I believe that I will be on my way," Yanick stated as he collected his winnings.

Redhot cleared his throat before he said, "You are not going anywhere until you give me the chance to win my money back."

"Unfortunately, it is getting late and I really must be going, my Chamyx friend."

"Not until we both get what is coming to us," said Redhot who then reached up and grabbed Yanick by the arm. As he squeezed Yanick's hand, a shower of Gurt–Duchene cards came flying out of Yanick's sleeve.

"Well, if that isn't the weirdest thing," smiled Yanick. Redhot grabbed Yanick by the throat, and lifted up in the air.

As he was gasping for what very likely might have been his last breath, Yanick said in a wisp of a voice, "You really don't want to do this, my friend. It will definitely end badly for you."

"That is very funny because I seem to be holding all the cards, so to speak," said Redhot.

"Except that I still have a Zenith in the hole," said Yanick. It was then that he bit down on a hollow fang that contained a potent knockout gas. As Yanick exhaled the gas into Redhot's face, he watched the large black Chamyx crumple to the ground like a Madagascan Xerevan flower.

In that moment, weeks before, Redhot had made his mind up in that he was going to take full advantage of any opportunities for revenge.

Yanick failed to take notice of Redhot as he once again became visible, hanging from a nearby wall and positioned himself so that he would be able to use his entire mass of six hundred pounds to come crashing down on the Trionyx.

"Yanick, you might want to move out of the way," said Buddash as he looked over to see Redhot.

"Buddash, I am really trying to focus."

"No, Yanick," said Buddash with a greater sense of urgency, "I really think you need to see this."

"Fine," said Yanick as he huffed an impatient sigh. As soon as he turned around, he recognized the large, black Chamyx hanging on the wall. The only verbalization that Yanick was able to muster was, "Oh, crasp."

"Now, you are going to see what cards I have up *my* sleeve, my little blue-and-green hustler," said Redhot. In one final maneuver, Redhot shifted his body about six inches until he was satisfied that he would land on top of Yanick, crushing him like a river melon. He took a flying leap towards Yanick.

Yanick watched transfixed and failed to notice as Buddash swung around to move him out of harm's way. All he managed to see was a black, and yellow colored blur flying past him as large pieces of metallic flooring were launched skyward.

As Buddash and Redhot fell through the newly formed crater, Yanick shouted, "Don't worry, Buddash. I'm coming down right now to save your shelled ass." However, a reply didn't come from Buddash. "How nice of you, my Trionyx friend. I believe that I will take you up on that generous offer." Before he even had a moment to react, a large black tail had wrapped itself around Yanick's mid-section. As Yanick went plummeting through the floor, he tried his best to maneuver away from his friend Buddash who had come to rest on a metal reading table. Yanick found himself in Minerva's prison library. Yanick managed to push himself past the table as he tucked and rolled along the plastic red tiled floor. Looking up towards the library's ceiling, Yanick knew that Redhot would come crashing down on him any second now. He looked over to see the metal hover-cart that contained a trifling of returned books; the prison library wasn't the most popular destination.

"How about taking in a good book for a change, you micro-brained Chamyx," Yanick said as he grabbed hold of the cart and sent it flying towards Redhot. The black Chamyx was thrown backward and crashed into the low-lying bookshelves behind him. Once Redhot recovered himself, he lifted up the cart, and flung it towards Yanick. With no effort at all, Yanick grabbed the metal table with both hands and feet as he balanced his weight on his tail.

"Careful. The tables are about to turn on you." retorted Yanick.

"Oh, I do believe that it is still your turn, Yanick," sneered Redhot. He jumped up with both muscular feet facing forward. Almost like an ancient bullet, Redhot slammed in the cart into Yanick and sent him crashing into the far wall of the library. Yanick lay unconscious on the other side of the library wall in the Prison's industrial laundry center.

"Daggit, does revenge taste sweet or what?" yelled Redhot.

"I wouldn't unwrap that vengeance candy, just yet." said Buddash.

"And what are you going to do to stop me?" asked Redhot as he turned back to face Buddash.

"Oh, just this," said Buddash as he leapt up from the table and into the air. As he landed onto Redhot's large back, extended his nails and dug them into Redhot's face, leaving four bloody lines that extended from his forehead to his chin. Buddash continued his assault by pulling his head into his shell by repeatedly slamming his shell into Redhot's face.

"Please stop, Cranitian. The pain is too much for me to bear. I surrender."

"Really? Did I just win?"

As Buddash produced his head from his shell, he saw that Redhot had a smirk on his face. "Sorry, but I am afraid that you didn't." Redhot spied the rows of dryers and washing machines through the hole in the wall created by the Yanick projectile. He watched with great satisfaction as he picked up Buddash and tossed him through the hole, knocking Buddash out cold. Redhot through the hole into the laundry center after his prey. "How to do away with you in a fittingly appropriate manner?" Redhot asked himself. "Ah, I think I have just gotten a slight notion." He picked up the limp body of Yanick in his arms. Like someone carrying a basket of dirty prison garbs, Redhot walked over to a row of massive industrial dryers, opened the door to the nearest one, flung Yanick's body inside, and set the drying cycle to maximum heat.

As Yanick was tossed around in the dryer, with pieces of his clothes and skin beginning to fly off like pieces of cloth being burned in a fire, Redhot laughed, "I hope you asked for no scorch for your clothes."

"Now what to do with you, my annoying little armored foe." Redhot looked up towards a large rectangular iron mass hanging from the ceiling of the laundry room. He instantly recognized that it was a steam iron used by the inmates who staffed the laundry room to fold and press the prisoners' uniforms. "It is about time that you were flattened and folded, my diminutive Cranitian friend," said Redhot as he placed Buddash in the over-sized round metal cradle that lay beneath the iron mass and fastened the latches on the outside, just in case Buddash did manage to awaken before becoming a steamed pancake.

Back in the Recreation Center, Captain Honeycomb was still laying on the floor feeling the after- effects of being knocked around by not one but two Chamyx during that morning. Buzz moved swiftly over to his comrade as he dodged the laser fire emanating from the guns of the Insectum guards who were trying to subdue the Reptilia prisoners and quell the near rebellion.

Buzz yelled to Honeycomb, "where the hell fire did that other Chamyx get to?"

"Daggit, If I know. Right now, I am more concerned about these other Reptilia in the room."

Honeycomb jumped into action. He motioned three Beetleguise guards over to him. "Someone or something made a hole in our lovely floor. Go find some metal and patch it up before we have multiple escapees on our hands."

"I can see you are going to prove handy to have around, my friend," said Buzz.

"Thank you for the compliment, Legate. What's next?"

"There is the matter of getting the prisoners back into their cells."

"How many have been put down, so far?" asked Captain Honeycomb.

"Well, here come four Reptilia who haven't been subdued yet," Legate Prime Buzz replied sarcastically. He and Captain Honeycomb looked up to see two blue-and-green skinned raptors who were similar in appearance to Yanick as well as two Cranitian who resembled Buddash Kyo. Quickly positioning themselves back to back, Captain Honeycomb and the Legate Prime quickly dispatched the foursome through several punches, the occasional Taser sting, and laser blasts.

Honeycomb looked over to see that the Beetleguise he had assigned to patch the escape hole were making slow progress. As he looked around, the Captain saw that other Polistines were engaged in hand to hand combat with detainees.

"This situation is absolutely intolerable," said Buzz. He flew up to a guard's crow's nest situated towards the top of the dome. He positioned himself mid-air as he aimed his blaster towards the protective glass. As he fired, the green laser cut a hole in the center, which fractured into a spider's web of cracks. With delicate but firm force, Buzz pressed his Taser into the small opening in the glass causing a rainstorm of shattered pieces to fall to the ground. Carefully covering his body with his wings as he bent down, Buzz climbed inside the nest and headed for the far wall of the chamber. With remarkable speed, he rebooted the tracking system using backup from the prison's mainframe computer. The Legate believed that the effect would be instantaneous but the computer informed him that the process of bringing the prisoners back under the behavioral modifications occurred in increments of five and ten percent.

"So much for modern technology," mumbled Buzz. He looked out the window to see that there were several circles of inmates and guards at various intervals standing around the Rec Center; the pattern was fairly consistent. Each group of guards had surrounded a number of prisoners and was trying to herd them back to their containment units.

In a quiet lament to himself, the Legate Prime saw no immediate end in sight for the standoff. He saw that there was an incoming communication from the Citadel and dared hope it was his salvation.

"Legate Prime, why are there prisoners still in the Rec Center at this late hour of the morning?" asked Warden Sobek.

"There was an issue with inmate 6610, the war criminal known as Hotfire. He activated the self-destruct on the prison transport, *Honeyvein One*. Captain Honeycomb and I have resolved that situation."

"What does that have to do with the fact that there are prisoners roaming loose in the Rec Center with deactivated trackers?" asked Sobek, who was becoming increasingly perturbed with his Legate Prime.

"Two Chamyx, Blight and Redhot, took advantage of the distraction and decided that today was a good day to start a riot," stated Legate Prime Buzz.

"I see. Dare I foolishly inquire where are they at the moment?"

"One is dead. The other is currently missing."

"It seems, Legate Prime Buzz that you require assistance in handling this situation. That assistance will be arriving at the Rec Center within the hour."

"For now. My guards are engaged in hand-to- hand combat with the prisoners."

"*My* guards, Legate Prime. Never forget who is truly in charge of Minerva. But for now, carry on, Legate. Assistance will be arriving shortly."

Back in the *Citadel*, Sobek pressed a few diodes on his command console, and his view of the Rec Center was replaced by an image of the Medical Bay. "Doctor Rabun, are you there? Please respond," asked Sobek. A sullen-looking creature with an elongated face, orange-colored-skin, and polished mirror eyes came into frame. "This is Doctor Rabun. How can I help you this morning, Warden? If it is regarding the use of the toxin, I must inform you that I am still considering the practicality of using the virus against Diabolix. I am also wondering what would be the consequences to our galaxy's population if the toxin fell into the wrong hands."

"The members of your species are forever reminding everyone how morally superior you are."

"I don't have time for one of our spirited debates so I will just get straight to the point. Besides, an update on the Diabolix toxin, how can I assist you?"

"I need you to activate project Xerxes."

"The subjects are still too difficult and violent to control outside a laboratory setting."

"Either you give me what I want, Doctor or I will introduce you to one of my enhanced creatures; as their next meal." said Sobek.

"I suppose that I could initiate the project in a limited fashion with a handful of participants."

"Very good. I will expect to see the project implemented at the Rec Center within the half hour. Sobek out."

"Damn you to the After burn," said Rabun as he headed down to the cryo-maintenance room."

After speaking with Warden Sobek, Legate Prime Buzz had returned to the floor of the Rec Center to assist the Polistine and Beetleguise centurions with prisoner containment and was currently engaged in appendage to claw combat with a large creature with an extended mouth approximately five- feet-long with six rows of razor-sharp teeth. The creature, known as a Quillian, also possessed a rather lengthy tail capable of knocking an opponent to the ground. This particular Quillian, Ractudo, was slamming his tail down repeatedly in an attempt to crush Buzz, but his opponent was refusing to stay still long enough for Ractudo to aim his tail in any sort of accurate manner.

As the Legate Prime watched Ractudo's tail about to come crashing down on his skull, he suddenly heard the sound of the klaxon and saw the large vault-styled door at the far side of the room begin to roll back to reveal four heavily armored individuals. In the doorway, there were four beings who wore red and yellow helmets with extended frills and three long horns above the eyes and nose. They were dressed in blue jumpsuits with plates of metal covering their knees, forearms and chests. One of these creatures stepped forward and announced that the prisoners needed to return to their cells immediately or face the consequences.

Ractudo stopped his tail in mid-air, "And what army exactly is going to make us?"

"Inmate 3551, Ractudo," said the Triceratopian soldier, "we four are the only army that is required." In the next instant, Legate Prime Buzz found himself involuntarily jumping back as a beam of blue light came out of one of the Triceratopian's horns. The beam crossed the room in a blink of an eye and landed on Ractudo's chest. The Centurions, including Legate Prime Buzz, and the prisoners watched in horror as the blue beam immediately began to dissolve pieces of the Quillian flesh until he had completely dissolved into thin air.

"There are only four of those goons," said another Trionyx raptor, Gabdulan. "And in my humble opinion, if we cannot deal with four horned faced thugs, then we are not worthy of calling ourselves "criminals." So, my fellow inmates, including my distant Chamyx and Quillian cousins, who will assist me in eliminating this threat to our ability to pursue our criminal ventures within our current confinement?"

"You are more than welcomed, inmate Gabdulan, to take a stab at eliminating me," said Alpha Triceratopian.

"It would be my absolute pleasure," said Gabdulan. The Trionyx picked up a nearby dumbbell weight and briefly bounced it up and down in his claw, before launching it directly at the head of Alpha Trike. The Triceratopian looked up toward the incoming weight as he reached his hand up to his helmet and launched two blue beams directly at the silver weight, disintegrating the iron projectile in mid-flight.

"Made you look," smirked Gabdulan. He flicked his tail and launched eight razor-sharp spikes at the Alpha Triceratopian. "Prepare to be sliced and diced, you ugly, horned freak!"

The Alpha Triceratopian glanced in the most casual manner at the oncoming spikes. As if he was getting ready to ask a question, the Alpha Trike raised his hand and silently addressed the deadly spikes flying towards him. In a manner that was unclear to the assembled Insectum and Reptilia, the Trike somehow requested that the spikes turn around and return to their point of origin.

"Oh, crasp," said Gabdulan. He could only watch helplessly as his own spikes came flying back, piercing his flesh. Bits and pieces of Gabdulan went flying everywhere. The Trionyx screamed in unholy terror as he was literally torn apart from the inside out.

Upon witnessing this atrocity, Legate Prime Buzz turned towards the remaining Beetleguise and Polistine centurions who had been attempting to contain the prisoners. "Everyone needs to fall back. Every Insectum guard needs to get as far away from those warriors as possible." Upon hearing the order to retreat, the Polistine and Beetleguise Centurions proceeded to the hidden doorways in the walls

"Honeycomb, you are with me. We need to get back to the control center," said Buzz.

"I wholeheartedly agree with that assessment of the situation," said Captain Honeycomb.

As Captain Honeycomb and Legate Prime Buzz flew up towards the broken window that led to the control room, the lead Triceratopian announced, "Let it not be said that the children of Xerxes are not capable of mercy." He touched his hand to his helmet once again and disintegrated Gabdulan. Following this mercy killing by the Alpha Trike, the other three warriors took this as a signal that it was time to begin corralling and disintegrating the prisoners who remained in the room.

As Legate Prime Buzz watched the carnage from high atop his perch in the Rec Center's control room, he knew that it could not allow it to continue. He searched around the control panel in a desperate attempt to see if there was anything that could possibly slow these warriors down. Checking in on the action, he noticed that the Trikes were standing near a fire-elimination hatch. "If I just alter the chemical composition of the fire-suppression foam then I just might be able to contain those things."

"Fingers crossed, I guess," said Captain Honeycomb.

The Legate Prime pressed a series of buttons before moving the evacuation lever on the fire suppression into the 'on' position. He watched as the suppression foam shot out of its chamber in its re-combinative, more gelatinous form and encased all four Trike soldiers in mounds of white, sticky foam that temporarily prevented them from moving around.

"Well done, Legate Prime," shouted Captain Honeycomb.

"Let's not congratulate ourselves too quickly, Captain. I am sure that the foam is only providing a temporary restraint for those creatures." The Legate Prime swiveled the comm microphone around to his face as he announced to his soldiers and the prisoners, "This is Legate Prime Buzz. Centurions, you are to immediately escort all prisoners of Minerva back to their containment units. Any prisoners who resist shall be left in the Rec Center to be dispatched by the Triceratopian warriors."

"Yeah," Captain Honeycomb smirked, "once they get free."

"I doubt that won't be in all that long a time," said Legate Prime Buzz. He watched as the Centurions escorted the 300 plus Reptilia prisoners out of the room and loaded them on small rhombus- shaped Trams carried on an anti-gravity track. The trams loaded with prisoners were driven by Beetleguise Centurions back to the main containment dome,

"There is one remaining question," said Legate Prime Buzz. "What are we supposed to do with our four new friends?"

"That is a good question," said Captain Honeycomb. "And I think it is one we need to answer right away," said the Captain as he watched the four Triceratopian begin to punch their way out of the now hardened cones of white suppression foam. "Legate Prime, if you have any good ideas about how to stop those things, this would be the perfect time to share."

The Alpha Triceratopian looked up at the window of the Rec Center's control room as he barked at the other Trikes, "You will eliminate the Legate Prime with extreme prejudice. Fire!"

Captain Honeycomb and the Legate Prime ducked under the console as the blue laser beams from the Trike helmets shattered the remaining glass. "Querzi, activate a localized containment sphere. Target those four Reptilia lifeforms in the Rec Center."

"I detect no Reptilia life signs in the room below," said Querzi.

"What the After burn? Are you telling me those creatures are not Reptilia?" asked Buzz.

"They are no elements of Reptilia genetic material present within their DNA,"

"Warden Sobek will have a lot of explaining to do once this is all said and done," said Buzz. He then returned to his discussion with the Querzi, "Just stick those things in a reinforced-amber cube."

"As you wish, Legate Prime." Querzi activated a hidden door that concealed what appeared to be a laser cannon. It did not produce an energy beam but instead shot an extremely strong plastic covering that enveloped the four Triceratopian.

"Polistine insect, you will not be able to contain me with your tricks. And once I am free, I promise you that I will kill you myself," said the Alpha Triceratopian.

"Put those Salamanders into the storage room by the hangar bay for the moment, Centurions." The Legate Prime slid down on his abdomen as four Beetleguise Centurions lifted the reinforced-amber cube containing the Triceratopian off the ground and guided it down the hall to a large empty cargo bay next to the room where Hotfire had tried to incinerate Minerva Penitentiary earlier that morning.

In a hesitant voice, Buzz spoke into the microphone attached to the console. "Warden Sobek, I have your warrior in the cargo bay. Feel free to send your personal guards over to collect them at your earliest convenience."

A booming voice nearly reached out from the intercom. "If they were unable to complete as simple a task as eliminating some rebellious prisoners, then I have no need or use for them. You may dispose of the four

Triceratopian at your earliest opportunity. That is, if you can kill them, which I highly doubt."

"I don't intend to eliminate them. I will be in contact with the Polistine Science Academy. They appear to be Reptilia but Querzi failed to detect any associated genetic material. Besides, a weapon of such violence and unpredictability should not be use as a tool in maintaining law and order."

"Those creatures, as you call them," said Warden Sobek, "are the property of the Hawking Brain Beetles. Therefore, no member of the Polistine Science Academy will be permitted to study the Triceratopian. And you Legate Prime would be well advise to mind your own business regarding the Triceratopian. That is if you still value your position. Sobek out."

As Buzz slid against the console of the control nest, he could not help but think back to a different battle on a different day, many years before. He had been stationed at Waspatoon on the southern continent of Nectaine for nine weeks. His training legion, the Yellow Z Swarm, had just returned from maneuvers in the Vitruvian expanse where the average temperature was 87 degrees Fahrenheit in the shade. At the time, Buzz was only a lowly Centurion. Centurion Buzz's extremities were bruised from carrying sixty pounds of equipment on his back; the aching of his wings was unbearable and there was no doubt in his mind that a Trionyx Mud Fish probably had a more appealing odor that he did. The only thing that he wanted to do was get the three-hour rest he and his company had been promised.

But it was not to be. "On your feet and in the air, your sorry excuses for Polistine excrement. We have been summoned for an important mission on the western continent. There has been an unprovoked attack by a Beetleguise battalion whose cruiser crashed near two Polistine villages out that way, Hutus and Frailin. We have been assigned to provide aid and support to the survivors. In addition, and this I believe is the fun part of the mission, we get to perform seek-and-destroy maneuvers of any Beetleguise dissident terrorists in the area. So, you Maggots have exactly ten minutes to pack your gear and meet me out by the air field. That's right. I am spoiling you larvae and allowing you take a transport. Alright, if there are no questions which I know there won't be, let's move out," the Drill Sergeant barked.

Centurion Buzz raised his hand, much to the annoyance of Maxizum, who flew over towards him and in a teasingly sweet voice said, "Oh, I am sorry. I just assumed that no one had any questions." Immediately he raised his voice and shouted in Buzz's face, "Because you all know by now that I become extremely upset when I have to take questions from larvae."

"Drill Sergeant, the only thing is that an attack on those villages makes no sense. Hutus grows river melons as its major export. And Frailin's major export is woven cotton. What would be the purpose of destroying either one of those villages?"

Maxizum put his hand on Buzz's shoulder. "Son, I can't argue with the fact that you raise a valid question. So let me think about it for a minute."

"Alright, that sounds reasonable, Drill Sergeant."

He shook his head as he hovered in the air. "I got nothing, Centurion. So here's what we are going to do." Maxizum dove right in his face shouting, "You are going to pack your stuff and get on that blastard ship in less than ten minutes. Or you are going to be doing a sentence of twenty-five years in the military prison on Hepatica."

Less than thirty minutes later, the transport ship was coming in for a landing a few clicks away from Hutus. Every soldier in Yellow Z Swarm company was able to witness that the village had been laid waste and that there were indeed survivors. Yet, the whole situation still didn't make any sense to Buzz.

As Yellow Z Swarm marched triumphantly into Hutus, they were surrounded by children, elderly male Polistine and their female companions, who hovered around them, offering gifts of melons and delivering praise to their saviors. As the congratulation fest continued, a Polistine who carried himself with an air of importance flew over to the Drill Sergeant. "I am Nector, chief administrator of the town. We are so relieved that the military received our distress call."

"We are happy to help hard-working colonists." Maxizum looked around the village and wondered how the citizens had survived before the attack. There were few luscious meadows, mostly low lying grasslands. The buildings looked rundown, like they had seen more than their fair share of decay over the years. The villagers themselves looked as if they hadn't had a decent meal for weeks. A youngster flew towards the Drill Sergeant, "Please save us."

"We will, son. These centurions will evacuate you as soon as your folks are all packed."

"No," the youngling shook his head. "They are going to send us back to the work camp."

As centurion Buzz screamed behind him, "It's a trap," the Chief Administrator turned around and vaporized the boy with his Madagascan blaster. The thirty soldiers of Yellow Z Swarm leapt into action, positioning blasters in a defensive posture.

The Beetleguise soldiers who emerged from the dilapidated huts were nothing like Drill Sergeant Maxizum had ever seen in his long career of military service. These Beetleguise soldiers were almost 11-feet long and wore reinforced armored shells. As the centurions fired on the Beetleguise soldiers they activated small camouflage devices that allowed them to blend in with their surrounding environment. In addition, the Beetleguise appeared to be capable of firing pink energy beams out of their mouths capable of instantly annihilating a Polistine Centurion.

In minutes, the Beetleguise soldiers had taken out a third of Yellow Z Swarm with the Polistine centurions unable to achieve a single enemy kill. Despite the Beetleguise Warriors' refusal to be dispatched, Maxizum was continually yelling at his troops to hold their ground. But at a certain point in the fight, centurion Buzz looked over and saw an expression on the Drill Sergeant's face, a look that he would never forget. It was the face of absolute terror.

Centurion Buzz took the action that would promote him to the status of hero among his fellow grunts at Waspatoon. With his still-aching wings, Buzz flew back to where the transport had been set down. Without hesitation, he ran into the cockpit where the pilot and co-pilot were waiting patiently.

"What are you doing back here, Maggot? Where is the rest of Yellow Z Swarm?" asked the pilot.

"We were ambushed. We need to go back to save the rest."

"You are full of dung, Maggot. And you are a dirty deserter."

"For the Great Hive Master's sake, I don't have time for this bull-dung." Buzz grabbed the pilot's pistol, quickly making sure that it was on stun. He aimed the blaster and with two shots for each, he knocked out the pilot and his associate.

When he returned, only six of the original 30 members of Yellow Z Swarm remained including the Drill Sergeant, still without a single Beetleguise casualty. Buzz landed the transport and yelled at his fellow Centurions to run for the ship. Once they had reached orbit, Drill Sergeant Maxizum made the executive decision to launch a thermal device that vaporized the remaining Polistine villagers and the eight Beetleguise super soldiers. Even after all these years, Buzz knew that things could have turned out for him very differently. He was lucky that he was given a medal instead of a date with a firing squad. But he was still troubled that somehow, some way, his past was reemerging. And he had a feeling it wasn't going to be a pleasant reunion.

Chapter 6
KASIDY VULKNER

As the monitors surrounding the ship's main propulsion system sat silent and blank after being drained by the Green Diamond, Captain Odinord of the *Mjölnir* resolved that he would indeed meet the challenge of restoring life to the spacecraft and preserving the lives of his crew.

Kon spoke first. "Captain, if we don't do something —."

"Yes, Lieutenant Kon, I know. We are all going to die and the *Mjölnir* will be our mausoleum," said Captain Odinord.

"Correct, Captain. So as our commanding officer, how do you propose to resolve this situation?"

"As a crew, we will think of a solution within the next eighteen minutes."

"And how can you be so sure of that, Captain?"

"Because I do not believe in a no-win situation," said Captain Odinord.

"Well, you must have gone to a different S.T.A.R. training academy than I did Captain, because I was taught that in space when the dung hits the asteroid, there is not a Daggit thing you can do about it."

"That is enough, Lieutenant. All this meaningless debate is only accomplishing one thing. And that is using up our supply of oxygen in an even faster manner than if we weren't standing here hypothesizing about how we were all going to die," said Engineer Kasidy Vulkner.

"Well said, Engineer Vulkner. Is there any way that we could siphon off energy from the gem? Maybe we could get just enough back to get some life support?" asked Captain Odinord.

"That Green Diamond already spent all the ship's power blowing up that Beetleguise star fighter. It has no energy left to return," said Kasidy. "Could we tap the atomic reserve in Querzi's protected memory core and just redirect some of the power to the life support?"

"You do realize that with all the power gone from the rest of the ship that Querzi will be less than generous with her atomic energy," said Captain Odinord.

"I am aware of that, Sir. But I think that it is our best play at the moment," said Kasidy.

"Well, the only way we are going to be able to access that protected memory core is by taking a little walk to the external data terminal," said Kon.

"Kon, I know the layout of this ship backwards and forwards with my eyes shut. I am pretty sure that I will be able to find it," smiled Kasidy.

"I would still feel better if I came with you to watch your back. Our sensors are down, so we have no idea what or who could be out there," said Kon.

"Negative, Kon. I will be accompanying Engineer Vulkner. It is my ship, so if anyone is going to be risking their life to fix this boat, it is going to be me," stated Captain Odinord.

Kon was about to object to the captain's decision yet again when an officer with pink skin and copper colored hair came into the room. The officer was dressed in a red tunic with a yellow vest that extended down to his knees. In a frantic tone, the ship's doctor, Tulare, went immediately into a detailed report of the health of the crew, casualties, and other concerns regarding the ship.

"Tulare, I share your concern for our fallen comrades. However, my top priority at this moment is the preservation of the lives of the remaining crew members. So can you please tell me, is there anywhere on the ship that has an oxygen supply that is not dependent on the life support?"

"Captain, that is a brilliant idea. I will gather the rest of the crew and take them there."

Odinord silently shook his head and tried to resist the urge to bark at his ship's physician. "Can you tell me where that independent oxygen source is located?"

"The decontamination sphere by the medical bay has its own external oxygen supply just in case a crew member is exposed to a pathogen and needs to remain isolated from the crew," stated Dr. Tulare.

"Kon, go with Dr. Tulare. Find as many crew members as you can and bring them down — "

Dr. Tulare interrupted the Captain. "There is very little room in that sphere, Captain. I think at maximum we could only fit six or seven crew in that sphere at a time."

Odinord paused, then dictated his orders. "Kon, you take charge. You will need to set up a rotation schedule for who is able to go into the sphere and for how long they can stay in there. Vulkner, you are with me. We are going to be following you toward the decontamination sphere, doctor, because we need to retrieve a pair of environmental suits. We can all collect stray crew members along the way. So let's get going. We have a lot to do and not a lot of time."

Defensive Officer Kon turned to Dr. Tulare, "I guess that means the discussion is over."

Back aboard the Polistine shuttlecraft, lieutenant Thorn felt as if he had lost so much within the course of a few hours. The *Honey Hive*, which had been his home for countless years, was becoming a distant memory as the battle cruiser burned in space. He had no real notion of how, or if, he'd ever see the Polistine home world again. And finally, there was the matter of witnessing an ancient weapon that had the capability of reducing an individual, a starcraft or probably even a planetoid to infinitesimal atoms within a matter of seconds. However, all these larger galactic issues were secondary to Thorn's more immediate concern: he was currently being crushed by a rather sizable piece of the ship's metal bulkhead. The lieutenant had begun to formulate a possible solution to his current predicament. He had spied a button on the console that operated a manual release for the shuttle's skylight. If he could reach it the vacuum of space would lift the piece of bulkhead off his body and carry it into space. However, there was one annoying detail in his risky plan — that the same force that would carry away the metal plate probably would also manage to propel him, too, out into space."

"Computer, this is Lieutenant Thorn of the *Honey Hive*."

"Glad to see that you are still fairly operational, Lieutenant. How can I serve you this morning?" asked Querzi.

"I was kind of in the mood for a glass of mead," Thorn said sarcastically. "And oh yes, there is the matter of the two-hundred-pound metal sheet that is currently crushing me."

"Unfortunately, my replicating system is down so I am unable to generate that glass of mead" stated Querzi. "But, we could have a pleasant chat since it is just the two of us. I am extremely knowledgeable about a great many subjects. And I have been told that I am simply a delight whenever I get the chance to chat on the Galaxanet."

"No, Querzi. There was actually another pressing matter,"

"That was a clever play on words, Lieutenant."

"It wasn't meant to be. Querzi, could you please assist me with getting this sheet off of me?"

"I was only trying to be sociable. And, as for the other issue, I do not possess any appendages that can assist you in removing the metal sheet."

"I am not expecting you to remove the sheet. I have my own plan for doing that and just need your assistance," said Thorn through gritted teeth.

"I don't think I appreciate your tone at the moment. I believe I need some A.I.M.T."

"What on Insectvore is A.I.M.T?" asked Thorn regretting it as soon as it left his lips.

"Artificial Intelligence Me Time. Goodbye, Lieutenant."

Without the assistance of Querzi, Thorn knew that it would be necessary to resort to less sophisticated tactics if he had any hope of freeing himself from this impromptu scrap metal press. He grabbed a hold of the chair legs behind him and pulled himself out as far as possible from underneath the fallen piece of metal debris. He found that he was able to clear his frame down to his last two appendages but no further. It was then that Lieutenant Thorn spied a utility closet at eye level which he opened it reveal an industrial hatchet.

"This isn't looking promising, but I guess that I will start to worry about the broken bones in my legs once I get free. Here goes nothing."

Lieutenant Thorn positioned the hatchet underneath the sheet metal, he alternated between chopping and recovering from the pain of removing his own lower wings. Thorn used the hatchet to cut through skin, muscle and bone in order to accomplish its assigned task of removing the lower wing. When Thorn was done a half hour later, he had managed to sever both sets of wings and was spewing yellow blood and cream plasma on both sides of his frame. He leaned forward on the floor, feeling pale and light headed. Right before he passed out, he heard Querzi: "Lieutenant, you appear to be in need of medical attention."

Dr. Tulare had managed to corral a good number of the crew members of the *Mjölnir*; a third of the crew had sustained serious injuries or been killed instantly by the collateral damage from the battle between the *Honey Hive* and the Beetleguise fighters. The remaining crew were led by Captain Odinord, Defensive Officer Kon, and Engineer Vulkner as they made their way towards the decontamination sphere located near the hangar bay. They were occasionally faced with having to remove fallen pieces of bulkhead or illumination units from their path. Yet, for the most part, the walk from the engineering section to the hangar bay was uneventful.

That was until they reached the main research center located just a few hundred feet from the hangar bay. "What in the name of the Arboreal Guardian is that supposed to be?" asked Kon.

The twenty remaining crew members collectively gasped at the sight that lay before them in the corridor. There was a black and grey swirling tornado ⊠ clouds and wind twisting and gyrating — directly in their path. Captain Odinord and Kasidy, along with their fellow shipmates, could only act as spectators as the black cloud reached out and snatched anything in its immediate vicinity. These suctioned objects were promptly picked up by the wind of the cloud and deposited in the center of the tornado.

"How did that get on-board?" asked Captain Odinord.

"I was working on perfecting a stable wormhole for transporting people, supplies, and even star craft over long distances," volunteered a science officer, Lieutenant Lokhra.

"It looks like you still have some perfecting to do, Lokhra. Let's move away from the sucking hole in space and find an alternate route to the hangar bay," said Kon.

"I fully concur, Defensive Officer," said Captain Odinord.

A tentacle of storm clouds reached out from the tornado and grabbed an ensign in a blue jumpsuit by both feet and began to pull her through the air towards the center of the tornado. Kasidy immediately leaped over and grabbed a nearby door frame with one hand and the Ensign's arm with her other.

"I've got you, Ensign Katjhon. Just hold onto me and don't let go!" said Kasidy.

"It is too strong. I can feel it pulling me in," cried Katjhon.

Captain Odinord realized that if he didn't act quickly that he would lose two crew members to the nameless void within the tornado. "Lokhra, this is your doing so you are going to help me fix it."

"What do you need me to do?"

"Get to that door behind, Kasidy and start pushing it open."

Within seconds, they had used a broken piece of metal as a wedge to force the door open. They, next, reached out to grab Kasidy and Katjhon. Unfortunately, as Kasidy fell back, Katjhon lost her grip and went flying directly into the center of the tornado.

"I tried to save her," Kasidy told Captain Odinord. "If she had just held on for a moment longer, she would have been all right."

"I know," said Captain Odinord. He immediately switched gears from a one-to-one dialogue to addressing the remainder of the crew. "Everyone get in here. Lieutenant Lokhra, get that door closed once everyone is inside."

"Very good, Captain," said Lieutenant Lokhra. He and Kon reached out with one hand and ushered the rest of the crew into the room. Both used the wedge to close the door once again. Unfortunately, three more of their shipmates were delivered to the center of ravenous cloud before they could close the door completely.

"How many did we lose, Kon?"

"Too many for my liking, Sir. But if you want numbers then we lost four good officers."

Captain Odinord knew that the rest of the crew would judge him as cold and uncaring for not even taking a moment to mourn. But he knew from years of command that taking a minute to reflect to acknowledge a fallen crew member might cost another individual's life somewhere down the line.

"We need to open up the drop ceiling and climb to the hangar bay. Tulare and Kon, we will proceed as we discussed. Engineer Vulkner and I will don our environmental suits so we can have a little discussion with the onboard Querzi about restoring the life support."

Within seven minutes, the remaining sixteen members of the *Mjölnir* crew were standing in the ship's hangar bay. The doctor was ushering five individuals at a time into the decompression chamber, that was being pushed to capacity.

As Captain Odinord got into his environmental suit, Kasidy said, "I guess in a perfect universe we could all just hang out in here and wait for the life support to reset."

"But you and I both know, as well as I am guessing most members of the crew, that our mental capacity is in the early stages of being adversely affected by the limited oxygen supply."

"Well, I did sign up for adventure when I decided to join the Ruddarian Space-fleet," said Kasidy.

"Then, would you care to accompany me outside, Engineer Vulkner?"

"I would be delighted, Captain. But I insist that you should go first, as the senior officer."

"If you insist."

Odinord turned to Kon, "if we haven't returned in ten minutes, I want you to get the rest of the crew to the escape pods. Find the nearest inhabitable planet and contact Space-Fleet."

"What about the Green Diamond?" asked Kon.

"Eject that little beauty into space," said Captain Odinord as he walked over to the air lock, followed closely behind by Kasidy who had finished putting on her environmental suit.

As they made their way along the bottom of the ship towards the auxiliary barrier generators, Kasidy began to have an unmistakable feeling of dread that their mission to access the Querzi's data core was proceeding way too uneventfully. As she moved just below the forward sensors and past the barrier generators, that nasty surprise made its grand entrance onto the scene.

"Captain, what the After burn are those supposed to be?"

"I am not sure, Kasidy. All I do know is that they don't look friendly."

Kasidy watched as a swarm of medium-sized mechanical robotic flies condensed into an arrow shaped formation as they flew directly towards her and the captain. The flies' abdomens flashed red, and green in a synchronized display.

"Run for cover, Kasidy. The flies seem to be somewhat perturbed at us."

Both Odinord and Kasidy had the same idea. They pushed off the saucer of the ship and made their way towards the other side of the observational dome at the far end of the ship. As Kasidy and Captain Odinord retreated, they shot laser blasts back at the flies, hitting a few but far from diminishing their numbers.

"Where the After burn did those things come from?" asked the captain.

"The Querzi must have created them in order to protect the memory core," said Kasidy. "But, I might have the perfect bit of insecticide for this little problem." Kasidy grabbed a scanner from her belt and scanned the signals in the immediate vicinity until she came across the signal that was being sent back and forth between the ship's computer and the flying robotic pests. Once she found it, she selected a virus that she had just removed earlier from a secondary program in the computer's subroutine. "There you go, my little virus. Go snack on some flies," said Kasidy as she watched them go dormant.

"You gave the robotic flies a virus?" asked Captain Odinord.

"Yes, I did, Captain," beamed Kasidy with a devilish grin.

"Well done, Vulkner. Now let's go do some reprogramming so our friends can get some air."

Kasidy had already activated her heel thrusters and pushed off towards the memory core when she was met with a very unpleasant surprise. Captain Odinord could only reach his hand out in a halting motion as Kasidy began to use her multi-tool with laser scalpel to undo the panel. With Querzi recognizing a violation of its precious power, Querzi began preparing a highly-charged pulse whose intention was to paralyze anyone trying to tamper with its system

"Look out, Kasidy," cautioned Captain Odinord. But Kasidy had already grabbed a nearby deactivated fly to absorb the electrical charge and then slammed it into the console, disabling Querzi's ability to defend itself from harm.

"Take that, you, micro-processor maniac," quipped Kasidy. She quickly pressed the final digits before Querzi had the opportunity to reboot its systems from the power supply for its protected memory. Before Querzi knew what was happening, Kasidy had successfully re-routed power to life support.

As Captain Odinord flew over behind Kasidy, he stated, "That was damn reckless, Vulkner. And on top of that you could have been fried like a Meditaplassen chicken."

"Anything else, Captain?" asked Kasidy.

"Well done."

Kasidy tapped the micro-comm in her helmet. "Kon, are you breathing any easier?"

"Yes, we are," said Kon.

Before Kasidy could reply, she heard strange voice that was in her headset. **"This is an emergency distress call. Does anyone read me?"**

"Who is this?" asked the captain, who was also receiving the message in his headset.

"I am the Querzi system located on the Polistine shuttle which is adjacent to your vessel."

"What can we do for you?" asked Captain Odinord.

"The Polistine Lieutenant aboard my vessel is in need of immediate emergency care."

The next conscious memory that Lieutenant Thorn was aware of was the sight of a pink-skinned Ruddarian standing over him. The one thought that presented itself immediately to Thorn was that he was no longer aboard the *Honey Hive's* shuttle.

"Hello there. I am Dr. Tulare. And you, my Polistine patient, are lucky to be alive."

In a raspy tone, Thorn asked, *"Clast butrize ru nol?"*

"Dammit, Querzi, I need you to try to reboot the translator circuits."

"Clust mo E? Surick tris gunga o?" Thorn said as he reached up and grabbed Tulare by the collar, an action the Polistine regretted almost immediately as a wave of nausea came over him.

"You may not want to get up so quickly next time. Querzi, I need those translator circuits as soon as you can," Dr. Tulare said as Thorn slumped back to the table.

"Your request for the translator circuits to be repaired has become irrelevant," said Querzi.

"I think that a short-tempered Polistine trying to kill me because he can't understand me kind of makes repairing the translator circuit a priority," expressed Dr. Tulare somewhat vehemently.

"Tell me what is going on or I will slowly slice you open, Pink-Monkey," spouted Thorn.

"Dr. Tulare, I was merely informing you that I had already complied with your request by repairing the translator circuits."

"Much obliged, Querzi," said Dr. Tulare. With an intentional motion of spinning on one heel, Dr. Tulare turned his attention back to his patient. "As I was telling you before, my Polistine friend —"

"It is lieutenant. You may address me as Lt. Thorn."

"Very well, Lt. Thorn, you are very lucky to be alive. Your Querzi contacted our ship while our crew were in the midst of essential repairs. In short, we were informed that you had lost a lot of blood and were dying. The Captain and Astral Engineer Vulkner, retrieved you from your ship and brought you to my medical bay. Let me say that given your condition at the time we found you, that is a miracle you are still alive. The only thing that I don't understand is what would possess you to slice off your own wings?"

"After the collapse of a bulkhead on my craft, I was trapped under a heavy metal sheet. In order to survive, I found it necessary to remove my wings to escape from my metal prison. However, this accident has stripped me of the right to call myself a true solider of the Polistine. Our wings are a symbol of our dominance over all other races and now they are gone forever. And in part, your crew is indirectly responsible for my accident."

"My crew and I didn't even know you existed fifteen minutes ago, so how are we responsible?"

"Because my injuries were indirectly caused by the activation of that weapon, the Eye of Hermes. A weapon, I might add, that your primitive Ruddarian race couldn't possibly begin to understand."

"I believe that we are slightly more advanced than you give us credit for, Lieutenant."

"The Polistine race is a few 100,000 years old, one of the oldest in the cosmos, and my people dare not even try to harness the Eye of Hermes. I must speak with your captain at his earliest convenience so we can determine the safest means of transporting the Green Diamond back to wherever you found it."

"The Green Diamond is scheduled to be delivered to the Ruddarian Scientific Complex on Madagascan for research and testing. The scientists at the facility have constructed a vault of reinforced dwarf-star palladium. Once the green diamond is placed within, it will not be able to harm anyone."

"Sadly, Ruddarian, walls even that thick will not be able to contain the Eye of Hermes if the legends are to be believed," said Lieutenant Thorn remorsefully.

"I will let the Captain Odinord that you urgently need to speak with him."

Odinord's voice crackled over the med bay's speaker, "Doctor, I need you to return to the decontamination bay. I still have crew who are suffering from the after-effects of oxygen deprivation."

Tulare pressed a button on a communication deck by the door. "I was just looking after our Polistine guest, Captain. But I will be up right away. Tulare out."

"You will be fine in here, Lieutenant. I will check in on you at my earliest convenience."

"It was most gracious of you not to eject me into space," said Thorn stoically.

"That's the closest you get to saying "Thank you?""

"If you choose to take it as such then that is your choice, not mine."

"Then I warmly accept your thanks."

Odinord interrupted at that moment. "Dr. Tulare, I needed you down here five minutes ago."

"Got to go," smiled Dr. Tulare.

Tulare grabbed his medical supply kit as he ran out the door. The moment the doors had closed, Thorn slipped gingerly off the bed. As a Polistine, it was unusual for him to rely solely on his lower appendages, or what Reptilia, and Hominoids, called legs, to do all the walking. He fell down a number of times before reaching the door, but he was up to the challenge of building up the muscles in his appendages. It was truly disheartening, though, that the Healer had sealed the door behind him. Typical Hominoid behavior was truly on display this day. They extend an olive branch with one appendage as they drive a slicing blade into your back with the other, he thought. Lt. Thorn hobbled back toward the bed. As he walked, he couldn't help but notice the differences between his own race and the doctor's. These Ruddarians wore decorative garments that served no purpose in assisting them to defend themselves. Among the Polistine race, a soldier would never leave himself so unprotected. Thorn's uniform was made of black ivory and gold-plated steel woven into a flexible material that only allowed spaces for his wings and appendages. When they went into battle, a Polistine always wore a protective helmet of gold-plated steel. The Centurions of his race had a variety of weapons at their disposal as well as their personal weapons: dual stingers, which could disable an opponent.

Despite the events of the last few hours, including the destruction of the *Honey Hive*, it was never more clear to Lt. Thorn as he examined the glaring contradictions between the Polistine race and these Ruddarians that he still had to eliminate the threat presented by the Eye of Hermes. He acknowledged that the first obstacle that needed to be overcome was that locked door.

In the decontamination bay, Odinord touched Dr. Tulare on the shoulder, "Glad you could tear yourself away from your newly found specimen."

"I was trying to assess his threat level to our crew," said Dr. Tulare.

"Is there something you are trying to tell me?"

"I have a duty to preserve all life, no matter if it has two, four or six legs. So even if that giant bee does wind up killing us all, I still believe that you made the right decision bring it aboard, Captain."

"Regardless of how any of our belief systems affected our decision making, unfortunately what's done is done. Now, does the Polistine seem like he might be a threat to us?" asked Captain Odinord.

"My response is that I feel like he holds a lot of resentment towards hominoids. He blames us for his injuries and says that we had no business using the Green Diamond to save the ship."

"Kind of getting the feeling that our precious cargo needs some extra security."

The captain tapped the comm in his ear, "Kon, think we need to get a few more men down to the cargo bay to keep an eye on the Green Diamond."

"Way ahead of you, Captain. I already have two more guards watching over it."

"Well done, Kon. Carry on."

Tulare turned around just in time to observe a woman with copper and silver hair trying to stumble off a hover medical bed. "Kon, needs my help in engineering, Captain. We need to fix the engine before more Polistine show up on our doorstep."

"Lay back down, Astral Engineer. You have done more than your share for this ship this morning. Right now, you need your rest."

"Doctor, I am going to be all right," shouted Kasidy before collapsing back on the bed.

"Lieutenant Lokhra, escort Vulkner, back to her quarters. And Lieutenant, make sure you place a timed lock of at least three hours on the door of her quarters so she doesn't make a break for it."

"Understood, Captain

Even as Lieutenant Lokhra was carrying her back to her quarters, Kasidy's mind returned to the time when she was fifteen-years-old living on Rogestran Five Colony and her father, Kabul, had died in that fateful encounter with three off-worlders. Despite her insistence that neither she nor her mother knew anything about her father's activities, they were both still periodically taken in for questioning by government officials in what they still considered an open investigation.

Kasidy's mother must have also held out some hope that her husband would return some day. She'd continued to work in the Ruddarian market making weave crafts to help support herself and her young daughter. There were customers who were so impressed with her work that she was able to expand her business somewhat off-world. She even ventured to Insectvore and Madagascan to peddle her wares. On a few trips off world, when the school calendar permitted, Kasidy would accompany her mother. However, many times Kasidy was left alone on Rogestran Five. She'd taken advantage of the opportunity to run with what her mother would call the "wrong crowd" by engaging in such elicit activities as experimenting with mind enhancing chemicals and participating in speeder racing on bikes with re-tooled engines. Basically, she engaged in any activity that took her mind off the pain of her everyday life.

This usual routine was forever changed after her mother returned home early from a trip to Höllenfeuerhalbinsel. As she reached their village and made her way through the park, Zanesta saw her daughter lying naked with a gentleman friend behind the gazebo.

With amazing speed, Zanesta reached over and grabbed the young man by the scruff of his neck and turned him around to face her, "Get your clothes on and get the After burn out of my daughter. I am in no mood."

"You are such an embarrassment, Mother. I am practically an adult and can make my own choices," shouted Kasidy.

"Not while you are under my custodianship, you don't."

"I hate you so much," screamed Kasidy. She jumped up and ran all the way back to their house, followed close behind by her mother, Zanesta. At the same time, the young man, Alexa hurriedly slipped on a pair of denim jeans and a black and red short sleeved "Imploding Satellites' shirt. But, Zanesta realized that her first priority was making sure her daughter was okay, even though she was tempted to give the boy a piece of her mind. However, Alexa apparently could not leave well enough alone. "Do you think Kasidy would be able to come to the Harvesting party next Saturnday night, Mrs. Vulkner?"

"She most certainly is not," said Zanesta as she turned and began to walk back home.

"I hate you more than words can describe!" Kasidy screamed at her mother as she walked into the house to see her daughter sitting on a futon. She got up to run after him but her mother stepped between her daughter and the door. Kasidy pushed against her, knocking her down. The young woman was halfway down the hallway to her room when her mother called after her, "Kasidy, I think I discovered a link that could help us find your Dad." Zanesta sat down on the futon and began telling her daughter her tale, a great portion of which Kasidy already knew. Her mother had been selling her weave craft in the market a week or so ago when a stranger in a hood approached her to inquire about her artistic creations."

"I have never seen a more spectacular mastery of the weave craft in my life. It is amazing how you are able to combine the colors to bring out the true beauty," said the stranger.

"You are too kind, my friend. But I am just a simple crafts maker who is trying to make her way in this world for herself and her daughter."

"Do you not have a man to support you?" asked the stranger.

"Unfortunately, my husband abandoned me and my daughter a number of years ago. And even before his untimely departure, we were not exactly experiencing the 'best of times.' I think my daughter believes that he is dead but I know better. Kabul was always a survivor."

"You are to be admired for staying resilient in the face of such adversity."

"I know it is just me being foolish, but I still carry a photo of my husband, Kabul."

Zanesta produced a holo-photo encased in a locket she wore on a chain. She carried the picture more out of sentiment than anything else because even after all these years, his image was burned into her memory. It was hard to forget those strong, broad shoulders, that blond silken hair the color of maize, and his piercing green eyes.

The stranger took a step back, her hood falling back around her shoulders to reveal an alien with spikes down her neck and smooth, scaly blue-and-green skin over her entire body, including her bald head. "I have glanced into those green eyes before, but they did not belong to a Ruddarian."

"I don't understand. If you know where my husband is, then I am begging you to please tell me."

As a grave look came over the alien's face, she pleaded with Zanesta, "You must give up your search for your husband for it is much too dangerous for you to continue."

"What do you mean. Is he being held somewhere?" asked Zanesta.

"No, but I assure you that if you continue this search, you will not be pleased with the results," said Kindlespark.

"Did you convince her to tell you where father could be found?" asked Kasidy.

"No, I did not. However, I proceeded to track this Trionyx's movements throughout the market in the hope that she would lead me to your father. And three days later, Kindlespark boarded a hover train to the province of Gryfanfire carrying a number of contraband items including a sample of your father's Enhanced Energy Gas."

"Did you follow her? Was she meeting father," inquired Kasidy.

"I followed Kindlespark to the outskirts of the Gryfanfire province to an abandoned space-yard. It was already getting dark when she arrived there with several cargo boxes. It is possible that Kindlespark was early for her meeting or the other party was running late, but it was over two hours before the actual meeting occurred."

"What did he look like?" asked Kasidy. "Was it father?"

"It was not your father. Kindlespark's buyer was over fourteen feet tall with a long black tail and Insectum appendages. He wore a purple and golden cloak exposing a blue chest plate that appeared to be made out of reconstituted platinum. But that was not the most haunting aspect of this being."

"What do you mean?"

"Kindlespark was right. When he turned to glance towards me, I think that I did see your father's eyes staring back at me. But I know that is an impossibility because this creature was the farthest thing from a Ruddarian that could be imagined."

"What happened next?" asked Kasidy.

"Kindlespark told this creature that there was a merchant from a Ruddarian colony who had been inquiring about him and that it would probably be best if the creature concluded his business and returned to Meditaplassen — the home world of the Hawking Brain Beetle ⊠ as soon as possible. The creature agreed with Kindlespark and proceeded to inquire what merchandise she had to sell him. Kindlespark produced some artwork and crafts that could bring them a pretty penny among the Hawking Brain

Beetle. The seller protested at first, saying that because he mainly dealt in intoxicants. However, Kindlespark convinced the creature to purchase the artwork by offering him Enhanced Energy Gas, as well."

As Zanesta remained perched on a worn plastic beam inside the abandoned space yard warehouse, she realized that she had been hunched in the same position for hours and that she desperately need to stretch her legs. But as she extended one of her legs, she heard a loud creak emanating from the board.

The creature immediately flew into a rage. "Kindlespark, you swore to me that you came alone. You have betrayed me! And for this action you will pay the ultimate price." The creature swooped his tail around Kindlespark's abdomen as he lifted her up into the air."

"I beg you, Lord Diabolix. Have mercy upon me," cried Kindlespark.

"I will show you mercy. my Dear. I will make your death a speedy affair." Zanesta heard a sickening crunch as Diabolix crushed Kindlespark's body like a crumpled piece of papyrus.

Diabolix turned towards where Zanesta was sitting high above on the plastic beam. She watched in horror as the fourteen-foot-long creature began to scale the wall, no doubt to eliminate all witnesses from the scene of his failed transaction. As she looked down, Zanesta knew that she had to overcome her fear and decide on a plan of action if she was to survive this encounter.

The creature looked up at her as he moved closer. And as he climbed, he uttered something that left utterly perplexed: "It has been years since I last saw you."

"Get away from me!" screamed Zanesta. She brought her fist crashing down on the beam, causing it to break away and send her falling towards the ground. As the plastic beam came flying down, it knocked the creature unconscious.

"I ran out of the warehouse and didn't look back. But I swear to you, Kasidy, that this encounter has only strengthened my resolve to find out what happened to your father."

Kasidy moved closer to her mother on the couch. It had been a long, long while since they had shared a moment when both considered each other to be mother and daughter. "It will be all right."

As the pair sat quietly on the couch, there was a sudden explosion that knocked the apartment's front door off its hinges. A group of six Security Squad officers came marching in with the lead officer handcuffing mother and daughter as he informed them, "Zanesta Vulkner, you and your daughter are under arrest. You will be sent immediately to a detainment camp for criminals involved in crimes against the State."

"That is ridiculous. On what charge are we being arrested?" asked Zanesta.

"We have learned that you have knowledge of the murder of a known smuggler named Kindlefire. Her body was found two days ago on Höllenfeuerhalbinsel in the province of Gryfanfire. She had pieces of your weave-craft in her possession at the time of her death. Take them out of my sight, Centurion." As Kasidy and Zanesta were placed in the transport, two of the officers from the Security Squad strapped gag-pieces over their mouths and blinders over their eyes. Even though she tried to remain strong for her mother, Kasidy believed that she had never been more afraid in her entire life, including her run-in the night her father had been murdered. Or had Kabul just been abducted? Kasidy was more convinced than ever that she did not truly know her father's fate. However, she knew that where she was going, she wouldn't be finding out any new information anytime soon.

Kasidy and her mother were fingerprinted, had their holo-mugshots taken and were placed in a small, confining windowless cell. Neither woman knew if they were still in the colony or had been taken to another part of Rogestran Five Colony. It was possible that they could have been dropped off on some distant asteroid or planetoid, like the supposed Polistine penal facility known as Minerva. However, Kasidy was able to determine from the sounds of the crashing waves and the howls of the Krakens that she and her mother had been taken to The Southern Sea holding facility.

Still blindfolded, Kasidy turned in her mother's general direction, "I should have told you something a long time ago, Mom about the night that father 'disappeared.' I saw a Chamyx named Hotfire incinerate father. That creature you saw couldn't possibly have been father. If you had known that then, you would have never gone looking for him. So, our incarceration is all my fault."

"Baby, don't say that. I would have gone looking for him even if you told me you were convinced that he was dead because it wouldn't have changed the fact that I still love him and miss him to this day."

"Are we going to get out of this, Mom?" Kasidy asked.

"I promise you that we will. I love you, Kats."

"I love you, too." In her waking life, Kasidy already knew that, through no fault of her own, Zanesta was making a promise that night to her daughter that she would never be given the opportunity to keep.

Chapter 7
THE PLEASURIST HUNASH

A few light years' away from where the crew of the *Mjölnir* were struggling for their very survival, the passengers of the luxury shuttle, *Charon*, were enjoying a fairly routine voyage. That is except for Hunash, who was becoming increasingly agitated. awaiting word from her cousin, Buddash. She knew that her main role in the dispensary robbery was to distract Rabun while Buddash and his business associate, Yanick, stole every drug that wasn't carbon-sealed to the shelves, but something was definitely wrong. And it didn't help lessen Hunash's worries about her cousin that the last time she had spoken to him, he had mentioned that now Lord Diabolix had taken responsibility as the robbery's main coordinator. Hunash just wished that she, or Buddash, knew more about why Lord Diabolix was so interested in this particular venture.

As she was lost in her thoughts, she noticed a tall, young Trionyx sitting across from her on the space flier commuter escorter. He was something she had never seen before; a Trionyx who had those ridiculous spikes on his back and head, but who was also dressed in a tailored pair of coveralls. He wore a lizard skin vest underneath and a pair of respectable combat business boots.

"My, the clientele has definitely gotten an upgrade since the last time I was on this shuttle," said Hunash.

The Trionyx looked over at the pleasurist, an orange-skinned Cranitian wearing a tortoise shell that teased at her well-endowed figure. She wore blue-and-orange gloves over the sleeves of her smart little crimson silk and velvet jacket. She wore an all-too-brief pink velvet skirt with green nylons underneath, pink lipstick and rouge on her cheeks. Despite her height of six-two, she remained a ravishing Reptilia creature.

"I was just about to say that I am enjoying the view *inside* the cabin this flight more than outside," stated the Trionyx.

"Hi, my name is Hunash. And who might you be?"

"Cassian Traggert. The pleasure is truly mine. Would you care to accompany me to dinner this evening, Ms. Hunash?"

"It would be my absolute delight."

"What time should I pick you up?"

"Aren't we the forward thinking one? How about I meet you in the dining compartment at a quarter to eight? Then we will see where the evening takes us from there."

"I look forward to seeing you then."

A few hours later, Cassian was sitting nervously at a small round table in the dining compartment of the space flier, *Charon*. The room was decorated in a style similar to ancient Normandy Pangean. There were crystal and diamond studded light fixtures hanging above each table with two lamp fixtures on each arm extending outward. The table itself was covered in a red-and-gold silk tablecloth, and the chairs were made from rare Pangea redwood, a cushion of velvet adorned every chair. The ship's clientele was treated to a fine dining experience every night amid the eloquent décor of embroidered wool carpets of intricate designs and handwoven curtains of cotton and silk. As Cassian fumbled with the platinum fork and knife by the fine china plate, he contemplated the possibility that Hunash may have had second thoughts about their impromptu get-together. But then he looked up and saw her walk into the room.

The young Cranitian was a vision in a gown of gold and green, draped around her naturally armored but still sensual orange-skinned frame. She had chosen a red hair piece to cover her natural baldness as well as a pair of red Reptilia heels to add to the grace of her presence. Finally, she wore a strand of ivory pearls around her neck and a set of matching earrings.

"You look absolutely stunning, Hunash."

"Thank you. That is extremely kind of you to say."

"The necklace complements your oval eyes beautifully."

"That is the sweetest thing I've heard in a very long time."

Realizing that he was sitting transfixed upon Hunash's image, Cassian suddenly realized that she was still standing in front of the table and he had remained seated. He jumped to his feet and moved to her side within an instant. "You must think me so rude. Please, let me get your chair."

She slid gracefully down into the chair as Cassian pushed her closer to the table.

"I know I sound like a skipping holo-recording but those pearls truly complement your beauty."

"You make me blush too much, sir." Hunash giggled. "This necklace was a gift from my mother. She gave it to me as a present for the 20th anniversary of my birth. My mother, Jundash, told me that she saved 2 pearls per year from the time I was born to construct this necklace. My mother Jundas had laid 70 eggs on the beach-head the year I was born, but only 28 of us survived to adulthood."

"If you don't mind me asking, what happened to the 47 kids?"

"Many of them were gobbled up by a hungry Quillian before they could even make it to the ocean on Leathershell."

"Well, after that lovely little tale, who's hungry?"

Hunash giggled in spite of herself. "I do have to admit that I was, excuse the pun, hardened at an early age to the cold, sometimes unforgiving reality of our worlds."

"And I must apologize. I was less than a proper gentleman for making light of your brothers' and sisters' untimely demises. But it must say that I am indeed happy tonight that you managed to survive."

"Thank you. May I say that your presence has made this voyage already more enjoyable than I had anticipated." Before he could continue the conversation, Cassian's pager unit began to flash, "I am so sorry, but I just received an important incoming message. I am afraid I must bid you a fond farewell for tonight."

"Good night, Cassian. We must do this again before our journey is over."

A Beetleguise waiter came over carrying a bottle of amber nectar, year 13,982. In a clicking voice, the Beetleguise inquired, "Will you be sampling the vintage tonight?"

"If you were not totally opposed to the notion, maybe we could adjourn to my cabin and continue our lovely evening there," Cassian said to Hunash.

"I think that I would like that," smiled Hunash.

Once they had returned to the privacy of Cassian's suite, they made themselves comfortable within the rock formation that enclosed the tidal pool waterbed. As quickly as they shed their inhibitions after consuming the nectar, that was how instinctively they chose to shed their external coverings, leaving her orange scales pressing against his blue-and-green leathery skin. She often felt that her life as a pleasurist had left her jaded to the excitement and passion of carnal sensations, but Cassian allowed her to experience feelings that night that oozed into her senses and encompassed her body in a state of euphoria.

As they lay together in the oval-shaped whirlpool, Hunash turned to Cassian, "I was a little Cranitian when I started as a pleasurist, no more than twelve years old. My mother knew she didn't have the means for taking care of all of us. So instead of caring for us, she provided us with her best advice for survival. She told each of us that we needed to find what we were best at in this world. I found that I was best at making other beings experience the sensations of copulation. The Zanuck Corporation seemed to agree and thus I began my life as a pleasurist. But tonight, Cassian, you have provided me with the opportunity to feel the pleasure that I have hopefully provided to so many others over the years."

"Your warm sweet touch and your beauty inspired me to express my desires in ways that I rarely have done throughout the years," said Cassian.

"I am so happy that I have made this night memorable for you as well." Hunash gently leaned in and began to plant small delicate kisses on Cassian's neck until she made her way to his imposing jaws. Carefully maneuvering around his teeth, she sensually embraced his mouth and lips with her own sizable mouth. After what seemed like an eternity, Hunash pulled away while still gazing into his eyes. "I feel myself getting a little bit hot and thirsty. Would you care for some more of that nectar?" asked Hunash.

"I think that I would like that. Besides, it would give me a chance to rest up for a second helping of something else as well."

"I will be right back," said Hunash.

In a single motion, Hunash threw on a golden robe that only came down to her thighs as she exited the whirlpool. She barely felt like she was walking on the ground as she made her way towards the small preservation unit by Cassian's bed that contained an additional bottle of nectar. Hunash was about to reach for it when she noticed a small flashing light connected to a black rectangular shape on his night table. As a pleasurist, she was conditioned to respond to any summons from what appeared to be a message device so she absently picked it up and read the screen.

"Fortress on Helvete Fredon has been breached. Methurazus Rejuvenate has been acquired by Purple L Swarm. Please advise?"

As Hunash tried to make sense of the cryptic message, she could sense Cassian behind her. "My sweet Hunash, I really wish that your curiosity had not gotten the better of you."

Dropping the messenger device to the floor, Hunash backed away from the Reptilia. "I don't know who you are, but I promise you that I am very good at keeping secrets."

"And I intend to make you even better," smiled Cassian.

Cassian reached out with his tail in an attempt to wrap it around Hunash's neck, but she'd already launched herself into the air and was aiming her foot directly at Cassian's head. Hunash's foot would have landed directly on its target if Cassian hadn't reached up and grabbed a pair of overhead lamps at the last moment. As Hunash crashed into a glass table, Cassian twisted his body around and threw himself directly onto her. Cassian pressed his muscular hands over Hunash's mouth and pressed down.

"My dear, I must admit that you have touched my heart tonight in ways that I thought were no longer possible. Therefore, I will share my most intimate secret." Hunash looked up and saw Cassian's features begin to morph. His blue-green complexion began to wash away only to be replaced by an orange tone. The spikes on his back and head dissolved away as they were replaced by leather scales and a shell. And finally, Cassian had traded genders and assumed Hunash's face as its own.

Hunash uttered a muffled scream as her newly arrived doppelgänger said, "Allow me introduce myself. I am a shape-shifting Clonstellar assassin, and my name is Second Skin."

Within the confines of The *Citadel*, Warden Sobek had taken a moment's respite in his private forest of mechanical trees and shrubbery. He watched with the joyous pleasure of a youngling as the branches of the trees quietly made rotational motions as the internal cogs and gears continuously propelled them in never ending circular loops. Sitting at the base of one of the massive trees, Sobek mused about how much the Omnipotent Hawking Brain Beetle Council depended on him to maintain order on Minerva. He told himself how little his cousins truly appreciated his efficient management of the facility and that if he were to disappear one day, possibly to a pleasurist planet, the members of the Omnipotent Hawking Brain Beetle Council would immediately regret how badly they had treated Warden Sobek Bokhun. As his mind lingered on his thoughts about his inflated level of importance to the Hawking Brain Beetles, he failed to notice that a blackened view-screen at the far side of the room began to flicker to life.

As he stared up through the metallic leaves of his artificial tree at a small lighted orb that was meant to represent a distant moon, he heard the voice of his cousin, Osiris. "Dear cousin Sobek, it fills my heart with such joy to know that, even in the midst of a crisis, you have found time to engage in one of your many daydreaming sessions."

"I was not daydreaming," stated Sobek as he stood up from the tree. "I was mentally preparing for my engagement with inmate 6610, the Abomination Hotfire. Once I am done with him, he will have choice, but to assist us in eliminating Diabolix."

"I do have faith in you, Cousin Sobek. Yet, there are members of the Omnipotent Council who are not completely convinced that you will be successful. In the spirit of quieting your critics on the Council, perhaps you could enlighten me about the details of your plan?"

"I will implant a psychic Arachnid like this one." Sobek pressed a button that produced a holo-image of a ten-legged brown spider.

"How will this ghostly creature control the Abomination?" asked Osiris.

"I assure you that the creature is very real. It is one of my most successful genetic hybrids. The psychic Arachnid is injected into a host creature as a tiny parasite. Once inside the host's body, it attacks nerve cells and cranial tissue as it continues to expand at an exponential rate."

"Very good, cousin. But you do realize that the Abomination is very adept at dealing with pain."

"And once again, Osiris, you have silenced me before allowing me to tell you the most nefarious part of my plan. If the Psychic Spider is not removed within 18 hours, then the host creature will perish."

"Sobek, you are indeed a devious Bokhun. It is for that reason that I take daily comfort daily that we are separated by several hundred light years."

"I am glad that I can oblige my dear cousin. Now you must excuse me. I must liberate some of my favorite pets from what my do-gooder Legate considers an inescapable cell.

"Well, I wish you only success in your endeavor, cousin Sobek. The Omnipotent Hawking Brain Beetle Council is depending upon your skills in removing the threat of Lord Diabolix from the galaxy. Do not disappoint us."

"As always, my dear cousin, I move forward as the hand of the Hawking Brain Beetle."

"May your hand cradle the universe itself," said Osiris as her image disappeared.

The Alpha Triceratopian paced around the perimeter of the cubed-shaped, gold-tinted enclosure. He was unable to look directly out due to the yellow coloring of the glass, but he was able to distinguish that the shadows buzzing around the cube belonged to approximately twenty Polistine centurions. His fellow Triceratopian brothers were alternating between banging on the glass and trying to evaporate the material with their blue laser beams, both with little success. As Alpha completed yet another lap around the cube, he could feel a vibration deep within his ear canal as his implanted ear-comm came back to life.

"I hope you have enjoyed your morning break, Alpha," jibed Warden Sobek. "You and your fellow Triceratopian have more work that needs to be done."

"Whatever you desire, Master Sobek."

"I need you to bring Hotfire to me. I have already calculated that the Legate Prime's attempt to do so is already doomed to failure," said Warden Sobek.

"Master, I am well aware of how much you detest 'failure,'" said Alpha.

"Then make sure that you do not provide me with any more examples this day."

"I will obey."

"Now, quickly. Tell your brothers to move towards the center of your cube prison. And they should also be prepared to engage in a bit of pest control as well."

In the *Citadel*, Sobek initiated a program on his large overhead computer that scanned for the material that composed the prison cube, namely transparent aluminum and gold. Sobek next instructed his Querzi to determine the heat evaporation point at which the material would begin to dissolve. Finally, Sobek reached up with his tentacle and fired a beam that shot out from the top of the *Citadel* and landed directly in the center of the cube.

"My children," cackled Sobek, "go forth and bring the Abomination before me."

Back in the hangar bay, the only warning that the Polistine Centurions received that anything was wrong was that they suddenly heard a high-pitched hum. And before they could even begin to comprehend what was happening, the impenetrable cube began to wither away. The twenty Polistine Centurions could only watch in dismay as the walls of the golden cube melted away as the four Triceratopian emerged from their impenetrable prison.

As they began to shoot down the numerous Polistine Centurions who were buzzing around them with their blue helmet lasers, The Alpha Triceratopian ordered the others, "Leave no flying Polistine pest alive. We'll then teach the Abomination how impolite it is to keep our Master waiting."

Not too far from where the Triceratopian were freeing themselves, Hotfire was awakening to find himself within a cylindrical energy containment field on board a Spartan transport vehicle known as a Tram. The tiny transport vessel had four to six navigation tubes that allowed a set of pilots to control the ship with their thoughts via a headset which descended from the top of a vacuum tube. Hotfire's confinement device was located at the rear of the Tram behind a massive central Artificial Intelligence processing unit that coordinated the actions of the various pilots, in order for the ship to operate in a smooth and efficient manner. The Tram was currently in the same tunnel following the same track that had carried the prisoners from the Rec Center to their containment cells about a half hour before and would eventually carry the prisoner, Hotfire, to the Warden's office.

"Would one of you lads be willing to rub my nose? I have the most terrible itch."

"Are you unaware that your reputation as a trickster is known throughout the galaxy?" asked Centurion Trazz.

"Not even one little scratch?" asked Hotfire with doe-like eyes.

"In addition, your request is most likely part of a rouse on your part to incapacitate us."

"You are probably right about that. I was just trying to make chit-chat," smiled Hotfire. "Are we almost to see the Warden? I would never forgive myself if I made him wait."

"Fear not, Abomination. You will not have to wait much longer to receive your judgement."

"I was judged as a villain a long time ago so I have my own obligation to fulfill."

"And what would that be?" inquired Lieutenant Trazz.

"Causing chaos," smirked Hotfire.

As the Beetleguise guards watched in horror, Hotfire vanished right in front of their multi-lensed eyes. Trazz rushed over to the apparently empty cylinder at the rear of the Tram only to be greeted by an orange fireball emerging from inside the field. He fell to the floor, stone dead.

Trazz's second in command, Hargot, climbed out of his vacuum tube to come to the aid of his fallen colleague. He ran toward the back of the ship, Hotfire reappeared within his cell and sent another fireball flying over Hargot's head, leaving singe marks on his antennae.

"Your accuracy seems to be slipping in your old age." taunted Hargot.

"Oh, you thought I was aiming for you? How easy it is to distract your tiny Insectum brain."

As Hargot pulled out his blaster and began to fire as he watched the protective containment field begin to dissolve around Hotfire. With every other step, Hotfire disappeared as Hargot fired and repeatedly missed. And every time Hotfire reappeared, he had moved a step or two closer to where Hargot stood, until he was close enough to pick the Beetleguise up by the scruff of his neck. In an act of desperation, Hargot fired his blaster one last time. Hotfire moved his shackled hands into the laser blast's path. When the shot severed his iron bonds, Hotfire held his hands up like a magician who had just accomplished a spectacular trick. And once the Beetleguise had served his purpose, Hotfire threw him against the far wall of the capsule and watched as the fallen Beetleguise oozed milky white blood.

The third Beetleguise guard smashed through a console on the control panel with the intention of electrocuting Hotfire.

"Aww, I feel bad that you are doing all my work for me," said Hotfire with a sneer. He grabbed the Beetleguise around the waist with his enormous tail and smacked him directly into the panel. The Beetleguise burned brightly with a white hot flame, ending up before being burned to a cinder.

"Any more takers?" asked Hotfire.

"I give my life willingly for the glory of the Beetleguise Trotsnexus," said the last Beetleguise as he grabbed a neutron grenade from a weapons cabinet and removed the pin. This action took even Hotfire by surprise because he had never witnessed such self-sacrifice in a Beetleguise before.

"I admire your bravery, Beetleguise, but I am afraid that your valor is for naught." Hotfire rechanneled the plasma energy that he normally emitted from his tail and began to send the fire up his trachea and out his mouth. This redirection would have incinerated the grenade and the Beetleguise who was holding it. However, before he even had the opportunity to release this terrible destructive force from within, Hotfire and the Beetleguise Centurion were distracted by the hissing of a high intensity laser beam piercing the far wall of the ship. Observing that the attention of the Beetleguise had been diverted from thoughts of assassination to pondering who could possibly be breaking into the transport pod, Hotfire took the opportunity to grab the thermal grenade out of the Centurion's appendage. Without missing a beat, he deposited the thermal grenade into a demolecularization disposal unit at the front of the Tram. Unfortunately, he was characteristically late in his timing, which resulted in the disposal unit being vaporized along with the front half of the ship. The force of the explosion knocked Hotfire and the fourth Beetleguise against the tubes at the far wall of the Tram.

"My Brothers and I had been more than willing to take the time to slice your craft in half, but we do appreciate you doing most of the work for the Triceratopian." said the Alpha Triceratopian.

"And who the Fuctur are you, might I ask?" Hotfire said as he looked at the latest arrival to the party.

"Ah, dear Hotfire, I am the one who will bring you to your knees," said Alpha Trike.

"It will be my absolute pleasure to see you try," smiled Hotfire. "But I would prepare myself if I were you, because you are about to have hellfire unleashed upon you and your brothers."

Hotfire jumped through the newly created skylight in the Tram and positioned himself so that he was sitting on the roof of the craft with his tail facing towards the Triceratopian. Like an astro-ball player at batting practice, he launched a dozen fireballs at the Trike. The Trike's expression grew intense as he fired blue lasers from his horns that caused most of Hotfire's fireballs to explode in mid-air. Faced with the possibility of being singed by the four surviving fireballs, he lifted up his hand to harness the invisible force of his telepathy to repel the remaining projectiles back at the Abomination.

"Oh, I am thinking that can't be a good thing," sighed Hotfire. He launched himself into the air just as the fireballs made their way back to him. As the projectiles flew by him, Hotfire jumped higher in the air to avoid the first two while completing a double somersault to dodge the final two.

"Most impressive, Abomination!" said Alpha Trike. "But your tricks will not be enough to save you." He motioned for two more of the Triceratopian, Beta and Gamma, to start ascending the Tram to retrieve Hotfire.

"Now you know I wasn't going to make it that easy for you to capture me," smirked Hotfire. He leapt off the roof of the Tram as he spun around in mid-air using his tail as a rather effective whip. Beta managed to avoid being knocked down by the tail, but Gamma was not so lucky. Hotfire's tail smacked Gamma directly in the face as he was pushed backward, and forced Beta down to the ground.

"Brothers, the only way that we will defeat this adversary is through the strength of our numbers."

"You have spoken truth this day, Alpha," concurred Beta Trike.

"Do the Horned-faced freaks know that their ugly faces are about be introduced to the floor? I think not," said Hotfire as he waved his hands dramatically in the air.

"Subdue the Abomination, my Brothers," said Alpha Trike.

"Methinks you talk way too much, you Horned-face Blastard," said Hotfire. "Let's cut the dialogue and just fight."

"Agreed," quipped Alpha Trike, as he aimed his blue lasers directly at Hotfire's head. As the beams came close to landing on their mark, the Abomination vanished before their eyes. He reappeared a moment later holding on to a rock formation above Alpha's head. "You must excuse me, I had some expired rodents for breakfast and now I have the worst case of Reptilia breath," Hotfire remarked right before releasing the fire in his trachea he had intended to use on the Beetleguise. The fire burned through the rock and sent a coned-shaped rock barreling down on Alpha Trike's head.

As Alpha turned towards Hotfire and the descending stone, he used his blue lasers to disintegrate the stony mass into harmless rubble. Having witnessed his projectile eliminated, Hotfire jumped down to face Alpha Trike directly. He slammed directly into the Trike and knocked him to the ground. Alpha immediately returned to his feet and began to charge towards Hotfire with his horns down in attack position. Before Hotfire even had a chance to move, he was sent hurtling up toward the top of the cavern. Hotfire was unable to gain control of his body, at first, as he went falling back down towards the ground, but at the last possible second he was able to right himself and land on his feet. Unfortunately, he landed directly in the middle of the Triceratopian foursome.

As Hotfire made his way clockwise around the circle of opponents, he kicked out with his tail and legs while defending himself from their blue lasers by hurling fireballs, most of which were disintegrated. To all outward appearances, the Abomination was making a valiant effort to keep this Triceratopian quartet at bay. Yet, it soon became apparent to Hotfire that there was an unnatural component to these Triceratopian that made them quicker than a normal adversary. As hard as he landed a punch or tried to take out their legs, these Trikes never truly succumbed to his assault upon them.

As Hotfire launched a final round of fireballs at the circle, the Alpha Trike yelled, "Concentrate, my Brothers. If we are able to deliver his flamed projectiles to his feet, we will defeat him."

Hotfire could only watch helplessly in his weakened state as the fireballs turned away from his horned adversaries and came directly back to him. Like a punch from a fiery beast, each fireball sent Hotfire staggering backwards as they landed on his chest with increasing force until the last remaining projectile sent him into a state of unconsciousness.

The Alpha Trike touched his finger to his ear to contact Sobek as he watched Hotfire laying motionlessly on the cavern floor. "Master Sobek, we have secured the Abomination for transport. We will be with you shortly."

"You have served me well this day," said Sobek.

At that moment, the last Beetleguise came running out of the half-destroyed Tram with a laser cannon screaming, "You will perish at the hands of the most valiant Beetleguise you've ever encountered." The four Triceratopian turned as one and the Centurion become nothing more than a puff of smoke.

While Hotfire was on the receiving end of a generous pummeling from the four Triceratopian, Buddash was slumbering in the prison's industrial iron, blissfully unaware that he was about to become significantly thinner.

Not even the sound of the industrial iron's motor beginning to rumble out of its slumber was enough to rouse the sleeping Cranitian. It was not until the machine released the lubricant grease, which prevented the machine's gears and cogs from freezing up, did Buddash awaken with a start. He had been unable to tolerate the smell of lubricant grease from the time that he was an adolescent and had been forced to spend countless summer hours working in his uncle's repair shop. Even upon waking, Buddash momentarily believed that he was back on Leathershell in his uncle's garage repairing hovercrafts for the measly wage his uncle reluctantly provided him. But as he looked around the darkened cylinder and felt the long, stiff plank beneath his shell, Buddash remembered where he was and how much trouble he truly was in at that moment.

As he looked up to see the heavy anvil rushing down towards him, he spoke aloud, "Come on, Buddash. You need to come up with an answer and you needed it two minutes ago." He glanced back up at the descending iron, hoping desperately for inspiration. "Nope. Nothing is coming to mind. Daggit!" But then he noticed three cables running from the iron up into the top of the machine.

"Well, I can't think of any more insane notions at the moment, I guess I'll go with this one."

Buddash stood up as best he could on the plank — because the press was already almost on top of him — and leapt. He grabbed the metal iron and, holding on for his very life, extended two of the spikes on his hand and slashed at the cables connecting the press to the roof of the machine. Immediately, as the cables were severed, the press began to swing in a wild, wide arc all around the chamber. Buddash struggled desperately to regain control of the iron press. He stood up on the metal iron, and Buddash coaxed it into greater and greater circles as it spun around the inside of the chamber. Finally, he rode the iron press through the circular glass door of the industrial press, sending him flying out of the press and onto the floor of the prison laundry room.

As Buddash was escaping the iron press, Yanick sat unconscious within the industrial washer/dryer as it turned around, tossing and removing the dampness from prison uniforms. In Yanick's catatonic state, he had no knowledge that his skin was starting to flake. He was literately being burned alive. But as he was tumbled here and there, Yanick's head occasionally made contact with the over-sized washer/dryer until he was finally jarred awake and back into reality. Naturally, the first thing he screamed when being exposed to the extreme heat was "Water! Oh for the sake of the Great Hive Master, someone get me some water." Unfortunately, the only portion of the plea that the washer/dryer's voice-activated sensor heard was water, and it immediately switched from the dry to wash cycle of the machine. The cylinder immediately began to fill with water that would soon fill the interior completely. Yanick swished through the laundry water to the clear window on the door. As Buddash had not yet been ejected from the industrial iron, Yanick saw no one else in the laundry room. He pushed with all his might to try to break the glass since Redhot had locked the laundry room door from the outside. Yanick backed down as far as he could into the bottom of the drum. Holding his breath, Yanick backed up and jumped into the filthy water, realizing when the washer/dryer was done with the clothes that they had to go somewhere. it occurred to Yanick that the filthy water had to go somewhere when it was done "washing" the clothes. Yanick began to claw at the pipe to increase the flow of water that was entering the drum of the washer/dryer. It was not long before the water pushed its' way out of the drum and exploding into the laundry room, carrying Yanick along with it.

When Yanick went crashing out of the drum of the washer/dryer, he discovered that Buddash had been swept up in the tidal wave of laundry water that now filled the laundry room. Yanick scanned his surroundings furiously for some sign of high ground, but there was none to be found. The single object which Yanick occasionally viewed among the torrent waves was Buddash, bobbing up and down, as he tried to swim with the current. He could only continue to try to keep his head above water as he floated from the laundry room into the lower technology fabrication shops where the inmates built inexpensive ship parts, entertainment devices and everyday convenience implements for export to the Polistine Empire. The most essential commodities created in the shop were pulse rifles and blasters.

As Yanick floated, he realized he needed to start paddling back upstream, an action Buddash immediately adopted as well. They were now moving furiously away from the exit of the room in order to avoid being sliced in half by the large metal door that was coming down to contain the water within the room. Yanick always considered himself more of a desert Reptilia because he seriously despised the water. Still, he realized that his options at this point were to tread water as long as he could or face drowning, which was just very unappealing at the moment.

As he swam around in circles, he swore that he could see something swimming beneath him, and was trying to reason out what it could possibly be. He was so busy trying to determine the identity of the creature that it didn't even dawn on him that it might be a good idea to try to avoid it. It was only after Yanick saw Buddash being pulled beneath the waves by the Chamyx, Redhot, that he decided that it might be a good idea to try to try to avoid the homicidal Reptilia in the water.

Just as Buzz was preparing to give himself a well-deserved pat on the wings for his ingenuity in capturing the four Triceratopian Super Soldiers, Captain Honeycomb contacted him and informed the Legate Prime that he needed to get down to the hangar bay right away.

After flying down to the hangar bay at top speed, Buzz was utterly appalled by the scene of carnage. The massive display of mangled, mutilated and broken Polistine centurions who laid dead around the perimeter of the cube drove Buzz immediately incensed the Polistine and filled him with the strongest need to seek retribution for this massacre.

"Sobek," whispered Buzz as he surveyed the fallen soldiers.

"You don't know that for a fact," Honeycomb said. He knew his old friend too well. Buzz was a gifted tactician when it came to military strategy, but he also was capable of acting very recklessly at times. Captain Honeycomb knew in that moment that the Legate Prime might be considering vengeance against the Hawking Brain Beetle as payment for the slaughter of his Centurions.

"You can be daggit sure that I am going to find out whether he was responsible."

At that moment, a young lieutenant named Zips, came flying furiously into the hangar bay. "Legate Prime, there has been some type of flood in the Machine Shop."

"How could there be a flood?" asked Buzz incredulously. "You do know that we are on an asteroid?"

"Yes, I know. However, the internal sensors are telling a different story. The storm doors have activated around the Shop section. The room is basically sealed."

"What is the status of the items within the Shop itself?"

"Unknown at this time," said Zips.

"If those items are damaged or the shipment is delayed, the three of us are going to wind up in the mines of Sisyphus, praying for a shovel. How well do you think the environmental survival suits could hold up in water rather than zero-gravity?"

Lieutenant Zips contemplated for a minute before stating," Pretty much the same set of variables: extreme pressure, lack of oxygen... I think they could work."

"Then let's get to it, Insect-men," exclaimed Buzz. "And bring a few spear stingers because we don't know who are what is down there waiting for us.

Honeycomb turned to Lieutenant Zips, "Did we just volunteer?"

"Nope, I think we were just drafted."

Legate Prime Buzz, Captain Honeycomb and Lieutenant Zips were sitting inside the emergency escape pod of the, *Honey Vein One*. Captain Honeycomb had provided each Polistine with an environmental suit for their "undersea" expedition, which they quickly put on over their uniforms. Fortunately for them, the suits were designed to accommodate the special features of Polistine anatomy, such as six appendages, four wings and stingers. Once their suits were on, Legate Prime Buzz and Lieutenant Zips fell in behind Captain Honeycomb as he climbed into the tiny three-seat capsule.

Once settled, Honeycomb turned to face Buzz to ask for directions to the Shop. "There is only one way to get there from here to there. We are going to have to bust through some plumbing."

"What do you mean?" asked Zips.

"Just let me drive," Buzz said with a determined look on his face

Quickly, the Legate Prime piloted the pod out of a hanger in the mid-portion of the trapezoid-shaped shuttle. It was already quiet unsettling to Buzz's pod mates as he backed up and put the craft into reverse in close proximity to the *Honey Vein One*, but he managed to heighten their level of discomfort when he informed them, "Okay, Insect-men, I would seriously think about holding my breath if I were you."

"Dare I ask why?" inquired Lieutenant Zips

"I wouldn't," said Honeycomb.

As Buzz pushed the accelerator control all the way to one hundred and twenty, the craft flew forward in a slingshot motion into an exhaust port in the side of the hanger, barely fitting within the circumference. "Captain, calibrate the pod's external sensors to identify any major water sources."

"Right away." After enabling and calibrating the pod's sensors, the on-board Querzi computer reported back to the crew that water had been found 400 feet ahead of them. Buzz re-adjusted the navigation system so that they could reach their destination in one piece.

Honeycomb and Zips sat in terror as Buzz twisted the ship around the metal catacombs of the prison's ventilation system. He called back to them at one point, "You may want to put a few appendages over your eyes for this one."

They accepted this suggestion, but it did not help at all as Buzz drove the pod straight up at a 90-degree angle and then proceeded to do a 180-degree turn before coming straight down at close to 90 mph. As they flew down, the three Polistines felt as if they were going to be ripped from their chairs and plastered onto the side of the craft. They entered one final long shaft at the end of the dive before Buzz announced, "Hold on to your antennae, Insect-men, we are going in for a splash down."

The pod came swiftly up onto the netting of the ventilation port at the end of the tunnel. With a tremendous amount of force, the tiny craft went crashing through the webbing to enter the now completely submerged Machine Shop.

With a sigh of relief, the Legate observed that the ship was indeed watertight and seaworthy. What was somewhat disconcerting though, was the fact that they were not alone. He saw three of his wayward detainees — Redhot, Yanick DcCullen, and Buddash Kyo — from the port side of the ship. That was good. But what he observed on the starboard side was troubling. Apparently, the event that had caused the Shop to flood had also caused some of the oversized fish tanks to burst in Warden Sobek's private aquarium where he kept some of his less-than-successful aquatic experiments. Buzz recognized Warden Sobek's favorite pet, the monstrosity known as the Kraken, as well as the transparent marine abhorrence named after an ancient Pangean god of sleep, Morpheus.

Before Buzz could react with any kind of defense posture, he watched in horror as the final marine experiment in this quartet of escapees, two

Porposians whose heads had been transformed into a mash up of horrors. broke off its pursuit of the Cranitian Buddash Kyo to head towards their tiny pod. They had rows of teeth as sharp as knives and an extended sword on the middle of its forehead.

The Legate Prime said grimly "Hold on, Insect-men, I think this is going to be pretty bad."

Chapter 8
SECOND SKIN

The pleasurist, Hunash, gazed up from the floor of her cabin and watched the being that a moment ago had been Cassian Traggert, but who now had an all-too-familiar face, try to force the life out of her with a firmly placed hand over her mouth. She imagined what she thought would be her last moments, that this is what it must feel like to slip into an alternate reality and meet your evil twin. She was also somewhat amazed, not by this creature's ability to transform but, rather, how much he was enjoying the act of snuffing the life out of her.

Second Skin, who was still wearing Hunash's face as he sat on top of the pleasurist, sneered, "If you could, you would thank me for taking your life if you knew what destruction I was sparing you from. There are very unpleasant things that I need to accomplish within the next few hours and there are very few of your fellow passengers who will survive. So take solace in the fact that your death will be the first of dozens aboard your precious *Charon*."

The absolute glee that this being was taking in the knowledge that he was to be the impetus for chaos was too much for Hunash. She determined in that moment that she had to find a way to take action to prevent the malicious mischief that this creature was planning for the passengers and crew. Hunash pulled her jaws back as far as she was capable of doing with Second Skin's hand covering her mouth.

"What are you trying to do you, Cranitian Slutas?" demanded Second Skin.

Hunash slammed her teeth into the hand of her assailant. The Clonstellar let out an unholy wail in Hunash's voice, and grabbed the injured hand with the fingers of his unaffected limb as she moved in violent circles around the cabin. Hunash instinctively made her way for the door as Second Skin continued to nurse his injured hand.

As she ran down the hallway, Hunash heard the door to her cabin slide open to see that Second Skin, who had wrapped his bloody hand in a scarf, had reverted back to his former self and as Cassian was shouting to everyone in the vicinity that Hunash had stolen all his credits. The co-pilot of the *Charon*, Lieutenant Commander Zappo, was coming out of his cabin to make his way up to the ship's cockpit. The Polistine Commander had agreed to work the night watch that late evening so a junior Polistine ensign could recover from a bout of the Yataxan flu, or so the ensign claimed. Zappo had a sneaking suspicion it was more likely that the ensign was recovering from shore leave. Despite the potential volatility of the scene, Zappo was secretly grateful for the small opportunity to feel useful.

"What seems to be the problem, sir?" asked Zappo.

"This Cranitian pleasurist was providing private entertainment for me in my quarters when I caught her downloading credits from my account to her Querzi tablet," said Cassian.

"That is a lie, Commander," said Hunash. "He is a homicidal shifter who just tried to choke me."

"Now why would he be trying to kill you over a few credits?" asked Zappo.

"Yes, Cranitian. Why would I do that?"

"Because you said yourself that you are some kind of assassin," said Hunash.

"Who would I be trying to kill aboard a transport shuttle? There is no one of great importance for me to eliminate on this ship. In fact, the only two individuals of any great importance aboard this ship are the pilot, Captain Hooms, and you, Lieutenant Commander Zappo. And the only purpose which I could achieve in killing either one of you would be to hijack this ship."

"Commander Zappo, run!" screamed Hunash.

As the warning passed over Hunash's lips, it was already too late for Zappo. Cassian had morphed into a nine-foot tall, red-skinned Quillian with a pale complexion. Now disguised as the Quillian, he wrapped his arm around Zappo's neck, twisted his head off his body like a thirsty bar patron.

"As they used to say, "you can't hijack a ship without cracking a few skulls," smiled the Quillian. "Now, the only thing left to do before I deliberately disable this ship is to eliminate you, my dear."

Hunash knew she needed to stop Second Skin, even at the cost of her own life. She reached behind her as she backed away to find a conduit pipe and slowly backed away as her attacker grew closer.

"Don't fight it, my dear. It's just so much quicker when you don't fight, my dear."

"Well, see how you feel about fighting this!" quipped Hunash as she extended the claws on her left hand and punctured the conduit behind Second Skin leapt forward and as she landed in front of the pipe. He was greeted by a stream of pressurized, scalding hot water pummeling him in the face. As Hunash turned to run down the hallway, she heard the ungodly screams of Second Skin echoing in her ears as she moved towards the escape pod.

"Come back here, you Cranitian. I will kill you slowly for this insult."

But Hunash already was aware that she needed to get help from an outside source in order to prevent Second Skin from going forward with his plan so, for now, she had to run away. She swore that she would return as soon as she was able as Hunash ran down the hallway towards a row of escape pods.

Back aboard the *Charon*, Second Skin, who had now assumed the form of Lieutenant Commander Zappo, made his way to the cockpit where he was greeted by the Polistine captain, Hooms.

"You oversleep again, old man?" asked Captain Hooms.

"Yes, you just know me so well!"

"Well, you know I don't mind covering for you. Just don't let it become a habit."

"Well, I can definitely assure you that I will never be late for another shift ever again."

"Well, you don't need to take it to that extreme." The captain was inexplicably overcome with the desire to get as far away from Zappo as possible, so he never saw Second Skin plotting an intercept course for the Purple L Swarm's vessel.

Chapter 9
LIEUTENANT THORN

Lieutenant Thorn emerged from his brief slumber on board the *Mjölnir* with a start. In a terrifying dream, he had encountered a mirror image of himself who was once again whole, but lacked any sense of honor or duty. Instead, this anti-Thorn craved only one thing in his life, the desire for conquest. This lust had a physical manifestation in the anti-Thorn: his eyes glowed with a bright green illumination. Thorn found himself wrestling with the anti-Thorn within the dream, with his antithesis pushing him into a deep cavern where he fell endlessly surrounded on all sides by an emerald light. He wondered what the meaning of this internal vision could be; was it a prophecy of things to come or a vision of things past?

Thorn sat on the medical bed contemplating. The door to the medical bay slid open to reveal a stately looking Ruddarian in a blue jumpsuit who introduced himself as Captain Relich Odinord.

"I am Lieutenant Thorn, formerly the Weapons Officer of the battle cruiser, *Honey Hive.*"

"I extend my deepest condolences to you regarding your fallen comrades. It is never easy to watch those you've served with perish in battle, even if they have died with honor."

"What do you know of combat or loss, Captain?"

"I have watched friends die in battle as they defended their homes on Sisyphus from members of Swarm battalions who had decided that they needed our food and medicine more than we did."

"Every citizen is required to make sacrifices in war, even cattle such as the Ruddarians."

"A matter to be discussed at another time, apparently. Anyway, Dr. Tulare informs me that you have some knowledge of our Green Diamond and, possibly, how we could more safely transport the item for the remainder of our voyage to Madagascan."

"Yes, your doctor has told me of your scientists' plans to encase it in a vault constructed of dwarf-star quartz. The Eye of Hermes will slice through such a vault like paper and then drain every last ounce of power from the Beetleguise home world."

"What can be done to combat the power of this Green Diamond?"

"That, I do not have the knowledge to answer with accuracy. Legends states that the ancient race known as the Queztalcoatin, who it is said were responsible for the engineering of the Polistine race itself, managed to create a power source that was able to prevent the explosion of a dying sun. Some of their finest scientific minds argued that they could forge a stone that could consume the energy of this explosion. The greatest mystics among the Queztalcoatin stated that the destruction of their world was pre-ordained according to the cosmic timelines and could not be averted."

"So what was the final decision?" asked Odinord.

"Captain, the scientists who favored the preservation of their world won the day. The Eye of Hermes was constructed from green carbon harvested from the deepest depths of their world. The green carbon was cooked in their hottest volcano, making it indestructible. It is said that a Mystic Queztalcoatin cursed the Green Diamond to have an insatiable craving for energy. The Eye of Hermes did stop the exploding sun, but then it came to cause havoc in its wake as it continued to drain power from other stars.

"How was it stopped from destroying the galaxy?"

"The Queztalcoatin Mystics magically bounded the Eye of Hermes' power. It is said that these Queztalcoatin Mystics sent it to the very heart of the Universe where it remained for tens of millennia," said Lieutenant Thorn.

"Somehow, it has re-emerged into our space," said Captain Odinord.

"The Green Diamond is said to be able to bewitch a being into becoming his servant. This Servant of the Eye of Hermes is used as a puppet by the Green Diamond to slowly make its way back to the Queztalcoatin home world. There is one being known as Diabolix. Some claim that he is capable of harnessing the power of the Eye of Hermes, and has the ability to use the Green Diamond to absorb the power of a star into his own body as easily as a Polistine blowing out a candle."

"Diabolix is in the most impenetrable prison in the galaxy. There is no way that he will ever be able to get his hands on the Eye of Hermes," said Captain Odinord.

"There are many individuals of all different races who would call you foolish for your presumption, dear Captain," smirked Thorn.

Before Odinord could ask the Polistine another question, it seemed that the Great Hive Master himself put his foot down and stated there had been enough discussion because numerous elements of chaos began to play out all around the Ruddarian science ship. Defensive Officer Kon was reporting that a Polistine battle cruiser had just come out of hyper-space directly along the *Mjölnir's* port side. Jonn Dansk, who was acting comm officer, replacing Jandar Weingarter, was reporting that a Polistine named Legate Prime Nectaxus, — Legate Prime of Purple L Swarm as well as commander of the Destroyer, *Pollister* — had informed them they were about to be boarded. As Odinord looked at Thorn, he shook his head, "You and I will be the first of billions of lifeforms to perish from the Eye of Hermes' devastation."

Chapter 10
YANICK DCCULLEN

Hotfire remained slightly disoriented after being subdued by the four Triceratopian, but he had a sneaking suspicion that the Triceratopian had been had assigned the same task as the four Beetleguise Centurions; namely bringing him before Warden Sobek. As he glanced around, he observed that he was in a deep metallic cylindrical shaft that lacked both windows and doors. Upon closer inspection, Hotfire was unable to determine how he had gotten in the chamber, and, worse yet, how he would ever get out. But there was the more immediate matter on Hotfire's mind; what were Warden Sobek's plans for him now that he was caught in his trap?

"Sobek, I am telling you right now that whatever you wanted me to do —"

Before Hotfire could even finish his sentence, the faceless voice of Warden Sobek reverberated throughout the chamber. "You refuse to help me. Is that what you were getting ready to say? Next, you'll probably tell me that you are going to resist me with every fiber of your being,"

"Yep, something to that effect," said Hotfire.

"And we both know that your only objection to helping me is that you won't make any profit," mocked Warden Sobek.

Hotfire stood on his hind legs and shook a finger at the disembodied voice, "No. I refuse to help you because I will be too preoccupied figuring out how to get off this floating prison. And once I escape from your little jail, I will make sure that you meet your end in the most painful manner possible."

"Unfortunately, I don't believe that you will be able to avail yourself of that opportunity."

"And why is that?" asked Hotfire.

"Because you will be too preoccupied fighting for your very life and sanity. See, I have been dabbling in biologic experimentation in recent years. These scientific studies currently include investigating the mental functioning of creatures with higher brain capabilities. More specifically, the impact of psychic organisms on sentient creatures like you, Hotfire. For this experiment, I am going to introduce a Psychic Spider into your brain through subdermal injection. I will then monitor your reactions with the Psychic spider over the course of eighteen hours as it grows to maturity. At the end of the eighteen hours, I will either sanction the removal of the Psychic Spider from your cranial cavity, if you refuse to carry out my simple task, I will sit back and watch your head explode."

"And how exactly do I change your mind about letting this spider kill me after eighteen hours?"

"You will enter a portal to X-Space and eliminate the repugnant creature known as Diabolix."

"Okay. I've already made up my mind. I am going to find a way to stop your little pet on my own. So, you can go Fuctur yourself."

"Oh, I am so sorry you feel that way because the Psychic Spider is programmed to obey my wishes and desires. Once you are injected with the Spider, you will be compelled to do my bidding."

"That does it! I am getting out of here, Sobek, right now."

Hotfire turned to the nearest wall and began launching fireballs towards it in an attempt to create his own exit. Two doors slid open on either side of him. Through these doors, Alpha and Beta Triceratopian casually walked over towards Hotfire with tranquilizer cannons and proceeded to shoot several knockout darts into his chest. As they carried him into a dark chamber with a silver recliner that had restraints on the feet and arms of the chair, Hotfire continued to mumble somewhat incoherently, "I am going to stop you all and then I am going to crush you. Do you have any idea who you are dealing with? I am The Abomination!"

Alpha Trike strapped Hotfire to the chair. "It is going to be absolute pleasure to see you in undying torment." He then brought down a needle that injected a small black ball into Hotfire's neck.

As the Psychic Spider made a path directly for his brain, Hotfire uttered an otherworldly scream as it attached itself to his dermal matter and immediately began to impose its will on him

"Is the procedure complete?" asked Warden Sobek.

Before Alpha Trike could speak, Hotfire replied, "I will obey you, Master Sobek.

Yanick felt like he was a pet Piscean who had met an untimely end and was being unceremoniously flushed down a toilet drain. Redhot's attention had abandoned any thoughts of revenge in favor of self-preservation upon seeing the voracious creatures who had entered the submerged Machine Shop. Instead, Redhot pushed Yanick against a nearby wall as he secured him using an industrial- sized vice around his mid-section. "Sobek's pets will deal with you soon enough. Meanwhile, I am going to take your friend to the bottom to make sure he meets his watery end."

"You haven't seen the last of me, you black Salamander," spouted Yanick.

"But I think that I have," said Redhot as he turned around and jumped onto the unsuspecting Buddash's back and began pushing him down to the bottom. Yanick immediately began to work deactivating the servo lock on the vice. But as he stared up he Yanick realized that there were perils in this manufactured ocean that were far worse than escaping his metal restraint. In the dark, he saw a pair of yellow eyes staring back at him. After a moment that seemed to last an eternity, the creature began puncturing the glass with its set of six clawed appendages until it had formed a hole large enough for it to squeeze its body into the Machine Shop.

Yanick had already managed to remove the panel from the servo-control of the vice using his claw as a makeshift screwdriver, but the glass began to crack with greater speed, the beast with the six appendages continued to press his enormous bulk against the glass with increasing force. The fracture lines grew longer and longer as the bellowing frustration of the beast appeared to grow in intensity despite the fact that it was muffled by the rising water. These utterances of irritation reached their climax as the beast drew back his top four limbs one last time and used all his might to finally pierce the aquarium glass.

As the glass exploded into a multitude of shards large and small, the beast came barreling into the Machine Shop with three other aquatic companions, two genetically modified Porposian and an enormous transparent cuddle Piscean, along with a few hundred more gallons of recycled water.

As Yanick's finally discovered the correct series of circuits that needed to be activated to release the vice, he found himself being swept up in the wake of the incoming flood that began to push him towards the bottom of the shop. But just like a child's yank-yank toy, Yanick felt himself being pulled back up, and he looked down in despair to see that the beast had wrapped an appendage around Yanick's mid-section as it began to squeeze. The beast, which Yanick was able to identify upon closer inspection as a Kraken, then commenced to slither its appendage up around Yanick's body. As he pondered the situation, he was unable to determine a means of escape as he observed the tip of the Kraken's tentacle moving towards his mouth. He looked next to the Kraken and saw an industrial fan still in operation, even submerged in the water. Seeing a chance for life, Yanick twisted slightly in the Kraken's grasp as much as he could and swung repeated blows with his tail against the beast.

The Kraken was amused that this little blue-and-green morsel was trying to fight him off right before he was getting ready to eat him. However, this amusement turned to annoyance as he suddenly felt "knives" digging into his back from behind. The Kraken turned to observe thin lines of green blood migrating into the water from its wounds, realizing only too late that its prey had managed to escape from its grasp. The Kraken lunged forward enormous jaws with rows and rows of razor-sharp teeth but, Yanick had already begun swimming towards the bottom of the shop. The Kraken remained confident in the face of this momentary setback as it had already determined that if he could not catch this morsel using his mouth then he would just have to employ another body part.

Yanick desperately hoped that he would be able to find some type of ventilation port that would allow him to escape this nightmarish game of Felindon and Piscean in that he was currently engaged. As he swam through the blackness of the murky water, he saw a set of goliath-sized mine launchers floating midstream in front of him. Sending up a silent prayer to the Great Hive Master, he reached down and slung the weapons over his shoulders.

Just as the Kraken turned towards Yanick, he launched a set of four mines at its hind quarters. Unfortunately, the mines did not have the desired effect. They merely landed along the Kraken's tail and caused what amounted to a slight burn. Still, this further source of irritation was enough to send the beast flying into a rage. It made a quick turn in the water so that his head was now facing the bottom and went darting down with the intention of swallowing Yanick whole. But it found that the fates seemed to favor those foolish enough to believe that they could survive his wraith. At the last possible second, a small metallic pea-shaped craft came hurtling out of an access tunnel in between the path of the Kraken and his intended prey.

Before Yanick even realized what had happened, a submergible vehicle was hanging in front of him in the water. As he watched the small transport, he realized that there was a downside to his good fortune: he recognized the pod as Polistine military-issued. But Yanick couldn't concern himself with that right now; it was more important to put some distance between himself and the Kraken.

Not far from where Yanick was trying to avoid becoming a Kraken snack, Redhot was pushing Buddash down to the bottom of the Machine Shop like a demented Polistine child trying to drown a pet centipede. As Redhot pressed down harder on his opponent's shell, Buddash realized that both he and Redhot were using their internal set of gills to function in the water. Therefore, he might be able to disrupt Redhot's ability to breath by hitting him in just the right spot.

Realizing that he would probably have only one chance before Redhot realized his intentions, Buddash retracted his head as far as he could and bashed into his target. The impact of Buddash's head caused Redhot to curl up in a ball as an immeasurable aching permeated his entire chest. This should have given Buddash the chance he needed to escape from him, but Redhot recovered almost instantly.

Redhot turned towards Buddash and used his tiny-but-powerful arm to knock him into a nearby wall. As Redhot swam towards the dazed Buddash to continue the pummeling, he was greeted in an unceremonious fashion as Buddash propelled himself like a missile, with appendages and head now within his shell, towards Redhot, slamming him into the opposite wall.

After a moment's recovery, Redhot spun in a 180 degree-motion in the water with the intention of whacking the Cranitian so hard that he would probably think he was a hatchling once again. But as he was moving towards Buddash, Redhot heard a whooshing sound in the water followed by a Porposian hurtling towards him. This new monstrosity had an extended sword on its nose that it used to impale Redhot. Possibly unhappy with having a Chamyx attached to its face, it then raced through the water went hurtling through the water before stopping short, sending his corpse flying into one of the lower industrial fans.

The Porposian then turned towards Buddash who used the unfortunate demise of Redhot to assist him in his own self-preservation. He once again pulled his head and appendages beneath his naturally occurring armor and turned his shell towards the genetically altered Porposian.

Having an awareness of what the Porposian was probably intending, Buddash waited until it was less than an inch from him before springing up and bringing both feet directly down on the Porposian's nose. Buddash then sent his body spinning with a kicking motion as he landed repeated kicks and hits onto the beast. Buddash was surprised to observe that the Porposian did not retaliate in any way but, instead, just continually stood its ground. It was only after the third or fourth such engagement between himself and the Porposian that Buddash began to suspect that something was very wrong.

Buddash turned to see that the Porposian was maneuvering his Cranitian prey into the teeth of a spinning power-saw that was floating in the space behind him. Buddash only came to this realization after he felt the burn of the spinning metal wheel on the edges of his shell. In desperation, Buddash reached out and smacked the Porposian on its nose, sending it into a blind rage. As the Porposian came charging towards him, it realized only too late that Buddash had already pulled up towards the roof, leaving the Porposian to be eviscerated by the spinning wheel of death.

As the passengers of the shuttle pod from the *Honey Vein One* watched a Cranitian sending a Porposian to its death with an assist from a power saw, it was only by the slightest bit of good fortune that Buzz saw the oncoming Kraken, who was agitated from having a Trionyx using it for target practice.

"Buzz, I got this. Putting us in full reverse," said Honeycomb.

"I think it might be a little too late for a tactical retreat, Honeycomb," said Buzz as the beast came nose-to-nose with the pod. It before extended its massive jaws and wrapped four of its six appendages around the hull of the ship.

"Hold on, boys. This is probably going to be bad," said Buzz.

"That just maybe the understatement of the year," sighed Honeycomb.

As the jaws of the Kraken tore into the roof of the pod, it ripped into the transport like a hungry raptor pulling apart an avian egg in search of a tender, young morsel. Buzz, Honeycomb and Zips were barely able to climb into their environmental suits and out into the filthy, cold water.

The three Polistines pushed up towards the roof of the Machine Shop at the greatest of speed. Yet, the Kraken's reflexes were too quick and it swooped Buzz up with one of its clawed appendages. As Buzz was brought closer and closer to its considerable jaws, he could feel the heat of the Kraken's breath, to sense the creature's anticipation at the thought of devouring him. But just as he was precariously dangling above the Kraken's jaws, Buzz felt himself jolted violently out of the creature's grasp and went flying backwards through the icy water.

A second or two after recovering his senses, Legate Prime Buzz glanced back in the direction of the Kraken to discover that his savior was the Trionyx, Yanick DcCullen, who was holding a mine launcher in each of his claws.

Just as it was dawning on Buzz that a prisoner was responsible for saving his exoskeleton, the Legate Prime observed that the Kraken had recovered from having his claw nearly being blown off and was swimming back around to claim Buzz as an afternoon snack.

"Just don't sit there, DcCullen," yelled Buzz. "Toss me one of those things!"

Yanick threw the mine launcher into the air as Buzz took off in the water to intercept it. As Buzz pushed himself forward, he observed out of the corner of his multi-lensed eye that the Kraken was moving towards the same target and was reaching up to grab the launcher in its powerful jaws.

At that moment, inspiration struck the Legate Prime. He swam in between the Kraken's jaws and twisted the mine launcher so that it was facing its throat. After taking a moment to position the launcher, he fired four mines directly down the throat of the beast.

Buzz quickly swam away from the beast and motioned for Yanick to follow his lead. He was unsure if the thick, draconian scales of the beast would contain the explosion, or would the Kraken merely implode? Neither of these events occurred. All that happened, much to Buzz's surprise, was that there was a small boom as the Kraken's stomach expanded for a moment before contracting; as a small puff of smoke escaped from his lips, followed by a nerve-shattering, siren-style scream.

Yanick swam over to Buzz. As the Trionyx positioned himself in front of the Kraken, he mouthed, "Great! Now he is really mad."

"Well, do you have any constructive suggestions?" asked Buzz as he motioned for Yanick to continue swimming away from the angry Kraken.

Buzz was somewhat disappointed with the response from the Trionyx as Yanick merely began swirling his hand around in the water.

"Well, that isn't very constructive to let me know that you could care less."

But Yanick could tell that Buzz was not getting that he was suggesting a plan of action rather than showing his disdain for the Legate Prime. So he decided to demonstrate his suggestion with a somewhat more elaborate gesture. Yanick began twisting his body in circular motions in the water while holding his nose. He then pointed at the smoke evacuation valves that served as a means for clearing the shop of smoke in the case of a fire.

"You may just have a notion there, DcCullen. Instead of using the valves to get smoke out of the shop, we just might be able to use them to drain all the water out of this little aquarium."

Yanick began to nod vehemently at Buzz. However, at the last second, Yanick reached out and grabbed him as the Kraken was bringing his claws down to crush the two of them. Buzz and Yanick turned in unison towards the Kraken and began to fire mines from their launchers as they moved up towards the first suppression valve. As they swam away, Buzz activated the ear-comm in his helmet. "Lieutenant Zips, I think we might have a workable plan for dealing with these creatures while, at the same time, draining the Machine Shop. I need you to activate the left corner evacuation valve. There should be a yellow lever on the far left wall of the shop that will activate the evacuation valve.

"Sir, that is a brilliant idea. I will make my way down to activate the valve as soon as possible. However, I am actually a little preoccupied at the moment," said Lieutenant Zips.

Having seen that Legate Prime Buzz was going after one of the fugitives, had taken the initiative to pursue the Cranitian being chased by the Porposian.

After disposing of the first Porposian, Buddash had found that the partner of the dearly departed Porposian had not taken kindly to having his friend being sliced to pieces by a table saw. Therefore, the second Porposian had begun to pursue Buddash along the bottom of the tank.

Zips found the Cranitian at the bottom of the Machine Shop He turned around to head towards the bottom of the Machine shop in order to intercept the Cranitian, but was unsure exactly what he would do to deal with the 200-pound Porposian, unaware that the Porposian had already detected that there was someone behind it and had turned around and swimming right at Zips. He was therefore taken completely by surprise. He realized that he needed to assume a defensive posture immediately. Looking around for a place to hid, he was swimming toward a fractured portion of the escape pod from the *Honey Hive One* when he received the order on his ear-comm to move down towards the bottom of the shop and release the valve.

The Porposian had already begun to slice the metal fragment of the *Honey Hive One* pod apart with its razor-sharp teeth when Zips decided that he needed to take aggressive action. He flipped a larger piece of metal towards the Porposian's head as he turned around and flew down towards the bottom of the tank. He could hear the Porposian uttering a deep, moaning set of clicks behind him in agitation before pushing forward into the water after him.

Zips was not exactly sure where he was headed but knew precisely what he was looking for beneath the artificially created depths. He continued to dodge to left and right as he swam away from the Porposian who was using his sword-like nose to continually attempt to poke holes in the Polistine's gut. As Zips swam down to the floor of the Machine shop, the Porposian continued to use a combination of its sword-like nose to impale Zips as well as its razor-sharp teeth to pull the Polistine apart. Within sight of the darken floor, the Porposian commenced what it believed would be its final assault on its black and yellow target. But unfortunately, just as it was ready to strike, a translucent tentacle reached up and wrapped around the head of the creature and pulled it towards its mouth, tearing the Porposian to shreds with its massive jaws. The squid-like creature Morpheus used its tentacles to retrieve loose chunks of flesh that were floating away and devoured them, too.

"I guess I'm the leader of the pack when it comes to activating levers," said Zips. "And just in time it seems because I can see that giant cuddle Piscean is almost done its snack." Zip twisted his body and headed towards the bottom of the room. Given that his stingers were contained within the environmental suit, he knew he was at a tactical disadvantage. Before Morpheus detected that there was another piece of prey in his vicinity, Zips moved as quickly as possible over to the far wall with the lever, until he got within a few feet of the left wall and felt his foot catch on a power generator cord within inches of his goal.

As the Lieutenant was in a state of entanglement, Morpheus launched one of its sharp-barbed stingers. As the tentacle dug into his back, Lieutenant Zips quickly experience two sensations that he believed were contributing to his rather painful death. These were: the spear-shaped tentacle in his back, and the expulsion of oxygen from his environmental suit. As he felt himself dying though, he knew that his final action would be one that would give his comrades the chance for life.

Zips ripped two slits in the environmental suit, which allowed his wings to function in the water. He took one final leap on the floor towards the emergency vent's access panel. Ripping it open with all his might, he pulled the yellow lever. In that instant, the water began to run past him through the newly exposed vent. Then he let go, and was swept away in the flood of rushing water.

Honeycomb swam as fast as possible to complete his assignment. The Legate Prime had instructed him to make his way to the right hand wall of the

Machine Shop where he would flip the switch that would start to drain the room liked a flushed waste disposal unit. He had no love for being in this submerged water tank. The faster that he, Zips and the Legate could get away from this watery battlefield, the happier that they would be.

But just as he was making his way to the wall, who should arrive on the scene but the overgrown six-armed aquatic monstrosity that Sobek affectionately called the Kraken. As soon as the Kraken laid his eyes on Captain Honeycomb, it became obvious that his mind was set on taking out his anger and frustrations on anything that resembled a Polistine.

The Kraken swam swiftly beneath where Honeycomb was hovering in the water; he flipped the captain up into the air with its massive tail. Once Honeycomb was tumbling end-over-end in the water, he could see that the Kraken was positioning its body so that he would land in his jaws. Honeycomb began to furiously flap his wings so that instead he'd come down next to the Kraken's uppermost left arm. In a twirling motion, Honeycomb spun next to the arm and slammed his two stingers directly into the beast's shoulder. As it was recovering from the pain, the Kraken brought his uppermost right arm around to protect the injured arm. Honeycomb proceeded to quickly sting the right arm as well. With both upper arms injured, the Kraken was vulnerable to attack as Honeycomb came slamming down on the mid-rift right arm and smacked a claw into the Kraken's chest, extracting more streams of green blood into the water.

Captain Honeycomb quickly realized though that, first, the Kraken was less incapacitated as it was leading him to believe and secondly, he was tired of losing this particular game of Reptilia versus Rodectos. While the Kraken was holding its three injured arms with his remaining healthy appendages, he leaned back and exhaled a mist of purplish smoke that enveloped Captain Honeycomb in a watery fog of miniscule particles causing paralysis in Honeycomb's exoskeleton.

As he was floating helplessly in the water, Honeycomb noticed that there were large bubbles floating towards the surface as an unseen force began to cause ripples in the blackness. Even before he was able to determine what was causing the disturbance, a translucent flipper attached to a long tentacle had wrapped itself around the captain's neck. There was a slight prick as the creature Morpheus injected a hallucinogenic into his system.

Honeycomb nodded off inside his helmet as if he was going to sleep. When he jolted awake a second later, he knew instantly that he was in a dream state because, instead of being enveloped by liquid, he was surrounded by nothing but endless miles of rocks and desert. He knew this landscape; It was the planet, Scaratutulo. He hadn't been here for 20 years. And only in his worst nightmares did he ever imagine returning.

He had been commanding a supply ship that was flying necessary rations, weapons and medicine to a battalion of Polistine centurions engaging the Eighth Legion of Beetleguise warriors on the Madagascan colony of Tubradon. He and his crew had encountered enemy fire from Beetleguise fighters. As a result of this military engagement, their ship, the *Pollenflorster* had been forced to crash land.

The veil of 20 years was quickly pulled away as Honeycomb recalled that he and his crew of 18 had been stranded on Scaratutulo for 10 days. He had believed that the lack of food and water would have been the greatest challenge to his crew's survival. But after they had been marooned for less than 2 days, Honeycomb came to understand what the true threat for anyone unlucky enough to land on Scaratutulo was: namely the enormous twelve-foot-long Robinator.

Honeycomb stared up at the sky in his dreamscape to discover to his horror that a Robinator had identified him as a source for a morning meal. As it swooped down, Honeycomb took flight and headed straight towards the twin suns. He moved back and forth to avoid the snapping jaws of the humongous avirat. If it flew down after him in the valley, Honeycomb rose towards the twin suns. When the Robinator rose back towards the bright suns, the captain sought safety beneath the rocks.

Just as he was ready to collapse, Honeycomb spied what he could only assume to be a mirage. It was an expanse of isolated and jagged mountains that had jutted out of the sand in anachronistic fashion.

"I'll be safe there. He won't find me," Honeycomb repeated to himself incessantly. He limped slowly up the mountain side until he came to rest on a soft mat of grass and twigs surrounded by blue speckled oval stones.

One of the blue speckled stones began to crack. Then another. And another. A look of horror came over Honeycomb's face. "Forgive my sins. I was only doing what I needed to survive."

But just as one of the babies moved forward to engulf Captain Honeycomb with its already enormous beak, he could feel a tightness building around his abdomen from a phantom source. The air carried a water plankton smell, which was an impossibility in the arid desert of Scaratutulo. This isn't real, thought Honeycomb, he glanced down to find that he was still wearing his environmental suit and had a Taser in his holster. It was that realization — that his encounter with the Robinator was just a ghost from his past — that erased the desert scene in front of him. Still the fact that he was in the grip of one of Morpheus' tentacles and was being pulled into the jaws of the overgrown cuddle fish was not reassuring.

"Thinking it is time that you had a little sleep, my friend," said Honeycomb.

Honeycomb sank all six appendages into Morpheus' side, which caused the beast to roar with unquestionable objection to the Polistine's course of action. Once Honeycomb planted his arms and feet firmly in place, he twisted his body around in order to stab Morpheus in the chest with his stingers, which he used as impromptu lightning rods, pressed his Taser gently in between them. As a charge of electricity traveled from the Taser down his stingers and into Morpheus, the great sea creature's body lit up like an atomic generator roaring to life. The shock of the voltage sent Captain Honeycomb flying backwards from the body of the sea creature into the blackness of the Machine Shop.

"Honeycomb, I have been trying to get in touch with you. Were you able to release the evacuation valve on the right hand wall?" Buzz's voice boomed into his ear.

"I encountered some difficulty down here. One of Sobek's pets was trying to make a meal out of me. Was Lieutenant Zips able to activate the lever on the left hand side?"

"Lieutenant Zips was able to loosen that lever but did so at the cost of his life."

"Then I will not let him or you, down, Sir," said Captain Honeycomb.

He pushed himself forward in the water towards the far right wall of the shop. He almost found himself being splat like the proverbial Polistine on the force field as the Kraken came swimming by him at the last moment, headed for the Legate Prime. He withdrew beneath a floating table to a more discreet observation point and allowed the six-appendage beast to swim out of sight before re-emerging from his hiding spot. But before he could even make his way towards the lever, a translucent tentacle shot past his head and ricocheted back towards where Morpheus was floating behind him. As he felt himself being pulled through the water, Honeycomb glanced over to see an exhaust fan switch on a nearby way. Honeycomb reached out with his left leg and kicked the switch to the 'on' position as he pushed with all his might out of Morpheus' grasp. He made his way to a parallel position by the fan. When Morpheus reached out with his tentacle to grab Honeycomb, the Captain kicked the tentacle directly into the fan. In the next moment, there were large chunks of almost invisible flesh being thrown into the water from the massive fan blades. Honeycomb turned and reached out for the fan switch once again, placing it now in the 'off' position.

Contemplating that he'd had more than his fair share of adventure for one day, Honeycomb limped over to the lever on the wall and pulled. "Sir, I activated the right-handed lever for the evacuation system. By the way, I think that the Kraken is headed straight towards you."

"Acknowledge, Captain. My prisoner and I will keep any eye out."

"Your prisoner? Is it Buddash Kyo or Yanick DcCullen?" asked Honeycomb.

As the water began to drain into the open vent, Honeycomb looked up to see Buddash flying towards him with his legs extended. Buddash kicked the Polistine guard forward, causing him to plunge into the newly exposed space at the floor of the shop and into a tunnel.

"Take a wild guess, Polistine," smirked Buddash.

At the top of the Machine Shop, Buzz found himself dealing with a number of mutually unsettling factors in what was becoming an increasingly difficult and challenging situation. First and foremost, the Polistine Legate Prime needed to reach the final lever that would facilitate the evacuation of the water from the shop. Secondly, he needed to determine how and when the Trionyx prisoner, Yanick DcCullen, would attempt to escape his custody.

And finally, he needed to formulate a strategy in order to avoid becoming an afternoon snack for the Kraken.

For now, Buzz chose not to deal with the disturbing fact that communications with Captain Honeycomb had been abruptly terminated. The only possibilities in the Legate Prime's mind was that either Captain Honeycomb had been consumed by one of the sea beasts or captured.

Buzz scanned the immediate area of the dark and desolate water before proceeding to the top of the tank to activate the evacuation lever. As he gazed out, his worst suspicion was realized as he looked over to see Yanick DcCullen aiming a mine launcher directly in his direction. What was truly unexpected was what happened next.

Before Yanick fired, he was waving his tail frantically to the left as he was mouthing either for Buzz to "move out of the way" or simply, "get down!"

As Buzz crouched down in the water, Yanick raised his mine launcher and aimed for the Kraken as it came within inches of bringing its jaws down on top of Buzz.

Yanick fired five or six mines towards the Kraken's head; as each mine approached, the Kraken continually swatted the small metal disk away with one of its tentacles, it pushed forward towards Yanick in an attempt to grab a hold of the little blue-and-green creature who was flicking the annoying disks it's general direction.

While this engagement was occurring between Yanick and the Kraken, the Legate Prime took advantage of the distraction and swam up towards the final evacuation lever and pulled it into the "on" position. As the few thousand gallons of water began to drain out of the room, Buzz turned on his external comm, "Inmate 3249, it is time to go."

Yanick turned towards the Legate Prime as he mouthed, "Who?"

"You. Yanick DcCullen, you need to come with me, right now."

A huge smile grew on Yanick's lips as he shook his head from side to side. Yanick pushed himself above the decreasing water line and said, "No, you Polistine pest, you're mistaken. I'm not going anywhere."

Thinking quickly as he watched Yanick aim the mine launcher at his head, Buzz reached for his Taser and placed it in the center section of his own mine launcher in the space where the mine would normally go, he launched the Taser at Yanick before the Trionyx was able to fire a single mine.

"No. You are coming with me whether you like it or not."

Buzz grabbed the limp Trionyx's body as he scanned his environment to determine a means for surviving the whirlpool of swirling artificial tides as the laundry water was being flushed from the room. He headed for the first thing that entered his field of vision, namely an oval, cylindrical container that was sealed at one end and hollow at the other. The Legate Prime instantly recognized it as a mortar shell for a blaster cannon that was used on Polistine Battle Cruisers. As he pushed his unconscious prisoner inside the container ahead of him, Buzz flipped a switch within the cylinder that activated the covering for the mortar that unfortunately only partially closed around the lid. As Buzz looked up, he could see that there was still a plate-sized opening in the cylinder. He resigned himself to the fact that some covering was better than none at all as they descended into the raging whirlpool that had been created by the drainage of the Machine Shop.

As he got closer to the bottom, Buzz could feel the pressure of the water intensifying on their metallic canister and squeezing him like someone making a fresh glass of sweet fruit juice. He felt as if his eyes were preparing to exit his skull. Despite the resistant force, the Legate braced all six appendages against the interior of the mortar as he struggled to steady himself during the horrific journey down into the bowls of the Machine Shop.

Just as he had convinced himself that he had regained some sense of equilibrium, his world literally began spinning out of control. Buzz looked up to the opening of the top of the mortar to see that the Kraken had knocked its tail against the side of the metal cylinder as it was rushing desperately towards the opening in the ceiling where it had exited Warden Sobek's aquarium. And unlike its three companions, the pair of Porposian and Morpheus, the Kraken would be able to survive on dry land for a short time before it was necessary to find another water source.

At the same time, Buzz watched as the mortar capsule was spinning away from his intended target. Specifically, he had been hoping that the tides would carry him and his prisoner back to the shaft where Captain Honeycomb, whom he prayed to the Great Hive Master was still alive, had guided the pod from the *Honey Vein One* into the formerly submerged Machine Shop.

As the endless waves of water passed by the mortar, Buzz began to doubt that he would be able to make his way back to the ventilation shaft where he and his fallen comrades had entered the sealed room. It was then that Buzz spied the mine launcher resting near DcCullen's sleeping form.

The Legate Prime knew from his military training that he would most likely have only one chance at success as he picked up the launcher and loaded a mine. He aimed as best he could for the small opening at the top of the mortar, and fired. As the mortar exited through the hole, Buzz knew instantly that he had succeeded as his view out of the canister changed from a sea of waves to a dark tunnel that led into the ventilation shaft. Shortly thereafter, Buzz was exiting the other end of the shaft into the launching bay. Regrettably, it had been less than a smooth landing.

The mortar bounced a number of times upon exiting the ventilation shaft, sending its occupants tumbling about within the compartment, as well as reviving Yanick from his slumber, before coming to rest within feet of the prison transport, *Honey Vein One*.

"I really need to put in for a vacation as soon as this all over," quipped Buzz.

Seeing an opportunity for escape while both of them were disoriented, Yanick reached for Buzz's blaster but the Polistine proved to be the one with the faster reflects. He pulled up the mine launcher and aimed it directly at Yanick's chest. As Buzz reached over to press the switch to retract the mortar's top, he stated, "you will be following me out of this capsule or I will blow your blue-and-green head off. Understood?"

As Buzz and Yanick crawled out of the snug mortar capsule, the Legate Prime was surprised to see Legate Beta Zook standing over him along with four Beetleguise centurions flanking his position.

"Zook, I was going to come find you as soon as I took inmate 3249 back into custody."

"Sir, I am very sorry about this. I wouldn't do this if I had any other choice."

Buzz shook his antennae at Zook. "You aren't making any sense. I want a sub-legion of fifteen Polistine guards assembled within the half hour and prepared for combat. Sobek's Triceratopian slaughtered twenty of my Insectum this morning and I am going to make sure he is made to answer for that crime, Warden or not."

"I can't let you do that, Sir," said Legate Beta Zook.

"Why the After burn not?" asked Legate Prime Buzz.

"Warden Sobek transmitted footage to the Insectvore military command this afternoon that distinctly shows you releasing the four Triceratopian from the plexi-cube. You are seen on the visual feed standing by as the Polistine Centurions are being slaughtering by the Triceratopian."

"That is an absolute falsehood. I found them dead in the hangar bay with Honeycomb."

"And where is the captain now, Legate Prime?"

"I lost communication with him in the Machine Shop."

"Very convenient. I regret that, by order of Warden Sobek and the Polistine High Command, I am placing you under arrest for being complacent in the murder of twenty Polistine Centurions. You will be placed on trial and exterminated at the Conglomerate's earliest convenience. Beetleguise Centurions, do your duty and take both criminals to cells within the containment dome."

As two Beetleguise Centurions grabbed Buzz, he shouted, "You need to let me go! Warden Sobek is trying to frame me." But before he could protest any more, a tranquilizer dart silenced him.

Chapter 11
AGENT HONEY RUNNER

Legate Prime Nectaxus, Commander of Purple L Swarm, had been cataloging the statistical information regarding Gladiator casualties, necessary repairs for his ship, and budgeting how much food, weapons and ammunitions, and other consumables would be needed for their next mission inside his War Study aboard the battle cruiser, *Pollister*. He felt a sense of relief to be going home, even if it would be for just a few weeks, after an extended tour of duty in the deepest portions of the barren nebula wastelands that lay between Madagascan and Insectvore.

The area of the wastelands had not always been so desolate. Until about 300 years' prior, there had been colonies of the Polistine Conglomerate and the Beetleguise Trotsnexus throughout that region of space. These colonies had been prospering until representatives from both militaries chose to conscript the majority of able-bodied Beetleguise and Polistines of both sexes from these colonies, leaving only the infirmed, the young, and the elderly to maintain the operation of the colonies. With the removal of all the individuals who could defend the colonies, they became easy targets for Reptilia raiders as well as Centurions of the opposing military, to plunder each of the remaining resources.

Nectaxus could only pray that when some sense of sanity was restored to the universe, Insectum life would once again begin to flourish not only in the wastelands but throughout the Conglomerate. But, he knew for now that his reality consisted of defeating the Beetleguise scourge once and for all.

As Nectaxus sat thinking about the events of the past few days, namely the recovery of Diabolix's Methurazus Rejuvenate from the Fortress on

Helvete Fredon, he tried desperately to remove the image of dozens of his Xeperian Gladiators in Purple L Swarm being torn apart by Diabolix's Quillian and Chamyx henchmen in a manner similar to a child ripping a piece of salt stretch candy into bits.

This quiet reflection was interrupted when Nectaxus' Legate Beta, Yodek, informed him via the conn that he had an incoming communication from Insectvore.

"Who is it from?" asked Nectaxus, as he thought himself couldn't he have five minutes of peace.

"The message is marked 'highly sensitive'," said Yodok.

"Very well. Redirect the communication signal down to my War Study."

"Very good, Sir."

The small screen before him flicked to life to reveal the image of agent Honey-Runner.

"Good afternoon, Agent Honey-Runner. We have retrieved the Methurazus Rejuvenate from the fortress on Helvete Fredon. How else may Purple L Swarm serve the Conglomerate this fine afternoon?"

"I am sensing a sarcastic tone in your voice, Legate Nectaxus. I cannot say that I appreciate it to any great degree," said Agent Honey-Runner.

"My Gladiators have been deployed for the last three weeks trying to prevent the return of Diabolix's return from X-Space by retrieving the only other known Methurazus Rejuvenate in existence outside of the one on Meditaplassen. I would greatly appreciate it if you just allowed my Gladiators to go home."

"My dear Legate Prime Nectaxus, what I am asking is so little. If, by some misfortune, Diabolix was able to escape X-Space then the first thing that he would probably do would be to go looking for the one weapon that could facilitate his conquering of every world in this space."

"You are obviously referring to the Eye of Hermes since Diabolix is the one being that can harness its' terrible destructive power," said Legate Nectaxus.

"I am so delighted that we are seeing multi-lensed eye to eye regarding this matter. Legate Nectaxus. And I must admit that I was slightly remiss in not informing you that your Gladiators will be compensated at 6 times their normal rate once you deliver the Eye of Hermes to section seventy-two," stated Agent Honey-Runner.

Nectaxus paused briefly as he considered the offer. Six times his normal amount of credits for a mission was definitely an offer that was hard to turn down. With a reluctant sigh, Nectaxus asked, "I believe that I speak for all my Gladiators when I state that we would be more than willing to retrieve the item."

"Very good. You will find what you seek aboard the Ruddarian research vessel, *Mjölnir*," said Agent Honey-Runner before Nectaxus screen went black.

On occasion, Kasidy Vulkner had heard it said that the outside world can influence the dreams of sleeping individuals. Yet, she had never experienced such a vivid demonstration of this phenomenon until today as her mind returned to 15 years prior when she and her mother had been held captive at the Southern Sea Polistine detention center on the Rogestran Five colony.

In her dream, Kasidy found herself being taken — blindfolded and handcuffed — to a small metallic room with two red chairs made of arboreal material and a long, rectangular metallic table. From the sound of a constant low buzzing, Kasidy made the assumption that her interrogator was a Polistine. He repeatedly asked her whether or not her father, Kabul, had contacted the family. Every time she had replied that he had not, the Polistine knocked her to the solid, stone floor.

This interrogation had lasted for hours, fifteen years ago. In comparison, reality came crashing through quickly as Kasidy awoke to find herself hurtling out of her bed and tumbling across the floor of her quarters by the force of some unknown projectile making contact with the ship.

Before she could even reach for the comm-panel on the wall, the door to her quarters slid open to reveal Defensive Officer Kon standing in the hallway with a long cylindrical blast rifle with an extended blade attached to the barrel.

"Do I even dare ask what is going on?"

"Vulkner, if we can make it to the flight deck, you just might be able to live to regret asking, but I will fill you in on the way down to the medical bay to grab the captain."

"I have a feeling that I will need to stop along the way to grab a weapon, too," said Kasidy.

As the adrenalin pumped through her veins, Kasidy momentarily forgot that she was still suffering from exhaustion as well as the wear-and-tear on her body from an extended astral environment walk to facilitate the repair of the life support. Kon moved his arm along Kasidy's waist as she suddenly began to fall.

"Just take it slow. You have already had a long day," said Kon.

"No guarantee that we are going to see the day's end," smile Kasidy.

"Don't even joke about that. As long as we keep an eye on each other, we'll make it through whatever the galaxy has in store for us."

"I didn't know you cared, Kon."

"I don't. But you watching out for me is my best option right now of not dying today."

"Then let's get me one of those rifles and fill me in on what has happened so far."

In a moment of frustration, Captain Relich Odinord permitted his veil of professional detachment to slip aside as he moved within inches of Lieutenant Thorn's large multi-lens eyes and said in an extremely irritated tone, "Who or what is attacking my ship now?"

Lieutenant Thorn began buzzing at an increased volume that indicated annoyance that he, a Polistine warrior, was begin challenged by this Pink Monkey. "The Polistine Conglomerate is aware that you are in possession of The Eye of Hermes. Therefore, they will do everything in their power to prevent it from ever coming anywhere near an inhabited world."

"And you would stand by as they murdered eleven innocent Ruddarians to accomplish this goal?"

"You are sacrificing your lives for the greater good of the galaxy. Your names will be honored in Polistine and Beetleguise songs for ages," said Lieutenant Thorn.

"And what happens to you? You'd just be another casualty in the Polistine's effort to prevent that Green Diamond from tearing the universe apart?"

"If that becomes necessary then I say "so be it," replied Thorn stoically.

"Beetle dung! I have seen over the last few hours how unflinchingly you've fought to survive. First on that shuttle of yours and then with the help of Dr. Tulare. Given the choice, I can tell that you'd rather preserve your existence than sacrifice it."

Thorn glared at Odinord for a long moment. For a Ruddarian, he did possess a keen sense for determining an individual's motivations and beliefs. Thorn decided that if it became necessary, he would destroy the Ruddarian ship himself. However, he was not completely sure that his Polistine comrades would destroy The Eye of Hermes. It was not beyond the realm of possibility that a Polistine government agency might attempt to utilize the Green Diamond as a weapon. He climbed down from his medical bed and limped over to the main viewer screen in the medical bay. After flipping a few switches, Thorn produced the image that was currently being displayed on the bridge's viewer down onto the smaller medical screen. The image that appeared was a large circular ship that resembled a wheel from a Höllenfeuerhalbinsel racer and had a central hub with eight spokes, with laser cannons around the edge.

Thorn motioned at the viewer with his antennae. "That, my dear Pink Monkey, is a Quartrack Light Destroyer. It has the ability to access a sub-nova pulsar generator to extinguish a community of 20 billion lifeforms without ever landing. When the ship's weapon is activated, it can turn a bustling metropolis into a barren lunar wasteland."

"But there has to be some sort of glitch that you aren't telling me about. Otherwise, the Polistine military would have marched right over to Madagascan and vaporized the entire population."

"Our scientists are still working on controlling the 'stability' of the reaction. There were unseen side effects when the weapon was first used; like, um... the crew of the test ship were vaporized. However, during a recent intelligence briefing, my former commander, Clack, was informed that a prototype Quartrack was being tested by the members of Purple L Swarm."

"So there are a bunch of Wasps over there running that ship? Doesn't mean that we can't reason with them," said Captain Odinord.

"You don't understand. The warriors aboard that ship are Xeperian Gladiators. When a Xeperian is killed in battle, a chemical is activated within in his circulatory systems that triggers a proto-genesis in their reproductive organs."

"You sound like you are talking, but you're not making any sense."

"As an Xeperian breathes their last breath, they are giving birth all the way to an adolescent Xeperian who devours the flesh of their parent and then moves on to devour whatever originally killed the mature Xeperian."

"Well, that's a new one, okay then," said Odinord, "we need to find a way to stop them before the Eye of Hermes decides to tap into the sub-nova power source."

"I whole-heartedly agree with you, pink-monkey."

"I won't even dare suggest that you need assistance making your way to the flight deck," said Odinord.

"A wise decision indeed, pink-monkey," said Lieutenant Thorn as the two of them exited the medical bay and made their way down the hall to the chute lift.

Vulkner and Kon were running down the corridor from the opposite direction when they spied Captain Odinord and the Polistine refugee. Kon immediately made his way to the Captain to brief him on the current situation, but was surprised when he barked at him: "Why aren't you already on the flight deck?"

"I was making my way to there when I remembered that Astral Engineer Vulkner was still in her quarters. I thought she might be able to provide some support in the present situation."

"I suppose that is an acceptable excuse. It is actually fortunate that you are still down here because I need you to take a few men and make your way to the Cargo Bay" said Captain Odinord. "Our Polistine guest seems to believe that there are highly trained warriors over there who are going to be coming for The Eye of Hermes."

"Polistine warriors, Sir?"

"Trust me, Lieutenant, they are far more deadly than any Insectum you have faced before."

"I'll reserve judgement on that until I see how easy it is to take care of them," said Kon.

"You might want to listen to him, Kon, because Lieutenant Thorn will be fighting alongside you. Vulkner, you'll accompany me to the flight deck," said Odinord

Thorn and Kon looked at each and simultaneously uttered, "What?"

"Get over it and get the job done!" replied Odinord.

They had made their way to the *Mjolnir's* Cargo Bay where Lieutenant Lokhra and Ensign Rajkvek were preparing to protect the mysterious Green Diamond as well as, hopefully, the ship.

Kasidy was standing behind the captain, occupying Lieutenant Kon's usual position, manning the ship's limited laser weapons and projectile mines. To the captain's left sat, Dr. Tulare, who had managed to bring his six remaining patients down to the Medical Bay where their conditions remained stable.

Even though his years of training at the Ruddarian Military Academy, S.T.A.R. — Space Travel and Alien Research — made negotiations with hostile species a routine function of his command, Odinord still felt it necessary to wear a mask of confidence. There was a tiny voice in the back of his mind telling him that if he screwed up, they could possibly all die. But for now, the captain was able to silence this doubting voice.

"Polistine vessel, this is Captain Relich Odinord of the Ruddarian Science Vessel, *Mjolnir.* As a vessel of scientific exploration, we seek only to exercise our right to pass through Polistine space as expediently as possible."

At that moment, Kasidy looked up from her console to see two blue projectiles emanating from the alien vessel. "Sir, I have two incoming torpedoes headed for the flight deck."

"Get those barriers up, Vulkner," said Captain Odinord. He swung around and pressed the conn on the arm of his chair, "Everybody, grab on for dear life."

The majority of the bridge crew were knocked to the ground as the torpedoes exploded adjacent to the underside of the saucer. The Captain, however, was merely thrown back in his chair,

"Report, Vulkner. What kind of damage are we looking at?"

Before Kasidy was able to reply, the image on the vessel's main viewer changed from the Quartrack Light Destroyer, *Pollister,* to the face of a

Polistine warrior. The Insectum in the frame had a set of extended mandibles on his face with huge multi-lensed eyes that shined in the darkness like lavanic rock. He wore a purple helmet with gold vertical stripes. He moved these mandibles in a horizontal motion as his uppermost appendages moved diagonally in and out of the frame.

"I am Legate Prime Nectaxus, commander of the Purple L Swarm. Lower your barriers and prepare to be boarded, pink-monkey."

"We have made no hostile action towards your vessel that would justify you boarding my vessel."

"It is unacceptable to the Polistine Conglomerate that such unevolved creatures such as yourselves are even within our borders. That is justification, enough, pink-monkey."

"Before, you board us, Nectaxus, there is one piece of information that I must share with you," said Captain Odinord.

"And what is that?"

"You should have never shot at us because you only made it angry," said Captain Odinord.

"What?"

Before Odinord could even provide an answer, The Eye of Hermes once again glowed bright with a luminous green light. The Eye of Hermes then produced a green, energized tentacle that passed through the outer hull of the *Mjölnir* and came to rest in the armament section of the *Pollister*. The beam headed directly for the strongest source of power on the ship, the sub-nova pulse generator as the Xeperian weapons officer, Cornco, could only look on in horror as the black spherical sleeping giant came to life with a menacing orange light.

"Legate Nectaxus, we have a problem down in the armament section. The sub-nova pulse generator just turned itself on."

Nectaxus pulled the long, thin communication fiber around to his mandible as he shouted, "It is my suggestion, as your executive officer, that you power the weapon down, Weapons Officer."

Legate Beta Yodok swung around in his chair to face Legate Prime Nectaxus, "It is not just the sub-nova pulse generator that has been activated. All major weapon, transport and propulsion systems have switched to active status."

"What purpose is served by turning on all our systems?" asked Legate Prime Nectaxus.

The answer came not from Yodok but from Astral Engineer Blast. "Sir, the beam is turning all energy settings at maximum and then siphoning off the power from each system. And that leads me to our next major issue."

"Which is what?" asked Legate Beta Yodok.

"All the power settings on the ship are going into feedback mode. This process will lead to a ship-wide implosion that will destroy half of the planetoids in this sector., many of which are inhabited.

"Have we lost molecular transport capability yet?" asked Legate Nectaxus.

"Not yet, Legate Nectaxus. I believe that the beam is going after higher energized systems."

"Then, Legate Beta, I want two squadrons of Xeperian Gladiators aboard that vessel immediately."

Back aboard the *Mjölnir*, the crew and Captain Odinord were dealing with their own consequences from awakening the power of the Green Diamond.

"Sir, the Green Diamond has locked onto all the *Pollister's* major systems. It appears that it is building up an energy reserve so that it can vaporize the destroyer in a similar fashion to Lieutenant Thorn's vessel, the *Honey Hive*.

Lieutenant Thorn's voice came over the comm, "Pink-Monkey, The Eye may not even get the opportunity to build up an energy supply before a feedback energy loop occurs."

Vulkner interrupted Lieutenant Thorn, "He is right, Captain. I am detecting a high-energy device on-board the alien vessel that looks likes it about to go critical. The device seems to possess a power 10 times the power of a typical atomic blast."

"Pink Chimpet, if that sub-nova generator explodes, you will be up close and in-person to witness the explosion of a star," said Lieutenant Thorn.

Defensive Officer Kon interrupted the discussion of the potential explosion, "Captain, our barriers were somehow just lowered remotely and 18 creatures who resemble walking black beverage protectors have just beamed aboard in the cargo bay."

"Understood. Engineer Vulkner, seal the Cargo Bay. Make sure none of those Xeperian get loose on the ship."

"Actually, captain, those Insectum transporting in just gave me a notion."

"What were you thinking, Vulkner?" asked Captain Odinord.

"We could re-install The Eye of Hermes in the main engine and use it to generate a wormhole that would allow us to escape from that ship filled with Xeperian," said Kasidy.

"How would you convince The Eye of Hermes to generate this hypothetical "wormhole?""

"According to our sensor scans, there is a sun, Zeta Sephi Three, that is in the final stages of becoming a white pulsar," said Astral Engineer Vulkner. "Right now, that sun is giving off a 100 times the energy of that sub-pulse generator on board the *Pollister*. With Zeta Sephi Three giving off that much energy, it will most likely be enough to divert the Green Diamond's attention away from the *Pollister*.

"I guess it isn't the absolute worst idea that I have heard all day," sighed Captain Odinord.

The captain turned around just in time to see Astral Engineer Kasidy Vulkner disappearing into the chute lift, heading down to the Cargo Bay.

Down in the Cargo Bay, Ensign Rajkvek began to maneuver back towards the shuttle pod of the *Honey Hive* as orange balls of transporter energy started to materialize within the room. Each orange ball quickly reformulated into an Insectum the color of midnight, that was slightly taller than a hominoid. The menacing Insectum had elongated oval heads, somewhat boxed shaped abdomens divided into two sections, and razor sharp prongs on their upper and middle appendages. Upon their arrival, he had heard both the captain as well as the injured Polistine Lieutenant Thorn refer to these soldiers as Xeperian Gladiators.

Ensign Rajkvek could hear Defensive Officer Kon shouting orders to him and Lieutenant Lokhra as soon as the Xeperian Gladiators appeared. The Gladiators' weapon of choice was an energized that they used as a baton but also extended in length to become an electrified whip.

Kon was instructing them that whenever possible that they needed to maim or wound the Gladiators rather than inflicting a mortal wound.

He told them that they needed to prevent the Xeperian from leaving the cargo bay because they could possibly overrun the ship. And finally, it was imperative to protect the Green Diamond at all cost and not allow it to fall into the hands of the Xeperian. Rajkvek wasn't exactly sure about whether this last order was the best idea. Why not just let them have the stone and let it suck all the power, including the life support, out of their ship?

"Get your head out of the stardust, Ensign," screamed Kon. Rajkvek turned around to find three Xeperian headed right for him with their batons extended. He raised his rifle at the last moment and, acting like he was a youngling back home on Rogestran Five with a snap-cap gun, Rajkvek fired the batons out of the claws of each Xeperian and then used one of the batons to slice off each of their legs until all three were lying on their backs like stranded baby Cranitian.

It was then that Rajkvek heard a clicking and clacking voice from above them shout, "There are four more Gladiators moving around the shuttle towards your position."

"Thanks for the heads up." Kon placed made a waving motion. "Let's go catch us, some bugs."

Lieutenant Kon and Ensign Rajkvek raced around the other side of the *Honey Hive* shuttle. They were faced with four more of the Xeperian scarabs carrying swords as well as the energy batons. The pair of Ruddarians aimed their rifles and began firing laser blasts at the Xeperian, making a temporary path for them to a more defendable position.

As Kon and Rajkvek made their way to the Cargo Bay door, Lieutenant Lokhra started to move forward toward his comrades in the center of the room. As they were repositioning themselves, Rajkvek continued to use the baton he'd acquired from the maimed Xeperian to remove the arms and legs from other Gladiators. Lieutenant Lokhra continued to complement the Ensign's efforts by skillfully removing arms and legs of various Xeperian attackers using a machete.

While in the intensity of this battle, Kon realized that he had become distracted by the Xeperian attack, an action that had taken his focus away from making sure that The Eye of Hermes was being protected. That was until Lieutenant Thorn began shouting down at him from his aerial vantage point.

"Lieutenant Pink Monkey, the strategy of the Xeperian seems to be shifting. They are coming together as a single unit. For what purpose, I do not know," yelled Thorn.

"Is there anything you can do to stop them?" Kon yelled back.

Kon, Lokhra, and Rajkvek realized that the time to prevent the Xeperian offensive had already passed as they watched their worst fear materialize before them. Three of the Xeperian had launched themselves in the air toward Rajkvek and Kon, who were still holding rifles with machete spears, landing onto the blades, impaling themselves with pinpoint accuracy. As they landed on the floor, a bubbling purple mist began to rise from their bodies.

"Eliminate those hatchlings!" yelled Kon.

"Negative, Lieutenant Kon," interjected Thorn. "If you kill those hatchlings, you'll only be creating more."

"Then how exactly are we supposed to stop them?"

It just so happened that Kasidy Vulkner, carrying a small metal container in one hand and a blaster in another, chose that instant to walk into the Cargo Bay. "Anything I can do to help?"

"Any ideas about how to remove these baby Xeperian from the ship without killing them would be greatly appreciated," said Kon.

"I think that I might have an idea."

"Give it your best shot, Kasidy."

The Astral Engineer raised her Taser-net cannon towards the baby Xeperian. Meanwhile, Kon, Lokhra, Rajkvek, and Thorn continued to slice and dice the Xeperian Gladiators, causing many of them to resemble a piece of crushed plum fruit. After a short delay, Kasidy trapped the Xeperian hatchlings by shooting electrified nets on top of them.

"What are we going to do with all these injured Xeperian?" asked Kon.

"I was thinking that we could send them back to where they came from," said Kasidy. She slid down a concealed panel by the door and pressed a button that revealed an emergency exit hatch.

"Everyone grab onto something. You as well, Thorn, if you know what's good for you," said Kasidy. She hit a final button that caused a hatch to retract in the floor. The plexi-plastic covering at the far end of the conduit rotated off, exposing the room to the vacuum of space. All five grabbed onto large heating and cooling pipes in the room as they watched the injured Xeperian go hurtling into space.

When the last of the Xeperian had been excised from the cargo bay, Kasidy could not close the panel since she had been sent flying across the room when it was first opened. She screamed at Thorn, "You need to get to the panel and hit code 75542. That will close the covering on the tube."

"I swear that I will complete the task or give my life in the attempt."

Lieutenant Thorn reached out with one of his lower appendages and grabbed a circular metal loop attached to the wall. Once he had a strong grasp on the pipe, he pulled the rest of his body down to the level of the metal out-cropping. He repeated this process several times before he made it to the panel. He then launched himself forward. He was at the mercy of the suction of space for what seemed like an eternity before he fell down, grabbed hold of the panel and entered the code.

All four Ruddarians simultaneously came crashing down to the floor, brushed themselves off, and checked for serious injuries.

"Thank you, Lieutenant. We could have not survived without your assistance," said Kasidy.

"I only acted in the name of self-preservation," said Thorn.

Captain Odinord's voice suddenly came over the comm. "The power levels on the alien vessel are continuing to fluctuate in a downward spiral. And our own systems, are beginning to be affected."

"Sir, we have dealt with the Gladiator incursion, for the moment. I am going to proceed as we previously discussed. I am going to try to tempt the Eye of Hermes with the Zeta Sephi Three star," said Kasidy.

"Pretty sure that the Green Diamond isn't going to allow you to move it," said Kon, not even believing himself what he was saying. "You know what I mean that the connection between the Destroyer and the Green Diamond is too strong for you to move it to the Engine Room."

"If you can't bring the evil Green Diamond to the ship's engine then all you can do is bring the ship's engine to the evil Green Diamond," smiled Kasidy.

Kasidy pulled out a medium sized silver capsule shaped device from the metal box. With a great deal of efficiency, she then removed four metal discs from the box and placed them on the Green Diamond's exterior of the gem that she attached with metal grabbers to create an electro-magnetic field.

"This remote navigational control will allow me to make a data link between the engine and the power of the stone. I'm hoping that the Eye will disconnect from the sub-nova generator as it realizes that the exploding star will make a better energy meal. Here goes nothing."

As Kasidy pressed the buttons on either side of the device, the Eye of Hermes activated a connection between itself and the main engine. However, instead of scanning the navigational database as well as accessing the ship's star-charts, the Eye of Hermes reached out and tapped directly into Kasidy's mind.

Captain Odinord watched with some trepidation but mainly an overwhelming sense of relief as the green energy beam leading from his ship to the *Pollister* dissolved like a spent firework falling from the sky. This relief lasted only moments, however, as every crew member was thrown backwards in their chair or knocked to the ground. As the Eye of Hermes created a wormhole between the *Mjölnir's* current location and the Zeta Sephi Three star. Within seconds, the *Mjölnir* emerged from the wormhole into normal space to face a large spherical inferno hanging in the blackness that was in the process of a mega-explosive event. An event that was occurring at a safe distance from the ship, for the moment.

"We have gone out of the fire and into an atomic explosion," Odinord mused to himself.

"Vulkner, I want a plan for returning the ship to a safe distance once we've dealt with the Green Diamond." The message was quickly acknowledged, but the response, much to Captain Odinord's surprise came from Defensive Officer Kon rather than Astral Engineer Vulkner.

'Captain, Kasidy has collapsed.

Chapter 12
WARDEN SOBEK

Given a choice when having to resolve a problem, Warden Sobek usually chose to delegate. Yet, in such a delicate matter as the resolution of the Diabolix/ Hotfire situation, he felt the most dependable hands were his own. Sobe+k momentarily allowed himself to enjoy imaging the master criminal Diabolix crying out unimaginable suffering as he was reduced to a bioplasmic mass. But there was one thing that he regretted about the whole messy affair. Namely, the Hawking Council had decided that the doctor was to be eliminated be- cause of his vocal resistance to using the toxin to eliminate Diabolix, and Cronos was being denied the opportunity to do it, personally. Of course, when the Warden said personally he meant having his Triceratopian's take care of it. It had been determined by the Omnipotent Hawking Brain Beetle Council that the appearance needed to be created that the doctor was facilitating the robbery of the prison dispensary by two inmates of Minerva. This appearance would be created by placing the doctor's access card in the possession of one of the criminals, once they were apprehended. This action would discredit the doctor within the medical community. In addition, the doctor would un- fortunately be a victim of a laser blast during the committing of this robbery, preventing the doctor from ever repairing his spotless reputation as a member of the Cranitian medical community.

As Warden Sobek sat in his office behind the half clam-shell desk con- templating the events to come, two jump-suited individuals wearing horned helmets with red and yellow decorative frills stood in the doorway of Sobek's office.

"The inmate, Hotfire, has been placed in the Ancient Western Scaratutulo cell as you instructed. Is there anything else that you require of us at this time, Warden Sobek?" asked Alpha Triceratopian.

"Yes, I was actually hoping the three of us could play a round of Five Card Gurt – Duchene."

"Really, Master? That is very kind of you," offered Beta Triceratopian.

Alpha Trike turned towards Beta Trike and gave him a not so gentle bop on the head, "No. He is not really offering. It is the Hawking form of speech known as *Hutanochen* or "sarcasm.""

"The two of you, go collect your brother Triceratopian and go down to the doctor's lab. Relieve him of the Diabolix toxin and bring it to me. I shall dispose of the doctor at my earliest convenience."

A look of displeasure came across the face of Alpha Triceratopian, "Didn't you tell us that the Hawking Brain Beetle Council was going to deal with the doctor?"

"Alpha, I am the supreme authority on Minerva. Therefore, I will do as I please. So, I am ordering you to bring the toxin to me. Is that understood?" asked Warden Sobek.

"As you wish, my Master," said Alpha Trike. "What if the doctor will not give us the toxin?"

"Then you will be permitted to use more persuasive tactics with the exception of killing him."

```"Master, I hope that you are able to kill the doctor," said Alpha Trike.

"And why do you hope that, my child?" asked Sobek.

"Because it would bring you so much joy to have his blood running through your tentacles."

"That it would, my child. That it would. Now, go complete your mission, my gallant warriors. I will meet you at the doctor's lab short-ly," said Sobek. "But first, I must pay our esteemed guest a visit in his holo-environment."

Despite waking up face down in a mixture of sand, mud and dried dung, Hotfire was almost positive that his last waking memory was being strapped to a long metallic slab. He distinctly remembered that both his hands and
```

feet had been securely attached to the sides of the table with metallic re-straints, and faintly recalled that there had been some discussion of him being injected with some creature that was growing exponentially inside his skull. In addition, he also had the nagging feeling that Sobek, was trying to con him into getting rid of Diabolix.

"Hate to be the one to tell you, Hombre. Your recollection of those events are a hundred percent accurate."

The rays of the two suns momentarily prevented Hotfire from being able to clearly determine the characteristics, let alone the species, of the individual who was currently addressing him.

"Who are you?" asked Hotfire. "Where am I?"

"I am the Psychic Spider."

It seemed that once Hotfire was aware that the image before him was being generated by his own sub-conscious, the spider's characteristics im-mediately began to sharpen and come into focus. His manifestation of the spider was a creature the color of deep brown, like a freshly made mud brick that had yet to dry, and possessed ten rather than eight legs. The spider was almost as tall as his one-time companion, Yanick DcCullen, and was wearing a broad-rimmed black hat that covered his eyes, along with a leather vest and a greyish belt that had loops for small, individual iron projectiles. He also had a firearm.

"Is that weapon what they used to call on ancient Scaratutulo —"

"A Gun," said the Psychic Spider.

"How did I get to Scaratutulo?"

"Didn't," said the Psychic Spider in an almost rhythmic, humming tone.

"Where am I then?"

"First, let's get out of this sun. I do believe that there is an establish-ment not too far from here that serves intoxicants. I believe that the ancient Scaratutulo referred to it as a tavern."

Hotfire pulled his massive legs underneath his frame as he tried to push himself up off the ground. Within seconds though, he fell to the ground under his own considerable weight. When the mental representation of the Psychic Spider reached out his arm in assistance. Hotfire knocked it away as he sneered, "Don't need your help, friend."

"Oh, when it comes to friends these days, Hotfire, you seem to be in short supply," laughed the Psychic Spider. "So if I were you, I would take any assistance that was offered to us."

Instead of offering a hand once again, though, the spider simply placed all ten legs on the ground and began to walk towards two lines of arboreal constructed buildings in the distance.

Hotfire managed to wrangle the last remnants of his strength and was able to slowly walk to the town. At first, he assumed he would be walking for hours, but he managed to reach the small western town in less than an hour, and the tavern that the Psychic Spider had described.

He was greeted by what could only be described as a family reunion. The tavern was populated by numerous versions of himself. There was a short, plump version behind the saloon bar wearing a grey apron as he dried a clear mug. There were four variations sitting at a small, circular table playing some type of cards and repeatedly throwing heavy gold credit bars that went thump on the metal table. Behind the bar, there was an ornate stage that appeared to have been carved out of the regional sandstone. Upon the stage were four variations of Hotfire wearing knee-high boots and short frilled red and black dresses with feathered head dresses; they were dancing to the music of the music box being played by yet another version of Hotfire. And, sitting at the bar, enjoying a bright blue-and-green concoction, was none other than Hotfire's new pal, the Psychic Spider.

"You look absolutely parched, my friend. Come slide up to the bar and have a —" he turned to the bartender — "what do you call this drink?"

"It is called a Hobbs Intoxicant.".

"Yes, one of those for my better half over here," said the spider.

"I've been to this tavern before, on Scaratutulo. Barkeep I'll have a shot of whiskey," said Hotfire.

"I make it a policy not to argue with the customers, especially when it is the customer who is mentally projecting me to life," said the Barkeep.

"Whatever," said Hotfire. "Just give me my shot. And put it on the spider's tab."

The Barkeep quickly complied with Hotfire's order and placed a small clear glass filled with golden brown liquid down on the bar. Hotfire was grateful for any sort of fluid to be introduced into his body, even if the liquid was imaginary. Hotfire contemplated as he drank: was his body really in this old western Scaratutulo town or was he still attached to one of Warden Sobek's mental probing devices? As he was trying to make sense of his reality, Hotfire suddenly felt a tremendous pain, like a white hot knife slicing into his skull.

"Oh for the love of the Hive Master, what now?" screamed Hotfire.

"Now that is being somewhat inhospitable of you, Hotfire."

As he recovered from the stabbing pain within his brain, Hotfire looked around to find that he was no longer in the tavern on Scaratutulo, but was once again in the cold, featureless tube-shaped room in the *Citadel*. Apparently, the harness that Hotfire had been strapped into during the injection procedure had now been moved to the outer room, and directly facing him was the shelled visage of a Hawking Brain Beetle.

"My dear Reptilia. Don't you think I can tell when you're trying to peek behind the veil?"

"I'd rather spend eternity in the Hellfire before I even raised a finger to help the Hawking Brain Beetles. Find another dupe to kill Diabolix."

"That is disappointing. I was led to believe from your illustrious reputation that you fancied yourself quite the mercenary. The Omnipotent Council, therefore, believed that you would be the perfect individual for this assignment."

"Sorry to disappoint them, especially since your Bokhun cousins sound like such fans. But, I will not be assisting the Omnipotent Council anytime in the near future," said Hotfire.

Warden Sobek pushed up on his tri-tentacles to move slightly closer as he stated in his deep, scratchy voice, "And by the near future, I assume that you are referring to the fifteen hours that you have before the Psychic Spider grows to full maturity and your head explodes?"

"Did I ever tell you that I prefer my Hawking Brain Beetles served extra crispy?"

"No, you never shared that particular fact with me. That is quite interesting," said Warden Sobek.

Hotfire had believed that he had made his intention very clear to Warden Sobek, he was somewhat perplexed as to why he was not moving out of the line of fire. Hotfire decided that if the Hawking Brain Beetle had a strong desire to be burned alive by his fireballs then there was nothing he could really do for him.

"I can't say that it has been a pleasure," smirked Hotfire.

As the Chamyx raised the tip of his tail and concentrated on generating a series of fireballs to launch towards Sobek, he suddenly realized that some eternal force was preventing him from generating a fireball.

"Are we experiencing some performance issues?" asked Sobek.

Hotfire's demeanor switched in an instant from one of playful Reptilia to an aggressive animal who was quickly flying into a red-hot blinding rage. At that moment, all he wanted to do was break free from that metallic slab, reach into that gigantic shell, and beat the evolved slug into an unrecognizable pulp.

Sobek began to chuckle, "I supposed that I forget to mention. The Psychic Spider is secreting a chemical into your brain that is inhibiting your ability to create your precious fireballs."

"Then how do you expect me to kill Diabolix without my fireballs?"

"You will be using a specially formulated toxin to defeat Diabolix rather than your fireballs. Your method for getting close to Diabolix will be left to your own discretion."

"And if I refuse to assist you?"

"As I previously stated, your head will explode in less than fifteen hours. However, if you succeed, you have my word that I will surgically remove the Psychic Spider. In addition, your confinement arrangement on Minerva will be in a holo-environment of your choosing. You have already received a small preview during your holo-experience in the Scaratutulo. But you can choose to occupy your mind over the decades in a Pleasurist resort for all I care. The point is that you will be segregated from the general population of Minerva."

"Why would I care about being isolated in your twisted mind-fuctur of a reality?"

"Because Hotfire." Sobek slid closer to the metallic slab as he extended a tentacle around Hotfire's shoulder, "You and I both know that there are dozens of Reptilia that you have cheated, beaten or otherwise generally wronged over the years. How long do you believe you would last in the general population?"

"I'll take my chances. So if you'd kindly take this spider out of my head!" shouted Hotfire. "I will begin my time with the general population as I continue to plan my escape."

"I am afraid, Hotfire, that it is not that simple. You and I both know that you are partially responsible, along with my grand-cousin Atlas, for the creation of Diabolix. So like it or not, you will be one of the individuals who will help to stop him, once and for all.

"I swear to you, here and now, Sobek. I will be holding your bloody, severed head very soon."

"Farewell for now, Hotfire."

As Hotfire throttled violently within in his restraints, Warden Sobek injected him with a neural sedative that made his mind susceptible to being integrated into the holo-environmental computer program. A moment later, Hotfire found himself once again in the old west Scaratutulo town of *Prosperity*. He was laying on a sizeable arboreal plank attached to the wall by two metal link chains with a blanket covering the hard surface. He looked around to discover that he was in a jail cell with metal bars preventing his escape. Just beyond the bars there was a Triceratopian sentry sitting in a blue jumpsuit with his feet up on the desk. He was wearing a large brimmed hat with two holes on either side of the hat and one in the middle to accommodate his long horns.

"Are you really here?" asked Hotfire.

"Nah, I am just another one of your mental representations. But if I were you, which technically I am, I would get some rest. You have a busy day tomorrow."

Chapter 13
METHUZARUS REJUVENATE

Yanick DcCullen, inmate 3249 thought that he had experienced the worst that Minerva Penitentiary had to offer a Reptilia criminal. That was until this moment. He knew he was in some kind of dream state, but that was all. He felt a chill; his entire body appeared to be frozen. Still, his current predicament was the least of his worries. It was very likely that he would be terminated for threating to kill a Legate. The rotten Insectum would probably even lie about the fact that Yanick had saved his exoskeleton by firing at the blasted Kraken.

To his own recollection, Yanick had not had a night this stressful in a very long time. The last time that he had been anywhere close had been 30 years ago.

It had been in the early morning hours on Rogestran Five Colony when they'd been scheduled to meet the Ruddarian Kabul Vulkner. It seemed, in those days, that he had been making credits claw over fist supplying weapons, drugs and conscious enhancing supplements to willing customers with the financial means. Their clientele included Centurions from the Polistine Conglomerate who required chemical assistance to make it through an extended tour of duty; Ruddarian customers who needed drugs to help them sojourn through 11 to 15 hour shifts deep inside volcanic moons; and finally, addicts who just needed an artificial assist to help them get through their lives.

Ten years before that ill-fated meeting with Kabul Vulkner, Yanick had been recruited off the streets of Belhimir on the Trionyx home world of

Mundilfarius by a young Chamyx with a penchant for trafficking in illegal substances. The Chamyx's given name was Hotfire. However, he'd often remind the other members of the team, a Hawking named Atlas Bokhun and his current companion, Buddash Kyo, that there was nothing that he wasn't willing to do in this life in order to ensure that he'd come out of any given situation as the winner. So much was his disregard for civil behavior in business negotiations that his enemies and associates adopted the practice of referring to Hotfire simply as the "Abomination."

And in the aftermath of that early morning encounter with Kabul Vulkner, it was the small yet powerful fist of the Abomination that was headed towards Yanick's face. Hotfire's punch packed the power of a discharging laser cannon as Yanick was knocked to the floor of Atlas Bokhun's ship, the *Doden Kriger*. Before Hotfire had time to even leap forward towards Yanick to finish his well-deserved beating, Yanick had used his own tail to bounce back to his feet. He broke into an energetic sprint towards Hotfire with his claws extended in attack mode. As he ran, he was building enough momentum that permitted him to launch his body into the air a mere foot or two from where Hotfire was standing his ground.

Hotfire swung his lengthy ebony tail around towards Yanick as the Trionyx came flying towards him so that Yanick grabbed onto Hotfire's tail upon landing instead of digging his claws into the Chamyx's face, which was his original intent.

As Hotfire looked over to discover that Yanick was firmly attached to his tail, a broad smile came over his face as a devilish notion entered his mind. He lifted his tail up with Yanick still attached and brought his massive appendage down to the ground with Yanick receiving the blunt of the blow. He quickly swung his powerful legs around on top of Yanick in order to prevent his escape.

"You took my blaster from me while I was hunting that little Ruddarian brat. For that alone, I should rip that tiny muscle you call a brain right out of your skull."

Yanick spat at him, "You wouldn't have been able to live with yourself if you had killed that kid.

Hotfire grinned. "Yanick, I cannot completely disagree with you."

Hotfire pulled his arm back as he determined the best position for maximum impact. "Guess I will just have to satisfy my bloodlust, this morning, by killing you."

Yanick preferred, whenever he could, not to witness the spilling of blood and especially not his own. Luckily, Hotfire never managed to land that punch.

Instead, the owner of a deep baritone voice yelled, "Get off of each other, you two halfwits. Both of you need to get over here and clean up the mess that we have all created."

Yanick got up off the floor after being released by Hotfire. As he glanced over towards the other side of the flight deck, Yanick observed Buddash carrying a Hominoid in his arms whose skin was a deep heart-fruit red with numerous patches of black. There were columns of steam rising from the body of the Hominoid, like heat escaping from a dissected body on a cold Mundilfarius morning.

"What do you expect us to do, Atlas?" asked Hotfire in a sarcastic tone.

"We need to figure out a means for saving him," said the Hawking Brain Beetle.

"There is nothing we can do for the poor blastard. Besides, Atlas, why do you give a damn whether or not he lives or dies."

"I have a very good reason. Our Hominoid associate, the soon to be departed Mr. Vulkner, didn't seem to trust our good faith arrangement as much as I had once believed."

"What the Hellfire are you saying, Atlas?' asked Yanick.

Atlas reached over with his tentacle and grabbed a slender flask on a nearby shelf that he proceeded to throw directly at Yanick's head.

"I am saying that the Ruddarian-Pink Monkey only gave us samples with half the ingredients for the Enhanced Energy Gas."

"Is there any way that I can extrapolate the other half from the available sample?" asked Hotfire.

"It seems that Vulkner mixed the formula in such a manner that the Querzi computer would be unable to determine the remaining ingredients."

"I vote that we kill the toasted Pink Monkey now and cut our losses," said Hotfire.

Atlas reached up and grabbed Hotfire by his throat. "You do realize that we have numerous clients who are expecting delivery of their orders? And of extra special concern to our well-being are those clients, who have homicidal tendencies."

"Oh, holy crasp!" exclaimed Yanick. "Now, what are we supposed to do?"

"Well my fellow villains," chimed Buddash, "the first thing we need to do is get him stabilized. And we aren't particularly doing Mr. Vulkner any favors standing around and debating his fate."

"Of course you are right, Buddash. Take him down to the infirmary and put him in the oxygen bed," said Hotfire.

"No, actually that would wind up killing him, Hotfire. The remnants of electricity in his tissue would interact with the oxygen in the chamber to light him up like a Polistine candle."

"Then what do you suggest, Mr. Med-tech?"

"Atlas, do we still have the ice tubs for transporting the Porposian meat from Leathershell on-board?" asked Buddash.

"Yeah, they are still on-board. Why? What were you thinking?"

"If we put Vulkner in an ice tub then we can cool his body down. At the same time, the ice will slow his metabolic function enough that he will be in a state of suspended animation, technically."

"And that will keep him alive until we figure out our next move. Get it done, Buddash, and quickly," stated Atlas.

"Right away," said Buddash. "Yanick, I am going to need your help to get the tank out of storage and fill it with ice."

"Right behind you, Brother."

Yanick walked behind Buddash still carrying Kabul in his arms as they headed for the chute lift. Before they entered, Yanick turned around gave Hotfire a parting glance that said spoke volumes. Yanick was trying to communicate with his stare, "I don't like you and I don't trust." What Yanick failed to realize was how right he was to mistrust Hotfire.

Once the door to the chute lift had closed, Hotfire turned to Atlas. "What are you planning to do about the fact that slime mocker of a Trionyx just tried to kill me?"

"From my point of view when I came up to the flight deck, you were trying to do the very same thing to him," said Atlas.

"I was trying to do the job that you need to finish, Atlas. He needs to be dealt with, permanently."

"Let me guess," hissed Atlas. "Either he is gone or you are going to be moving on."

"And I would love to watch you try to find another chemist with my fighting ability," smirked Hotfire.

"Hotfire, I will dispose of Mr. Yanick DcCullen at my earliest convenience."

"That is why I like working with you, Hawking Brain Beetle. You just always aim to please."

"You're welcome. Now that we have settled that, how do you suggest we deal with our other major problem?"

"You mean getting rid of the Cranitian?"

"No, you Cro-Reptilia ignoramus. How do we save Vulkner?"

"What a minute. How exactly do your people extend their lives so long?" asked Hotfire.

"The Hawking Brain Beetle possess a technique for the rejuvenating of cells and tissue that was handed down from the time when most of the orbs in the galaxy including Insectvore, Leathershell, Höllenfeuerhalbinsel, and Mundilfarius were merely hot lavanic balls of gas. In ancient times, the Hawking Brain Beetle were able to manifest this ability by activating the neurons within our own bodies. But the more that our biology has evolved from its original design, the less control we have over our ability to repair our own bodies."

"So how are you able to extend your lives, now that you can't do it with your own bodies?"

"My species possesses a machine known as Methurazus Rejuvenate. There is the possibility that the device could restore Vulkner to health and save his life. The only wrinkle is that it has never been used on off-worlders," mused Atlas.

"Really? That is the only wrinkle, Atlas? The last time I checked your sorry shell was banned from returning to your home world," sneered Hotfire.

"I have an associate on the Omnipotent Council who will be able to facilitate my return."

"You mean you've got a cousin on the Council who can sneak you back on the planet."

"Yes. Desperate times do require desperate measures. We will place Kabul Vulkner in the Methurazus Rejuvenate and hope for the best."

Atlas moved back into a dish-shaped seat in the middle of the flight deck of the *Doden Kriger*. As cables extended from the ceiling of the ship to provide him with a psychic connection with the ship, "Querzi, plot a course for the Hawking Brain Beetle home world of Meditaplassen.

If Yanick's recollection was accurate, Atlas Bokhun had informed him and Buddash Kyo about three hours after they left Rogestran Five that *the Doden Kriger* was currently in orbit around Meditaplassen. Atlas had made contact with a member of the Omnipotent Council, Apollos Bokhun, who had informed him that a slave freighter with a group of Reptilia slaves on board was returning that morning from a mining asteroid, Eurodan Seven. Apollos suggested that if Atlas could manage to stow away on the freighter, they would be able to slip past security and make their way to the chamber.

Shortly before the beginning of the mission, Yanick learned that Hotfire would be going down to the planet. "Buddash and I will be remaining on board for the moment. Once you and Hotfire have reached the Methurazus chamber, you will lower the barriers. I will then teleport Mr. Vulkner down in stasis." said Atlas.

"Wouldn't it make more sense for you to go down to the planet on the freighter with Vulkner?"

"Remember, there will be Reptilia slave miners on board the freight so I would stick out like a Madagascan fungiroom."

"I guess that I am going to have to take your word for that," said Yanick.

"Do as you're told for once, you blue-green salamander," snapped Atlas. "Now Buddash, get to that artillery console because I need you to fire a shot across that ship's bow."

Buddash started to ask, "what ship?" when a small box-shaped vessel — an amalgamation of various sheets of platinadium, steel, and copper plates

— came noisily out of a sub-phase jump. Buddash swore from the look of the vessel that a strong breeze could have shaken the craft apart.

"Buddash, I ordered you to fire at that ship," insisted Atlas.

"Here goes nothing," said Buddash as he pressed down on the lever to activate the main lasers.

All three Reptilia were somewhat surprised to observe that the small craft was turning around to return fire. In his mind, Yanick was equating the encounter with a Rodectos turning tail and actually coming after the carnivore that was chasing it.

"Just don't stand there you two," barked Atlas. "The ship is so old that it only has energy to maintain one system at a time. If they are using their defensive lasers, that means their barriers are down."

Hotfire grabbed Yanick by the neck and pulled him into the lift chute. A minute later, the doors to the chute reopened to face the ship's teleport console. Hotfire pulled Yanick to the chamber and instantly, they were teleporting over to the slave freighter.

Back on the flight deck, Buddash was maneuvering the ship away from the laser bolts being fired from the aging slave freighter. Surprisingly, the slave freighter still packed a punch.

"Activate our heat barriers, Buddash. We are going to drop into the upper atmosphere," commanded Atlas.

"Will do," said Buddash as he sent a barrage of three torpedoes from the ship's rear launchers. The torpedoes barely managed to scratch the surface of the slave freighter. But the brief engagement did provide Buddash with the opportunity to put some distance between themselves and the freighter.

"Did you manage to repair the perception reflectors like I asked you to do?"

"Yep, they are functional once again."

"Then I suggest you activate them so we can disappear," said Atlas.

As the old slave freighter moved towards the outer edge of Meditaplassen's atmosphere, the freighter's captain was bewildered to find that the vessel they were pursuing had managed to somehow disappear. He made the fateful decision at that moment to continue on with his original mission rather than going to chasing after invisible ships.

Unbeknownst to the captain, Hotfire and Yanick had made their way down to the holding cells where they were trying their best to blend in. These Reptilia were considered to be inferior by species such as the Polistine, Xeperian and Beetleguise. As the two of them stood by the door leading to the containment cells trying to find a way in, there was suddenly a deep baritone voice coming from behind.

"How did the two of you get out?" asked a Hawking Brain Beetle guard.

"Allow me to demonstrate," sneered Hotfire.

Before the Hawking could react, Hotfire snapped his tail backwards, knocking the Hawking to the ground. The Hawking quickly tried to use his tentacles to right himself, but Yanick was on him in an instant and dug his claws into the soft exposed flesh of the Hawking. Within a few swipes, Yanick had pulled the slug-like body from its protective shell.

"So I guess that is what Atlas looks like out of his platinum can of a shell," said Hotfire.

"Nice," quipped Yanick. "Can you please help me pull this the body the rest of the way out. I just might have an idea about how we can get out of this mess."

If Hotfire could masquerade beneath the Hawking Brain Beetle shell and Yanick posed as his prisoner, it could hopefully, allow them to move throughout the streets of the capital city, Dakplassen, without being hassled by the local security force.

"You know we do make a good team when you make an effort," said Hotfire

"A discussion to be continued at a more appropriate time."

The plan did go off fairly smoothly with both Hotfire and Yanick being able to exit the slave freighter, with Hotfire only occasionally having to direct a slave Reptilia of the Quillian, Trionyx, or Cranitian variety to fall back into line — Chamyx were rarely used as slaves due to their volatile nature.

As Hotfire moved the prisoners down a long walkway bordered on either side by large stone walls, he and two other actual Hawking Brain Beetles herded the Reptilia slaves into a walled compound. Once inside the walled arena, the Hawking Brain Beetles used long taser sticks to escort the slaves back to small dark cells located at the end of extended hallways that were covered in black tar. As Yanick was walking in front of Hotfire, he felt Hotfire's large Reptilia foot kick him into a ditch. Hotfire turned back to Yanick and put a foot up out of his fake-shell in a motion which meant for Yanick to stay put for the moment.

Yanick truly did not appreciate being abandoned, and could only try to assure himself that Hotfire would return for him at some point; otherwise, he would have to explain to Atlas why he'd left him on the planet. The main problem with this theory was that Yanick knew for a fact that Hotfire was capable of talking himself out of most tight situations. So explaining how he accidently left Yanick behind on this miserable rock would be child's play for him. It was then Yanick heard a burst of gunfire accompanied by the sound of footfalls. He looked up to see Hotfire standing over him, having already removed his Hawking Brain Beetle disguise.

"Are you just going to lay in that hole all day?" asked Hotfire.

"What the crasp happened back there?"

"Apparently, one of the other guards didn't take too kindly to the fact that I prevented him from whipping one of the Trionyx," stated Hotfire.

Before Yanick could even respond, a laser bolt passed between the two hitchhikers. Requiring no more encouragement, Hotfire turned to Yanick. "Time to go."

"I couldn't agree more," said Yanick.

Hotfire grabbed Yanick and pulled him out of the ditch. The two of them retraced their steps as best they could back up the long dark hallways, barely dodging the weapons' fire. Both Yanick and Hotfire stumbled several times, quickly pulling themselves back up before they became sitting targets. And after what seemed like an eternity but was actually only a matter of minutes, Hotfire and Yanick saw a yellowish-white light at the end of the tunnel that indicated the entrance to the large bowl-shaped arena. And as they moved closer, Hotfire turned to Yanick in what appeared to be a completely spontaneous fashion. "When we reach the entrance, just follow my lead."

"I guess so," said Yanick in an uncertain voice. "What did you have in mind?"

"Can you just listen to me for once?"

"Sure. Why not," said Yanick. "We are probably going to die horrible deaths anyway so in the end it doesn't matter."

Distracted by thoughts of his impending demise, Yanick failed to notice that he and Hotfire had already reached the entrance when he was lifted up by Hotfire wrapping his tail around his midsection. As he was being pulled up, Yanick saw blue laser shots above his head. These shots had the effect of dislodging the stones that supported the arch. Despite the ensuing avalanche, Hotfire continued to push forward, continually knocking stones out of the way until they had made it past the cascade of falling stones to reach the dirt and sand of the stone arena. Once the two of them had successfully made it past the stone cascade, they landed with a thud.

As they lay on the ground, Hotfire looked back at the newly-collapsed arch, "It is definitely going to take more than a minute or two for those Hawkings to dig their way out from there."

"What about all the slaves that you just buried alive?" asked Yanick.

"Oh please. You are tearing my heart out. I have never met a Reptilia worth his spit that couldn't dig a hole in order to get out. They will be free in a few hours."

"You just don't give a Daggit about who you hurt, even indirectly?"

"That is my secret for surviving this long," smiled Hotfire.

"Incredible," said Yanick as he shook his head.

"Thank you for the compliment." Hotfire changed his demeanor to one of all business in the next second. "Can we please get to the Methurazus chamber so we can get out of here?"

"How do you propose that we get out of this arena?"

"Just trust me," smiled Hotfire.

"How did I know that you were going to say that?".

Hotfire led Yanick over to a large metal hatch at the rear of the arena. As Hotfire removed the hatch, Yanick looked down to see a ladder attached to the wall of the long vertical passageway.

As they stood gazing down into the darkness, Hotfire said, "I snagged a pair of lanterns when we boarded the ship for just such an occasion. We can take this sewage tunnel straight from here to the Methurazus tunnel. It should take us all of five minutes."

Yanick remembered that the journey through the sewers was only a matter of minutes; however, much like Warden Sobek, his Bokhun cousins were fond of flushing their failed biological experiments down the refuse chute. And those failures were quite adept at The aforementioned experiments seemed to quiet adapt at making themselves at home.

Suffice it to say, Yanick was none too happy about the route that Hotfire had chosen for them to get to the Methurazus. There was a horrible smell throughout the tunnels, and Yanick could only imagine what rotting carcasses were littered there. And if that wasn't bad enough, Yanick's hypersensitive hearing was picking up an almost continuous cacophony of growls, groans and the sound of flesh being torn apart.

"Are we almost there, Hotfire?" asked Yanick. "I am not getting the most warm and fuzzy feeling being down here with whatever the fuctur is moving around."

"There is nothing down here that could hurt you. It's all in your head."

But his very next step, Yanick's fears were validated as a giant pink tongue shot out of the water. The pink monstrosity came hurtling towards his legs as the long, thick flab of flesh grabbed his legs and began to pull him down.

"Is that one of your imaginary creatures?" screamed Yanick.

Hotfire turned around to his companion just in time to see a large green head with two pink beady eyes, whip-shaped whiskers, two lengthy torpedo-shaped ears, and a jaw with enormous fangs emerge from the water. The creature was using his extended tongue to pull Yanick into its waiting jaws.

"Just hang on, Yanick," shouted Hotfire. "It is going to be okay. Just. Don't. Panic."

"Don't panic?" He was bobbing up and down in the sewer water attached to the pink appendage.

"Just hold on a minute," said Hotfire.

"I doubt that I even have a minute," cried Yanick.

"No need to start name calling."

"Do something now or I am going to die!"

Hotfire picked up the Taser spear that he had kept after killing the Hawking to discover that there was a range setting on the grip. He quickly turned the knob all the way to maximum as he aimed it at the enormous green head. Blue lightening came out of the slender blade and struck the creature's head right between the eyes. The creature released Yanick from its tongue and dove back down into the muddy water.

After recovering in the water for a brief time, Yanick rose to his feet and headed back toward Hotfire. When he passed directly by the Chamyx, he softly said, "Nothing down here to hurt me, huh?"

"Whatever," sighed Hotfire.

Yanick followed Hotfire for the rest of their brief journey up to the Methurazus chamber. He could detect when the two of them were leaving the sewer behind as the light around them seemed to grow a little brighter and his sense of dread began to subside.

"I think I found the ladder back up to the surface. But how do we know that it is the Methurazus chamber?" asked Yanick.

"Leave that to me," said Hotfire as he produced a small transistor unit from his belt. "Atlas, are you detecting regenerating particles in the vicinity?"

"The machine should be directly above you," boomed Atlas Bokhun.

"What did I tell you. We are going to have Vulkner back to his old annoying self in no time," said Hotfire. "Atlas, prepare to teleport the prisoner to this location once I lower the barrier as we discussed."

"Very good, my son," said Atlas Bokhun.

As Yanick followed Hotfire up the ladder to the Methurazus chamber, he got a cold chill down his back that wasn't coming from the drafty sewer. Once inside the ante-chamber, Hotfire quickly lowered the barriers that protected the Methurazus Rejuvenate device. As soon as Buddash received Hotfire's signal, he teleported Vulkner down to the room inside his stasis torpedo.

The Methurazus Rejuvenate occupied a prominent place in the center of the chamber. The red-tiled room glistened as the early morning sun that shone in through eight small oval windows. There was a large metal door near the southern portion of the room that appeared to slide down on two

157

tracks. The machine was a large cube that opened into two sections on a set of hinges on either side. The forward sections of the Methurazus were able to be pulled aside to reveal a central table that could be expanded or retracted in length depending on the height of the individual. Near the machine was a console that Hotfire determined was the means for controlling the device itself.

As Hotfire was familiarizing himself with the controls on the Methurazus console, Yanick moved over to the capsule containing Kabul Vulkner to slowly increase its temperature in three-minute increments until Vulkner's skin was changed from frosty blue back to deep pink.

But before Yanick could completely finish reviving him, Hotfire grew impatient with the defrosting process. He pushed past Yanick and scooped up Vulkner in his arms, took three big strides across the room, and deposited him on the table at the center of the Methurazus.

"You can't just drop him in there like you are cooking a fish over the fire."

"We don't have time to play around and make sure everything is just right," snapped Hotfire. "It isn't going to take those Hawking Brain Beetles too long to figure out where we've gone. We need to heal Vulkner and get the fuctur out of here."

"Just take two seconds to at least make sure that it is the right setting."

"Let me think about that," said Hotfire as he put his hand under his chin. "Ah, I don't agree with your assessment."

Yanick held his breath as Hotfire raced over to the Methurazus Rejuvenate and began throwing levers and switches. The operation of the machine continued to progress as Yanick scanned the console to determine what the Methurazus was doing to Vulkner. But it didn't take very long to realize that it was nothing good as they both could hear Vulkner's screams.

As Yanick continued to scan the console, he glanced over to see that the regenerative setting had been set for Reptilia. Apparently, the Hawking used the machine to not only repair their own bodies, but those of their Reptilia slaves as well.

"The machine is set for Reptilia! We have to get him out of there!" screamed Yanick.

"We can't take him out until he gets fixed."

"It is killing him, you dim salamander!"

Yanick had pondered long and hard over the next 30 years what occurred in that chamber. He wasn't sure if he had unleashed a plague upon the galaxy. He often reassured himself that he had no idea what was about to be unleashed. It just seemed to Yanick, at the time, like the right thing to do. He reached over past Hotfire and turned the dial back toward a setting of "other." However, Hotfire grabbed his hand in mid-turn and tried to pull it away from the knob, yelling "Leave it alone. You don't know what you're doing."

Yanick leaned back against the console, using his tail as a tripod, so that his legs were up in the air. With all his might, Yanick kicked Hotfire in the gut, knocking him across the room.

"You can't just leave it on any old setting and hope for the best."

"You are a dead Trionyx, Yanick DcCullen."

Yanick reached behind him on the console and set the knob back to the other setting. This action seemed to lessen the screaming from inside the cube. However, Yanick had a completely different problem since Hotfire was starting to get back on his feet.

"I am going to finish what I was planning to do to you after we left the Rogestran Five Colony."

"I am not scared of you, Hotfire."

"Well, that is your first mistake," smirked Hotfire as he walked toward Yanick with a look of malice in his eyes and thoughts of murder on his mind.

`"If that is my first mistake, then yours is underestimating how dangerous I can be," replied Yanick. It was then that Yanick spied the Taser spear that Hotfire had rested against the console. Unfortunately, Hotfire saw the weapon at the same time.

They both sprinted for the spear at the same time, but Yanick managed to reach it first. He quickly turned towards Hotfire and turned the knob to maximum, sending a long thread of lightening into Hotfire's chest. Yanick watched as the lightening propelled the oversized Chamyx across the room.

As he looked at the still body of his long-time associate, Yanick realized that he could not simply leave Hotfire to die, no matter how betrayed either of them felt by the actions of the morning.

He continued to question his next action to the present day and would probably continue to ponder if it was the right decision for the rest of his days. He dragged the unconscious Hotfire into the Methurazus Rejuvenate after the process had completed with Kabul Vulkner, who was still screaming hysterically even after being removed from the device.

After giving Kabul a sedative that had been provided by Atlas and placing him momentarily in a nearby metal chair, Yanick returned to the console to begin activating the sequence that would hopefully revive Hotfire. Once the chamber was closed and the processes were active again, everything began to spiral out of control.

During Yanick's monitoring of the regeneration process, he began to hear a pounding from inside the Methurazus device. It was Hotfire screaming that he wasn't injured and wasn't dead. What the machine was doing was turning him inside out and replacing his bones, muscles, and blood with new and improved versions. All Yanick heard was Hotfire screaming to let him out. But just as Yanick was about to comply with this request, the door to the chamber was blasted off as a group of Hawking Beetle Brain came crawling through.

Yanick decided to choose his own life over his associate's and activated the teleport device on Vulkner's cryo-torpedo. He grabbed Vulkner as he dove inside the empty torpedo chamber that vanished from the chamber and reappeared back on board the *Doden Kriger*.

The Hawking Brain Beetle surrounded the Methurazus chamber as the process slowly came to its conclusion with the reluctant Chamyx inside. As the device went quiet, the chamber doors swung open to reveal that the machine had exchanged the right external portion of his body for the internal right half so the organs on Hotfire's right side, including his brain, heart, and lungs were now exposed on the outside of his body.

"Somebody help me," screamed Hotfire.

"Guard, prepare a stasis tube for this abomination of a Reptilia and take him to the nearest healing facility."

The shelled Hawking Brain Beetle moved close to Hotfire as he lay half-dead on the floor of the chamber. "We, Hawking Brain Beetle, swear that you will be restored. However, the price of that bargain is that your life now belongs to the Hawking race. You are our creature now. You will therefore go forth into the galaxy once you are healed and do the bidding of the Hawking Brain Beetle."

Chapter 14
LEGATE PRIME BUZZ

Legate Prime Buzz awoke in the Tram with a headache that could easily have ranked among the ones he used to find himself with after a night of liberty and too much fermented nectar. He looked around his immediate surroundings; Beetleguise centurions, who he'd make sure were each terminated at his earliest convenience, had placed him in a synthetic restraint vest that restricted his entire upper torso and appendages.

Buzz's first instinct was to reach around with his stingers to use the barbs located along their spines to slice through the straight vest, but someone had anticipated this maneuver, most likely Legate Beta Zook, and had tethered his stingers.

Glancing around the cabin, he was unable to immediately determine if there were any implements or tools within the room that could assist him in facilitating his escape. However, he was certain of one thing. Warden Sobek was not going to permit him to be sent back to Insectvore to be "executed." All he had to do was take one look at Zook to tell that the warden had influenced his recollection of events. And Sobek was aware that he needed to remove the one Insectum, Buzz, who would be calling for his removal as warden of Minerva Penitentiary.

`Buzz knew that his innocence was an incidental fact at the moment because Warden Sobek was probably even now in the process of devising a means of facilitating the Legate Prime's untimely death. He could not think like an officer in a situation such as this one. For crasp sake, he couldn't even permit himself to think like a correctional officer. No. On this occasion, the

Legate Prime Buzz need to think like a criminal. And after briefly considering his dilemma, he was able to formulate a solution to his problem, worthy of a Reptilia mastermind.

"Centurion," shouted Buzz, "I have a pain in my abdomen."

After waiting a few minutes, during which no one came into the room, Buzz decided to up his game.

"Centurion, I think I am bleeding in here. I am telling you I really wouldn't want to be the one to clean up this mess," he said, putting an extra measure of anxiety in his voice.

A moment later, a Beetleguise centurion in a brown jumpsuit with gold stripes opened the door to the Legate Prime's cell. After taking a brief look around, the centurion walked up to Buzz proclaiming, "I don't see any blood."

Buzz lowered his head and brought it up underneath the Beetleguise centurion's head, knocking him backwards. Buzz then lowered his head to a horizontal position as he knocked his head forward into the centurion's face, rendering him unconscious.

"Do you see any blood, now? Oh, of course, that would be yours all over the ground."

The Legate Prime knew that he had to work quickly, since no doubt another centurion would be coming to investigate what was causing the disturbance. He reached into the pocket of the Beetleguise with his leg appendages in the hope that it held what he needed. By the grace of the Great Hive Master, Buzz was not disappointed as he pulled a slender yellow card.

"You beautiful piece of quartzix. I could almost kiss you."

Buzz lifted the yellow card up to his mandibles with his leg appendages. As he held the card in his mouth, he turned his head around to the rear panel as far as he could reach. With his powerful proboscis, he pushed the card into a rear panel, there was an audible click.

The moment that the yellow card entered the panel also happened to be when a second Beetleguise came walking around the corner. "Hey, you aren't supposed to be out of that vest."

Without missing a beat, Buzz picked up the first centurion's blaster and fired. As the Beetleguise centurion fell to the ground, Buzz replied, "you probably have a point." He then returned to liberating himself from the restraints with his final action being to use the centurion's blaster to free himself from the shackles.

Buzz ran out of his containment cell on board the Tram, he made sure to pocket the blaster that he had relieved from Beetleguise centurion, as he made his way down the hall. He had decided that it was necessary to take control of the command center. But, the more he considered this plan, the more he was convinced that he couldn't accomplish it alone.

Fate seemed to take him by the appendage because Buzz happened to glance through a small round window as he moved down the corridor to find that inmate 3249 was being kept in cryo-stasis on- board this Tram. He quickly pulled out his blaster and fired at the door lock.

Suffice it to say, Yanick DcCullen was shocked to see that the Legate Prime was the one who was reviving him out of the cryo-tube.

After being liberated from the ice-preservation, Yanick could feel his whole body shake as his skin, blood, and muscles began to receive the warmth of the artificial heating system. Despite the fact that he was still wet, exhausted, and famished, Yanick managed to tell Buzz, "Fine, you are taking me to the containment unit, probably to execute me. I am telling you now though that before I take my last breath, that I will make sure the warden knows that I was the one who saved your life."

"If I have my way, Sobek might not be warden for too much longer," said Buzz.

"What the fuctur are you talking about?"

"Before I was called away while pulling you and your fellow inmate, 3360, out of that artificially created ocean —"

"You know that he does have a name, you egotistical Wasp. It is Buddash Kyo."

"— yes, prior to having to rescue you and Buddash, there was a terrible incident. Some of my centurions were attacked by those genetic beings from the Rec Center this morning. They are called Triceratopian."

"Terrible? Guess it depends on your point of view," smirked Yanick.

The Polistine jammed his stingers into Yanick's gut in response to his indifference. However, Buzz reflected in hindsight that was probably not the best way to gain his trust. "Look, when this Afterburn of a day is over, you are going back to your cell. In the meantime —"

"You need my help to gain control of this ship. And possibly for something else?"

Buzz decided reluctantly that he needed to share a little more with this Reptilia ally, who was probably the best he was going to get at this juncture. "We need to take the Tram to the *Citadel*. Once we are there, I need to persuade the warden that he needs to destroy these Triceratopian, once and for all."

"Of course, you mean that "we" need to convince him," smirked Yanick.

"If 'we' can't convince the Warden to end the program, then "we" are going to have to find a way to stop them on our own," replied Buzz.

"Your own centurions are dropping like house bugs when they fighting those things. How are we supposed to stop them?"

"I am really not sure. But if you and I put our heads together, I am sure that we can think of something."

"Great. Just when I thought this day couldn't get any worse," moaned Yanick.

"Hush your moaning. I think we are about to have more unwanted company," said Buzz.

"Do you even have a plan for when they get in here?" asked Yanick.

"Nothing in particular springs to mind."

A wide grin came over Yanick's face, "In that case, it is your lucky day since you happen to be in the presence of a criminal mastermind. Now here's what I am going to need from you..."

Legate Beta Zook had been trying to contact the Beetleguise centurion, J'nox for close to five minutes so he could allow Zook to take a much needed break from piloting the Tram, but J'nox didn't seem to be answering his ear-comm at the moment.

Even more unsettling than his missing centurion was the fact that just after Zook completed liftoff, he had received an urgent directive that he was now supposed to deliver the prisoners to the *Citadel* for interrogation rather than taking them to solitary confinement in the Repose of Solace, located in a sub-chamber below the confinement cells and the auxiliary feeding chamber.

As Zook stood beneath the navigation helmet that guided the movement of the Tram, he suddenly heard what sounded like a door opening and closing. Then he heard voices. He quickly disengaged from the cables that connected him to the main operational Querzi as he set his helmet on a nearby hook.

"Centurions J'nox and Razz, this is Legate Zook, meet me in the rear hallway behind navigation. Just heard a disturbance in the back section."

"Can you not resolve the issue on your own, Legate?" asked centurion J'nox said, finally answering Zook's call. "We have gone without sustenance for several hours. J'nox and Razz are just sitting down for replenishment."

"I could care less about your hunger pains. You two worthless Beetleguise get up here and make sure to bring charged blasters, this time."

"It was not J'nox's fault that his blaster was de-charged the last time. J'nox cannot help it if the blaster is poorly made Polistine technology," said J'nox.

"Just get up here! Now."

"As Zook wishes," said J'nox.

As he left the navigation system on automatic and headed down towards the containment cells, Zook mused that one of the most frustrating aspects of his average work routine on Minerva was dealing with the Beetleguise centurions. They had no sense of seeking personal glory or providing service to their world in order for their culture to remain the dominant species in the galaxy. The Beetleguise did none of that. They simply built their machines, gathered food, and procreated. An absolutely pointless existence that did nothing to raise their standing as a species. It turned Zook's stomachs just thinking about their repugnant culture.

Once he made it down to the containment cells, Zook's opinion of the two Beetleguise centurions plummeted even further as he observed that they had not yet even arrived.

It was then that Zook heard a frantic knocking coming from inside the compartment where the Trionyx, inmate 3249, was being held in the stasis tube. Zook quietly removed his blaster from his holster and gingerly hovered into the room. Once inside, he looked around to observe that everything appeared to be in order.

It was then that he heard a scream mixed with fear and adrenaline emanating from above. Zook looked up to see his former commanding officer, Buzz, flying towards him with his Taser extended. Buzz slammed into Zook, knocking him to the floor of the cell. Zook instinctively grabbed for his blaster, but it was already too late. Buzz swung around his abdomen and knocked his junior officer with a powerful thrust, rendering Zook unconscious.

"I did what I had to with a heavy heart. You are a fine and noble warrior, Zook." Buzz picked up Zook's unconscious frame and lifted him over his shoulder as he flew towards an empty cryo-chamber. As he pressed the cover-release switch and placed him inside, Buzz said to his sleeping colleague, "I just hope that one day you will once again look upon me with honor." He flipped the switch again and the door slammed shut.

J'nox and Razz happened to choose that time to finally make their appearance. As they watched one of the prisoners placing their Polistine Legate into the cryo-tube, J'nox pulled his blaster and shouted, "J'nox demands that you release Zook now. Buzz will then come quietly without resistance."

"I doubt that will be happening today."

The two Beetleguise watched in stunned disbelief as the rear door opened and the Trionyx prisoner launched himself out of the tube and landed on top of them. The centurions grabbed a hold of each other and cowered pitifully as Yanick growled at them and flashed his menacing teeth.

"Please do not harm us, blue beast. We are willing to succumb to your demands," said Razz.

"That would be an extremely wise move," said Yanick.

"We implore you, Trionyx, that you grant us one request," said J'nox.

"I will think about it. What is your request?" growled Yanick.

"Do not crush our bodies under your enormous, ignorant frame," said J'nox in a confident tone.

"What?"

A second later, Yanick's body was shaking and gyrating uncontrollably as two Tasers were jammed into his sides. J'nox and Razz watched in great amusement as the simpleton of a Reptilia convulsed on the floor. So much was their enjoyment that they two failed to notice their disgraced Legate Prime pick up a blaster, set it to stun, and fire.

As Buzz came flying over to the Trionyx who now had two sleeping Beetleguise on either side of him, he casually looked down as Yanick was still shaking from the Tasers. In a tone that Buzz meant to be playful but just came out condescending, he said, "Just shake it off, Yanick. We've got work to do."

"You called me Yanick. Thannk Yooou!" he said as his teeth chattered.

Mercifully, the effects of the Taser, including the uncontrollable shaking and impaired speech, managed to shortly subside. But the experience further demonstrated to Yanick that he could only expect one frustrating event after another for the remains of the day. These turbulent difficulties would reach their inevitable conclusion at some point in the foreseeable future. For the time being, Yanick picked himself up slowly and headed onto the Tram to find out what had become of the whimsical Legate Prime. He did not have to look for long. He had taken the chute lift up to the Tram's central command center, and the lift's reflective platinum doors slid back, Yanick found the Legate Prime Buzz already activated the navigation system and connecting to the Querzi by the tubular cables. Yanick made his way into the room and circled the central control on his hind legs with his claws extended like an ancient Pangean predator.

"Is there something on your mind, inmate 3249?".

"I was wondering when you would be escorting me back to my cell?" asked Yanick.

"Not exactly at this moment. There is still the matter of dealing with Sobek,"

"You do realize that those horned Triceratopian freaks will probably be protecting him?" asked Yanick.

"I realize that. That is the main reason I need him to see reason. Sobek is not going to be able to control those freaks forever. And once they turn on him, it won't be long before all of us will be on the chopping block."

"How do you know that this is the right time to strike?" asked Yanick.

"I'm hoping that he will be so distracted dealing with inmate 6610 that he will just give into my demands so he can focus on him," said Legate Prime Buzz.

"Who the crasp is inmate 6610?" asked Yanick.

"The war criminal known as Hotfire," stated Legate Prime Buzz.

Before the name finished passing Buzz's mandibles, Yanick had reached out and grabbed Buzz's Taser from his holster, "I am not going within a hundred lightyears of that manic! So just turn this ship around, this instant! You get me!" yelled Yanick.

Seeing that Yanick was distracted, Buzz reached out and tried to grab the Taser from his claw. It was only at the last second that the appendage came into Yanick's field of vision. In an instinctive fashion, Yanick pulled back on the Taser, causing it to discharge a burst of electricity into the panel.

"Great going! You just fried the forward thrusters, Reptilia." shouted Buzz.

"What exactly does that mean?" asked Yanick.

"It means that we are about to have a very bumpy landing."

Chapter 15
CAPTAIN HONEYCOMB

The captain felt like he had been falling forever.

Struggling to gain any kind of grip hold for himself, Captain Honeycomb continued to slide down the winding tunnel toward what he could only assume was the center of the Minerva asteroid. He had no recollection of a tunnel this long within the schematics of the penitentiary, so he could only figure that the force of the flooding in the Machine Shop had uncovered a previously buried chamber.

Even in the blackness of the tunnel, unsure of where he was going or what lay ahead, Honeycomb was aware of one indisputable fact: there was someone following behind him. He was certain that there was someone else in the tunnel because he would periodically hear the sound of a very large object bouncing off the walls of the chamber. In his mind, Honeycomb was making the likely supposition that the Cranitian in the android green jumpsuit had followed him down the hole for one reason or another, possibly thinking that the tunnel led to a means of escape.

While Honeycomb tumbled deeper and deeper into Minerva's heart, he felt himself beginning to accelerate. He had a disturbing inclination that whatever was happening could not be good. It was then that he saw a curve at the bottom of the slope.

Honeycomb realized that if he didn't act fast, he would slam into the wall at the junction of the curve at a very high rate of speed. The best solution he could come up in this limited amount of time was to extend the three appendages on his left side so he would gently shift. Just as he was about to make contact, he moved his large frame over and avoided being splat like a gnat on an external viewer.

In the darkness, Honeycomb managed to yell back at his pursuer, "If you want to live, you might seriously consider moving to the left."

The heavy object, or being, in the tunnel could be heard shifting its weight a minute or so after the captain. However, it appeared that neither one of them had managed to overcome all the obstacles that the tunnel had to offer. Honeycomb glanced in front of him to see that there were a number of loops that lay ahead. He once again braced himself to the left as he was repeatedly spun downward on a natural slope that led him, finally, to an opening at the end of the tunnel. Honeycomb had no idea how deep the drop would be once he exited this thin, long slippery tunnel so he spun himself forward while there was still room available. At the very least, he would be facing forward when he came hurling out. And precisely not a moment too soon, he saw that the circle of light was growing brighter. Rust and silver replaced a continuous curtain of blackness.

At the last possible moment, right before Honeycomb would have dropped off the edge of the tunnel, he launched himself up toward the roof of the massive cavern. As he had observed through the tunnel's forward opening, he was surrounded by rust and silver colored rock, but there were golden, and brilliant red rocks at a higher level. Honeycomb assumed from the varied colors of rock that this cavern contained a wellspring of mineral riches just waiting to be tapped. Honeycomb also found himself having to avoid massive slagamites that descended from the cavern's ceiling as well as slagacites, arising from the floor. Honeycomb recalled from his early educa- tion at the Hive school that the presence of these formations in the cavern indicated that there had to be some form of oxygen and water within the cavern system.

Turning back toward the exposed tunnel opening in the rock wall, Honeycomb could distinctly hear the sound of someone shouting frantically for "help." He swooped back down and managed to catch the large Reptilia Cranitian as it exited the tunnel.

"You are a little bit heavier than you look," quipped Honeycomb.

"I have been meaning to cut down on my portions," said Buddash.

"It will definitely help you to live longer," smirked Honeycomb.

"You know what else would help me to do that? Getting me down to the ground!"

"I am definitely trying, but this extra weight is not helping. If I get a little lower, do you think you can tuck and roll?"

"What am I, a menagerie acrobat? I will bust my cranium for sure."

"Well," sighed Honeycomb, "I don't see many other options. Besides, I can already feel you slipping out of my appendages."

"Fine. Drop me, but please try to do it as gently as possible."

"All right. Here goes nothing. I will let you go on the count of five," said Honeycomb as he continued to move down in ever decreasing spirals.

"That sounds like a good plan."

"Okay, one, two, three —," said Honeycomb as he released Buddash and watched him curl up into a ball and roll along the cavern floor.

"What the Hellfire happened to four and five?" screamed Buddash.

"My instructors always did say that I was lousy at numeric functioning."

"Blastard," shouted Buddash.

Coming in for a soft landing a foot or two from the Cranitian, Honeycomb added, "You may want to keep your voice down. We have no idea who or what may be lurking around."

As the words exited his lips, there was the sound of a weapon being energized coming from behind them. The Polistine and Cranitian turned to face a ten-foot-tall satanic red Quillian with an extended pair of jaws and two marble black eyes. "You may want to take Captain Honeycomb's advice about being quiet," he said.

"Wait just one, daggit minute. Who exactly are you? And how do you know who I am?"

"My name is Multiverse."

Honeycomb watched as the being in front of him began to decrease slightly in stature while two sets of wings emerged from his back. At the same time, his arms and legs began to decrease in diameter and he acquired extra sets. Honeycomb looked on in amazement as the creature had changed before the original Honeycomb's multi-lensed eyes into a duplicate of himself.

"I am a Clonstellar, and I am aware of a great many things. Among the facts within my extensive knowledge is that you have been presumed dead, drown in the Machine Shop. So there will be no one to come looking for you, Captain Honeycomb."

At that moment, Buddash and Honeycomb could hear more blaster weapons being energized behind them. Buddash glanced behind him to see a Cranitian who was at least a head taller than him, a sorely looking Trionyx who could have been Yanick's evil twin, and two large Chamyx who were holding blasters big enough to be mounted on his old ship, the *Doden Kriger*.

Still appearing as Honeycomb and mimicking his voice, Multiverse faced Buddash Kyo. "My employer, Lord Diabolix, is in a current state of extreme displeasure with you, Mr. Buddash."

"I haven't done anything wrong. There were just a few items that I needed to take care of before I could fulfill our agreement."

"Inmate 3360, to what agreement is this Clonstellar referring?"

Captain Honeycomb was suddenly facing the Clonstellar-Honeycomb, like a Polistine glancing in the mirror in preparation for the day. In his best Honeycomb voice, Multiverse stated, "That is none of your concern, my dear captain. All you need to know is that Lord Diabolix's spies witnessed, you and Mr. DcCullen in the Recreation center this morning making your escape attempt. And at the time of this attempt, you had not yet concluded your business with Lord Diabolix."

"So, Diabolix doesn't have the stomach to do his own killing anymore. You know they say that's a sign that a proper villain is losing it," smiled Buddash.

"I will be sure to make Lord Diabolix aware of your concerns, once our business is done. And If I were you, I would not permit myself to succumb to the delusion that just because Diabolix is not in this room that you are beyond his reach. Trust me when I tell you that, one way or other, Buddash Kyo, you will shortly die by his claw."

Multiverse swung in a circle away from Buddash. During this pirouette, the Clonstellar reverted from his disguise as Honeycomb back to his form as a ten-foot-tall red Quillian. "For now, my Lord has decreed that my Reptilia and I may gain some amusement at your expense, upon the condition that you are kept alive." Multiverse turned around to face the Polistine Honeycomb. "Lord Diabolix made no pre-conditional statements regarding the need to keep the valiant Captain Honeycomb alive." Multiverse changed his voice to a whimpering tone, "So sorry about the oversight."

"Don't feel too bad. I have been told that I am kind of hard to kill," said Honeycomb.

"We shall see," said Multiverse as he wiggled his right hand in the air. "We shall see."

Multiverse flicked his hand up again in a casual manner as he informed his henchmen to take them to the holding area. Multiverse turned to the Chamyx who had a mixture of blue and gold stripes down his back. "Hot-streak, prepare the magna-dome. It seems that fate has provided us with some new opponents."

"Opponents?" Honeycomb yelled to Multiverse as the large Chamyx pulled him down a corridor. "Are you going to have us fight each other?"

"You may be fighting each other at some point. But probably only to get away from something far worse. Take them out of my sight, Hot-Streak, and allow them to make their peace with the Great Hive Master."

The ten-foot Cranitian and the disagreeable Trionyx raised their blasters to Honeycomb and Buddash's backs as Multiverse turned towards a walkway that had been carved in the rock face, Honeycomb was guessing maybe decades or centuries before. As Multiverse walked up the rock path and proceeded to a small box-shaped shuttle that had had its rear thruster portion removed and replaced with a sheet of protective golden plexiglass. Upon entering the vehicle, Multiverse set to work at a Querzi computer console by the far wall of the shuttle.

Having been distracted by trying to determine what the Shapeshifter was doing, Captain Honeycomb did not notice the Trionyx moving closer to him until he felt the cold snap of steel around his lower two appendages that was followed by an electronic humming from the bands that caused Honeycomb's legs to begin to vibrate.

"Those are gravity bands on your legs to prevent you from flying away, little Wasp," said the Trionyx.

Buddash noticed that the menacing-looking Chamyx that Multiverse had referred to as Hot-streak had made his way up to the shuttle enclosure to join the Clonstellar.

"They are initializing the magna-dome so that the two of you will be able to meet your demise in honorable combat," explained the Trionyx in answer to Buddash's quizzical. "Well, at least, the Polistine. The disposal of the Cranitian will have to wait till later."

"Is Multiverse going to try to dispose of me personally?" asked Buddash

"No, Cranitian. You will be dispatched from this life by the mighty Lord Diabolix."

"But, for crasp sake, we had a deal. My accounts would be cleared …"

The second Chamyx turned around and punched Buddash in the gut with his tail. "You talk way too much, Cranitian. His business is not our concern."

Buddash could feel a few drops of green blood dropping on his lips as he emitted a hacking cough. "Message received and understood."

The second Chamyx motioned with his blaster, "Now get going, Polistine and Cranitian. You both need to recover your strength."

As they walked forward, Buddash and Honeycomb were surprised to discover that the solid rock beneath them had ended, on to be replaced by a primitive canvas walkway. Honeycomb looked down to find that the walkway was propelled by a set of large wheels and gears that moved them forward.

"I demand to know where you are taking us," stated Honeycomb in his sternest tone.

"You shall see soon enough, Polistine. But once you gain the knowledge you seek, you may wish that you had remained ignorant," said the second Chamyx.

The moving walkway carried the three guards, Buddash Kyo and Captain Honeycomb over a deep gorge before depositing them onto a narrow ledge. The five of them walked down a path between two cliffs, where Buddash thought he could see oval-shaped depressions in the rock face. After a few minutes, the ten-foot Cranitian and the Chamyx pressed their blasters into their prisoners' backs. "This is where the two of you get off."

"Just please make it quick," said Buddash.

"No, you shell-head," quipped the Chamyx who pressed a black button that blended in with the rock. A door slid open to reveal a square, white room with two cream-colored benches on either side. "Your accommodations for this evening, Sir Polistine and noble Cranitian. It will take a few hours to siphon enough magnetic energy off the core of the asteroid to get the magna-dome to function properly. And Polistine, I suggest that you do as Multiverse advised and make peace with your maker."

The door slammed down in front of Buddash and Honeycomb like the lid of a coffin.

"We've got to get out of here. I don't like the sound of that Magna-dome thing in the least."

"Well what do you suggest we do?" asked Buddash.

"First, you need to level with me inmate 3360. What business do you have with Diabolix?"

"I can't tell you that. Even thieves, like me and Yanick, need to maintain a sense of honor."

"So, Yanick DcCullen is involved in the plot," said Captain Honeycomb. "You might as well tell me the rest because I am going to find out everything eventually."

"Diabolix will kill me if I spill the turtle eggs. And then he'll grind my bones into meat-dust before sprinkling me into the Southern Sea on Leathershell. And that is if he is in a good mood."

Honeycomb swung around and pressed his foot-and-a-half long stingers against Buddash's neck, "Diabolix is going to have to wait his turn because I am in here with you at the moment. And I promise you that I will drive these stingers into your thick skull if you don't tell me what I want to know. Since I am such an agreeable Insectum, I will give you to the count of five."

"You and your counting to five. Is that how high you learned to count in school," laughed Buddash.

"I am down to four. Now tell me what I want to know before there is a hole in the spot that your head resided."

"I wish I could, but I am sworn to secrecy," Buddash said as he shook his head.

"Three. If I were you I'd start talking before my stinger 'accidently' slipped."

"You know that this kind of torture is forbidden by the Hawking Pact regarding the treatment of prisoners."

"Two. The Hawking Pact only applies to prisoners-of-war, not Reptilia scum like you. Now start talking." Honeycomb moved his stingers into the flesh of Buddash's neck.

"Ouch! I'll tell you whatever you want to know, just make it stop."

"Start talking, Cranitian. And if I think you are holding back any details then I will dispose of you on general principle."

Buddash sat down on the bench as he related the entire narrative about he and Yanick's plan to rob the pharmacy while his cousin distracted Dr. Rabun. His explanation included how they were planning to insert themselves into the mining crew working at junction 42 in The *Citadel*. And finally, Buddash described how he had been coerced into getting a specific item, some kind of experimental toxin, that Diabolix had wished to acquire in exchange for erasing Buddash's debt instead of erasing Buddash himself.

"When is this 'job' supposed to happen?" asked Honeycomb.

"Haven't I've told you enough?"

"You are already in for a credit, in my book. So might as well be in for a gold bar."

"Fine. The job was supposed to take place tomorrow afternoon. But I have a feeling that Lord Diabolix might be moving up the timing to early tomorrow morning."

"We've got to find a way out of here," said Honeycomb. "I have to let Buzz know what Diabolix is planning and I've got to try to stop it."

"I may have an idea, Polistine, about how to get that door open. But you are going to have to trust me," said Buddash.

"I guess I would be able to give you at least the benefit of the doubt," said Honeycomb.

"Okay. Our jailors' first mistake was to leave that little electronic gadget around your leg."

As Honeycomb watched, Buddash removed a spike from his wrist. Almost effortlessly, the Cranitian had sliced through the electronic band

and pulled it off Honeycomb's leg appendage, Buddash then extended one of his fingernails to begin to recalibrate the energy output of the band.

"What are you doing with that thing?" asked Honeycomb.

"I am creating a feedback loop within the band that will hopefully create a strong enough electrical charge to produce a reaction that will short-circuit the lock. Would you happen to have anything sticky handy?"

"I have something. But we are going to have coordinate."

"Just tell me what I have to do."

Honeycomb directed Buddash to take the band over to the pad next to the door and hold it just above the lock. Honeycomb then turned towards Buddash so he was facing him. "Now when I tell you, let go of the band and run for cover."

"I don't know how I feel about that. It sounds kind of dangerous," said Buddash.

"Too late," said Honeycomb. Buddash watched as Honeycomb produced a wad of wax from between his mandible and chucked it at the band, slamming it against the door.

"Now, run!" shouted Buddash who'd managed to dive out of the way just as the band exploded and projected the door outwards. "A little more advanced warning would have been helpful."

"Duly noted for next time. Now just get this other band off my leg."

Buddash removed the other electronic band from Honeycomb's leg. "Now that I am free of my bondage, how were you planning to get out of here?"

"We are going to use that magna-dome device to ride our way out of here."

Buddash and Honeycomb hastily made their way back up the pathway between the two chasms towards the moving walkway. Buddash realized that the hour was late, and that there were probably only a handful of sentries guarding the other prisoners during the late shift. It then occurred to him that he and the Polistine might be Multiverse's only prisoners. Who could tell for sure? What Buddash did know for certain was that it was very suspicious that no one had challenged him or Honeycomb up to this point.

Honeycomb had moved slightly ahead of Buddash while he'd been contemplating the current lack of resistance to their escape plan. He was turning back to motion for Buddash to hurry up when Buddash saw a long dark figure holding a blaster materialize directly behind Honeycomb. Buddash tried desperately to calm himself enough so that he could alert Honeycomb to the danger, but all that he was able to produce were some whimpering sounds.

"Speak up, Cranitian. Use your words and tell me what you are trying to say."

The black figure perched behind Honeycomb wore a smirk as he said, "I think he is trying to encourage you to look behind you."

As Captain Honeycomb swung around, the large Chamyx lifted his massive tail and knocked Honeycomb to the ground. "Knock, Knock." Honeycomb started to rise from the ground, but the black figure pushed forward and head-butted him in the face as he continued to taunt, "Who's there?" Honeycomb spun around on the ground to try to knock the legs out from underneath the black figure, but before he could, the Chamyx put his foot onto his abdomen. At that point, he was probably getting ready to introduce himself, but never got the chance. Buddash had taken this moment of distraction to leap over his body and grab onto his tail. While holding the very tip of the Chamyx's tail, Buddash threaded it into the gears of the walkway like a seamstress threading the eye of a needle.

As he pressed down on Captain Honeycomb's abdomen, he felt a sudden pressure pulling on his tail. Mere moments passed before his massive frame was pulled into the mechanical under-workings of the walkway.

Buddash ran up and grabbed Captain Honeycomb by the arm as he guided him across the now- motionless walkway. "We need to get out of here before any of more of his friends show up."

"Well we already know that the Chamyx "Hot-streak" is working with Multiverse. But where is your slightly larger cousin, I wonder?"

Buddash looked up as he and Captain Honeycomb walked along the path. As Buddash scanned the rock face, he saw that a large stone-looking object had separated from the existing wall and was rolling down the hill.

"You just had to go and ask where my big cousin was, didn't you?"

"Do you think that is him?"

"If it turns out to be the tall-Cranitian then I might have a suggestion."

"And what is that?" asked Honeycomb.

"Let's get out of here!" yelled Buddash.

As the large Cranitian came closer, he could be heard yelling, "Don't run away, little lizard and tiny gnat. My name is Goltish and I wish to play with you."

Before Buddash and Honeycomb could get off the bridge, Goltish had landed straight in their path. "Goltish will teach you a lesson with his pads and feet before he takes your broken bodies back to your cell."

Before they could move out of his path, Goltish brought both fists down on the walkway, an action that sent Buddash and Honeycomb up into the air and crashing back down on the bridge. As Honeycomb noticed that there were a number of cracks that had formed after they had landed.

"Buddash, you remember what happened when you came out of the tunnel?"

"Yeah, I do. You need to spend some more time practicing your power lifting."

"Yes. I do. But do you see how that could help us in this situation?" asked Honeycomb.

"Ah, I do see your point," said Buddash.

Buddash quickly turned around toward the wall, and jumped up to the nearest rock, and began to climb. "Don't even try to catch me, you overgrown hatchling," yelled Buddash.

"Get down here, now!" bellowed Goltish.

"You are just going to have to come catch me," taunted Buddash.

Goltish saw no other alternative but to mount the rocks and begin to try to chase down the smaller Cranitian. However, there was an unsuspected snag in Goltish attempt to retrieve Buddash as Honeycomb suddenly launched himself and started to fly away.

"So long, Inmate 6630. Have fun being the giant Cranitian's plaything for a few days. That is until he accidently squashes you."

"Not so fast, you overgrown Wasp," yelled Buddash. "Are you going to let that Insectum taunted you like that, Goltish."

Goltish reached out to grab the Polistine as he was flying away, but Honeycomb turned around and lifted Goltish into the air. He needed to concentrate with every fiber of his being to lift the massive Cranitian aloft for a few precious seconds before dropping him directly onto the center of the moving walkway, causing the entire structure to go crashing down to the cavern floor.

After lifting something so heavy, Honeycomb found that he was having difficulty staying up in the air. He tried desperately to flap his wings in order to make a safe landing. Despite this effort, he suddenly realized that he had spent all his energy and would be following Goltish down to the bottom of the gorge. Just as he started to fall, though, he glanced up to find that Buddash had swung down to catch him on a rubber pulley that had been liberated from the newly-broken moving walkway.

"The only reason I caught you is because the sight of bug intestines turns my stomach," Buddash said

"Your concern is touching. Now let's just get to this magna-dome so we can get out of here."

"I could not agree more."

Back at the shuttle-complex, Multiverse's thoughts were immersed in determining the correct calculations for the activation of the magna-dome when he was interrupted by the sound of a massive crash. He ran out of the shuttle enclosure and up the path to see that the walkway he had spent countless hours in constructing, was now dipping down into the gorge in tatters.

"Diabolix can serve my head on a platter for all I care for my disobedience. But Buddash and Honeycomb's demise is an occurrence that is now pre-ordained, as far as I am concerned."

Multiverse smiled to himself as he realized that Honeycomb was not aware that he had detected the Polistine sneaking up behind him, "I see that you are a very punctual Insectum, captain. Even for your own funeral."

Honeycomb aimed and fired the energy blaster as Multiverse swung back towards him. As the blaster shots flew towards Multiverse, currently in the form of the nine-foot-tall Quillian, he changed his appearance within seconds to a Hawking Brain Beetle. In this form, Multiverse absorbed the laser blasts into his newly acquired tentacles before blasting his own electrical charge back at Captain Honeycomb who managed to jump clear of the shot, just in time.

Multiverse turned back around towards Honeycomb with the intention of firing another electrical bolt, only to find that Buddash was perched on a nearby wall, waiting to jump down on him. The Clonstellar decided to change into a mobile form in order to deal with two opponents. Buddash looked up to see that Multiverse had changed into a Black Chamyx. Multiverse turned and knocked Buddash down to the ground with his tail before disappearing.

"That is just perfect. Now how do we find him?" asked Buddash.

"I am a Clonstellar who keeps his promises, Mr. Buddash, and I swore to you that I would kill you as soon as I got the chance," said Multiverse soberly. Without warning, Buddash went flying across the room, slamming against the rock wall. He barely had time to turn himself over and move out of the way when the Chamyx-Multiverse came slamming down on top of him. Once he landed on top of Buddash, he turned around to stomp on him again, an action that he came to regret as Buddash reached up with his padded feet and arms to push the Chamyx-Multiverse crashing to the ground.

"Find something heavy to hold him down," yelled Captain Honeycomb.

Buddash jumped over to where Multiverse was still recovering from his crash landing. Just for good measure, Buddash kicked Multiverse again before looking around for something to keep him down. But apparently it was already too late because just as Buddash knocked a boulder off its mooring and picked it up with the intention of slamming it down on Multiverse, he'd managed to change from a large Chamyx to a tiny lizard and just slipped out.

Captain Honeycomb refused to let this Multiverse creature escape from his custody. He looked around the immediate area to find that there was a discarded glass tube that had probably recently been replaced in some piece of machinery. Honeycomb quickly removed the plastic bottom from the tube and plopped it on top of the tiny Lizard-Multiverse.

"Come on, Buddash. I doubt we have a lot of time," said Captain Honeycomb as he deposited the glass tube with Multiverse into an open panel that Honeycomb proceeded to seal shut with a nearby blow-torch.

Buddash looked at the settings for the magna-dome before declaring, "yep, I recalibrated a device similar to this one on Mundilfarius. Different function, but similar principle. Looks like Multiverse was ready to use leadronum sheets to create a mechanical worm with magnetic capabilities."

"How does that help us, though?"

"I can rearrange the elongated structure of the worm to a more spherical, dare I say snail-like configuration," said Buddash as his pads danced across the keyboard. "And our chariot awaits, as they used to say in the ancient Pangean expression.

Almost simultaneously, the large pieces of leadronum congealed together to form a large sphere inside the magna-dome that would provide Buddash and Honeycomb with a means of escape while at the same time there was a gigantic explosion in the shuttle as a large flying Reptilia with massive wings and an extended beak came flying out of the shuttle.

"Time to get going, I think," said Buddash as the two of them made it inside the sphere moments before the flying Reptilia, which was a long-extinct creature known as an Archeoptrexis, landed on the leadronum sphere.

As Buddash activated a number of switches, he reassured Honeycomb, "They haven't constructed a ship yet that I am not able to fly."

"Whatever you are going to do, I am pretty sure you need to do it quick."

"Calm down," said Buddash said as he casually turned over a few of the leadronum plates on the front of the sphere. "There you go. I reversed the polarity of the ship. Now just hold onto your wingtips."

Just as the Archeoptrexis pushed its beak through the sphere, the object went flying forward into the long tunnel that Buddash and Honeycomb had exited a few hours before, knocking the Archeoptrexis- Multiverse down to the ground of the cavern.

Within the confines of the Holo-environment, Hotfire awoke with a start to find the Psychic Spider on the edge of the metal plank that was currently serving as his bed. An unsettling feeling washed over him at that moment as he wondered how long the Psychic Spider had been watching him sleep. What thoughts had been going through the spider's mind as he was sitting there watching him sleep? Was he deciding whether or not to place one of his extended appendages down Hotfire's throat and choke him as he slept?

The ten-limbed brown Psychic Spider glanced over to the eleven-foot-long black Chamyx. "It just amazes me how quickly we forget. Or more specifically, how quickly your mind has forgotten that none of this is real. It is merely a fantasy."

Hotfire reached out and grabbed the Psychic Spider by one of its upper arms. "I know that I am not on Scaratutulo. I am imprisoned in the Minerva Penitentiary in one of Sobek's laboratory."

"And given the fact that you are most likely being sent off to your death in a parallel dimension, what are you sitting here worrying about?" asked the Psychic Spider.

"I don't know. Why don't you tell me what I am thinking?" spat Hotfire.

"You are worried about whether or not I am going to try to kill you in your sleep."

"That is a legitimate concern that shouldn't be taken at all lightly," stated Hotfire.

"Look! First of all, I am not really here in any physical form. This image is just a mental representation of how you see me."

"And what is your second point?"

The Psychic Spider smirked. "I was killing you yesterday. In fact, I am still killing you today. And, I will keep on killing you until you've experienced the most horrible painful death imaginable."

"So, how the fuctur do I stop you from killing me?" yelled Hotfire.

"I don't have that answer," replied the Psychic Spider, "All I can you is that you already know had to kill Diabolix because you have seen it before. But, here is an interesting fact The same method that you'll need to use to defeat Diabolix is probably the one chance you have to save your own sorry life."

"Can you explain to me what exactly you are saying? And could you possibly make sense while you are doing it this time," implored Hotfire.

"There is no more time. There are chemicals being introduced into your brain. If I am not mistaken, the purpose of the chemicals is to discontinue your brain's operation from the holo-environment's Querzi computer."

"What does that even mean?" asked Hotfire.

"Someone is trying to wake you up," said the Psychic Spider, before he vanished into thin air.

After his companion disappeared, the brick and stone jail cell as well as the constable's office on Scaratutulo vanished into the ether. Hotfire found himself strapped to a silver metal table in a sanitized room within *the Citadel*.

"Good morning, Hotfire," said Warden Sobek. "Your time has come to make a worthy contribution to the Venusian galaxy."

Hotfire peered behind Warden Sobek's massive shell to the two soldiers flanking him. Much like the soldiers that had attacked him on the Tram, these creatures wore green jumpsuits and helmets with multi-colored frills; three horns protruding through their head gear and were carrying blasters.

"You brought a little muscle with you. Doesn't matter, though, because I still am going to kill you."

"Yes. I know that you'll try," said Warden Sobek.

"Let me just take a moment to spell it out for you. I am going to make my way back from the hole that you are going to drop me down," sneered Hotfire.

"I doubt that you will survive the trip back because you will probably meet your own demise as you are eliminating Diabolix," said Warden Sobek.

"Why do you Hawking want Diabolix out of the way, so badly?" asked Hotfire.

"The reason is that the last time the Hawking faced Diabolix, we barely able defeated him. And, that defeat required the combined forces of the Xeperian, Polistine, and ourselves. The final battle, which occurred with the Ganmillcian nebula, lasted six days. The only reason that the forces of light were able to prevail was a bit of blind luck."

"Which was what exactly?"

"The Polistine detonated an atomic device that created a breach in normal space, opening a temporary rift into X-Space. Diabolix's main ship, the *Dolgthrasir*, was rammed by a Quartrack Destroyer, the *Pollencollect*, and knocked into this rift. And once both vessels were inside the rift —"

"Yes, I can figure the rest out, Sobek. The captain of the Destroyer probably activated the self-destruct," said Hotfire.

"No, but you are close. He overloaded an experimental engine that had the effect of closing the rift."

"So," said Hotfire. "Diabolix is trapped in another dimension and cannot hurt anybody. Therefore, if you follow that logic, then I should be free to go on my way," said Hotfire.

"Ah, there is the rub, so sayeth the ancient Pangean Bard," said Sobek. "Diabolix has a number of Lieutenants acting in his name on this side of the dimensional barrier, including two particular dangerous Clonstellars named Second Skin and Multiverse. Actually, they are employing two old associates of yours; Yanick DcCullen and Buddash Kyo. The Clonstellars are having DcCullen and Kyoto steal the Diabolix toxin before it can ever be used."

"I have a number of scores that I wouldn't mind settling with DcCullen and Kyo."

Sobek smirked, "Trust me when I tell you that they will both be taken care of very shortly."

"Do these two Clonstellars have a plan for getting Diabolix out of X-Space?" asked Hotfire.

"A Hawking Brain Beetle ship carrying a Methurazus Rejuvenate was hijacked by a group of Diabolix's forces approximately six months ago. It was only recovered very recently at the cost of many Xeperian lives. In process of recovering the Methurazus Device, it was discovered that another Clonstellar was sent on a one-way mission to X-Space to send a message to Diabolix. The message was that Multiverse and Second Skin were trying to use the Methurazus device to transport their Lord back to normal space. That is where you come in, Hotfire. You are going to enter X-Space to kill Diabolix before the Clonstellars have the chance to recover him."

"So, your plan for killing Diabolix is to stick me into one of those Methurazus Chambers?" asked Hotfire. In that moment, Warden Sobek could detect that there was a definite shift in Hotfire's demeanor. Up to that point, the conversation between them had been a mostly civil affair. But upon the mentioning of the Methurazus device, Hotfire slid into a more defensive posture.

"There is no way that I am ever getting into one of those things again. The last time I did, I literally came out as half a Chamyx."

"And our best Hawking Brain Beetle scientists used their considerable scientific knowledge to repair you to health. So therefore, you owe the Hawking Brain Beetle your life."

Hotfire positioned his tail towards the Triceratopian as they moved closer. It was only then that, he recalled that the Psychic Spider was currently inhibiting his fire power. Hotfire could only hope that he still possessed the ability to cloak.

Warden Sobek moved towards him as he lay strapped to the table, "It will make it so much easier on all of us if you chose not to resist."

"I regret to inform you that I won't be coming quietly. Not in this lifetime," said Hotfire as he vanished from the table. Sobek and the two Triceratopian watched as two chairs and a console were knocked over and an invisible Hotfire knocked diodes and controls off the wall as he scaled the dome.

One of the newly activated Triceratopian, Epsilon, asked, "Master Sobek, do you wish us to retrieve him?"

"That won't be necessary. Hotfire is still carrying the Psychic Spider. Therefore, I will merely need to have my creature increase the stimulation of the pain receptors within his brain."

Sobek watched Hotfire as he rematerialized and fell to the floor uttering a gut-wrenching wail. "Restrain that piece of Reptilia filth and bring it to the medical dispensary," he said to the Triceratopian.

"Sobek, if you are so opposed to Diabolix coming back and rebuilding an army, what are you doing growing these test-tube Reptilia?" asked the still-suffering Hotfire.

Epsilon Trike turned around and punched the Black Chamyx squarely in the chest, but Sobek replied, "Diabolix is far from mistaken that the galaxy is in chaos. Therefore, once again, the Hawking Brain Beetle must show the lower races the way."

Sobek dismissively waved a tentacle, "Take him out of my sight." With a barely audible sigh, Sobek thought to himself, "Such a busy morning. Just so many little details to take care of just for a plan to come together."

Chapter 16
KASIDY VULKNER

Onboard the *Mjölnir*, a nine-foot wasp-like Polistine named Thorn, a six-foot pink bi-pedal Ruddarian with copper and silver hair named Kon, and crew members Lieutenant Lokhra and Ensign Rajkvek, were hovering nervously over a female Ruddarian laying on the floor: Kasidy Vulkner. Dr. Tulare had been summoned to the Cargo Bay. When he arrived, Kon provided him with a synopsis of recent events. Kasidy had slipped into a coma after remotely connecting an alien device, the Eye of Hermes, to the ship's engine. Secretly, Thorn and Kon could not help also being concerned with the activity of the star currently in the last gasps of its stellar life that lay directly outside the *Mjölnir*. Despite Zeta Sephi Three being an ample source of energy, the Eye of Hermes had made no effort to drain the star of its' power. And no one was aware that despite being in what appeared to be a comatose state, Kasidy was actually experiencing what could only be called a state of waking R.E.M. sleep that included dreaming.

She could see a vision of future events, or a possible future. She saw Lieutenant Thorn, holding an appendage to his chest as blood emptied out of his body. For some reason, Kasidy was able to detect that the *Mjölnir* was hurtling out of control towards the exploding star. She then watched Thorn flying toward the Green Diamond. After appearing to be lifeless, Thorn sat up with a vacant expression on his face. Leaning against the Green Diamond, Thorn announced in a strange tone that he'd awaken from a long slumber. In her dream, Kasidy begged Thorn to clarify what he meant by this statement, but he only stated that his title was now, Thorn of Hermes, and he served the Eye. reveal more of Thorn's future. She had the most awful feeling that whatever happened to Thorn would have an impact on the well-being of her people, as well as the Polistine, the Beetleguise, the Xeperian and the Reptilia races.

The image of Thorn disappeared before she could make any more inquiries. Kasidy, next, found herself in a prison cell on Rogestran Five on the night when the Ministry of Justice had come for her and her mother.

For two and a half months, Kasidy and her mother had been detained in a prison camp located on a self-contained holding facility on board a hovering saucer on Rogestran Five's south plasma sea. According to the Polistine colonial charter, even enemies of the state — which now included Kasidy and her mother, Zanesta — were entitled to legal representation. Though they were blindfolded and gagged during their entire stay, they were informed by Commissioner Neptunian Bokhun, a member of the same race as the criminal Atlas who had killed her father, that an extremely competent legal representative had been assigned to handle their case. However, this specialist turned out to be less highly qualified than advertised and Kasidy and Zanesta were soon exiled to the penal vulcanic moon of Bengkulu where they were expected to begin a new life.

Kasidy had become solid, hardened among the rocky cliffs, vulcanic pools and bottomless craters of the unstable and angry moon of Bengkulu. In order to deal with the harsh terrain, she'd been required to become an expert on maintaining the life-support equipment in their small cottage in the mountains of Dreki Buror. Thus an astral engineer was born at the tender age of fifteen. Word of Kasidy's skill spread quickly among the residents of Bengkulu. She became a local legend among the Ruddarian prisoners, who stated that there was no generator or another machine that Kasidy could not mend. But her new-found fame gave her little solace. Kasidy lived every day with the knowledge that she was indirectly responsible for her father's death. But, as she would probably meet her own demise on this rock, she would have to wait until after death to be reunited.

There were indeed few things that brought Kasidy solace in her own little corner of the After burn. Surprisingly, one of the few happy times was when she watched the twin moons of Papyesis and Galilei rise in the sky at nightfall. Kasidy would set the stage in her vast imagination: the twin orbs were two magnificent Insectum racing each other across the orange horizon. The spewing vulcano below played the part of a fierce and angry Quillian, producing a constant stream of fire. Every night, Kasidy imagined, one of the moons would be able to fly fast enough to escape the vengeful Quillian. While the other orb was consumed by fire and dragged beneath the veil of everyday life to the After burn, the faster moon flew among the stars.

The other light in her life had been Graf. Kasidy had met him shortly after she and her mother had come to Bengkulu. To Kasidy, Graf was the most amazing person to ever grace the moon of Papyesis. Graf's father had supported his family by working as a navigator on a merchant freighter that shipped Ruddarian-made goods to various home worlds, such as Insectvore, Madagascan, and Meditaplassen. Their family — Graf, his mother, his father and his brother, Frein — led a quiet existence until late one night when two Xeperian Gladiators came knocking on their door. Graf's mother was informed that her husband had been killed during an attack by two Beetleguise battle fighters, and had been accused of abandoning his post during the attack. The Hawking Brain Beetle governor of Papyesis, Shesmus Bokhun, had decided that Graf's family would pay the penalty for his father's act of betrayal. They were detained for several months in a containment facility similar to the one Kasidy and Zanesta had been held in before being shipped to Bengkulu. The containment facility on Papyesis was on a giant boulder the size of a small nation-state and was supported in the upper atmosphere by propulsion engines located strategically around the boulder.

Graf had spent the majority of his stay at the Papyesis facility with a blindfold over his eyes, in a small ten-by-twelve-foot cell. He and Frein had no contact with their mother, so they had no idea whether she was alive or dead. They only learned her fate when they had been herded into a waiting transport to take them to Bengkulu some four months after their detention had begun. The boys were still blindfolded but recognized their mother's cries of joy when she heard her young sons' voices. That had been three years ago.

Kasidy and Graf had both worked in the mines of Bengkulu located inside the mountains of Dreki Buror. There was little opportunity for socializing while they were extracting precious minerals, common elements like leadronum and platinum and crystals that could be infused with Enhanced Energy Gas to provide energy to star crafts. Even though they rarely talked, they had a connection; they could see it in each other's eyes. They knew that they were meant to be together but had little chance of realizing that dream as long as they were prisoners under the oppressive guardianship of Neptunian Bokhun. Kasidy was convinced that she might never have the opportunity to develop a real bond with her soulmate, Graf. But destiny was not to be denied.

This turn of fate occurred after a particularly grueling eight-hour shift in the mines. Zanesta and her daughter's pink faces had almost turned black with soot, dirt and debris. Every time that Kasidy took a step, every joint in her body ached. She was not even sure that she would be able to make it back to their modest cottage, but she refused to allow this place to get the best of her.

While Kasidy was mentally pushing herself on, she heard a loud thud next to her, like someone had dropped a bag full of dirt taters. She looked on the ground to see that her mother, Zanesta, had collapsed.

"Mother!" screamed Kasidy.

"I must have over exerted myself a little during this shift," said Zanesta as she started to climb back to her feet, only to collapse once again.

"Mother, you are not well. The Warden needs to give you a hardship pardon so you can finish out your sentence in a medical facility."

"I refuse to leave my only daughter," Zanesta said as she reached up to place her bound hands around Kasidy's face.

"Get yourself from the floor, pink monkey, and get moving. We have orders that you prisoners need to be locked back in your cottages before dark," said a Xeperian guard named Asizit. She could only watch helplessly as the Xeperian extended his energy whip and slapped Zanesta in the back to encourage her to get moving.

"Leave her alone, you Scarab!" yelled Kasidy.

"Maybe she'd be better off if I just left her to rot in this cave. Bet some interesting minerals come out of her pink body," sneered Asizit.

"You have to help her get back. Your Polistine overlords would be displeased if you lost a prisoner," said Kasidy.

The Xeperian rose up in the air on his wings and began to whip Zanesta repeatedly. "The Polistine know that accidents happen in the mines. If I come back with one less, they will not make a fuss." The whipping grew more intense with every slice of the energy whip.

"Get away from her!" Kasidy rushed towards Asizit. As he was getting ready to bring his whip down on Zanesta's back, Kasidy smacked him against the cavern wall. Asizit managed to recover quickly and moved toward Kasidy, with the intent of snapping her neck.

Kasidy had braced herself. But she found herself being spared as Graf charged towards Asizit with a large rock in his bound hands. He slammed the purple gem repeatedly into the black dome-shaped protrusion that was the Xeperian's head, sending yellow blood streaming down his abdomen.

"Thank you for saving our lives," said Kasidy as she recovered her senses.

"I am sure that you would have done the same for me," said Graf. "We really should move deeper into the tunnels. It won't be too long before they realize that the Xeperian guard is overdue."

Graf turned to the rest of the prisoners, "An opportunity has presented itself. Whether you take advantage of it is up to each of you. I'd suggest that you, at least, try to seek a better life outside the compound."

"What if we choose to wait here for that Xeperian's replacement to come and collect us?" shouted a middle-aged Ruddarian.

"Then I would move as close to the mine entrance as possible," stated Graf as he grabbed Asizit's blaster who was already producing Xeperian hatchlings, "because there is about to be a cave-in."

Kasidy ran up behind Graf and grabbed a hold of the blaster before he was able to discharge the weapon. "Please. Just let me go with my mother. She is not in good health and I need to take care of her."

"Are you out of your mind?" asked Graf. "Warden Neptunian will have you executed once he learns that we have attacked and killed one of his soldiers."

"I can't leave my mother alone. I am all she has left in this galaxy," said Kasidy.

Zanesta slowly rose to her feet and quietly came over to her daughter. She took Kasidy's face in her hands once again. "All that I truly care about in this galaxy is that you are protected and you are safe. My days are nearly at an end. My only wish is to have the knowledge that you will be protected. Go with him, now. I will be all right."

"Mother, I refuse to abandon you and swear to you that I will find a way to get off this Hive-forsaken planet. Once I do then I will come back for you. You have my word that you'll breath the sweet air of freedom before your days are done." Kasidy hugged her mother tightly in a firm embrace until Graf moved behind her and pulled her away. As Graf held her, he used the energy whip to repeatedly strike the ceiling of the mine until rocks were knocked loose and came raining down, creating a solid wall of debris and burying the corpse of the spiteful Xeperian, and his offspring, beneath a makeshift stone grave.

"We have got to get moving. It is not going to be long before Neptunian realizes we are overdue. And I am sure at least one of our fellow prisoners will be informing him about our crime."

"How do I know that you won't turn me over to Warden Neptunian?" asked Kasidy.

"That is a possibility. Maybe you should listen to what your gut is telling you," said Graf.

"I suppose it would not hurt me to trust you for now," said Kasidy.

"Then let's get going."

As Graf took her hand, Kasidy felt a tingle move up her arm. How many times had she deliberately brushed up against him in the mines just to feel the sensation of his touch? And now here she was holding Graf's hand, yet she was unable to savor the experience.

Graf guided Kasidy down the corridor leading to the heart of the Kavadon mine. She realized they were headed deeper underground, and hesitated. She did not have many choices expect to place her life in this young man's hands. Despite her willingness to trust Graf, she felt as if they had been running blindly for hours. And just when Kasidy reached the point when she had convinced herself that she could not take another step, the pair came to a turn in the path that led down to a steep slope.

"We need to make our way down to the bottom of the ravine just over that next hill," Graf said as he pointed his finger forward. "There should be an escape route towards the floor of the canyon."

"Are you positive that there is a way out down there?" asked Kasidy in a skeptical tone.

"There have been stories among the older residents that have been retold for decades about an abandoned gas mine near the heart of the Dreki Buror mountains that leads to the western lava pools," said Graf.

"So, we are relying on popular folklore that has been passed down over the decades by Ruddarian prisoners who were probably drinking fermented heart fruit around a campfire?" asked Kasidy.

"Pretty much. There have been prisoners who have gone missing over the years in the mines with no explanation."

"Yes, it is called "being executed," said Kasidy.

"Look, if you had managed to keep your cool back there, we wouldn't be in this mess."

"Oh, yeah. I should have just let that Xeperian whip my mother to death."

"The bottom line is that right now I am your best chance of making it out of this situation alive."

"Funny. I don't remember asking for your help. I'm a pretty decent fighter in my own right, so fortunately I don't need someone to fight my battles," said Kasidy as she walked farther down the path.

"I am shocked that someone hasn't tried to kill you before today."

"Oh, don't fool yourself. There have been attempts."

Graf looked up to see three Xeperian guards turning the corner as Kasidy was walking down the path. "Kasidy, get back here, now!"

Just as she was getting ready to inform Graf that she wasn't going to have a boy tell her what to do, one of the Xeperian soldiers sent a shot of blue lightening from his whip that barely missed her head

"Halt and drop your weapons, Ruddarians. You are not authorized to be down here."

"Guess you are going to show me your fighting skills after all," said Graf.

"You take the leader; I will take his two underlings," smiled Kasidy.

Before Graf could object, Kasidy had already started running towards the Xeperian that were moving towards her. Just before she reached them, she dropped to the floor of the corridor and went sliding into them, knocking both to the ground. Before they could react, Kasidy jumped to her feet and pushed her foot into one of the Xeperian's chest, knocking him backward. As the other Xeperian tried to sneak up on her, she moved her fist backwards and punched him in the head, slamming to the floor.

"She is merely a hominoid girl you, fools!" yelled the leader. "Are you telling me that you cannot contain her."

The Xeperian that had been kicked in the chest recovered his senses as he pulled out his energy whip and flung it towards Kasidy, who saw the energy beam coming at her head. She flung her hands up in the air just as the beam came towards her, and sliced through her iron bands. She reached forward and grabbed the energy whip from the first Xeperian, and wrapped it around his neck. Before Graf could stop her, Kasidy had pulled off the Xeperian's head and juvenile had begun to emerge from its' corpse.

"Kasidy, we really need to run!" yelled Graf.

They headed down the path as dozens of Xeperian children, who had emerged after the adult Xeperian had been decapitated by Kasidy. She yelled back to Graf, "Why didn't that first guard that we killed lay those little monsters?"

"Because I buried it with the avalanche before any of those junior Xeperian could emerge."

"Right. But what are we supposed to do now?"

"We keep running until we think of something," yelled Graf, who then veered off the path when he saw a large stone pillar in the path. He climbed up the pillar and waited until one of the adult Xeperian came running past him. Just as the Xeperian moved within range, Graf produced his energy whip and slung it towards him, vaporizing his legs. As the Xeperian lay on the ground, screaming in pain, Graf jumped down and stomped on the large bug's chest.

"That is how you deal with a Xeperian. Always maimed. Never killed," said Graf.

"That little maneuver just gave me a bright idea. Let me hold that energy whip," said Kasidy.

"What are you going to do with it?"

"Just leaving a surprise for our Xeperian friends," smiled Kasidy.

Kasidy picked up her pace as she rounded the corner. When Graf caught up, he found her arranging the whip between two rocks and lining it up so it faced the wall. She placed the whip low enough so it would be at the level of a child. Kasidy motioned for Graf to place his whip on a rock that was directly opposite her own.

"What are you planning to do?' asked Graf.

"I have a plan for stopping those Xeperian babies, but it is going to require us to work together."

Kasidy and Graf hunched down behind their respective boulders on either side of the path. They did not have to wait for very long. The stampede of junior Xeperian came charging around the corner, and as they moved up the path between the two opposing boulders, Kasidy yelled to Graf, "Turn it on now."

They both watched as their whips connected and created a field of blue energy that encompassed the entire group of junior Xeperian. Kasidy watched as the bugs went into shock from being electrocuted, causing some of them to be killed. However, the offspring from the killed Xeperian were also electrocuted before they could make it out of the field. After five minutes or so, the entire horde of Xeperian lay dead in a pile on the cavern floor.

"What happened to that third adult Xeperian?" asked Kasidy.

"Doesn't matter right now," said Graf, as he led Kasidy up a steep slope to a large ravine inside a cavern that could have fit at least three or four Polistine battle cruisers.

"How are we supposed to get down to the bottom of the canyon?" Kasidy regretted asking as soon as the words came out of her mouth.

Graf simply smiled as he walked over to a large basket. "The Xeperian have a pulley system for transporting minerals and ore down to their ships. We are going to ride the baskets down; We can pretend we are Apollosian Bokhun and Dadertho Bokhun."

"Which one of those thought that he could race across the sky faster than the setting of the moon of Juneter? asked Kasidy.

"The merchant, Dadertho Bokhun, had such an intense rivalry with his cousin, Apollosian, that he was constantly bragging about his superior skills as a trade and a merchant. After many years of listening to these boasts by Dadertho, Apollosian challenged his cousin to race to see whose cargo ships was the fastest. It was agreed that the first merchant to arrive on the Juneter with the most merchandise aboard their ship would be declared the winner. His cousin, Apollosian, expressed to Dadertho that he understood his desire to win, but that they both should avoid the cosmic tides between Meditaplassen and the moon Juneter because it was nearly impossible to navigate their ships within the turbulent waves. Dadertho initially avoided the cosmic tides. But as Dadertho got closer to the tides, his desire to beat his cousin grew too overwhelming and he navigated his merchant craft into the cosmic tides. Despite his skill as a navigator, the cosmic waves ultimately tore his ship apart, sending it to the four corners of the galaxy. In the end, Apollosian could only watch helplessly as his cousin's ship was torn apart." related Graf.

"That was an excellent retelling of the myth, young Ruddarian," said a voice from behind Graf and Kasidy.

Kasidy turned to see the lead Xeperian that they had met on the path holding an energy blaster directly facing them. Swarming around the adult Xeperian's legs were a few hundred juveniles, "Now if you will kindly come with me, I will be able to expedite your execution for crimes against the state."

And as young Kasidy Vulkner glanced around for a possible solution, adult Kasidy Vulkner, the Astral Engineer on board the *Mjölnir*, heard a voice inside her head.

"Face the facts, Kasidy Vulkner. You were meant to perish long ago on that vulcanic moon. You have just been living on borrowed time." The voice was not hers.

"I have always been, and will always be a survivor," said Kasidy.

"We shall see about that," said the voice.

Back within the vision of her younger self, Kasidy watched as Graf put himself in harm's way to save both of their lives. Graf turned around and punched the lead Xeperian directly in the chest. He then crouched down to retrieve the laser whip as he lassoed the laser beam around a nearby stalactite.

"Over here, kids," yelled Graf. "You better come and grab me before I get away."

As he lowered himself over the side of the ledge, Graf could hear the patter of junior Xeperian making their way towards the cliff. Graf swung himself to the far edge and grabbed a piece of sharp obsidian from its resting place on a ledge. When the first junior Xeperian peered over the ledge, Graf swung back over and stabbed him in the chest, making sure not to cause a mortal wound. Graf then pulled the Xeperian off the jagged stone and threw it back onto the outcropping of the cliff. He repeated this process several times, before realizing that Kasidy was not following him down.

"Kasidy, where are you? You've got to get to the pulley system and slid down in the basket."

It was not Kasidy who replied, "I am afraid that your friend, Kasidy, is indisposed right now."

Graf climbed back up to see the Xeperian with this claw around her neck, "You will either surrender peacefully or I will snap her neck," said the Lead Xeperian.

"No need for violence. I will come with you quietly," said Graf as he walked towards the Xeperian. The last thing he remembered was being butted on the head with the handle of an energy whip.

Kasidy Vulkner was violently yanked from her dream state. She awoke on the floor of the Cargo Bay of the *Mjölnir* to discover a face with two enormous multi-lensed eyes staring back down at her. The eyes were alight with a green glow, much like in her premonition. She used her legs and posterior to move as quickly as possible away from Weapons Officer Thorn.

Dr. Tulare, observing Kasidy's disorientation, raced over and grabbed Kasidy with both arms, pulling her up to eye-level.

"What is going on?" asked Dr. Tulare.

With a wild, frantic look in her eyes, Kasidy spoke incoherently, "His eyes. Thorn's eyes. They were glowing, like the Green Diamond."

"My dear, Thorn very well may have saved your life. He was able to adapt my Neuro-reviver to access your deeper cerebellum, the part of your brain responsible for memory and R.E.M. sleep, to bring you back to a waking state. It was quite amazing."

"Doctor, I saw his eyes. They were glowing green like the diamond. It has a hold of Thorn's mind," said Kasidy.

"A Polistine would rather die than allow an alien force to possess his mind," said Thorn. "I still stand with your Ruddarian crew until this crisis has passed."

"Yeah," said Defensive Officer Kon said as he moved forward. "There is that little issue of the exploding star that is about to blow us all to the Afterburn."

"I don't understand," said Kasidy. "The Eye of Hermes should have been attracted to the more plentiful source of energy, namely the star, and disengage from our operating systems."

"Apparently, the Eye of Hermes believes in finishing what it has started," said Kon.

At that moment, both Kon's and Astral Kasidy's comm began broadcasting the voice of Captain Odinord. Kasidy quickly tapped her comm badge off and allowed Kon to intercept the message.

"Senior crew members Lokhra, Vulkner, and Kon, and Dr. Tulare, as well as our Polistine guest, report to the flight deck immediately. We have just lost barriers, propulsion and stabilization. Ensign Rajkvek, you keep an eye on the Green Diamond."

"We will be right there, Sir," replied Kon. "All five of us."

"And there is one more thing," stated Captain Odinord.

"What is that, captain?" asked Kasidy.

You all may want to switch on individual gravity units on your flight suits because I have a feeling that the artificial gravity is about to go next," said Captain Odinord.

Just as the words came out of Captain Odinord's mouth, the five Ruddarian crew and one Polistine watched as the Eye of Hermes shot out another tendril of green energy, up through the ceiling of the Cargo Bay. Before any of the crew could react, the *Mjölnir* tilted and the six occupants were sent sliding along the floor towards a set of large storage crates, knocking the containers to the ground."

"We have a problem, people," said Captain Odinord. "The star's gravity apparently just grabbed a hold of us."

Kasidy happened to glance at a nearby viewer screen at the enormous red, exploding star.

"And the star is pulling us in for the kill," she said.

Chapter 17
THE PLEASURIST HUNASH

The Cranitian Pleasurist, Hunash, had made a promise to her cousin, Buddash Kyo, that she would assist him in stealing pharmaceuticals and other assorted drugs from the Minerva Penitentiary's medical dispensary. This was a promise that, unfortunately, she now was unable to keep.

Hunash found herself aboard the *Charon* escape pod from the Zanuck Corporation shuttle. There were no weapons systems aboard and no protective barrier systems. The pod did possess a navigational system that was comparable to a small freighter, as well as a barely functioning communication system. Fortunately for Hunash, she had a wristband communicator that she carried for emergencies; she clicked on the wrist communicator that beeped for a second or two before the screen activated. On the tiny video screen, Hunash saw the oval-shaped, cheddar face of her client, Dr. Rabun, a fellow Cranitian. She quickly centered herself so Rabun would be unable to detect how stressful the events of the last few hours had been. Her large, reflective saucer eyes were the textbook image of calm and collected.

"My dear sweet Doctor, I am afraid that I will need to disappoint you, my love. I have had an emergency that has arisen and will not be able to come visit you tonight on Minerva Penitentiary," she said in her sweetish voice.

"Is everything alright, my lily flower?" Rabun inquired of Hunash.

"There has been a problem with the Zanuck corporation shuttle. It has been diverted."

"I am sorry to hear that. I am sure that we can make up for our missed time in a week or so," said Rabun.

That is my dear, sweet Rabun, Hunash thought, always putting his carnal desires, first.

"Doctor, can you do me one huge favor? I was supposed to drop an item off to one of the inmates, Buddash Kyo." The last thing that Rabun needed to know was that she had a relative who was a convict, Hunash thought to herself. She'd probably lose the great majority of her clients if this association came to light. "Can you let him know that I will be delayed for a few days?"

Instead of a response though, Hunash heard some type of chaotic disruption, with Rabun telling someone that he would sacrifice his life rather than give them the toxin. Had Yanick and Buddash decided to go ahead with the robbery without her? After a minute, her wrist communicator went blank.

As Hunash sat contemplating how she was going to make it out of her current situation, her wrist communicator began to hum with static once again. Maybe it was Rabun calling back to reassure her that he was alright. But, the message was only voices without pictures; apparently Hunash was picking up a nearby communication.

"Code Repose, Delta, Prime, can you read me?" said Zappo-Second Skin.

"Code Solace, Gamma, Beta, I can read you. This channel is secure." said the Clonstellar, Multiverse.

"Is the plan moving forward successfully to assist Lord Diabolix?" asked Second Skin.

"There has been a delay. The Cranitian Buddash has escaped from our custody. We may need to find an alternative means for obtaining the toxin."

Unable to control her emotions, Hunash let out an audible gasp regarding her cousin's situation.

"Second Skin, I thought you said that this channel was secure? Who was that?" asked Multiverse.

"I believe that I know exactly which Pleasurist is listening in. Hello again, Hunash. You should have made your way to the wastelands or some other remote spot. Instead I will have to deal with you." said Second Skin.

"Just make sure that you reclaim the item and bring it to the appointed spot," said Multiverse.

"Shut up, Multiverse, you fool. There is nothing that will prevent the return of our Lord," said Second Skin.

"His return will be truly glorious. End of communication."

There was a long unsettling silence. From her unfortunate encounter with this Clonstellar creature, Second Skin, silence in battle did not seem to be his preferred way of operating.

"Aren't you coming after me then, or have you decided to leave me alone?" asked Hunash.

"Oh, you are definitely to be dealt with, my dear Hunash," said Second Skin, who still had the appearance of Commander Zappo. He brought the *Charon* back around to face Hunash's escape pod.

"Here I come for you, my poor, sweet Cranitian Horash," smiled Zappo-Second Skin.

He increased the speed of the *Charon* to its highest level — a sub-space factor of five — as he aimed the ship directly at the escape pod. Hunash was barely able to roll the escape pod on its axis to move out of the way of the shuttle before it came barreling past.

"Just stay right where you are, dear Hunash. I will be back with you in a moment. Just as soon as I turn around," said the Clonstellar. Even as fast as Zappo-Second Skin was able to turn *the Charon* around for another pass, it was just as quickly as the ship's Captain, Hooms, was able to use his wings to race up to the ship's cockpit.

"Zappo, are you drunk on fermented pit fruit or something?" asked Captain Hooms.

"No, Sir. I am as sober as a friar giving a sermon," said Zappo-Second Skin.

"Then explain to me in simple language why you are driving so erratically?" demanded Hooms.

Before Zappo-Second Skin could respond, a voice on the ship's comm pleaded, "Get out of there, Captain. Zappo is dead. This creature will kill you."

Captain Hooms watched in horror as his pilot morphed into a Cranitian that was twice the size of the captain. "Sorry. That Pleasurist Hunash just gave you more information than you needed to know." Second Skin reached out and grabbed Captain Hooms by the neck and twisted it off like a Reptilia popping a sweet, ginger beer.

As Hunash listened as Second Skin sadistically dealt with Captain Hooms, she realized that she could not let his death be in vain. She needed to use the opportunity to sneak back aboard the *Charon* so she could deal with him, once and for all. To Hellfire with the consequences to her own safety. Unfortunately, the only systems that she had to work with onboard the escape pod were the antiquated communication system and the navigation system that could only reach velocity two. As she sat bemoaning the lack of modern technology, inspiration came. She reached forward on the panel. "Hunash to Charon's Querzi. Do you read me?"

Second Skin reached down towards the floor of the cockpit to grab the lifeless body of the Polistine, Captain Hooms. He hadn't made up his mind yet whether he was going to use the husk of the Polistine to work out a few of his frustrations. He quickly decided he would save his pent-up anger for when he had the opportunity to deprive the meddling pleasurist of her life.

Just as he went to lift Captain Hooms, he saw out of the corner of his reflective eye a small escape pod, which was occupied by Hunash, streaking across the sky as it prepared to go into sub-space. "Oh no. You don't get to escape from me that easily." He ran over to the control panel. As his fingers moved with incredible speed, he activated another escape pod. He aimed the second pod directly at Hunash's small ship and set the pod to exit the ship at top speed.

"Farewell, dear Hunash. Just remember, you brought this on yourself."

Second Skin watched in twisted amusement as the escape pod sped directly into Hunash's escape pod, causing the poor pleasurist's craft to deteriorate within seconds into a flaming fire ball. He laughed to himself as the burning ship dropped out of its sub-space stream and went plummeting through the night sky.

"That is the last of that particular annoyance." said Second Skin. "Now to deal with the rest of the crew and passengers." As he walked out of the cockpit, he casually removed a large energy blaster rifle as he strolled down the hallway. As he walked, Second Skin decided that the occasion probably called for a hefty-sized red-skinned Quillian.

The red-skinned Quillian that was currently the exterior appearance of the Clonstellar, Second Skin, moved throughout the *Charon* in a systematic fashion as he rounded up the rest of the passengers and crew. The eleven Pleasurists on board were wrestled from their guest quarters, frequently to the sound of laser blasts from Second Skin's blaster. The seven members of the ship's hospitality staff were easily located at a late-night game of Five Card Gurt–Duchene. The *Charon's* Steward, a Cranitian, had a hand of three Zeniths and two Emperors when the hostile-looking Quillian came bursting into the kitchen behind the primary level passengers' dining room, the same dining room that Second Skin had been enjoying a romantic late night dinner with Hunash on the previous evening. Quillian-Second Skin escorted the crew at gunpoint to the observation lounge, where he had pre-viously taken the Pleasurists. Finally, Quillian-Second Skin made his way to the engine room and secondary flight deck to acquire the remaining astral engineering staff and flight crew, a group of nine Beetleguise and Polistine. He followed a similar procedure as he had with the hospitality staff until he had everyone in one location.

Upon entering the observation deck with the 9 members of the flight and engineering crew, Quillian-Second Skin observed that the Cranitian and Trionyx Pleasurists were huddled in the corners of the room, repeatedly requesting that Quillian-Second Skin let them go. Other Pleasurists were promising him that they had wealthy clients who could make him rich beyond his imagination. Second Skin's response was to lower the weapon's power to the minimal setting and fire off a round of blasts into a nearby column.

As a hush fell over the room, a steward asked him his name. Second Skin moved his head from side to side and cleared his throat. "My name is of no consequence to anyone in this room, so I will not waste time giving it."

"How can you expect us to respect you if you won't even give us your name?" asked the steward.

Quillian-Second Skin wheeled around on his heel as he fired a blast from his rifle at maximum level directly at the steward. As the steward reached his hand up to his chest to touch the fiery hole where his heart once was, he dropped dead to the floor. Quillian-Second Skin pointed to him with a Reptilia finger, "I have no desire to injure or kill anyone else. But if my demands are not met, I *will* take further lives."

The *Charon's* executive chef, a Cranitian named Tulash, raised his hands slowly as he looked at Second Skin, "What do any of us in this room have that you could possibly desire?" Tulash moved forward with his pads above his head. "Whatever it is then I know I speak for all of us when I state —"

"We are in no way equals, Cranitian. You will all do exactly what you are told to do by me. If any of you fail to comply, another being in this room will die." Second Skin reached out with his long Quillian tail to grab a pleasurist Cranitian by the neck and pull her to him. Once the pleasurist was next to Quillian-Second Skin, he aimed the blaster directly at her elongated face.

"Do we understand each other?" said Second Skin as the pleasurist began crying hysterically. "Stop your blabbering, you Horash, or I swear I will blow your head off right now."

"I am so sorry. I can't stop myself from crying," pleaded the pleasurist, Gowanda.

"Too bad," smiled Second Skin. "Guess this is goodbye for you."

"No, please don't," yelled Tulash.

Gowanda closed her eyes as she waited for the Clonstellar to pull the trigger, but all she heard was a click.

Second Skin chuckled to himself. "I must have left the inhibitor switch on the gun," he said as he pushed Gowanda to the ground. She crawled back to a corner of the room, putting her pad in her mouth to prevent herself from crying aloud.

"As I said before, if my demands are not met then I will kill all of you one by one," said Second Skin. "Now, I need to find the right representative to communicate my demands." Second Skin glanced over at the *Charon's* Chief Engineer. "You will do nicely."

Second Skin pointed at the engineer. "What is your name?"

"Are you talking to me?" asked the Polistine Engineer.

"I told you to state your name," said Quillian-Second Skin as he fired a blaster shot into the engineer's lower appendage, "and you failed to follow my directions."

"Are you out of your mind?" yelled the engineer.

"See, my dear bugs and lizards, that attitude there," the Quillian-Second Skin said as he pointed at the Engineer, "That attitude is what is going to get you all killed."

Second Skin casually strolled over to the engineer. When he was right next to him, he grabbed the Polistine by the wings and pinned him against the wall. "Now let's try this one more time, my friend. What is your name?"

"It is Humzed. Humzed."

"Very good, Humzed. Now, your military has taken something of great importance to my employer, Lord Diabolix. You will contact the Ministry of Justice on Insectvore using your lovely communication system. At that time, you will inform the Justice Minister that Lord Diabolix's property will be returned or you will all be killed by my hand."

"How are they supposed to know what was taken from Diabolix?" asked Humzed.

Second Skin swiftly turned around towards Humzed as he fired a blast into his other lower appendage. "What did I tell you about asking questions?"

"Don't!" cried Humzed.

Second Skin placed his hand up to his left ear in comical fashion as he fired another blast into Humzed's left appendage. "I am sorry. I didn't quite hear you. One more time."

"Don't ask questions," sobbed Humzed.

"Very good. Unfortunately, I believe friend Humzed that you have a problem with following directions."

"No, I am begging you, Sir," said Humzed.

"Goodbye," said Quillian-Second Skin as Humzed tendered his resignation at the barrel of a gun.

Second Skin turned towards the remaining Polistine in a cheerful, yet serious manner. "Now. Who among you is better at following directions than the dearly departed astral engineer?"

Within the halls of the Ministry of Justice, in the capital city of Linnaeus on Insectvore, a covert police lieutenant, Zamber, was flying swiftly down a spiral staircase that encompassed the central rotunda from roof to floor. Once he reached the bottom of the stairs, he made directly for a row of shelves that contained yellow-beam diskettes with information on numerous enemies of the Polistine Conglomerate. He pulled a group of ten diskettes off one of the upper rows of the platinum shelves, and took a step backward as the shelf slid down to the right to reveal a hidden corridor. The shelves obediently returned to their original position as Zamber entered the corridor and flipped a switch on the wall.

After a brief walk down the hallway, Zamber encountered a junior agent filing papers at his golden cube-shaped desk. "I need to see your superior, Agent Honey-Runner, right away."

"That is quite impossible at this time," said the junior agent. "She is engaged in a highly sensitive matter that requires her absolute attention."

"You little nursery bee-ling, there are Polistine lives at risk, and the only Insectum who can resolve this situation is Honey-Runner," yelled Zamber.

Just then, Zamber felt a long, silky appendage on the back of his neck that slowly went down to his upper fertilizers as the hairs on his abdomen came to attention.

"Are you giving this young bug a difficult time, Lieutenant Zamber? He is only truly acting in my best interest because there are serious matters being handled right now," said Honey-Runner. She then stated in a baby-doll, bee-ling voice, "the things that I am dealing with are way above your clearance level. Oh yes, they are."

"Ma'am, I realize that other operations may be in play. However, we were contacted by a junior engineer, Dozor, on board the *Charon*, not fifteen minutes ago. There is currently a hostage situation and the individual who is orchestrating the hostage situation has already taken lives."

"Did those lives belong to citizens of the Conglomerate?" asked Honey-Runner.

"I believe that there are Polistines aboard the ship, yes. But the main point is that this individual has specifically stated that all hostages will be executed if we do not return a piece of property that belongs to the war criminal known as Diabolix," said Zamber as he handed a portable communication tablet to Agent Honey-Runner.

Honey Runner pressed a few buttons on the tablet and activated the interstellar connection signal that would link her office with Dozor.

"Ensign Dozor, I am Agent Honey-Runner. I represent an agency that has dealt with situations like this before. Are you currently unharmed?"

"I am fine, but he has already murdered the Chief Astral Engineer and the ship's steward. In addition, he scared a Cranitian pleasurist half to death."

Before Agent Honey Runner could respond, Engineer Dozer began to disappear from the viewer screen as the images in the background began to move downward, and Dozer's face was replaced by that of Captain Hooms.

Agent Honey Runner breathed a sigh of relief as a Polistine face, even if it was one she didn't recognize with a traditional Polistine Captain's uniform and awards of service on the left lapel, came into view.

"Captain, thank goodness that you are unharmed."

"Ah my dear agent, your Captain Hooms is very much deceased. I am only wearing his face because I found it pleasant," said Captain Hooms-Second Skin.

"Whoever you are, my suggestion to you is that you savor these last moments of your life. I tell you this as a representative of Polistine Intelligence so I would listen very careful," said Honey Runner.

"You have my undivided attention."

"If you harm another passenger on that shuttle, there will be nowhere in this galaxy where you'll be able to hide from my personal vengeance," said Honey-Runner.

She could feel the veins in her antennae bulging up to the surface as she watched the imposter's head move up and down as he laughed while clapping two appendages together. "Well stated, Agent Honey-Runner. Your point was excellently expressed. Now," he said as his expression turned became very serious, "allow me to instruct you on how you can avoid any further loss of life."

"You have my attention. But what exactly do I call you?" asked Honey-Runner.

"My name is not important. I am Nobody."

"Very well, Mr. Nobody. What are your demands for the safe release of the hostages?"

"A unit of the Polistine Military, known as Purple L Swarm, recently acquired a device known as a Methurazus Rejuvenate from my employer's residence on Helvete Fredon. If you want to keep these people safe and unharmed, the Commander of Purple L Swarm will deliver the Methurazus Rejuvenate to this ship no later than two hours past midday, Venusian standard time."

"And who exactly is your employer?" asked Agent Honey Runner.

"None of us are children, Agent Honey Runner. You know very well who my employer is and what he is capable of doing to this galaxy." Hooms-Second Skin reached over and positioned his abdomen behind one of the pleasurists. "Now, Agent Honey-Runner, you apparently require a demonstration of what lengths I will go, to do my master's will." Captain Hooms-Second Skin moved his abdomen forward as he sank both eighteen-inch stingers into the pleasurist's chest. Honey Runner instinctively closed her eyes as the poor Reptilia was murdered in front of her. This action did not prevent Honey-Runner from hearing the pleasurist's haunting screams.

"I killed her and don't even know her name," said Captain Hooms-Second Skin

"Her name was Vashtan, you animal," screamed a Trionyx pleasurist named Titanice.

Ignoring Titanice's objections, Second Skin told Honey-Runner, "You have five standard hours to return Lord Diabolix's property."

"Sadly, Purple L Swarm is currently out of range," said Honey-Runner. "There is no way that we can get you the Methurazus Device within five hours. We need more time."

"Ah, you need more time so that you can put together a military taskforce to bring me down. I don't see that happening," said Second Skin.

"There is no way that we can meet your request within the allotted amount of time."

"Then my suggestion to you is that you better start getting creative, fast. Otherwise, everyone else on this ship will meet a death similar to Vashtan's.

Just not as fast, and, definitely not as pleasant. Nobody, over and out," he said as the screen went blank."

"What are we going to do?" asked Lieutenant Zamber.

"Tell you what we aren't going to do. We are going to find a way to save those people without giving into the demands of that ..." Honey Runner paused.

"Don't feel bad. I have no idea what the hell fire to call "it" either," said Zamber.

"While we are figuring that out, Zamber, get a representative from Beetleguise intelligence, MH-19, on the video screen. We have a lot of work to do and not a lot of time."

Before Zamber could retrieve the tablet, it began to hum to life once again in his hands.

"My name is Hunash. I am a pleasurist aboard the *Charon*. I am in hiding on the ship and was monitoring your communication with that creature."

"Wherever you are, just stay out of sight. My agency will find a way to rescue you from —."

"He is called "Second Skin" and I am tired of hiding from him. I want to be the one to stop him."

Chapter 18
WARDEN SOBEK

Warden Sobek glanced through a small window in his office, the Warden searching the heavens for his home world of Meditaplassen in the morning sky, but it was too far away. He could only glimpse the coin-sized orange and pink orb of Insectvore that lay at a very distant corner of the horizon. Insectvore was almost completely devoid of natural water sources; there were no rivers, lakes or oceans, so it relied on artificial irrigation and water from conquered planets. From beneath his massive shell. Sobek's gaze wandered to his left as he saw the larger green and blue orb of Madagascan. The Beetleguise homeworld, Madagascan had hundreds of island-like land-masses and fifteen oceans.

According to legend, the asteroid on which now Sobek now stood, Minerva was created by the ancient Pangeans hundreds of thousands of years ago in order for their race to understand how objects from space could destroy their world. The Queztalcoatin, whom the Pangeans, as recorded in the ancient text, merely referred to as "The Grays", plucked the asteroid out of the planet's orbit. It was then a simple matter of teleporting the asteroid via extended range transport to the Venusian star system.

After the fall of the Queztalcoatin race, the artificial asteroid, which was maintained in position by hundreds of stabilizers and gravity engines, was acquired by the genetic children of the Queztalcoatin; the Polistine. Their race converted the asteroid into the Minerva Penitentiary fifteen hundred years ago. Even Sobek, who believed that the Hawkings were superior to all other races, admitted that the prison's construction was an impressive feat of engineering.

Sobek's mind was brought back to reality by a flashing blue button on his desk. He pressed the button that activated a flat monitor and saw the image of one of his Polistine employees, a Centurion.

As Sobek rubbed his orb-shaped green eyes under his shell, he asked in a tired voice, "How can I help you this morning, Centurion?"

"Sir, there is no sign of Legates Buzz or Zook this morning in the Penitentiary. The prisoners will need to be transported to the morning feeding chamber in approximately an hour."

Sobek was suddenly jolted awake. "Centurion, what do you mean that there is no sign of Legate Zook. He should have returned to the administrative office hours ago."

"What are we going to do about the morning feeding?" asked the Centurion

But by that time, Sobek had already muted the sound on the video screen. "Querzi, was Legate Prime Buzz delivered to my custody, last night?"

"The Polistine, Legate Prime Buzz, has not yet been scheduled for processing into my system and subsequent execution."

"Daggit," yelled Sobek. "Where was his last location?"

"Approximately twenty miles from the *Citadel* near the Galerius crater formation."

Sobek pressed raised the volume as he ordered, "this message is to be shared and reposted to every Beetleguise and Polistine centurion in the prison. Message follows. From Warden Sobek Bokhun. The Minerva Penitentiary is currently in state of Hawking Law. No one is to enter or leave their offices or containment areas. Travel to the *Citadel* is strictly forbidden, except in extreme emergencies. Management of the prisoners will be assigned to a unit of Project Xerxes, specifically Triceratopian, until further notice."

"Sir, a Tram that already left this morning for emergency repair work to junction 42 in the *Citadel*. A group of Rancoran have broken loose from their enclosure and need to be recaptured."

Warden Sobek opened his mouth with the intention of directing the Tram to return to the Containment/Feeding Dome when it dawned on him that his two would-be burglars may be aboard that particular transport. It would be considerably more plausible if Dr. Rabun met his end when there were prisoners actually present in the *Citadel*. In fact, the Rancoran, might even assist in disposing of these hapless burglars in the process. After a brief pause, Sobek retracted his previous command, "That is fine. I will inform the Triceratopian that once the work is completed then the members of the repair team will be detained in the *Citadel* until further notice. And finally —"

"Yes, Warden Sobek."

"Inform all Beetleguise and Polistine centurions that your former Legate Prime Buzz is to be shot on sight. No questions asked. I am counting on you, did I ask you your name, centurion?" asked Sobek.

"It is Dronok, Sir."

"I am counting on you, my new Legate Beta. Don't let me down."

Almost immediately after Sobek concluded his conversation with his newly appointed Legate Beta, the blue button by his video screen began to flash once again. After pressing the button, the formidable visage of Alpha Triceratopian appeared on the screen.

"Master Sobek, my fellow Triceratopian have been trying to convince Rabun to produce the formula for the Diabolix toxin for close to half an hour."

"And I assume that he has been less than forthcoming."

"The Doctor has been non-compliant. He has secured himself within the medical dispensary, and, to this point, we have failed to gain entry. My brother Beta and I have used threats of bodily harm, but he has refused to unlock the door."

"For all your noble strength, my Alpha Trike, how wisdom and sense continue to elude you," said Warden Sobek who realized that he was taking an extreme risk insulting his servant who was capable of crushing his skull with his bare hands.

"Maintain your position at the dispensary, I will join you and your brothers shortly."

"I obey your command, Master Sobek, in this matter as in all things," said Alpha Trike, before the screen switched to a blue field.

"I guess with that much brute strength at their disposal, there had to be a compromise somewhere," mused Warden Sobek to himself.

With the pushing of a few buttons, Warden Sobek converted the platform behind his desk into a hover-discus that would carry him quickly and easily to the doctor's medical dispensary; there was no point in exerting so much extra energy by even trying to walk there. He used his tentacles to operate a stick-controller at the base of the hover-discus. With the aptitude of a holo-game expert, he guided the device above his desk, out the door, and on his way to the dispensary where he would persuade Doctor Rabun to see reason, even if it was through the use of extreme force.

Warden Sobek came upon a sight that in another context might have been considered almost social as he glided towards the silver-and-platinum, trapezoid-shaped doors of the medical dispensary. Standing around the door were six Triceratopian soldiers in green fatigues; two of the trikes held four lengthy poles that contained cloaking restrictors that prevented cloaking around the Abomination Hotfire.

"What seems to be the difficulty?" asked Warden Sobek.

"He won't come out, Master," growled Beta Trike.

"Have you tried breaking down the fuctur door?"

"We tried that, first, but you might want to take a step back," said Beta Trike. "Go ahead and show the warden, Gamma Triceratopian."

"If you insist," said Gamma Triceratopian. He fired three shots from his horns. The blasts immediately reached their target and bounced off a translucent force field before ricocheting off the walls. The group outside the door managed to dive for cover in the last possible instant.

"For the love of the Great Hive Master, have you tried to use your telekinetic powers?"

"The Doctor is using some type of malicious trick to keep us from pulling off the door," said Alpha Trike.

Warden Sobek discovered that Rabun had been monitoring their conversation at that point. "You really believe that I would create these genetic beings and not put safeguards in place for my own protection?" shouted Rabun through the video screen above the dispensary door.

"I applaud your tenacity and ingenuity, Doctor," praised Warden Sobek. "But, the hour has become too late and there is a threat that needs to be dealt just beyond our own dimension."

"Yes, I know, Sobek. I have heard the rumors as well that the followers of Diabolix are trying to find a method for bringing him back from X-Space, and the Hawkings wish to prevent this return."

"If you know this, doctor," said Warden Sobek, "permit me to have the toxin, so this — he pointed at Hotfire — Abomination can use it to stop the threat."

"Because if the toxin doesn't work on Diabolix then you are delivering a compound into the hands of an individual who would have no qualms about starting a plague that could wipe out two-thirds of the civilized worlds in the universe."

"Come Triceratopian, I must return to my office. The doctor has provided me with new insight. I must convene these new concerns to the Omnipotent Hawking Council immediately," said Sobek.

The Alpha Triceratopian leaned his head down to the bottom of Sobek's shell as he asked in a whisper, "Are we really leaving Master?"

"Oh, we have yet to begun to outwit the good Dr. Rabun," said Warden Sobek as he motioned the company to begin walking up the hallway. He stated in a whisper, "Take Hotfire around to the rear access vent and shove him in there. If he doesn't open that door in an expedient matter, you crawl through the vent to the dispensary. Then, you kill him and the doctor."

"Come, freak," said Alpha Trike as he grabbed Hotfire, "we are going for a little walk."

Dr. Rabun scratched the barnacles beneath his chin as he strained to see through the video screen if any individuals from Sobek's group were still outside his door.

"For the sake of the Hive Master, I suppose I am going to have to go out sometime."

He made his way to the rear of the dispensary to a yellow, non-descript closet next to a large metallic device that had a large drill-shaped tube hanging over a platform. The device was a molecular recombinator that Rabun used to process minerals and chemicals into invaluable pharmaceuticals that were required to maintain the health of the criminals within his medical charge. Past the recombinator, the yellow closet had a single digital scanner-lock that held the two doors of the cabinet together. Doctor Rabun removed a small flash-lock from the pocket of his orange tunic and swiped it beneath the scanner-lock. He opened the cabinet to reveal a miniature combination safe. Next to the strong box on the top shelf was a test tube rack with six vials of the Diabolix toxin. Rabun grabbed a large Taser blaster from a side compartment beneath the shelf. Before Rabun could deactivating the force field, a large black mass dropped out of the sky.

"Oh, Crasp," bemoaned the Doctor as he watched Hotfire leaping toward him.

In a reflexive motion, Dr. Rabun aimed the blaster at Hotfire and fired.

"Oh, my dear Doctor, it is already so late for that."

Hotfire rolled himself into a ball as the shots flew past him. He then rolled his body in a straight line towards Dr. Rabun with the intent of slamming him into the nearby wall. Rabun jumped up and grabbed the upper trim that ran along the door frame, dropping the blaster to the ground. With the agility of an Reptilia athlete, Hotfire slid underneath Dr. Rabun and retrieved his weapon before swinging back around to face him.

"You might want to get down from there, doctor, before I get an itchy trigger claw." smiled Hotfire as he turned around and deactivated the force field. He pressed a button to open the door as Sobek came hovering down the hallway on his hover-discus, putting his tentacles together in appreciation for the Abomination's ability in battle. "Now Doctor, if you would be so kind to tell me where you've hidden the toxin. Get down from the doorway and tell us where you have stored the toxin?"

"He has it in his tunic, Sobek," said Hotfire.

"Your cooperation is most appreciated, Hotfire," said Sobek.

"But there is one last thing that I need to discuss with you, Sobek."

There is one minor issue before we discuss that," interrupted Hotfire

"And what is that exactly?" asked Sobek.

"That I am using this rifle as my ticket out of here," smiled Hotfire.

"I don't have the time to do this right now, child," said Sobek to Hotfire. "Alpha Trike, increase the intensity of pain from the Psychic Spider by a factor of five."

The Alpha Trike reached in his vest pocket and pulled out a dial mounted on a black box. He then decided that he was going to personally teach the black salamander a lesson by dialing the pain level all the way up to nine. He gleefully watched as Hotfire dropped the rifle and crumpled to the floor.

"That is enough, Alpha," yelled Warden Sobek. "He is still of value to me so I need him undamaged."

Inside Hotfire's head, the image of the Psychic Spider with his brown and black hat and ten appendages kicked him, "Listen, Hotfire, you might want to get up now."

"And why is that?" asked Hotfire as he lay on the floor of the dispensary.

"Because we have a Hellfire of lot of stuff to get done before I kill you in four and half hours."

As Hotfire felt himself being lifted into the air and then coming to rest on a soft surface, he heard Sobek tell his Triceratopian servants that now that they had recovered the toxin from the doctor that there was only one chore left. They needed to handle the disposal of the Doctor.

"Sleep tight, little Prince," said Alpha Trike. "You should definitely take the chance to get some rest."

"But then again, he'll be able to have plenty of time once he's done," said Epsilon Trike.

"You mean after his head explodes?" laughed Alpha Trike.

Hotfire was disappointed that he really didn't even get a chance to recover his strength. He could see the image of the Psychic Spider before his eyes almost constantly now. He also felt that the creature had grown exponentially in the last fifteen hours. The Psychic Spider had squeezed its head and abdomen underneath the top of his skull so it was pressing down on his brain. The legs of the Psychic Spider were radiated down from the top of his cranium and wrapped around the sides of his brain. Hotfire could feel that he was no longer in control of his own mind.

As he opened his eyes, he glanced over to see Sobek on his hover-discus. He barely caught sight of the room as it faded from a white, sanitary chamber to a dark room that contained a group of computers whose diodes flickered on and off with purple lights.

"Your abilities have been underestimated by your Bokhun cousin, Sobek," said Osiris Bokhun.

"You have my forgiveness, dear Bokhun cousins. I have retrieved the toxin."

"Have you left the doctor unharmed as you were instructed?" asked Ra Bokhun.

"Not to worry, Cousins. He is safely imprisoned in the *Citadel* for the moment."

"Very well. If this toxin is not effective then we will need his services, once again," said Ra Bokhun.

"I wholeheartedly agree, Cousin Ra. You have my solemn word that he will remain unharmed."

"Are you prepared to deliver the Abomination to complete his task?" asked Osiris.

Sobek reached over in the darkness towards where Hotfire was still crumpled in pain, and injected a trans-molecular compound into Hotfire's neck. "He is prepared for transport.".

"You are all out of your shells," mocked Hotfire. "I am not going anywhere."

But in the next instant, Hotfire felt every molecule in his body being pulled apart as it was sent flying through space and time to Meditaplassen, the home world of the Hawking Brain Beetle. The journey was instantaneous though Hotfire felt the effects of disorientation long afterwards.

As he lay on the floor of the Omnipotent Hawking Council chamber before a group of twelve shelled creatures similar in appearance to Sobek, one of the three supreme disciples moved forward to speak. "Hello Hotfire. I am Cousin Osiris Bokhun. Many years ago, you swore a pledge to serve the Hawking Brain Beetle in exchange for saving your life. You have been somewhat negligent in this commitment to our race, but today you will demonstrate your allegiance to us by eliminating the war criminal known as Diabolix.

"Sobek already told me that you were going to put me back in that Methurazus Rejuvenate to take me to X-Space. I'd rather die than go back into that thing that twisted me inside out."

"Hotfire, you might yet get your wish. But for the moment, you will do as the Hawking Brain Beetle and this Omnipotent Council command you, for once in your life," said Ra.

"Guards, take the Hotfire Abomination to the Methurazus Rejuvenate," said another Bokhun, Ramses.

Hotfire was lifted off the floor of the Council Chamber. He looked up to see three massive yellow-skinned Cranitians wearing a purple breast plates, green helmets with visor, and holstered weapons.

As Hotfire looked up the hallway, he saw the same sight that he had seen some fifteen years before, a Methurazus Rejuvenate. The guards moved quickly and efficiently to strap him to the cockpit- style seat at the center of the cube while activating the console to close it.

Hotfire frantically began screaming from inside of the Methurazus device as he heard the Cranitian moving back and forward outside. But as he pleaded with his captors, he was suddenly bathed in an eerie yellow glow as felt his molecules were being transported again

As he pressed one last time against the restraints, they inexplicably retracted. The door to the device opened to reveal a blinding white light. As his small, black-marble eyeballs adjusted to the light, he was able to distinguish that he was on a dirt road in the middle of a desolate landscape. It was one that he recognized without having to take a second look.

"I am on Scaratutulo," sighed Hotfire.

"Nope, you are in X-Space, and you've just landed on Diabolix's world."

Hotfire turned around to see the Psychic Spider sitting on a large rock, laughing hysterically.

Chapter 19
YANICK DCCULLEN

"Legate Prime, I would consider it an extremely generous gesture if you could take me back to my cell now," pleaded Yanick DcCullen.

Legate Prime Buzz regarded the situation he was currently in as an inconceivable turn of events. Buzz had been able to follow the chain of events of the day very clearly, but despite understanding the consequence of cause to effect, namely that Sobek had betrayed him, he felt that it was just surreal to be plunging to his death aboard a hijacked Tram with one of his Reptilia prisoners in tow.

"It's just a perfect metaphor for my day that we are spinning out of control," quipped Buzz.

"That is just great news," yelled Yanick.

"You are the one who threw a Taser into the forward thrusters," the Legate Prime reminded Yanick. "So, I would quit your yelling if I were you, and think of something."

"I am doing the best I can. I should have been able to think of something by now because I do really well at problem-solving under stress," said Yanick.

"Then why haven't you?" asked Legate Prime Buzz.

"Probably because someone is standing around blaming me for the whole mess," said Yanick. "And that has been known to interfere with my ability to think clearly."

"Oh, I feel so bad for you," said Buzz sarcastically.

"You do?" asked Yanick as he reciprocated the sarcastic tone.

The Legate Prime suddenly glanced back up at the viewer screen, just in time to view a spherical rock formation headed straight for the Tram. "We might be in just a little bit of trouble. And if I were you I would definitely grab onto something."

"You mean as we go slamming into a rock wall at top speed?" asked Yanick.

"Just brace for impact."

"I swear that if I survive this, I am filing a complaint with the Zanuck Corporation about your flying skills," yelled Yanick. "That thing looks like it is getting awfully close to the ship."

"Maybe if we can't keep from falling towards it we might be able to get out of its way," said Buzz.

"You have lost your senses, Legate," screamed Yanick. "That rock is coming right for us."

As he glanced at the settings on his visor that were controlling the motion of the ship, Buzz used the optical control to change the ship's trajectory. "Since the Tram is already in a roll, then it should just be a small matter of changing from down to up trajectory."

Yanick was tossed up against the banks of consoles and computers as the ship changed from an end over end to sideways maneuver.

"Can you please stop with the aerial acrobatics and just find somewhere we can set down to repair the ship?" asked Yanick. "Then I will go quietly into custody as you take me back to prison."

"Can you fix the forward thrusters, Inmate 3249?"

"It is probably a simple matter of re-routing energetic pathways from an alternative electric system as well as welding shut any loose connections that are interfering with circuit completion. That said, I am not willing to do a daggit bit of that for you until —"

"Until what?"

"You stop referring to me by that loathsome number, for Hive Masters sake," said Yanick.

"Fine, DcCullen. Can you fix the ship?" Legate Prime Buzz reluctantly asked for a second time. This time though, it was definitely in a more begrudging manner.

"I can indeed. But you might want to watch it because we are headed towards the rock shelf pretty fast," said Yanick.

"Hang on," advised Buzz. "Going to need to activate the buffers to smooth out our landing." Buzz activated four inflatable rubberdonian pads that then, released around the rim of the Tram, cushioned the ship's landing on the rock shelf approximately 85 miles from the *Citadel*.

"Now that we are safe and sound for the moment, you might want to get to work, Yanick," said Buzz.

Yanick went to reach down to a supply locker located at the rear of the flight deck, but when he lifted his gaze, he was greeted by the cold, hard steel of a disruptive blaster in the hands of a disgruntled Legate Zook. "Yeah, I am thinking that there might be a flaw in that plan, Legate Prime," said Zook.

Buzz removed his control helmet as he was turning around to find out what exactly was bothering his reluctant prisoner now, only to face his former subordinate with his two Beetleguise Centurions, Razz and J'nox. "How the hellfire did the three of you get loose?"

"The Warden provided me with a verbal access code for the Querzi that will open any door on this Tram. Now, you will surrender yourself this instant, former Legate Prime, and return to your cell along with this lowly, scourdash of a Reptilia. I will then escort you to the *Citadel* where you will answer for your crimes," said Zook.

"And you thought it was bad when I referred to you just as a number," smirked Buzz.

"We are about to have a problem in a minute, Mr. big deal Legate, because nobody talks to me that way," retorted Yanick.

"Your mother would have been more blessed if you had been absorbed back into her innards rather than been a burden upon her for your whole miserable life," said Legate Beta Zook.

"That is it! That is the last piece of stalk," said Yanick. He reached back with his tail and launched himself into the air, landing on top of Zook. "No one talks about my mother!"

Zook wrapped his appendages around the Trionyx as they both ascended towards the roof of the ship. Yanick pummeled Zook in the face with repeated blows to the head and chest. Zook slammed his wings alternately into Yanick's side as he tried to pry the Trionyx loose from his body.

Buzz was watching the whole spectacle unfold before him when his ear-comm, that he had completely forgotten was still there, suddenly vibrated to life.

"Hey, Buzz. Thought you'd never hear from the old Captain Honeycomb ever again, huh?"

In a state of shock, Buzz moved forward a step or two towards the Beetleguise centurions who immediately held their Tasers at attention. "It is okay. This is me, not going anywhere," he assured the centurions.

"Where are you, Buzz. What is going on?" asked Captain Honeycomb.

"Long story. Suffice it to say, I am a steeldonian can ration right about now, and could really use an opener." said Legate Prime Zook.

"I can definitely loan you a can opener, old buddy," said Captain Honeycomb.

"That would be great. What is your location?"

"We are flying blind in a magna-sphere, and we are headed your way."

"I can give you some landing lights to show you the way, Honeycomb," said Buzz.

"That would be most appreciated, Buzz. Looking forward to that light in the dark," said Honeycomb.

The Legate Prime looked over to Yanick as he was climbing up a wall with the Polistine Zook wrapped inside his tail. Yanick was slamming Zook against the side of the Tram wall, and Zook was retaliating by pushing Yanick hard against the consoles and fixtures inside the flight deck. As Yanick went to slam Zook down to the floor with his tail, Zook reached up and grabbed Yanick with his appendages and threw him down to the ground.

Yanick looked over at Buzz. "A little help," mouthed Yanick.

"Help is on the way," Buzz mouthed back.

Zook turned to the two Beetleguise centurions, Razz and J'nox, "I am dealing with the Trionyx. You, Fools! You need to handle the Legate Prime,"

Yanick leaned back on his haunches as he launched himself towards the Polistine, Legate Beta Zook hovering in the corner. Zook watched as Yanick came flying towards him, then just before Yanick was getting ready to grab him, he zapped Yanick with an energy blast that sent him tumbling to the floor.

Buzz, meanwhile, found himself flanked on either side by Razz and J'nox who both had their Tasers extended. "We do not wish to harm the former Legate Prime. You may assist us in preserving your health, former Legate Prime, by coming with us back to your cell," said centurion J'nox.

"I would rather take my chances going on the run then with you two bugs," said Legate Buzz.

"I respect your choice to engage in combat, Polistine," said Razz.

"We'll see about that."

Centurion Razz pushed his Taser onto the ground and used it to catapult himself towards the Legate Prime. As Buzz watched Razz coming towards him, he lifted himself up into the air and began to flap his wings furiously in the direction of the oncoming Beetleguise causing the centurion to roll into a ball and fall to the ground like a stone. Before Razz could recover himself, as well as the Taser that he had dropped, Buzz pressed the code on the flight deck's main access door, kicked Razz down the ramp that led to the containment cells and swiped the door closed setting the lock once again.

"It was with ease that you dispatched centurion Razz," said J'nox. "With centurion J'nox, you will not find it to be so easy."

"We shall see about that, Beetleguise," said Buzz. It was then than Buzz looked over to see that Yanick was still dodging laser bolts from Zook's blaster. He thought to himself that Yanick could have easily evade Zook if he had only made his way down to the bottom of the cabin. Then it dawned on Buzz what Yanick was doing. He noticed that the Trionyx was positioning himself under a ventilation shaft. "So," Buzz said to himself, "you are obviously setting some kind of trap…but what?"

Legate Prime Buzz turned towards J'nox. "You may be able to defend yourself, J'nox. But what is to stop me from neutralizing your commander, Zook?"

"This is an action that not even you would dare, Polistine," said Centurion J'nox.

"Just watch my pollen dust, Beetleguise."

As Buzz moved away from J'nox, he backed himself into the command chamber at the center of the room while quickly donning the control headset once again. He began scrolled through the communication options until he reached external detection.

"Come out of there and face me like a warrior, Polistine," said J'nox as he pounded on the glass.

As he finished adjusting the external beacon, Buzz touched his appendage to the top of his antennae. "The beacon is lit. You are going to have two packages if all goes well."

"I confirm reception of that directive. We are two minutes away," said Honeycomb.

Outside the command chamber, J'nox was yelling at the top of his spiracles, "I will crush the tube with you inside it, Polistine. Now come face me in combat as the Great Hive Master intended."

"If the Great Hive Master had intended to fight, then why did he make me so much cleverer than you, Beetleguise?"

As Buzz activated the internal speaker, he shouted, "Yanick, time to eject the trash." He activated a suction tube that grabbed a hold of J'nox and sucked him out of the ship. Almost in the same instant, Yanick punched Zook in the face and then pushed him back towards the ventilation port in the ceiling. When he turned around and hit the activation button, he watched as Zook went flying off into the vacuum that was Minerva's sky. Using his tail to anchor himself, Yanick crawled forward and pressed the button that re-sealed the port.

As Legate Prime Buzz emerged from the command chamber, Yanick said to him, "you do know that you just sent them to their death."

"I am fully aware of my actions, Trionyx," replied Buzz.

"That is pretty cold, even for a Polistine," stated Yanick.

"Not as cold as you think," smirked Buzz. "Honeycomb, are your guest secured aboard the sphere?" asked the Legate Prime.

"Yes, and thanks to the Cranitian Buddash, we already have a flight plan that will take them back to the Containment/Feeding dome," said Honeycomb.

"Very good, Captain. The Trionyx Yanick needs to do some minor repairs to the Tram. After they are completed, I have every intention of confronting Sobek about the blood on his tentacles."

"I will teleport to your location, just as soon as I have our two guests fully settled in," said Honeycomb.

"What did you do to them?" asked Buzz.

"I might have pocketed a couple of vials of sedative while I was fighting with the Abomination yesterday," said Honeycomb. "Now that they are sleeping soundly, I can teleport over."

"That is a negative, Captain. I am giving you a direct order to make your way back to the *Honeyvein One* and prep her for liftoff. If things with Warden Sobek don't go our way, we are going to need to get off this asteroid in a big hurry."

"Buzz, are you sure that is the smartest move?" asked Captain Honeycomb, "There are a million things that could go wrong when you face a Hawking Brain Beetle."

"It is most appreciated, Captain, but right now I just need you to follow my orders. You take the Buddash back to the containment cell. Then, start prepping the *Honeyvein One*. "

"What about DcCullen?"

"Oh, he's coming with me," said Buzz with a smirk in his voice.

"Copy that, Sir. We are headed for the Containment/Feeding dome."

Buzz watched through a rounded window port near the front of the Tram as the black magna-sphere sped off towards the twin reflective domes on the horizon.

"Now, Yanick, we need to fix these forward stabilizers because, apparently, we are late for a robbery at the dispensary," Buzz said in a deadpan tone.

Yanick vehemently shook his head. "You are out of your Bumblebee mind. I don't know anything about any robbery or getting any drugs for Diabolix."

"Don't try to deny it, Yanick. Your partner, Buddash, already spilled the eggs to Captain Honeycomb."

"And why exactly are you not trying to stop me?" asked Yanick.

"Because, believe or not, there is something in that medical dispensary that might actually help me to deal with Sobek," replied Legate Prime Buzz.

Chapter 20
DOCTOR RABUN

Legate Prime Buzz, a laser rifle resting on his shoulder, pushed forward through the hallway toward the trapezoid doors of the medical dispensary. He kept looking from side to side to see if he was being followed. A number of false alarms had already occurred including a fire compressor system beeped as it reset itself. However, there had been indication up to that point of actual resistance.

Buzz flew quietly toward a nearby storage closet that faced the door of the medical dispensary at a diagonal. Pressing his body close against the door of the closet, Buzz cocked his rifle in preparation to fire, but did not release the pre-firing switch on the butt of the gun.

After taking a deep breath, he flew to the door and moved to pull a pass card from his pocket, but the doors to the medical dispensary inexplicably slid open.

Buzz looked around the dispensary in a state of awed bewilderment. All of the chemicals required for the fabrication of pharmaceuticals had been removed from the glass cabinets surrounding the three medical beds. In addition, all of the narcotics in the dispensary — the pain meds, sleep meds, aphidian relievers, medical hallucinogens, and holistic pain relievers —had vanished from the cabinets.

As he looked around, he heard someone or something moving around in the darkness of the room. He silently glided to the center of the room with his rifle positioned to deal with whatever threat presented itself. It was then that he looked up to see an unwelcomed site.

Yanick DcCullen was standing with his back to the Legate Prime. Buzz raised his rifle and positioned it in line with Yanick's head for a clean shot.

"Don't move, Yanick."

Yanick spun around to face him as he placed his hands on his head yelling, "Don't shoot! For the Hive Master's sake, Don't shoot!"

THREE HOURS EARLIER

Yanick worked feverishly on soldering the severed electrical connections in the circuit box for the forward thrusters. He really would have preferred if the Legate Prime had sent him back to his cell. Mainly, Yanick already had a bad feeling about the whole nature of this mission. What would be the repercussions from defying the will of a Hawking Brain Beetle warden? Whatever they were going to be, they wouldn't be good. In addition, there was his possible reunion with Hotfire. The few times he had encountered the Abomination since their unceremonious parting had been far from pleasant.

"Trionyx, are you almost done with those repairs? Time is growing short," barked Legate Prime Buzz.

"It is slow going, but I should be done within the half hour," said Yanick.

"You have 15 minutes, 20 minutes at the most, before I shoot you out a waste chute," said Buzz.

"Fine! I will get the repairs done in 15, but all this side conversation is not helping."

"Besides," Yanick thought aloud, "it really should be Buddash under this panel, he's the one who is always bragging about how he could have been an astral engineer."

"Well, the Cranitian isn't the one who threw a Taser in there, so stop your yapping and get to work," said Buzz.

"I get time off my sentence for helping you out, right?" asked Yanick.

"Just pray to the Hive Master that we don't both wind up in front of an elimination squad."

Presented with several more incidences of forceful encouragement, Yanick was motivated to complete the necessary repairs ahead of schedule. At their completion, Yanick advised, "It might not necessarily be pretty, but it will get us to the *Citadel*."

WILLIAM HOWARD

"Great. Let's get underway."

"You are welcome, Yanick," mumbled the Trionyx. "Glad you were here to get me back in the air."

"You do realize that Polistines have excellent auditory organs in our antennae?" said Buzz as he climbed back into the command chamber. Buzz and Yanick were not in the air for more than 5 minutes when the Legate Prime viewed a disturbing sight on the viewer shield of his helmet. A prisoner Tram was moving up, and immediately opened communications.

In Legate Prime Buzz's helmet, he saw the image of a Polistine centurion, "Legate Prime, I am surprised to see you out here?"

"I was unaware that it was now customary for Legates to explain their presence to lowly centurions?"

"No, of course not, Legate," said the Polistine centurion.

"What is your name and designation, son?"

"I am HumBuzt, centurion, first class, Legate."

"You may find that your designation will be lowered in rank if I hear even a hint of insubordination from you HumBuzt," stated Buzz.

"I completely understand, Legate. I apologize for my informal tone."

"Is there a particular reason why you are piloting a Tram this early?" asked Buzz.

"Some of Warden Sobek's Rancoran have gotten lose in the *Citadel* and we've been ordered to escort a group of Reptilia prisoners to recapture them, as well as repairing their enclosure by junction42." replied HumBuzt. "Due to the volatile nature of the beasts, Sobek has given us special permission to complete our task, despite the recently imposed restriction prohibiting travel to the *Citadel*.

"I have been on special assignment for the Warden for the last few hours, Centurion HumBuzt. What is the cause of the travel restriction?"

"Apparently, one of the high-ranking centurions went on a killing spree."

"I see."

Thank goodness that his centurions couldn't keep their gossip straight, though Buzz. Apparently, HumBuzt had no clue that he was speaking to a rogue, homicidal Legate.

230

"I suppose that is why I have been recalled to the *Citadel* by Warden Sobek. He probably wishes to discuss how we will apprehend this villainous individual."

"I think it is Legate Zook, sir. I never liked him," said centurion HumBuzt.

"That is enough, centurion. I will not have you besmirch another Legate, is that understood?"

"Sorry, Legate Prime," said centurion HumBuzt.

"Centurion HumBuzt, I am due to meet with Warden Sobek within the hour. I have inmate 3249 aboard my vessel, whom I am returning from a medical exam at the *Citadel*. He claimed that he was experiencing gastro distress when, in fact, it was only probably some bad fish, according to the doctor. Could you return him to the Containment dome once you have done your work?" asked Buzz.

Yanick grabbed at one of Buzz's appendages. "Have you lost your Insectum mind?"

"Is inmate 3249 able-bodied enough to assist with the Rancoran internment?" asked HumBuzt.

"I believe that the exercise will do him a world of good, actually," said Buzz.

"Then I will be more than happy to teleport him aboard and add him to the work detail."

"He will be ready for transport to your Tram in 5 minutes," said Buzz.

"Thank you, Legate Prime, for the additional worker. And I apologize for my earlier informality."

"Just don't let it happen again," said Buzz, closing communication with HumBuzt.

"What is going on?" asked Yanick.

"What is going on is that you'll be going through with your original plan. There is an exhaust tube in the top of the Rancoran enclosure that you will be able to follow directly to the dispensary. I will be leading Sobek and his Triceratopian on a merry chase so they will be distracted from your activities."

"Which will be what exactly?" asked Yanick.

Yanick could not help but be impressed as Buzz explained his plan to deal with Sobek. Once Yanick was taken aboard the prisoner Tram, Buzz directed his own Tram's navigation to set a flight path towards the towering building known as the *Citadel* located to the west of both the containment and administrative domes of the Minerva Penitentiary. The internal structure had been blasted out of solid nickel, gneiss, and hornsfels. The exterior of the *Citadel* was encased in a double-thick layer of steeldonian and platinum. The building itself was designed to resemble an inverted Hawking Brain Beetle shell with several domed-shaped chambers reaching up to the heavens.

"Now, here comes the tricky part," said Buzz came into sensor range of the warden's enclave that included his testing and research facility for his experimental pets, private offices, and the medical dispensary."

The communication system began broadcasting a deep voice: "Vessel, this is Epsilon Trike. State your business at the *Citadel*?"

Buzz disabled the Tram's viewer and set it into all audio mode, "This is Legate Beta Zook, you simple Beast. I am expected by your master, Sobek."

"You are extremely overdue. Master Sobek had become concerned about your fate."

"You can tell Sobek that he can sedate and transport his own Polistine prisoners next time. Buzz managed to get free from his cell and attacked me. Knocked out half the ship's systems in the process."

"Legate Zook, I am not able to establish visual communication with your ship," said Epsilon.

"That is one of the daggit systems that the Legate Prime knocked out during his brief escape. I managed to sedate him and put him back in his cell. But I am running low on Enhanced Gas. I need to either land this Tram or just park it through the window of Sobek's private office."

"You are cleared for landing, Legate Beta. I will inform Beta Trike and Theta Trike to meet your party at landing bay C in 20 minutes," said Epsilon.

"That sounds just wonderful," said Buzz as he groaned to himself.

Onboard the Prisoner Tram, Yanick had been unceremoniously thrown into a cell with a red-Quillian, another Trionyx, and two Cranitian. HumBuzt had informed Yanick, "Don't get too comfortable, Trionyx. You will soon be doing back-breaking work or being eaten by a Rancoran. Either way, your afternoon isn't looking too promising,"

Minutes after Legate Prime Buzz had spoken to Trike Epsilon regarding landing, it was HumBuzt's turn to gain clearance to *the Citadel*. "Hello control, I have a group of prisoners that are scheduled to repair the Rancoran enclosure at junction 42."

"What was your delay, Polistine centurion? The Master is most displeased because a few of his personal Beetleguise attendants have already been snacked on by the Rancoran."

"I actually picked up an additional prisoner from Legate —."

But before he could inform Epsilon that he spoken to Buzz, the conversation was interrupted by Gamma Trike, "Where the hellfire are those workers? A Polistine pleasurist was just ripped in half."

"Master will be most displeased. Prisoner Tram, you have clearance to landing Bay D," said Epsilon Trike. "And get down to the research level with your prison workers as soon as possible."

Buzz was continuing to formulate his plan as he flew his Tram down into the *Citadel*. As soon as he flew past the opening down into a corridor of exposed rock with orange guiding lights embedded in the wall, Buzz switched on the Tram's running lights. As he maneuvered the Tram towards the bottom, he observed two hexagonal, metallic doors sliding back to reveal a large, round, landing pad.

Outside hangar bay C, two of the Triceratopian, Theta and Beta, looked around slightly confused. They had been instructed by Epsilon Trike to meet the Legate Zook and his prisoners in the bay and escort them to holding, but the entire Bay appeared to be deserted except for the Tram.

"Where do you think they are?" asked Beta Trike.

"There is something definitely not right, Beta," said Theta. "We should consult Alpha."

"Alpha doesn't think we can think for ourselves. Do you want to hand him more proof?" asked Beta. "I am going in the ship, are you coming with me?"

"I suppose that I have no other choice, do I?"

"You could always let me disintegrate you," laughed Beta.

"That proposal continues to be unfunny, no matter how many times you suggest it," said Theta.

Theta Trike followed behind Beta Trike as he manually lowered the landing ramp at the front of the ship that led the two Trikes into the cargo hold. Both Theta and Beta went to get two pulse rifles from a cabinet but to Beta's surprise it was already open and one pulse rifle had been taken out."

"What do you think happened to the other one?" asked Theta Trike.

From the ceiling, Buzz zoomed down with a pulse rifle in his hand and laid down a line of energy fire along the floor of the cargo hold.

"I am actually the one who borrowed it," he said.

"Fortunately, we have spares," said Beta Trike. "Aim at that wasp and fire."

Buzz dove down towards Theta and Beta as he laid down another round of fire. Theta placed his hand up to his horns and been shot several blue blasts of laser bolts that singed the hair on Buzz's appendages and wings. He pulled back up towards the ceiling as Beta began to launch blue blasts into Buzz's wings. He dove back down again to the floor as he continued to fire the pulse shots from his rifle. Both Beta and Theta Trike continued to shoot laser blasts from their horns. Unable to escape from the barrage of laser blasts from both Triceratopian, Buzz was knocked to the ground.

"We have him, Brother. Wasp, prepare to meet your doom," said Beta Trike as he reached with his mind towards the semi-conscious Legate Prime.

Legate Prime Buzz could feel his whole body being pulled back toward Beta.

"Help me, Brother," said Beta Trike, "Only together, Theta, can we bring this unruly Polistine to his knees."

"Agreed," said Theta Trike who began to use his telekinesis on Buzz.

The trikes reached out with their minds as they beckoned Legate Prime Buzz to begin to move towards them. Buzz found that their powers of attraction very hard to resist as he felt the power of their Triceratopian minds moving his Polistine body towards them. Buzz found himself floating in mid-air across the cargo hold to his Triceratopian assailants.

"Sobek will be most pleased when he sees the great gift we have brought him," said Beta.

"Yes, he will be most pleased," said Theta.

"I wouldn't count on victory too soon," said Buzz as he suddenly sent his body into a horizontal spinning motion that began to knock aluminum and plastidon crates from their shelves. The Triceratopian, Buzz had deduced, were casting a wide psychic field; he had noticed that small objects in the hold had begun to move towards them as well. He reached down for a smaller group of crates that were marked Medical Supplies. He quickly opened the crate by pushing his stinger into the lid and removing one or two small items that were meant to be delivered to the dispensary. In one fluent movement, he placed the items into his jacket pocket.

Meanwhile, Theta and Beta found themselves quickly bombarded with heavy crates, knocking them to the floor. As they tried to climb to their feet, the boxes continued to fly off the shelves at them.

After they were sufficiently subdued, Buzz flew back up towards the ceiling. He angled himself just so that he would come down at a direct angle to the groggy Trikes and began to fly at top speed, flapping his wings as hard as he could. Beta Trike was able to recover long enough to get off a few blasts from his horns but Buzz was able to easily dodge them by moving from side to side. Just before Buzz reached the ground where the Triceratopian were lying, he swung back around to a set of crates that were marked Remote Observation Devices. He lifted the top off the crate and took two flying drones out of the box. He deposited two of the items from his pocket, syringes filled with a sedative into the drones and threw them into the air, whereby they obediently flew down to the Trikes and injected them with the strong tranquilizers.

Buzz dropped down by the two Trikes who were now resting somewhat comfortably courtesy of the tranquilizers. Even though Buzz had believed that these tranquilizers would have completely neutralized them, he was shocked when they both briefly turned over and grunted in their sleep.

"Why do I think that those tranquilizer darts are not going completely do the trick?" asked Buzz,

He was not looking forward to dragging the Triceratopian to the containment cells. Fortunately, he was able to find a hover-pallet in the cargo hold. With a great deal of effort, he dumped each Trike on the hover-pallet and guided it up to the containment cell. Buzz could see that the hover-pallet was straining under the weight of the two Triceratopian; he kept his antennae crossed that the hover-pallet would not break down under the strain in the middle of the corridor. Thankfully, he was able to carry them on the hover-pallet and place them both in cryo-chambers without incident.

"Now that the two of you are tucked away, I'm off to find your Master," said Buzz.

Centurion HumBuzt, along with two Beetleguise centurions, J'azz and Turg, escorted their thirteen prisoners down to the research laboratory where the Rancoran had broken through their glass enclosure. HumBuzt's complement of prison workforce included a red Quillian, four Chamyx —some deep blue and others midnight black — four cheddar-hued Cranitian, and four Trionyx, including Yanick. J'azz and Turg were pushing their charges forward towards their assigned location.

"Come on, you Reptilia scum," taunted J'azz, "Rancoran hasn't had scales and leather for bit of time now. Be nice and give them treat. Put self out of own misery."

"Why don't you mind your own business?" asked the Red Quillian called Leathrdo.

J'azz pulled out a blaster. "Why J'azz not just blow head off now. Let Rancoran come find you?"

"I'd like to see you try, little bug splat," growled Leathrdo.

J'azz fired his blaster on stun setting. "J'azz far from little. Maybe remember his sting now?"

"That is enough, J'azz," barked centurion HumBuzt. "We are going to need each of these Reptilia if we are going to contain this situation."

"Polistine think that he is master of J'azz. Polistine might want to check fact about that," smirked J'azz.

"All of us need to work together to get this job done. The faster we complete this task, the better," said HumBuzt.

"Turg say that hard to argue with. Want to get done. Want to get home," said Turg.

HumBuzt said, "want to tell you how much Zanuck appreciates your help, and possible sacrifice."

"Yes, J'azz really broken up about not seeing some of you again," he said glancing at Leathrdo.

"I said that is enough," said HumBuzt.

"If HumBuzt says so, then it must be true for J'azz." quipped J'azz

Yanick and the other prisoners moved down a long path, Yanick observed a change in architecture. The corridor that their party was in had changed from rock walls to ones that were an antiseptic white. Scattered on the walls were off-gray discus aligned in a horizontal pattern on either side.

Looking forward, he saw that there was an irondoan door that had turned green and oxidized with age. It appeared that someone — or something — had turned and opened the large circular handle on the door. The wheel had three metal radii that met in the center at a smaller circle that had visible claw marks around its perimeter.

Yanick watched helplessly as one of the Cranitian, Bokjat, upon witnessing this sight of the forcefully opened door, yelled, "I am not dealing with whatever that is." Bokjat turned and ran down the corridor, his irondoan appendage restraints jangling.

In a tone of mock concern, J'azz called after him, "No. Stop or you make J'azz shoot you, Cranitian." This only made Bokjat pick up his pace.

"Fine. J'azz gave you chance to come back," J'azz yelled.

J'azz methodically raised his blaster, clicked the gun up to the highest setting, aimed and fired. The Cranitian was probably not even cognizant of what was happening as he disintegrated in a puff of smoke before the eyes of his fellow workers.

"J'azz never care for Cranitian. Have no backbone. Have no sense of glory," said J'azz.

"That is no excuse to kill him," offered Yanick.

"Maybe J'azz hand slip while point gun at you too, Trionyx," J'azz said to Yanick.

"Like to see you try," said Yanick.

"J'azz spin wheel of fate for you and see if you win or lose."

As J'azz raised his blaster to fire, a large object slammed down from above and landed directly on him flattening him and spreading his yellow blood all over the corridor.

"What in the Hive's Master's name is that supposed to be?" asked Leathrdo.

"I think that is meant to be a Rancoran," replied Yanick.

The large creature began to rip portions of J'azz flesh, and organs out of his abdomen. The Rancoran proceeded to devour the unfortunate Beetleguise while he remained conscious, making him a witness to his own demise. The brown and purple beast had an oversized head with a massive snout and serrated teeth, claws on each appendage, and had an extended tail that it used to beat its prey into submission. It also had two oval-shaped feet that allowed it to pounce on its' prey and further subdue their unfortunate victims.

"I am guessing that it is not going to be too long before that thing finishes with the Beetleguise," said Leathrdo. "So I think we should probably be making a run for it."

"Anyone who runs, including Beetleguise centurions," said HumBuzt with a sideways look," will be summarily executed by yours truly. Just think on that for a moment."

"If Turg can't run, then what are we supposed to do?" asked Turg.

"We use centurion J'azz's sacrifice to our benefit," said centurion HumBuzt. He reached over to two of the Chamyx and deactivated the cloaking inhibitors on their collars. "Blackfire and HotCrozz use your camouflage abilities to disable the Rancoran with these paralytic darts. You dare try to use them on me, there will be consequences. I will send fifty thousand volts of electricity through your implants."

"Point taken, centurion," said HotCrozz.

Yanick watched as the two Chamyx moved closer to the feasting Rancoran. When they were nearly on top of him, they climbed the walls on either side, in tandem, before disappearing. The Rancoran looked around for a minute like it seemed to detect the marsh-like smell of the Chamyx, but then went back to its meal.

HumBuzt watched closely for a minute to determine when the Rancoran was coming up for air. He watched it raise its head and then yelled, "Now!"

Yanick watched as a look of utter surprise came across the face of the Rancoran when the beast was suddenly lifted up into the air. It was unable to determine who or what was attacking it when HotCrozz and Blackfire reappeared with their tails wrapped around the waist of the beast, who kicked at the Chamyx with its over-sized feet and chomped at them with its blood-stained teeth.

"Shoot it now!" screamed HotCrozz at Blackfire.

"As soon as it stops beating me," Blackfire screamed back.

"There is no time, you dope. Shoot him!"

The two Chamyx fired half a dozen tranquilizer darts apiece before the Rancoran finally collapsed to the ground, next to the bleeding remains of the Beetleguise.

"One down, five more of these critters to go," smiled HumBuzt.

"You've got to be kidding me," said Leathrdo.

Yanick knew that he had to take his chance to make his move soon, or the time would pass. HumBuzt quickly and efficiently ushered the remaining twelve prisoners inside the dark chamber. There was a large wading pond larger than some imperial flying enclosures that Yanick had seen from time to time on Polistine colonies. At the far end of the room was a rectangular container with clear reinforced glass on its horizontal sides. On each end of the rectangular aquarium as well as on top, there were dull gray irondoan plates that were meant to prevent the inhabitants of the tank from getting loose, a premise that had been disproven by the Rancoran who had ripped a hole and escaped.

HumBuzt announced to the prisoners that once the Rancoran were contained, Warden Sobek had ordered the room sealed because his pets had just proved too dangerous to sentient life.

Yanick saw his chance and decided to take it.

"You can't fool me, Bug. Sobek probably told you to wall them up with us on the inside."

"No, you will be using stones to wall it up from the outside," said HumBuzt.

"No way, Polistine. Sobek wouldn't leave his precious creatures in here without fresh meat. And we are the fresh meat, my dear Reptilia," said Yanick in false hysterics.

"Pull yourself together, Trionyx, and get to work. Nobody is leaving anyone for dead."

"Well, I am telling you this, Bug! No one is taking —"

Yanick, unfortunately, didn't have the opportunity to finish his defiant proclamation as a Rancoran jumped out of the over-sized pool and dragged Yanick into the water in its oversized jaws. Yanick immediately began to attempt to pull away by forcing the spikes on his legs and hands into the face and eyes of the Rancoran, temporarily blinding him.

The beast flailed around in large circular motions, using its sense of smell to detect the mixture of musky oil and mud scent that was the signature smell of the Trionyx. As it moved deeper in the water, ready to sink its teeth into Yanick's hide, there was a barrage of laser blasts through the water that found the large skull of the Rancoran.

Thinking quickly, Yanick hid beneath the leathery flesh of the Rancoran until he was able to determine that the weapons fire had come to an end. He could tell it was time to leave when the Rancoran had finally stopped twitching about.

In a muffled voice, Yanick heard someone deliver the order that the prisoners needed to recover his body, either dead or alive. They probably wouldn't be satisfied until they saw blood in the water, and he was reluctant to shed his own blood since he was not a fan of the sight of his own blood. It was then that he noticed that the creature was spilling violet-colored blood, the same as his own. He twisted his spike deeper into one of the wounds of the dead Rancoran and allowed its blood to fill the pool.

"Wait a minute," stated HumBuzt. "Don't think that there is much left of the Trionyx. Let's wrangle the three other Rancoran and wall up the room before there are any more causalities."

According to Legate Prime Buzz's instructions, Yanick recovered a small acetylene torch from a false stone by the pond. He then made his way for the drainage port at the bottom of the swimming pond. Using his thumb spike, he twisted the bolts out of the screw holes and moved the screen aside. Once he squeezed his sizeable frame into the medium-sized pipe on the other side of the access point, he pulled the screen back toward him as he secured the plate with the torch.

Yanick swam up the tube that led to the exhaust port beneath the medical dispensary. Even though he had previously been feigning distress over the walls closing in around him, Yanick was now beginning to feel the sensation for real. He pushed himself to move faster because the quicker that he was out of the tube, the better.

"Can't go forward. Can't go back. Now what" said Yanick.

He carefully brought the lower part of his body to just above the water line in the horizontal pipe. In preparation for making his exit, he pulled his legs back to gain momentum and extra strength. He took one last deep breath for luck before pushing his feet forward with all his might. To his surprise, the metal grate slid up into a recess in the pipe, leaving his path clear to go flying into the room. Yanick landed, seconds later, on the tile floor of the medical dispensary.

"Who the hellfire opened that gate?"

The last thing that Yanick was expecting was an answer to his rhetorical question, but that is exactly what he got though. He heard the voice of the Medical Dispensary manager, Dr. Rabun, from above him. "The gate was rigged to open upon contact by Warden Sobek."

Yanick looked up to see that the Cranitian Dr. Rabun was strapped to one of his medical beds with canvas restraints and a metal dome covering his head. There were seven black floating drones with rows of syringes encircling their midsection. Apparently, once Yanick had made contact with the grate, the drones' automated program had been activated by the Medical Querzi. They were all headed in the same general direction, towards Dr. Rabun on the table.

"You, Trionyx! Help me!" Rabun screamed.

"What do you want me to do?"

"Take out the drones, however you can."

The drones were going to be on top of the doctor at any moment so Yanick knew that there was no time to lose. He knocked two of the nearest flying drones to the floor, smashing them with his tail. As he swung back toward the table, Yanick sent spikes flying from his tail, pinning two more drones against the wall. As he watched the drones crumple into scrap metal, two more drones flew directly at him, pushing him into a nearby cabinet.

Yanick pushed himself as close as he could to the cabinet doors. With less than an inch to spare between himself and the cabinet, Yanick reached up and tore off the cabinet door and flung it at the two offending drones. He looked on in relief as they were crushed.

It was then that Yanick heard a cry from across the room: "A little help would be nice."

He looked over to see that a final black and gray drone was seconds from pressing a syringe into the doctor's neck. Yanick climbed over the medical bed in front of him and launched himself up toward the laser scalpel above where Rabun was restrained.

"It is starting to pinch the slightest bit," yelled the doctor.

"Alright, just stop getting your shell in a bunch," said Yanick. He grabbed a hold of the control panel that he found on top of the laser scalpel. "Which buttons do I push, Doctor?"

"The orange and red ones. The orange and red ones!"

"Oh, I see," said Yanick. At the last possible second, Yanick activated the orange laser. As it radiated down from the scalpel, it cut the drone into two halves, sending it crashing to the floor.

"Dr. Rabun, are you alright?" asked Yanick as he jumped down and began to unloosen the straps on the medical bed.

"Do I look alright?" asked Rabun sarcastically. "The Warden Sobek imprisoned me in my own laboratory. He set up those motion-activated Drones to pump me full of enough barbiturates to kill me while making it look like some patsy, guessing you, murdered me. My genetically enhanced Triceratopian are running amuck. And to top it off, Warden Sobek sent some homicidal Chamyx —"

"That would be Hotfire, I am guessing," mused Yanick.

"Yes, Hotfire, off on a suicide mission armed with my Diabolix toxin."

"Well, doctor, you need to make your way down to hangar bay C. There is a Tram there that will take you back to the administrative dome. The most important thing is that you are not here in about five minutes," said Yanick.

"You are coming with me?"

"No, I was given very specific instructions to remain here."

"Well, I can tell you that there is no way that is happening," said Dr. Rabun.

"Doctor," said Yanick as he grabbed his orange smock, "you don't have time to think right now. If you want to make it through this day alive then you need to listen to me. But more importantly, you need to listen to the Legate Prime."

"Very well. Do you need anything else from me?"

"I just need you to show me how to operate the remote viewing feed."

"That is no problem. I can activate the viewing system before I leave and show you how to use it. Was there anything else?"

"Yes. A little Polistine told me you were investigating compression technology."

THIRTY MINUTES LATER

In the hangar bay C, Buzz walked over to one of the crates marked 'blasters' in the Tram and retrieved a Pulse Rifle from inside. He made his way up the Chute Lift to the executive wing of the *Citadel*, but as soon as he stepped out alarms started going off.

As he ran down the hall, Buzz was thinking to himself that he may have been better off if he'd let Yanick do the running and he dealt with the Rancoran instead. Just as he finished his thought, what should come busting through the door but a Rancoran.

"For the Hive Master's sake, I wasn't putting forth an invitation!"

The Rancoran immediately turned his head and extended his sizeable jaws. At the very last second, Buzz managed to step back and jump towards the ceiling. The Rancoran leapt up as well and followed him up toward the ceiling. It pressed back on its hind legs to give its body a little more leverage, then started stabbing at the flying Polistine.

Buzz continued to alternately maneuver to the left and right, choosing in each particular instance whatever direction was farthest away from the Rancoran. Realizing that he could not keep up this game of misdirection, Buzz conceived of a desperate ploy to escape. The only downside to this gambit was that he would most likely be killed in the execution of his brilliant plan.

Buzz backed himself into a corner of the metallic corridor where he spied a junction box that had come loose, probably from overuse of the palladium sliding doors. He grabbed the grey box off the wall and launched it directly at the head of the Rancoran, a decision that he regretted immediately. Apparently being hit in the head by a blunt object did little to slow down the raging beast and, in fact, seemed to strength his resolve to capture its prey.

The Rancoran propelled itself through the air to where Buzz was currently hovering, only to land flat on his face as Buzz stepped aside. When the Rancoran raised his head, Buzz could see that it was mad.

"Guess it's time to run," he said.

What the Rancoran did not know was that Buzz had flown through these corridors so often during the last fifteen years that he possessed an extra sensory ability to know exactly where he was in the *Citadel* at any given time. The Legate Prime turned the corner at the end of the hallway, making sure that he was still being pursued. Sure enough, the Rancoran was right behind him as he turned the corner and made his way up the adjoining hallway, where Warden Sobek kept supplemental food rations, additional uniforms, and emergency provisions. The Rancoran was now close enough to chomp at Buzz's legs motivating him to move even faster toward the circular door.

Within sight of the round metal door, Buzz tripped over his own feet and began to skid. He had to push his body forward just before reaching his destination so he could grab the handle, in order to avoid becoming a permanent decorative covering. He turned around to see that the Rancoran was at his heels. With a mighty leap, Buzz jumped over the Rancoran, crashing down by its tail, and quickly scrambled up above the entrance to the room — a decompression chamber — but not before slamming the door.

As Buzz listened to the beast trying to force its way out, he jumped down in front of the control panel. "This is nothing personal, my large-head friend. Just survival of the smartest," he said Buzz as he pressed the button that released the inner door, sending the Rancoran flying into the vacuum of space.

Buzz heard a familiar, ominous voice behind him at that moment, "Legate Prime, I was just getting ready to express the self-same sentiment regarding your disposal."

Legate Prime Buzz turned around to see Warden Sobek, flanked by two more of his Triceratopian. "Trikes open the door to the compression chamber and toss him into space e. I regret that I will be seeing the demise of three worthy adversaries this day. Hotfire has likely been already been sent to his death. Dr. Rabun has been taken care of with great efficiency. And you, my do-gooder Legate, will be the last to die today."

"Not if I have anything to say about it," said Buzz as one of the Trikes opened the door while the other grabbed Buzz by the appendage, proceeding to shove him inside the chamber. "You should have restrained me before sending me to my doom."

Buzz reached his leg into his pocket and pulled out the final tranquilizer dart. In a fluid motion, he pressed the syringe into the neck of Delta Trike. As the needle went in, Delta Trike let out a haunting scream before crumpling to the floor. Epsilon Trike immediately began using his telekinetic ability to bring Buzz towards him. While witnessing this exchange, Warden Sobek was screaming, "Enough of that, just shoot him!"

As Buzz watched the two Trikes preparing to use their laser blasts, Buzz decided to use the momentum against his attacker. He backed up as far as he could against the far wall, and sent his body hurdling towards his Triceratopian attackers, knocking them to the ground.

"You idiots, one of you needs to get up and stop him," shouted Warden Sobek.

Epsilon and Delta Trike were momentarily only able to remain in a dazed state on the ground as Buzz picked up one of the Trikes pulse rifles as he made his way down the corridor towards the medical dispensary.

As he looked around, Buzz heard someone moving around. He silently glided to the center of the room with his rifle positioned to deal with whatever threat presented itself. It was then that he looked up to see an unwelcomed site.

Yanick DcCullen was standing with his back to the Legate Prime. He raised his rifle as he positioned it in line with Yanick's head for a clean shot.

"Don't move, Yanick."

"For the Hive Master's Sake, just don't shoot me!"

"This dispensary was full of drugs this morning. What have you done with them?"

"I don't know what you are talking about. It was empty when I got here," said Yanick.

"And where is Rabun? What have you done with him?"

"There were a bunch of drones in here. One of them incinerated him before my eyes."

Buzz turned towards the door of the medical dispensary as it opened once again to reveal Warden Sobek upon his hover-discus with the two Triceratopian on either side of him. Before he could even approach Buzz though, a number of familiar holographic figures surround him; the members of the Hawking Brain Beetle Council.

"Cousin Sobek," said Osiris Bokhun, "how do you account for the disappearance of Dr. Rabun?"

"What has happened to the medical supplies that were shipped to you earlier this month?" asked Council Member Ra Bokhun.

"Before he was exterminated by the drones, the doctor did say there was a recording," stated Yanick.

"Be silent, you maggot Reptilia," said Epsilon Trike, "before you are walking around without a head." As Epsilon Trike raised his weapon, the hologram of Osiris Bokhun commanded with a deafening roar, "Stand down, foul Triceratopian! The Hawking Brain Beetle Council will hear this recording.!"

"Cousin Osiris, dare you trust the word of this criminal?" asked Warden Sobek.

"Oh, the Hawking won't be trusting my words," whispered Yanick. "She'll be hearing it from your own voice."

"Play the recording. Now!" demanded Osiris Bokhun.

Yanick kept his hands above his head. "Legate Prime, I am telling the truth. Please obey your Hawking masters and press the green button on the console."

"For your sake, you better not be lying, Reptilia," said Buzz as he pressed the green button. From internal speakers in the walls, the Hawking heard the conversation between Doctor Rabun and Sobek earlier in the morning.

Doctor Rabun; "Because if the toxin doesn't work on Diabolix then you are delivering a compound into the hands of an individual who would have no qualms about starting a galactic plague. He could wipe out two thirds of the population of the known galaxy,"

Warden Sobek: "Come Triceratopian, I must return to my office. The Doctor has provided me with new insight. I must convene these new concerns to the Omnipotent Hawking Council, immediately,"

The Alpha Triceratopian: "Are we really leaving Master?"

Warden Sobek: "Oh, we have yet to begun to outwit the good Dr. Rabun. (Whispering): Take Hotfire around to the rear access vent and shove him in there. If he doesn't open that door in an expedient matter, you crawl through the vent to the dispensary. Then, you kill him and the Doctor."

"What exactly are you referring to when you said you were going to outwit Dr. Rabun?" asked Osiris Bokhun.

"Did you possibly mean that you would stage a robbery and blame the good Doctor for the crime?" suggested Legate Prime Buzz.

"The Hawking Omnipotent Council has determined that there are questions to be resolved. Legate Prime Buzz, you will assume the post of acting warden until this issue is resolved," said Osiris Bokhun.

"It is a heavy responsibility, Bokhun, but I will try my very best to fulfill my duties in an admirable fashion," said Warden Buzz.

"Cousin Sobek, there are questions that need to be asked. And it seems you are the only individual who can answer them. Prepare to return to the homeworld," said Osiris Bokhun.

"I haven't done anything wrong," yelled Sobek.

"Your Trike servants may also have information, so they will need to accompany you," said Ra Bokhun.

"You cannot do this to me! I am warden of Minerva Penitentiary," screamed Sobek.

"No, shell-head, there is a new warden in the galaxy, and his name is Buzz," said Yanick.

Yanick and Warden Buzz watched as a blue sphere encompassed the two Trikes and Sobek Bokhun inside a bubble. The sphere glistened and crackled for a moment before it disappeared into the air. Unbeknownst to Yanick and Warden Buzz, the bubble reappeared moments later in a prison compound on the Hawking home world of Meditaplassen where the trio were escorted to waiting cells.

Once the two Triceratopian and the Hawking Brain Beetle had vanished, the holographic image of the members of the Omnipotent Hawking Council flickered away, save for one representative.

"Polistine, you have undertaken a great responsibility with the administration of this facility," said Osiris Bokhun.

"I swear to my allegiance to the Omnipotent Hawking Brain Beetle Council."

"Make sure that you do. Your predecessor became negligent in the disposition of his duties. And for his negligence, I assure you he will pay dearly."

Yanick and Warden Buzz watched as the Hawking Brain Beetle vanished into the ether.

It was then that Buzz turned to Yanick, "Trionyx, you truly gave a flawless performance. I believe that the Council really believes that the Doctor is really dead. Now where exactly is he?"

"He is waiting for you by the Tram in hangar bay C."

Warden Buzz sighed, "He is going to need to be stowed away in a distant portion of the Conglomerate. No one can ever know that Rabun is still alive."

"Or the Hawking Brain Beetle will declare war on the Polistines?" asked Yanick.

"To say the least. Now secondly, what happened to the contents of my dispensary?"

"I don't know exactly what you are talking about?" asked Yanick.

"Sobek was right about one thing. The dispensary was full this morning. So where are all my chemicals and pharmaceuticals?" said Buzz as he cocked the pulse rifle and placed it against Yanick's head.

"For the Hive Master's sake —"

"If you want to keep your head, then I suggest you tell me what happened to the drugs."

"I can't tell you because I don't know," said Yanick.

The Polistine touched his appendage to his antennae to activate his ear-comm, "HumBuzt, this is Legate Prime Buzz, do you read me?"

"You are coming in loud and clear, Legate Prime. How can I help you?"

"Actually, I have assumed the position of acting warden. Sobek was re-called to Meditaplassen."

"Very good, Warden buzz. How may I be of service?" asked centurion HumBuzt.

"First and foremost, were you able to facilitate the repairs at junction 42?" asked Warden Buzz.

"We were unable to recover two Rancoran, but the rest are permanently sealed in that room."

"Very good. Secondly, I am standing here with my gun trained on in-mate 3249."

"Yep, that Trionyx was a skittish one. Thought he was eaten by the Rancoran," said HumBuzt.

"You can come collect him in the medical dispensary," said Warden Buzz.

"I am on my way. Warden Buzz," said HumBuzt as the screen went blank.

A spiteful sneer crossed Yanick's face upon hearing that he was going back to his cell. "You know that you'll never see those drugs again if I can help it."

"I look forward to seeing how that turns out for you." said Warden Buzz.

Yanick realized only too late that Buzz had just stuck him with the last tranquilizer dart.

Chapter 21
THE EYE OF HERMES

Like a greedy child preparing to consume the last bite of a saccharine cracker, the dying star Zeta Sephi Three pulled the unfortunate science vessel, *Mjölnir* closer to the sun's fiery dying heart.

Inside the *Mjölnir* cargo hold, the casual observer would be witness to the improbable scenario of watching five pink Ruddarian aliens walking down a wall with their gravity boots. Following these Ruddarians was a Polistine, Lieutenant Thorn, who was trying to fly the best he could, using his broken wings.

"Captain, we are still upside down. Can you do something about getting the horizontal stabilizers back online so we don't have to scale this wall like we are climbing Mount Yggdrasil?" complained Defensive Officer Kon.

"I swear that I will render your body unconscious this very second, Pink Monkey Kon, if you do not cease your incessant complaining," said Thorn.

"Could both of you stop using up the oxygen with your nonsensical babble?" Kasidy interjected herself into the conversation.

"I will be quiet out of respect for you, Pink Monkey Vulkner," said Thorn.

"Is it me?" asked Ensign Rajkvek. "Or is it getting harder to walk?"

"As we are getting pulled closer to the star going supernova, the external gravity keeps doubling exponentially," said Lieutenant Lokhra. "Pretty soon, we will not even be able to stand up straight."

"Then why did we go flying across the room before?" asked Kon.

"The star's gravity wasn't able to locate us in space initially. But it knows exactly where we are and won't let go," said Lokhra.

"That's just great to know," said Kasidy. "But does anyone have any idea how to either get that Green Diamond to stop draining all the energy from the ship's system, preferably, find a way to get the ship free from being pulled into the heart of a dying star?"

"Wasn't that daggit diamond supposed to snuff the star out like a spent candle?" asked Kon.

"At least, I had a more feasible idea than 'just blow something up.'"

"Quiet, all of you!" exclaimed Thorn. "Your vessel has acquired greater vibratory motion."

"What does that mean, exactly?" asked Kasidy.

"The arrival of a new vessel to this area of space." stated Thorn.

Junior navigator, Ensign Thetan, watched in dismay at her station on the flight deck of the *Mjölnir* as a large circular craft, emerged from sub-space. The Quartrack Light Destroyer shot a warning blast across the bow of the Ruddarian science vessel.

"Sir, our scarab friends appear to have followed us," said Thetan.

"Sir, we are being hailed by their captain," said Communication Officer Weingarter.

"***Noes tega mortag expo Xeperian. E promcuck noes thich balwa fum heu Actkocos,***" proclaimed Nectaxus as he appeared on the *Mjölnir* viewer screen.

"Are the blastard translator circuits down again?" cried Captain Odinord.

"I think that the Polistine is seeking revenge for the death of his soldiers. Saying something about blowing us out of the sky," said Weingarter.

"I really don't care at this point," stated Captain Odinord.

"Sir, it looks like he is preparing to fire on us," said Thetan.

"Do we have any power that the Green Diamond hasn't taken from our systems yet?" asked Captain Odinord.

"Even if we did, Captain, our spacecraft is still being pulled into the star. We would never be able to get even a halfway-decent target lock," said Weingarter.

"Captain, they are firing once again," said Thetan.

"All hands, grab onto something solid," said Captain Odinord.

Captain Odinord quickly grabbed the sides of his throne-like command chair as he watched the flight deck shake back and forth at an even steeper angle. He watched helplessly as the four remaining crew members rolled out of their chairs onto the floor.

"We can't take another hit, like that, Captain. The gravity from the star is already beginning to tear us apart," said Thetan.

"You said that the Zeta Sephi star is still pulling us in, right, Thetan?"

"Yes, sir. The only thing that is keeping us from being pulled in is the repulse thrusters and they are probably going to go any minute,"

"Think it is time that we evened the playing field between us and the Polistine captain. Shut down the repulse thrusters for fifteen to twenty seconds, Thetan," said Captain Odinord.

"Sir, without those thrusters in operation, we will go flying into the star," said Thetan.

"Junior Navigator Thetan, I gave you a direct order. Now, either follow my order or I will have you relieved of duty!"

"Yes, Captain," said Thetan. She switched off the repulse thrusters on the *Mjölnir*, causing the Ruddarian vessel to violently lurch forward. It felt to the crew like the *Mjölnir* had re-entered sub-space."

"Thetan, re-engage the repulse thrusters!" yelled Odinord.

"We are going too fast, Captain," she said. "They won't be enough to stop us."

Captain Odinord leapt out of his chair, pushing Thetan aside, as he activated the repulse thrusters. The ship continued to lurch forward momentarily before stopping in space at an angle.

"I apologize, Captain," said Thetan. "I suppose I panicked."

"It is alright, Junior Navigator. We have all been there before. The most important thing is we are at a stop-gap for the moment," said Captain Odinord. "Now let's see if our Scarab friends take the bait."

On board the Quartrack Light Destroyer, the *Pollister*, Legate Nectaxus, was looking on in disbelief as the Ruddarian science vessel moved closer to the collapsing star.

"What could those Ruddarian Pink Monkeys be thinking?" asked Legate Prime Nectaxus.

"I do not know but, I would advise that we don't pursue," replied Yodok.

"And why is that?" asked Legate Nectaxus.

"Because the Ruddarian vessel is in imminent danger of being destroyed., And if our ship is sucked into the star along with them when we will have failed in our mission," commented Yodok.

"Keep up that questioning about the purpose of our mission, and you'll find your next assignment will be cleaning out the inside of exhaust tubes on Polistine Battle cruisers," sneered Nectaxus.

"Whatever our goal is, Sir, my suggestion is that we wait until they destroy themselves and then just recover it from the debris," suggested Yodok.

"There are twenty of my best Xeperian Gladiators floating in space like common garbage. I will not dishonor their memory by allowing those Ruddarians to have a peaceful end at the center of a star."

"Legate, I believe that vengeance is clouding your judgement," said Yodok.

"Then it might just be the hour to exhale our last breath," said Nectaxus.

Nectaxus turned towards the black scarab-like creature who was his Xeperian Astral Engineer. "Bratox, I crave Ruddarian blood this day. Bring that ship to me!"

"I wish to have it noted in the spacecraft's record that I am extremely opposed to this action," clucked Bratox.

"Duly noted. Now bring me my prize, Astral Engineer Bratox."

"Very well, Legate Prime," said Bratox.

As Bratox disengaged the engine restrictors that were preventing the ship from being drawn into Zeta Sephi Three, the Quartrack Light Destroyer *Pollister* was lurched forward in space. The remaining Xeperian Gladiators of Purple L Swarn found themselves tossed about their workstations like youngling's rag dolls. Some Xeperian were slammed into walls so hard that there was nothing left but bug splats.

Once Nectaxus recovered his senses, he looked around to see that Yodok, had been thrown forward and impaled on the spike of an irondoan railing. Poor Yodok was staring back at him with a blank expression. Bratox had met a similar fate when he had been thrown from his chair and broken his neck.

Nectaxus had to look away as baby Xeperians were coming out of Bratox's body, devouring his remains.

He checked his console to determine whether the *Pollister* still possessed teleport capability. By some miracle, the system was still operational.

"Bratox's younglings, I apologize for placing you in harm's way so early in your life, but your sacrifice will be remembered in story and song for time and immemorial. Farewell!"

Nectaxus pressed three buttons on his console; orange beams appeared, surrounding him and transporting the 40 Xeperian offspring over to the *Mjölnir*.

Nectaxus barely had time to lament his decision when he was knocked backwards as a massive green beam punched its way out of the lower portion of the Ruddarian science vessel, landing directly in the mid-section of the *Pollister*.

Kon and Kasidy had just reached the door of the cargo bay when the repulse thrusters had been disengaged. Kon could only watch helplessly as Rajkvek was crushed by a number of falling containers.

Kon looked up at the wall to see that Dr. Tulare's gravity boots began to fail, and he was slipping off the smooth surface like an Trionyx fried egg. Unable to reach him, Lieutenant Kon could only stretch out his hand as he called, "Doctor Tulare!"

Dr. Tulare began to scream as he felt himself falling, "Somebody! Help me!" yelled Dr. Tulare as The ceiling of the cargo hold came racing towards him at greater and greater speed. Suddenly though, he found himself suspended in mid-air.

"I have you, Tulare Pink Monkey," said Lieutenant Thorn.

Lieutenant Kon was so fixed on Tulare's drama that he practically jumped into the air when he heard a voice coming from behind. "That was a close one!" Kon turned with his blaster drawn to find Lieutenant Lokhra standing there. "Calm down, Kon. It is only me."

"Don't ever sneak up on me like that again, Lokhra!" yelled Kon.

Lokhra suddenly looked down to the ceiling of the cargo hold to see orange teleport beams appearing. As the orange lights began to coalesce into solid figures, they saw Xeperian Gladiators surrounding them with their claws drawn for combat.

"Captain, we've got big problems down here," said Kon as he touched his ear-comm.

"Guessing the Green Diamond has already managed to disrupt communications," said Kasidy.

"It would seem that is the case. Guessing we are on our own."

"This is how combat should be," said Lieutenant Thorn.

As Thorn flew downwards, he handed Kon and Kasidy each a broad sword from his belt.

"Defend yourselves well, Pink Monkeys," quipped Thorn. "If not, then meet your demise well."

"What are you supposed to use to defend yourself?" asked Kasidy.

"I will use what evolution has provided me with in her infinite wisdom: my dual stingers!"

Kasidy turned to face three Xeperians clawing and scratching her legs and arms. She sliced through the lower half of one and watched as it dropped to the ceiling while his upper half flew up toward the floor. Kasidy pushed her sword forward to impale a 2nd Xeperian, then cut off the legs of the final Xeperian.

Lieutenant Lokhra found himself surrounded by four Xeperian who were snapping their claws at his head. Lokhra kicked at one of them, knocking it to the floor and giving it a non-lethal blow to the chest. Lokhra grabbed another Xeperian by the legs.

"Make a wish, you scarab," he yelled as he pulled each of its legs in opposite directions.

Before Lokhra could even turn around, another of Bratox's younglings grabbed Lokhra by the arms as another grabbed his legs. "Now, we shall be the one making a wish," said the third Xeperian.

"I don't see that happening any time soon," said Lokhra, as he shot off one of the Xeperian's arms, then turned the blaster towards the other Xeperian. He managed to shoot this Xeperian in the gut, and watched as the scarab collapse to the floor.

Kon grabbed the broad sword he'd received from Lieutenant Thorn and began slicing and dicing Xeperian opponents like he was making his way through a Maize field back home on Galilei. The Xeperian younglings of Bratox kept trying to latch onto Kon's arms or legs, but he continued to slice them in half, leaving them writhing in pain on the floor.

Facing yet another Xeperian opponent, Kon saw out of the corner of his eye that two others were making their way across the cargo hold to ambush Lieutenant Thorn. He called out to Thorn, but it was already too late.

Thorn looked down at his abdomen at the sets of Xeperian pinchers came bursting through his chest; yellow blood came spewing out of him and onto the floor.

"Thorn, no!" screamed Lieutenant Kon.

"I have had an honorable death, Pink Monkey Kon. Make sure they sing songs of my glory!" said Thorn.

He was holding an appendage to his chest as blood emptied out of his body when the *Mjölnir* suddenly lurched forward, throwing Thorn through the air, without the assistance of his wings, towards the Green Diamond.

Lokhra, Kon, Vulkner, and Tulare turned in unison towards the Green Diamond. Thorn's body now was lying upon the Eye of Hermes. It hummed for a moment. Then a green, other-worldly beam shot through Thorn's body, then through the ceiling of the cargo hold and out into space.

Kon, along with the others, looked on in shock and amazement as Thorn sat up, his wound completely mended. Despite his multi-lensed eyes and already stoic expression, Kon sensed that there was something different about Thorn. But Kasidy knew right away what was coming next. It was what she had glimpsed when the Eye had invaded her mind. Kasidy knew what she would see when she gazed upon Thorn's face.

"Behold Ruddarians, I have arisen from my long slumber," said Thorn. As he turned in a circular motion around the room, the possessed Polistine completely incinerated each remaining Xeperian.

"Who the Hellfire are you?" asked Kon incredulously.

"No, don't," yelled Kasidy.

"No. I would like to know. Who are the Hellfire are you? And what have you done to Thorn?" asked Kon.

"We are Thorn of Hermes, and we will be leaving with our property now," said the newly merged creature.

"You have to come through me, first," said Kon as he shot several laser blasts into Thorn's chest.

"We are glad to oblige," said Thorn of Hermes as he reached out to evaporate Kon.

Kasidy hoped that she was still connected in some way to the Eye of Hermes.

"Lokhra, do you think the force field came down again on your wormhole?"

"It probably did, why?" asked Lokhra.

"Just cover me if my plan blows up in my face," said Kasidy.

"Hey, Green Eyes. You lose something?" she asked as she reached out and picked up the diamond.

"You shall return our property this instant," yelled Thorn of Hermes.

"In a Moosran's eye, I will. You are going to have to catch me."

"I command you to stop!" screamed Thorn of Hermes.

Kasidy jumped down to the entrance of the cargo hold and made her way down the hallway toward the swirling tornado of cosmic energy that had just yesterday swallowed up Ensign Karajan. Kasidy could hear the Thorn of Hermes' cries as she carried the precious Eye of Hermes, the haunting cries imploring her to stop. She didn't know where her journey would take her next, but Kasidy did know that the Eye of Hermes would not be a threat to this universe for, hopefully, a very, very long time.

Thorn of Hermes saw Kasidy running down the hallway towards the Tornado vortex. With his wings fully restored, he reached out and grabbed Kasidy's leg but, to his surprise, Kasidy grabbed his leg and they went sailing into the vortex together. The swirling cosmic energy began to close in on itself — sending a wave of powerful energy — from the vortex or the Eye of Hermes, out into the surrounding space.

On the flight deck of the *Mjölnir*, Captain Odinord watched as a wave of energy suddenly burst into existence around his ship and the Quartrack Light Destroyer, pushing them like youngling's playthings far away from the Zeta Sephi Three star, to opposite ends of the Cosmos.

"Captain, this is Lieutenant Kon. What is the situation on the flight deck?"

"Never mind our situation. Where did that wave come from?"

"Engineer Vulkner managed to close Lieutenant Lokhra's wormhole, Sir. Must have been happened when the Vortex closed in on itself," said Kon.

"How did we get back power?" asked Captain Odinord.

"Vulkner entered the Vortex with the Eye of Hermes, followed by the Polistine, Thorn, who now, it seems is possessed by the Eye."

"How are we supposed to stop a nine-foot-tall Polistine possessed by an ancient entity?" asked Captain Odinord.

"Vulkner already did that job for us. Think she might have dragged Thorn into the Vortex."

"Well for the Hive Master's Sake, where is she?"

"Unknown, Captain Odinord. Unknown," said Kon.

Chapter 22
HUNASH'S LAST STAND

Second Skin, who had reassumed the visage of a ten-foot-tall red Quillian, was reluctant to divert his attention from guarding his remaining twenty-two hostages, but he was aware how impatient Lord Diabolix, and his First Lieutenant, Multiverse, could become when they were not constantly updated about whether or not he'd acquired the Methurazus Rejuvenate.

"I must momentarily tear myself away from the pleasure of your company," he told his prisoners. "Though I feel compelled to remind you that in my present form as a Quillian, I possess exceptional hearing, so I would suggest that none of you make a fool-hearted heroic plan to subdue me."

He removed a pulse blaster from a grey long coat that he had procured from the luggage compartment. With a sufficient amount of bravado, Second Skin sprayed a volley of laser blasts above his head in an effort to punctuate his point.

Most of the hostages held their appendages over their heads at the incredibly loud sound of the weapons fire while a few of the Cranitian pleasurists merely stuck their heads inside their shells.

"Wonderful to see that we understand one another," smiled Second Skin.

He moved to the rear of the Observation Deck and removed a square, flat-screen remote tablet from below the upper storage cabinet. He'd stored the device there in case there'd complications in retrieving the Methurazus Device. Once again, his instincts were right.

He used his chubby red fingers to operate the controls, and the image of a blue-and-black striped Chamyx appeared on the screen.

"Who am I speaking to?" inquired Second Skin.

"I could ask the very same question," said Multiverse.

"Very well," sighed Second Skin, always annoyed with having to go through this hood and blaster charade. "The Xeperian howls at Midnight."

"The Quillian laughs with delight at the Café," replied Multiverse.

"Now that we have established who everyone is, I have a slight problem," said Second Skin.

"That is not good. The Hawking infidels are preparing to move against the Master. If we wish to retrieve him, it needs to be now or never."

"The Polistine vessel *Pollister* is nowhere to be found in this quadrant," said Second Skin.

"It might be necessary to implement our alternate plan. How far away are you from Meditaplassen?" asked Multiverse.

"Less than two light years," said Second Skin.

"Then proceed as we discussed. However, you must stage your actions as if they are occurring by our enemies' design." said Multiverse.

"I understand. The hand of Diabolix will once again cradle the Universe," smiled Second Skin.

"Is there anything I can do for you, Gowanda?" asked Roethroba.

Gowanda, who had been the unfortunate victim of Second Skin's abuse, sat quietly in a corner with a fellow pleasurist, Roethroba — who had aqua-blue skin with red strips along her back, and wore red-thigh boots and an orange one-piece jumpsuit with the center of her back exposed.

"I am still in a great deal of pain, Sweetie, but I think I will survive it," said Gowanda

Gowanda, who had gold and orange skin and was wearing a low-cut green skirt with numerous holes in the back for the humps of her slender shell, looked at Roethroba with her pupil-less, large eyes.

"Trust me. We are going to make it out of this, all of us," smiled Roethroba.

Roethroba suddenly felt the small, fin-like plates along her spine being pulled backwards. She cocked her head to the side, but was only able to hear the voice of the red Quillian in her ear slit. "Not necessarily. Some of us might find ourselves dead by the time it is all over."

"Please don't hurt her," cried Gowanda. "It is my fault."

"This should be good," smiled the Quillian-Second Skin. "How it is your fault, my dear?"

"She was asking me how I was feeling," said Gowanda.

"Very well. Since it would be extremely unchivalrous of me to teach you another lesson —"

"Don't! Whatever you are going to do, Don't" cried Gowanda.

"It is alright, Gowanda. Whatever he does to me, I can deal with the pain," smiled Roethroba.

"Brave Reptilia. Fool hearted, but still brave none the less," said Second Skin as he wrapped his hand around her neck. "Prepare yourself for the Afterburn, my dear," said Second Skin.

"I am not just ready to go, as of yet," barked Roethroba as she extended her jaws and closed her mouth around Second Skin's nose. She looked to see that she had caused more than a flesh wound before Roethroba tried to grab Gowanda by the hand to run from the Observation Deck.

"No!" yelled Gowanda. "Save yourself!"

"I am saving both of us," said Roethroba. She pulled on Gowanda's paws, but she refused to move. Just as Roethroba gave up on trying to persuade Gowanda to come, Quillian-Second Skin recovered his senses, as he nursed his bitten nose with his claw. In the next moment, Second Skin had switched his appearance from a red Quillian into a grey Chamyx.

Chamyx-Second Skin was at his most vulnerable during the conversion from one bodily shape to another, which made what came next all the more devastating. A panel dropped down from the Observation Deck's ceiling as a Cranitian wearing a pink skirt, crimson jacket, and pink blouse came bursting through the ceiling firing a pulse rifle.

Chamyx-Second Skin was knocked back several steps before recovering his balance and firing his own pulse rifle at Hunash. "Sweet Hunash. I don't know how to put it more plainly. We had fun, but the romance is over."

"It is only over when I blow your head off!" exclaimed Hunash.

"You first."

The Chamyx-Second Skin whipped his five-foot long tail in a lasso-fashion up into the ceiling as Hunash disappeared under the coverings. Chamyx-Second Skin used his tail in a methodical fashion to punch out each square in the ceiling in rapid succession. After pushing out ten to twelve squares, he identified the square where Hunash was hiding, and reached up with his tail and grabbed Hunash from the ceiling, bringing her down to his eye level.

"I regret to inform you that I will take a considerable bit of delight in ending you. But, it is nothing personal."

The Chamyx-Second Skin cradled the Cranitian Pleasurist in his arms as he raised her above his head. But as he prepared to break her back, Gowanda grabbed Hunash's discarded weapon and fired it at Second Skin's legs. Hunash tumbled down to the floor before recovering a moment later. She quickly ushered Roethroba and Gowanda towards the door of the Observation Deck. Hunash tried to calm herself while trying to recall the unlock code, but was unable to remember the digits.

"The code is 6587, Hunash," provided Roethroba.

"Quick," yelled Gowanda. "I think he's getting up."

"Going as fast as I can!" yelled Hunash.

"You might want to go a little faster," interjected Roethroba.

The Chamyx-Second Skin had evolved once again. This time, Second Skin had taken on the appearance of an extremely large, extremely mobile combination of a Madagascan multi-crawler and a Beetleguise with a total of eight limbs. The Beetle-Crawler-Second Skin was climbing the walls in a circular motion as he made his way towards the three pleasurists trying to exit the room.

"Come back, my sweet pleasurists. I haven't yet begun to play!"

Hunash looked back at the Beetle-Crawler as she was entering the code, but was redirected by Gowanda. "You work on getting that door open. I'll deal with that," she said blasting off several shots.

Hunash took a deep breath. She had to trust that Gowanda would handle the situation. She decided that she would focus on the entry of one number at a time; she even managed to block out the sounds of the pulse blasts. She also refused to allow herself by the screams for pleasurists' blood.

"6-5-8-7," Hunash said slowly to herself. Despite the fact that she was aware that she had taken her time, it still came as a surprise to her when the door to the Observation Deck finally slid open.

"Let's go!" Roethroba yelled as the three ran, slamming the door behind them.

The pleasurists ran, but grabbing the pulse-rifle from Gowanda's hands, Roethroba swung on her heels to discharge the weapon at the door panel. An explosion of sparks emanated from the small box.

"You realize that you just sealed the crew and our friends in there with that fiend," said Gowanda.

"If this all works out; I am guessing that it won't be for very long. Am I right about that, Hunash?" Roethroba asked as she stared into Hunash's large saucer-shaped eyes.

"I need to get to a communication station," said Hunash as she led Gowanda and Roethroba down the hallway. "But you're right, Roethroba. He is more interested in dealing with us than killing anyone in the room right now."

The remaining hostages moved closer toward the walls, struggling to find any recesses to huddle in as the Beetle-Crawler-Second Skin took out his displeasure on being bested. He picked up three tables with the Crawler portion of his body and slammed them to pieces on the floor. He threw five or six chairs up against the shatter-resistant clear aluminuminix windows before his rage subsided.

"Junior Engineer Dozor, activate the communication system. I wish to speak with the beguiling Agent Honey-Runner," smiled Beetle-Crawler-Second Skin.

"I will do as you command, Mr. Nobody," Dozer said, using Second Skin's alias.

"Very good, Bug," said Second Skin as he patted Dozor on the antennae with an appendage.

The two-way viewer screen hummed to life. "Mr. Nobody wishes to speak to Agent Honey-Runner."

The multi-lensed face of Lieutenant Zamber appeared on the screen. "She is dealing with an internal administrative issue at the moment. Tell Mr. Nobody that she will be with him shortly."

"I will speak with Agent Honey-Runner underling's. But just make sure that I am able to speak with your superior as soon as she becomes available," interjected Second Skin.

Second Skin could hear the voice of Agent Honey Runner in the background, "Your efforts may have been admirable, but the fact remains that you still fail me, Commander Nectaxus."

"I am deeply sorry for causing you disappointment," said the Polistine Commander, Nectaxus.

"I am deeply sorry for having to cause you pain, but I can assure you that it never lasts for long."

There was a choking, gurgling sound off-screen, followed by a loud thud. Honey-Runner flew into view as she brushed herself off. "Mr. Nobody, I appreciate your patience. I regret to inform you that we have not yet retrieved the Methurazus Device."

Second Skin debated whether or not it was the best idea to negotiate with an individual as ruthless as Agent Honey-Runner seemed to be. But the thought was fleeting since Second Skin knew that after 600 years of existence in the universe that there was no creature more cunning or ruthless than a Clonstellar.

"It seems that some of the hostages are being disagreeable, Agent Honey-Runner," said Second Skin. "Therefore I find it necessary to activate this vessel's self-destruct if I do not have Diabolix's property in 30 minutes."

"Go ahead," said Agent Honey-Runner.

"Excuse me, Agent? I just thought I heard you tell me to blow up the ship."

"Yes, Mr. Nobody, you heard me right. There is nothing of value on that vessel that can't be replaced. Besides, I will be daggit if I allow you to get your appendages on a Methurazus Rejuvenate."

"Give me back that device!" screamed Second Skin. "Or I will kill another hostage."

"I would be more than happy to assist you," said Honey Runner. "Mr. Dozor are you still there?"

"Yes, I am Agent Honey-Runner," said Junior Engineer Dozor.

"Do you have a W-192 pill available?"

"Yes, I do. I carry it always." said Junior Engineer Dozor.

"Then I need you to swallow it, to demonstrate to Second Skin that we are serious," said Agent Honey-Runner.

"I really would prefer not to have to swallow that pill," said Junior Engineer Dozor.

"I am giving you an order, Lieutenant," said Agent Honey-Runner.

"If you insist —" stammered Junior Engineer Dozor.

"Excuse me! Agent Honey-Runner, did you just call me Second Skin?"

"Of course not. How would I know your name?"

"Because the only person who I told my real name was —," Second Skin paused. "Again and again that Monash of a Cranitian Monash interferes with my plan."

"Pleasurist Hunash, if you can hear me, you need to hurry disabling the auto-pilot," yelled Junior Engineer Dozor.

Inside the flight deck of the *Charon*, Hunash was working feverishly to release the locks on the ship's auto-pilot. Her cousin, Buddash, had provided her with some instruction regarding technical matters over the decades, but she was still a novice at best.

"Gowanda, how mechanically inclined are you?" asked Hunash.

"I have fixed a Querzi tablet in my day," said Gowanda.

"That's a start," said Hunash.

"Why is the Querzi computer counting?" asked Gowanda.

"Because the Clonstellar just remotely activated the self-destruct," said Hunash. "But Gowanda, I need you to focus on me."

"I am focused. What did you need to know?" asked Gowanda.

"Do you have technical experience?" asked Hunash.

"I had to get myself and a Polistine client out of a locked steam-pool once," said Gowanda.

"Perfect. You take over trying to release the access codes for the auto-pilot," smiled Hunash, as she turned to Roethroba, "Honey, I need you to hack into the system and try to disable the auto-destruct on the ship."

"In under two minutes?" asked Roethroba.

"The more we stand around and argue, the more seconds will tick by."

"Fine, I will see what I can do," said Roethroba as she slid down on her haunches. She removed the panel from underneath the main control panel and began to determine how to tackle the problem.

"What were you planning to do?" asked Gowanda.

"Nothing special" quipped Hunash. "Querzi, activate emergency teleport."

"Where is your intended destination?"

"I need you to delivery me to the Observation Deck. There is someone I need to speak to," she said as her molecules began to dissolve.

After 600 years, there was very little in the galaxy that would manage to surprise Second Skin. However, Hunash reappearing before him on the Observation Deck was one of those rare exceptions."

"I thought that the next time I saw you, my dear, that I'd be standing over your lifeless body."

"Even for a pleasurist, it is considered 'bad form' to not finish what you've started," said Hunash.

"Sweet Hunash, there have been so many before you who have tried to end me. What makes you any different?" asked Second Skin.

"Because I have always been and always will be a survivor."

Second Skin brought the muscular back portion of his body down on top of Hunash, moments before she managed to bring her body into her shell and roll away.

"Why can't we just be friends?" asked Second Skin as he lunged forward to press the weight of his chest against Hunash. Once again, though, he was too slow for Hunash's agile reflexes. She jumped over him as he lunged forward to encompass her in his eight appendages. Hunash jumped up to the hole in the drop ceiling where she had previously entered the Observation Deck.

"My dear Hunash, there is nowhere left to run that I will not find you," yelled Second Skin as he assumed she was making her escape. To his disbelief though, Hunash re-emerged, an instant later, with two long, irondoan pipes, one in each hand. "You two-faced piece of indeterminate creepiness. I am so through running from the likes of you!" said Hunash.

Second Skin extended his jaws around Hunash's head as he once again insisted, "you still haven't told me why we could not just be friends?"

As he was bringing his jaws down on her head, Hunash tucked her head into her shell and butted him in his long head.

"Dear Hunash, you think that would really stop me?"

"No, but this probably will," said Hunash as she placed the iron pipes between the claws on her feet. She brought each foot up in rapid succession and stabbed Second Skin in the chest. As she looked at the now motionless Second Skin, she smiled "That's why we could never be friends. I don't associate with beings whose heart I have to break."

Hunash teleported herself back down the hallway to the flight deck. She immediately saw that Gowanda had managed to re-route the controls of the ship's auto-pilot. Satisfied that she was making progress, Hunash turned to the more immediate problem: the auto-destruct system was down to **sixteen**.

"Let me get, Dozor up here. He should know how to deactivate this thing," offered Hunash.

The Trionyx cocked her head. "By the time, he gets up here, we will all be space dust."

"But you are cutting it really close to the wire, so to speak," said Hunash,

"And the more mental energy I waste talking to you."

"I just hope you're right," said Hunash as she glanced to see that the countdown clock now read **"twelve."**

"Just give me about ten more seconds to lick this problem," sighed Roethroba.

"That's about all that you have," replied Hunash.

"Thanks for the update," said Roethroba as she examined the connection to a particular wire. "I don't have enough pressure on me."

Hunash glanced over to see the clock now read **"eight."**

"I really think that it is still not too late to call for help," said Hunash.

"It is already way too late," said Roethroba.

"Hunash watched in horror as the number on the clock began to change from **"three"** to **"two."** As the **"two"** began to morph into a **"one,"** Roethroba cut two final wires under the console. The numeral **"two"** froze in mid-change as the Querzi announced to the three pleasurists in the cockpit, **"Self-destruct aborted."**

"You are the luckiest Trionyx I know,' said Hunash to Roethroba.

"If you have no respect for my skills, Cranitian, then I have no time for you," said Roethroba.

"Gowanda, we need to get Dozor up here so he can undo the damage Second Skin did."

"Lieutenant Dozor, do you read me?" asked Hunash as she spoke into the comm.

"Yep, I am right here. I imagine the *Charon*, poor old girl, is probably to need a major overhaul."

"Junior Engineer," said Agent Honey-Runner, "you are only one and a half light years from Meditaplassen. I will contact the Omnipotent Hawking Council for permission to put down for repairs."

"Thank you, Madam Agent. That is most kind of you."

"Don't thank me yet, Junior Engineer Dozor. I may be asking for the assistance of the *Charon* in a special mission in the near future," said Honey Runner.

"Yes, Agent Honey-Runner. I will be happy to serve," said Dozor.

"Ms. Hunash, may I speak to you on a discreet channel?" asked Honey-Runner.

"Yes, Agent Honey-Runner," said Hunash.

Hunash hit one or two buttons that converted the communication from a public to private channel.

"Engineer Dozor, tells me that you managed to survive not one, but two attacks from that Clonstellar?"

"I have always had a strong survival instinct, Agent Honey-Runner."

"I believe," said Agent Honey-Runner," that you are minimalizing your role in dealing with this incident. I would not do that if I were you. You should take pride in your skills and accomplishments."

"Yes, Agent Honey-Runner," said Hunash.

"If it wasn't for your intervention, there would probably be a lot more fatalities. I need to ask you how you'd feel about leaving the Pleasurist Corps and coming to work for me at Section Seventy-Two?"

Epilogue
DIABOLIX'S WORLD

Hotfire was lying face down in the street of a deserted town on Diabolix's World.

In his jacket, Hotfire could feel the twin syringes pressing against his breast. It was only then, feeling his life force slipping away, that he acknowledged the truth. Sobek was not only removing two individuals who continually threatened the peace and tranquility of the galaxy, he was also eliminating two anarchists who continually thwarted the efforts of the Hawking Brain Beetle to successfully influence the unfolding of galactic politics and relations among the races.

Hotfire looked up from the dirt to see the almost-mirage like figure of the Psychic Spider standing over him. "That is just amazing," the spider said, clapping four of his ten appendages. "You used that tiny river melon you call a brain to figure out that Sobek wanted you dead?"

"He hasn't killed me yet," whispered Hotfire.

"Besides the fact that I am an hour away from bursting out of your skull?" asked the Psychic Spider. "No, other than that you are totally right: you aren't dead yet."

Hotfire whipped his tail around the Psychic Spider to try to pull himself up. But as soon as Hotfire began to use the Psychic Spider as a brace, he fell back down into the dust.

"Oh, my lord! Did we happen to forget that I am nothing more than a mental projection? Dear me! That is just classic Hotfire."

"Not as classic as this, my ten-limbed friend," smiled Hotfire as he rolled his body over on his back and reached down with his tail to retrieve a syringe from a band on his ankle.

The Psychic Spider gasped, "You stole a sample of Enhanced Energy Gas from the laboratory on Minerva. You are going to use it to temporarily give you enough energy to deliver the toxin to Diabolix."

"You bet your Höllenfeuerhalbinsel heart that I am going to do just that," smirked Hotfire.

"You can't do that. Sobek promised me that you would be my host. He never mentioned anything about you surviving."

"Even I knew that he never intended to let me live," said Hotfire in a whisper.

"This is not fair!" yelled the Psychic Spider.

"Next time, pick a sap who doesn't have such a strong will to live."

With every last ounce of energy, Hotfire placed the vial of Enhanced Energy Gas into the syringe and brought it up to his neck. He began to scream for mercy as the energy gas flooded his cells with adrenaline and began to initiate cellular repair throughout his weary body.

The voice of the Psychic Spider remained in his brain, but was momentarily pushed aside. Unfortunately, the spider's growth continued uninterrupted y the effects of the gas. But at least, its ability to inflict pain was briefly suspended.

Hotfire got to his feet and looked around the Scaratutulo-inspired landscape of Diabolix's World. He saw two groups of older arboreal buildings on either side of a communal compound, that was once referred to in the ancient vernacular as a *town*. In front of the buildings, was a large metallic object protruding out of the ground; at first glance, it looked to be the remains of an extremely large star-craft. It turned out to be Diabolix's warship, the *Dolgthrasir*, emerging from the planet. Some distance away, the Quartrack Destroyer, the *Pollencollect* appeared to be laying on its side.

Hotfire ached from the experience of being transported to X-Space by the Methurazus Rejuvenate. He told himself that going through that infernal machine was more than enough for one lifetime.

As Hotfire walked towards the remains of the *Dolgthrasir*, his memories returned to the morning that he and Yanick DcCullen had made their way down to Meditaplassen. It was the day that they had attempted to save the life of the inventor of the Enhanced Energy Gas. Hotfire never did learn what became of Kabul Vulkner.

In any case, Yanick, believing that he had killed Hotfire in a physical engagement, had placed him in the Methurazus Rejuvenate, but instead of healing him, he'd managed to horribly disfigure Hotfire, with half of his body being transposed so the right side of his innards were on the outside.

Before being removed from the chamber, Hotfire's last fleeting memory of that day was that three Hawkings sprayed his body with a cold, wet gel. that covered his entire body. He'd felt his body growing colder before being slipped into a long clear container and sealed in like a preserved canister of rodenies.

Hotfire was unsure how much later his next memory occurred. He awoke in a clear chrysalis suspended above a large, circular medical scanner with red and blue lights moving around the scanner's perimeter. Once the lights reached the end of their cycle, there were blue beams that emanated from the device that moved up and down along the chrysalis. After a momentary scan, there was a loud beep before the lights began chasing each other once again.

Hotfire next remembered the first time that he heard a voice that he would come to dread.

"Hello there, Chamyx. You are extremely lucky to be alive. It took thirteen hours of extensive reconstruction to make you whole again," said a Hawking Brain Beetle.

Hotfire remembered that when he had regained consciousness he could only speak in a whisper, "Where am I?" he asked.

"You are in a healing facility in Dakplassen on Meditaplassen. You have been here for quite some time," said the Hawking Brain Beetle.

Hotfire happened to glance down at his left leg crammed into the chrysalis. He noticed that there were a number of protrusions emanating from his tail. As he examined them, a flaming object came out of one of the protrusions and tore a hole in the chrysalis.

"What have you done to me?" whispered Hotfire.

"Given the fact that I had the unprecedented opportunity to repair a living Reptilia, I simply couldn't resist the urge to experiment slightly with your genetic code. Now, you have the ability to use your internal chemistry to generate fireballs."

"Why? Why would you do this to me?"

"Because it is an opportunity to advance both metabolic and cellular science. This work could one day allow me to create an invincible army of fire-breathing dragonian. You are the first child of a new enhanced Reptilia race. You are my first Xerxes."

"Who are you?" asked Hotfire.

"My name is Sobek Bokhun. And I can tell that we are going to have a fruitful relationship."

Back on Diabolix's World, Hotfire could already feel the effects of the Enhanced Energy Gas beginning to subsidy. The Psychic Spider was whispering in his ear, telling him that he should not waste the last of his energy, that he should just allow himself to die in peace.

"I am almost to my goal, so you can keep your comments to yourself," said Hotfire. He had managed to walk towards one of the buildings in the faux-version of *Prosperity*. The town had appeared to be just a few steps away, but the journey had taken Hotfire the better part of half an hour. The Psychic Spider was pressing against his forehead and he could feel himself weakened again.

The building on the outskirts of the town had a number of slender, long arboreal boxes low to the ground. Hotfire remembered from his brief time in daily formative sessions when he was a young Reptilia that these boxes were used to bury the dead when a being's body became damaged beyond repair, either from age or by accident.

As he examined the worn and weathered boxes, he barely even registered that a purple swirling Vortex was replacing several of the solid arboreal planks in the bottom of the low boxes. Before Hotfire knew what was happening, several tentacle appendages pushed up through the boxes, shot up in the air and lifted Hotfire up into the dry Scaratutulo western sky. As he was held in the air, he heard a voice being broadcast from the arboreal boxes that made any sane individual cringe in terror.

"You dare to come into X-Space and challenge me in my own reality?"

"Lord Diabolix, I would never think of even trying to harm you," gasped Hotfire.

"I can sense that you have a drug. A drug that someone believes can kill me," said Lord Diabolix. "How dare you presume that you can kill the ultimate being in the universe?"

"I am so weak that I could not harm even the lowest Ruddarian in my condition."

"That is truly a disappointment to me," said Lord Diabolix.

"Why is that?" asked Hotfire.

"I have often heard tales of the exploits of the legendary Hotfire. I had hoped one day to have a meeting of our incredible minds. But now, you are sick and broken. Therefore, I will do you the mercy of destroying you quickly." Then, a massive tail came out of the ground, grabbing Hotfire's waist.

"One thing that I failed to mention Lord Diabolix," said Hotfire.

"What would that thing be?" asked Lord Diabolix.

"This arid western air has given me some of my old vigor back," smiled Hotfire. He swung his tail around towards Lord Diabolix as he launched dozens of fireballs. As the fireballs disappeared beneath the surface, a violent roar could be heard coming from the Vortex, I can play this game as well."

Hotfire felt himself being thrown to the ground as the dirt and mud parted and a fourteen-foot visage in a black, ribbed environmental suit with six pairs of claws and six pairs of appendages emerged.

"I will vaporize you, Abomination and use your dust to cleanse my skin in this heat!" as he launched silverdron blasts from his tail at Hotfire.

Thinking quickly, Hotfire instinctively jumped into the Vortex and reappeared inside the engine room of the *Dolgthrasir*. Hotfire looked at the main propulsion unit and surrounding area before laying eyes on what he hoped he would see: a Methurazus Rejuvenate. Hotfire rushed over to the console and placed the small amount of remaining Enhanced Energy Gas into the chemical-enabling chamber. He watched as the Methurazus roared to life. He set the Methurazus for his own dimension before stepping inside. Before he closed the door, he placed a syringe into one of the condensation chambers between the tubing and the corner of the Methurazus square. As he closed the chamber doors, he watched as Diabolix came through the vortex.

"You dare try to escape from me, Abomination," yelled Lord Diabolix.

"I dare and I shall," said Hotfire.

As Hotfire began demolecularization within the chamber, he could feel the Psychic Spider scream in pain inside his mind as the Enhanced Energy Gas began to infect every cell in the spider's body, causing him to disintegrate within Hotfire's brain.

Lord Diabolix ripped open the Methurazus Chamber and stepped inside. Hotfire had made a pivotal mistake. There was still a sample of the Enhanced Energy Gas remaining in the chamber that would allow him to use the device to transport himself out of X-Space to his dimension of origin.

"Lord Diabolix will rise once again."

The Methurazus roared to life with a flurry of lights and calculations. Before Diabolix could be transported anywhere, he was enveloped in a toxic gas. The toxin permeated every cell in his body before he disappeared into nothingness.

The shuttle, *Charon*, gracefully entered orbit around Meditaplassen shortly after Hunash's final confrontation with the Clonstellar known as Second Skin. The pleasurist Hunash, who had been assigned the designation of field agent by Agent Honey-Runner, activated the communication viewer in the ship's cockpit so she could inform the Omnipotent Hawking Brain Beetle council of their ship's arrival.

The image of a Hawking Brain Beetle appeared on the screen, "This is Ra Bokhun of the Omnipotent Hawking Brain Beetle Council. We were informed by Agent Honey-Runner of Section Seventy-Two that your ship was in need of repairs."

"Yes, there was extensive damaged done to our ship's auto-pilot by a particularly troublesome Clonstellar. In addition, we have a number of structural elements that are in need of repair. But first and foremost, we have passengers and crew who are in need of medical attention."

"We will do our utmost to meet your needs, Agent. Now if you would be so kind, please maneuver your vessel into our orbiting maintenance dock so that our engineers may begin the repairs."

"Certainly. And the Polistine Security Agency extends its thanks once again," said Hunash.

The screen had just switched off when the Polistine Junior Engineer, Dozor peered his head in the cabin door, "One of the Hawking scientists just sent a message from his shuttle requesting that we release the remains of the Clonstellar. He said that he was doing a study on methods for regenerating dead cells. He seems to believe that studying the dead Clonstellar would provide some significant insights."

"Look at you, lieutenant. Just mastering the techie-talk," smiled Hunash.

"Well, what can I say? Science and engineering are my passions."

"Just let me contact, Agent Honey-Runner, and then I should be able to release the body."

"Where is the body being kept exactly?" asked Dozor.

"In the refrigeration unit below the dining room. But I will go with you as soon as I get authorization," said Hunash.

Hunash didn't manage to see Dozor's right hand morph into a large Lobsterian claw as she turned towards the viewer. Dozor-Clonstellar raised his enlarged claw up in the air and smacked her to the ground, rendering her unconscious.

He moved Hunash out of the way as he activated the comm, "Multiverse, this is Engimus. Have you arrived at the Methurazus Rejuvenate chamber on Meditaplassen?"

"I am in position. Engimus, have you located Second Skin's body?"

"Yes, I am headed there now. I will take a pod down to the surface and see you within the hour."

"Very good. I look forward to seeing you then," said Multiverse —who had assumed the form of a Hawking Brain Beetle.

"Was the Lord able to return from his exile in X-Space?" asked Engimus.

"Unfortunately, not. Once we revive Second Skin, we will need to begin formulating a new plan for facilitating Lord Diabolix's return."

"There is nothing that can prevent his return so our only task is to determine the means for achieving that goal," said Engimus.

"You speak truth, brother Engimus. I will see you shortly," said Multiverse as the screen went blank.

As the Multiverse terminated the connection with Engimus, the Methurazus Rejuvenate roared back to life, emitting a hot white light from its closed chamber. After a brief flurry of electrical sparks encompassing the cube, the doors slowly opened to reveal a large black Chamyx sitting on the metal table within.

"Well I be a Hellfire's lizard, I actually made it back in one piece," said Hotfire.

"Where is Lord Diabolix?" demanded Multiverse, still maintain the form of a Hawking Brain Beetle.

"I did what you asked me to do. I used the toxin to kill him," said Hotfire.

"You lie, Abomination! Lord Diabolix cannot be killed! He is immortal!"

"Ah, fuctur. I am guessing you aren't really a Hawking."

"You are right, Abomination. And now you shall die," said Multiverse.

Hotfire jumped up toward the ceiling, using the metal table as a launching pad. As he flew through the air, he camouflaged his body while launching fireballs towards the Hawking impostor. The fireballs did manage to slightly singe the Hawking-Multiverse's shell, but it was no match for the three bolts of electricity that Hawking-Multiverse sent flying into Hotfire's back. He watched with great satisfaction as Hotfire came flying back down to the ground, slamming his head on one of the doors of the Methurazus. As he lay motionless on the floor, Multiverse shot Hotfire with an electric bolt one last time, for good measure.

As Multiverse waited for Engimus to arrive with the body of Second Skin, he kept himself occupied by placing Hotfire's unconscious form in an office at the rear of the chamber and locking the door. Once he and Engimus had completed their business, he would deal with the Abomination in a more permanent manner.

By the time, Multiverse had returned from the office, Engimus had arrived in the chamber holding Second Skin's corpse. Upon his death, his body had reverted to its original state; a silver, featureless form. His head had a small slit of a mouth, two tiny dots for nostrils and large oval eyes.

Noticing the burn marks on the floor, Engimus inquired, "Did something happen?"

"Yes, the Abomination returned from X-Space. He claims that he killed Lord Diabolix."

"That cannot be true."

"Well once we're done, you, Second Skin and I will put an end to Hotfire. For now, though, placed our comrade's body in the chamber."

Engimus placed Second Skin's body into the Methurazus Rejuvenate as Multiverse activated the controls. After a frenzy of electrical activity within the cube, the white light began to dim as the doors began to open. Both Clonstellars watched with anxious anticipation as Second Skin, who was still in his featureless silver form, sat up on the metal table.

"Second Skin, we are so relieved that we were able to revive you," said Engimus.

"I realize that you need time to recover, but I must share some grave news with you. The Abomination Hotfire may have killed Lord Diabolix," said Multiverse.

"No, Diabolix is very much alive, reborn in the body of this fool. And now that I have returned, the galaxy will flow with the blood of my enemies."

ACKNOWLEDGEMENTS

I must concede that there was no singular moment in my life when I decided that I wanted to write a novel. It was just something that I have always wanted to do. As a young child growing up in the East Oak Lane section of Philadelphia, I was fortunate enough to have individuals in my life who encouraged my love of reading and books. There was my father, Franklin. He encouraged me through both action and example. He would take me to the local Atlantic bookstore on Route 309, three times a month. Invariably, I would walk out of the store with no less than seven books. I can never remember a time when I was growing up that my father did not have a 2-dollar pulp adventure novel sitting on his cherry-wood nightstand. The next biggest influence in promoting my love of reading was my mother, Ann. I guess that she observed early on in my life, when I was attending Finletter elementary, and later John Story Jenks elementary school, that I was more likely to pick up a sci-fi or fantasy novel than crack a textbook. To remedy this situation, she worked out an arrangement. My reward for completing my school work was that I was allowed to finish reading my sci-fi book. Mom also gave me my first typewriter —my younger readers should know that this device is a manually-operated version of Microsoft Office — and showed me how to replace the ribbon. I reached the point through trial and error where I managed to complete several stories. Yet, my mind was always moving onto the next idea so I left some unfinished. My mother would reassure me that many of the greatest authors had manuscripts that were collecting dust.

Finally, I had three amazing English teachers during my school career that I would be remiss if I didn't acknowledge at the completion of this first novel. In seventh grade, my English teacher, Mr. James Broderick, introduced me to the genre of the fantasy novel as social commentary. He introduced me to Madeleine L'Engle's *A Wrinkle in Time*, Norton Juster's *The Phantom Tollbooth*, and J.RR. Tolkien's *the Hobbit*. These books provided me with an understanding that there were magical wondrous worlds that were no farther away than within the covers of a novel.

Once I reached high school, I was lucky enough to have a teacher who was an authority on the novelists of the early 20th century. Mr. Floyd Blythewood introduced my young mind to Erich Maria Remarque's *All Quiet on the Western Front*, a brutal examination of the consequences of war, the hardship of the oppressed by having us read Steinbeck's *Of Mice and Men* and *the Grapes of Wrath, and* the struggles of the outsider that were demonstrated in such classics as *Flowers for Algernon*. My other incredible English teacher was Mrs. Maxine Greene. I will always remember her as the teacher who gave us books we really shouldn't be reading, like Bradbury's *Fahrenheit 451*, Orwell's *Animal Farm*, Camus' *the Stranger* and, of course, Kafka's *Metamorphosis*.

However, my idea for this novel, *The Eye of Hermes*, actually is in some part due to the late British actor, William Hartnell, and Verity Lambert. The notion came to me in my room on an October evening when I was 16 years old when I was watching a rebroadcasted episode of Doctor Who from 1965, entitled *The Web Planet*. In this particular adventure, the Doctor, Barbara, Ian and Vicki had landed on the planet Vortis, being drawn there by a mysterious power. The time-travelers banded together with a group of insectoid races, including the butterfly-like Menoptra and underground-dwelling Optra in order to free their planet from a spider-like race known as the Aminus who were encompassing the planet with an enormous web. I can remember my 16-year old self sitting transfixed in front of my small television. There were aliens on my screen who on Earth were insignificant bugs who were determining the fate of their alien world. Amazing!

It would take thirty some years before the stars would align, namely having retired from 20 years of teaching, having just finished a second Masters' in education, and my wife, Bonnie Gold, wondering what I would be doing with my newly acquired degree. The answer came when we were walking through the local Barnes and Noble bookstore, one Sunday afternoon in 2014. There were a group of individuals, who I would later become friends with who included Theresa Gauthier, Rich Weiss and Julie Greenbaum, sitting at a table with their laptops and notepads. I went over to inquire what they were doing. One of the group members told me that this writers' group met on a monthly basis. I told the gentleman that I had a few pages of a novel at home, and, as they say, the rest is history.

With all these various supports and influences there is no way that I would have ever completed this novel without the support and understanding of my wife, Bonnie Gold. She demonstrated patience and understanding above and beyond the call. It was her loving support that permitted me to spend my weekends during the school year slowly completing this narrative, keeping me company while I wrote on almost a daily basis during the summer.

Once I had completed the first draft, my fellow writer, Marie Gilbert, who was encouraging me through the entire process, introduced me to my amazing editor, Patti O'Brien. She is the singular reason that I have a completed manuscript rather than a draft that is gathering dust on a shelf. She challenged me, supported me, and guided me in the revision of this novel.

This novel would also not have been possible without the love and support of my friends and family. First and foremost, there is my understanding wife who would only occasionally ask me if I was considering getting a summer job. Next, there is my mom, Ann, and sister, Shari, who provided me with encouragement as I continued to move forward towards this novel's conclusion. And after meeting my sister's literary hero in December 2016, Diana Gabaldon, I do concede that she is kind of awesome. I also need to acknowledge my Uncle Phil and Aunt Connie, who would ask me on a regular basis how the book was coming, supported me throughout the process. Finally, there is my surrogate-sister, Sharon Hoelzle, who inspires me every day with her positive attitude and steadfast demeanor. Sharon has my eternal gratitude for being willing to read the first thirty pages of *The Eye of Hermes* before I even knew whether it was a workable novel.

Thank you to Steve, Lori, Ryan and Kristen Link. Thanks to my in-laws, Sandi and Stewart Melrose. Thanks to Shannon and Edward Rothschild.

My extreme gratitude to Uncle Bob and Aunt Judi Duboff. Immense gratitude to cousins Irene and David Symons. Scott Washburn, you rock. Keep fighting those Wellsian Martians. Ian Williams, thank you for the support on Facebook. Malcolm Shabazz Hoover, thank you for showing me the love on the Central Facebook page. Mom, Bonnie and Shari, the three of you keep me writing every day.

ABOUT THE AUTHOR

William Howard has always found opportunities to both learn and teach throughout his life. A graduate of Temple University with a bachelors' degree in education and two educational-related masters' degrees from LaSalle University in Philadelphia PA, he also often traveled the road less taken. He has volunteered at the Historical Society of Pennsylvania where he wrote online articles about the Germantown and Mount Airy sections of Philadelphia. He has been an educational volunteer at the Academy of Natural Sciences and the National Museum of American Jewish History. In his spare time, he writes short stories and attends the Neshaminy Writers' Group on a monthly basis. He currently resides in Philadelphia, PA where he lives with his wife, Bonnie.